BIG SEXY LOVE

KIRSTY GREENWOOD

For my dad, Dave Greenwood, who taught me how to be funny. And how to be weird. And that I should always look for the positives in every situation. I love you, Dad.

CHAPTER ONE

I'm calling it. This year is officially my most rubbish year yet.

Olive Brewster's Most Rubbish Year Yet.

My top five reasons for this declaration are as follows:

Reason Number One: My brother Alex and his girlfriend Donna are kicking me into the teeny box room of the house we share. Donna wants to use my big room as a studio for her new scented-candle business. She hasn't even started making any scented candles yet! But apparently they 'want to be prepared for when it happens' and need me 'not to be a dick about it'.

Reason Number Two: I'm twenty-seven years old and I work as a fishmonger in Manchester Indoor Market. It was supposed to be a temporary job to help me pay my way through university. Nine years later I'm still here. It's not terrible, I suppose. But it's not exactly captivating either. The regular customers are pretty sweet and I know the job back to front, but mostly I'm skint and spend way too much time elbow-deep in cod, avoiding eye contact with all the fish who still have their heads and are definitely staring at me.

Reason Number Three: I haven't had sex in almost ten years. Not even a tiny bit of sex. The entire world tells me it's something that would make me feel amazing if I did it. But I'm entirely convinced that sex is a really dumb idea. I've seen first-hand how it makes people lose control, become selfish, turns them into reckless boneheads ruled only by their peens and vajeens. I don't want to be like that! I like my life simple. Safe and sure and certain… and sex-free. Or at least I thought I did… Because the thing is, last month I watched *Atonement* for the first time, and you know that scene where Keira Knightley and James McAvoy do it standing up in that posh library? Well, it gave me a rather pleasant and curious sensation in my very own vajeen. A rather pleasant and curious sensation indeed. My sans-sex lifestyle has never, ever bothered me before. My first time was fumbly and awkward and not something I was eager to repeat. Plus, I've not met anyone I fancied in years, so it's never really been an issue. But… now I'm starting to wonder. What if everyone is right and I've been missing out? I can't get the thought of that steamy library sex out of my mind. I think of it multiple times a day and it won't bugger off.

Reason Number Four: Last month I did one of those

Buzzfeed quizzes that let you know which Harry Potter character you are. I got Buckbeak. Yeah, I know. I couldn't remember Buckbeak either. Not even one of the main players. Not even a *human.* I mean, why even include that as a possible result on the quiz? It's just hurtful. I only thank God that I wasn't in Hufflepuff. Ain't nobody want that shit.

Reason Number Five: My best friend Birdie is dying.

* * *

'Are you all right, dear? You look like you're about to cry.'

I'm tugged out of my melancholic daydreaming by the customer I'm serving – an elderly fellow called Norris who comes to the market every single Thursday afternoon to buy a peppered tuna steak for his supper. He's been coming here for as long as I've been working at this place. Always Thursday afternoon, always a peppered tuna steak. I find the routine of his turning up so regularly, always choosing a certain dish on a certain day very comforting. He's a man after my own heart. Where possible, it's nice to know what to expect! Birdie objects when I say this. She reckons the fun of living is all about the unexpected. But I've experienced the unexpected and let me tell you, I am not about that life.

'Oops, sorry, Norris.' I smile at him. 'My mind was somewhere else! Tuna steak, yes?'

I reach into the chilled counter to grab the fish fillet when Norris's gravelly voice stops me.

'Actually, love, I think I'll go for a seabass today.'

I freeze, my hand dangling mid-air inside the counter, my eyes sliding across to my colleague Tall Joan and then to my boss Taller Joan. They don't seem to notice that

Norris, who has been getting the same tuna for time immemorial, has suddenly changed his regular order to sea bass.

'What's going on?' I ask suspiciously, wondering what on earth has caused Norris's unforeseen change of habit. 'Are… are you… is everything okay, Norris?'

I think my question comes out more accusatory than I intend it to, because Norris frowns, his thick white eyebrows lowering so much that they almost obscure his heavy lidded blue eyes. 'I just fancied something different is all, Olive. Nice to switch things up once in a blue moon.'

Nice to switch things up? The last time I switched things up was in 2010 when I bought some coloured contact lenses on a 'whim' and people thought I had glaucoma.

'Oh.' I say, fumbling over his new order. 'Cool. Totally! Great!'

Something different.

Fancy that.

* * *

On my way home from work that evening, I button up my plum-coloured duffle coat and wander through central Manchester towards the tram stop that will take me back to the rural suburb of Saddleworth where I live. The sky is still blue and bright, the springtime weather crunchy and fresh like a Granny Smith apple right out of the fridge. I amble through Piccadilly Gardens, saying hello to the friendly florist with her pretty pop-up flower shop. At Café Milo, I stop, as I do each week, to pick up a big cup of tea, cheese and ham baguette and custard tart for Mickey, the homeless man who can always be found on the benches by the fountains.

I smile as I approach the busking cello player outside Superdrug. He's there playing for the commuters every Thursday night without fail. I toss a pound coin into his cello case.

'Thanks, Olive!' he yells cheerfully as I pass.

'Cool cello playing, George!' I call back, giving him a thumbs up. I have Fridays and Saturdays off work so I won't see him again until next week. 'Have a brilliant weekend, George!'

'You too!'

I'm about to reach the tram stop but, before I do, a smiley-faced woman jumps right in front of me and blocks my path. Who is this person? What does she want from me? Why is she in my face, smiling so loudly? If I were a cat, I'd be all puffed up right now, fur on end, hissing, all of that.

'I'm not looking to invite Jesus into my life at the moment,' I explain, concluding that a person so smiley can only be someone who has recently discovered the lord and wants me to do the same.

'Ha ha! Good one!' the girl says, handing me a paper flyer printed with the words 'Secret Comedy!!!'

'Secret Comedy, three exclamation points?' I ask, intrigued. 'Why is the comedy a secret? Who is it a secret from?'

'It's just a marketing trick,' the girl explains. 'Secret stuff is all the rage nowadays, right? Secret bars and secret speakeasies, secret gardens, secret cinema, secret pot brownie in your bottom desk drawer at work for when your boss is talking about Excel macros and you wonder how long it will be until your head pops off with boredom, you know? Ha ha.'

'Oh!'

'Anyway, it's a free improv comedy show we're putting

on. And there's usually an open mic session afterwards, if you're up for it?'

I feel a little frisson of interest somewhere deep in my stomach. But it's Thursday night and that's always *The Big Bang Theory* night with Alex and Donna who are obsessed with *The Big Bang Theory*. We have dinner and then we watch it together as a family. They're expecting me to be there. And even if I wanted to go to this secret show, I really need a shower because, let's face it, eau de seafood is not a good bouquet on anyone. Plus, I can hardly go to a comedy club on my own. That would just be strange. What if more strangers tried to talk to me? Or the comedy folk peer-pressured me to getting on the open mic? And somehow I decided that that was the time to spew out all of my worried thoughts about poor Birdie into the ether. And someone in the audience shouted 'What do you think this is? The damn therapist's office?' And everybody laughed *at* me, instead of *with* me. And I became the joke of Manchester and probably the entire secret comedy world at large?

'Ah, it's all a bit last minute for me, to be honest,' I say eventually, backing away from smiley woman. 'But thanks for the invite!'

The girl shrugs and wanders off to some other Manchester commuter, chirpily convincing them to come to her gig, expecting them to abandon their prior plans on a weeknight, like that's such a simple thing to do. I watch, and for a moment wonder, enviously, what it would be like to be her. Brave enough to stand in front of people and be funny. Confident enough to approach strangers and boldly ask them to come see it! Someone completely unafraid.

With a wistful sigh, I turn on my favourite distracting 90s pop playlist, reach my tram stop and wait patiently for the tram to arrive and take me back to real life.

CHAPTER TWO

Olive's phone Reminders:

Book dental check-up (Filling needed? Skanky tooth?)
Order that rose gold Kate Spade coffee mug for Birdie
Download 'Still Minds' meditation app
Listen to Day 1 of 'Still Minds' meditation app

If my home life were a sitcom it would be called *The Alex and Donna Show*. Which is a shit title for a sitcom, I know, but you get my point. I would be the pale, oddball sister living in the basement, popping up occasionally to make some dry remark but mainly serving as the audience for Alex and Donna to act out in front of.

If it were *Friends*, I'd be Gunther.

I've been living in this house since I was born. It used to belong to my parents. And then, two weeks after I started university in Manchester, we found out Mum had been having a sordid affair (is there any other kind?) with a French man who had been visiting the city on business. Out of nowhere she decided to leave dad, my brother Alex and me for a new life in Marseille with her rando French fancy. Her whole family carelessly left behind because of a stupid affair! She only stayed with Luc for a year, but she met someone else in France and still lives there.

Dad was so broken about it all that he spent most of the next six months eating tinned pies in the living room with the curtains closed. And then, just as I was doing my first-year exams, he transferred the mortgage to Alex and upped and moved back to his home town of Scotland where he now goes from girlfriend to girlfriend to girlfriend, desperately unhappy and bitter about how things turned out.

So then it was just me and Alex.

I don't really speak to my parents anymore. Everything kind of fragmented after Mum bailed. Not that I'm still messed up about it. (Except that, of course, I totally am.) Once, when she was drunk, Birdie said that all of my current foibles can be traced back to the unexpected break-up of my family, that I was 'emotionally traumatised'. It's a bit of a Psychology 101 suggestion in my opinion, but... I did used to be a lot braver when I was younger. I was the girl who, at the park, ran *up* the slide rather than slide down it. Badass.

I like it here at the house in Saddleworth, despite the shit that went down here. It's home: a nice roomy semi-detached, on a quiet street, with a pretty gravelled garden, countryside not too far away. Inside it feels cosy and full of memories that were happy and safe, of times before our family's sudden split. I know the place so well that I can find my way to the bathroom in the dark without even using my hands to feel along the wall.

As I enter the floral papered hallway, I smell the delicious tomatoey scent of Donna's lasagne wafting through the house. I yell a quick hello into the kitchen and dive upstairs so I can shower off the day's work.

Afterwards, in my room, I get changed into my comfy navy jersey dress and dry and comb my ginormous wilful russet curls up into a ponytail, securing them tightly with a retro scrunchy.

Down in the kitchen, I do my duty and offer to help Donna with the cooking. She shrugs, blowing her wispy blonde fringe out of her face as she stretches and rolls her home-made focaccia dough out onto the floured kitchen island.

'All the hard stuff is done,' she answers with a worthy smile. 'A truly authentic *lasagna* takes a very particular set of culinary skills.' She says 'lasagna' in a terrible, over-the-top Italian accent, and she's not even messing about. 'You could set the table, I suppose? If that's not too much trouble for you, Olive?'

She's an odd one, is Donna. I don't think she likes me very much. I mean, everything that comes out of her mouth is *technically* nice and perfectly polite. But there's this underlying antagonism which makes me constantly feel like I've done something to upset her. She always acts so formal with me and she says my name a lot, which creeps me out. I know she'd much rather have this house for her and Alex without me cramping their style and taking up the big room that, for the record, I've been sleeping in *since I was born.*

'No probs,' I say, grabbing the cutlery out of the drawer and laying three places at the kitchen table. 'How was your day at work?'

Donna sighs wearily, opening the oven door to check on her authentic lasagna. She's an Information Strategy Manager at a supermarket head office in Chester and pretty high up in the pecking order, by all (her own) accounts. 'Busy and exhausting as usual,' she answers, closing the oven. 'My brain is fried!' She gives me an envious glance. 'Gosh, it must be so *relaxing* to not have to think too much at your job, Olive!'

'Um…'

I go to protest, but she's right. My job doesn't take a whole lot of thinking. Mega knife skills, extensive crab knowledge, expert de-scaling abilities? Absolutely. But brain-frying levels of thinking? Not so much.

'Well,' Donna continues. 'I suppose when my candle venture takes off things will get better. You wouldn't *believe* how hard it is, Olive, doing a corporate job when your soul is as deeply artistic as mine.'

'Mmhhmm!' I say, sitting down at the table and nibbling at one of the breadsticks that have been laid out in a shabby chic jar.

'Napkins!' Donna says with a smile. 'Don't forget the napkins, Olive.'

Alex and I never used napkins before Donna moved in last year. If we were eating messy food, we'd use a bit of kitchen towel or, sometimes in a pinch, toilet roll. But Donna insists on actual cloth napkins, which she starches and irons and everything.

'What's up, guys!' Alex strides into the kitchen, setting down his briefcase by the tumble dryer and heading over to give Donna a kiss on the cheek. His gentle round face is pink-cheeked and beaming, his usually neat auburn hair a little sweaty at the front. 'Big Bang Theory night! I can't wait!'

'Me too!' Donna says, clapping her hands together so that a cloud of flour poofs up around her. Her face breaks into a genuinely excited smile. 'Bazinga!'

'Bazinga!' Alex adds.

The pair of them turn to me expectantly.

'Bazinga,' I say with a smile that attempts to be as psyched as theirs.

'Oh, Sheldon,' Donna laughs, shaking her head as if she's recalling a fond personal memory. 'What a stand-out character!'

'We're living in a golden age of sitcoms, for sure!' Alex adds, loosening his tie and grabbing a bottle of beer from the fridge.

I lay out the napkins on the table and wonder how many more episodes of *The Big Bang Theory* there will be until the season ends and we can finally watch a new box set.

* * *

'The great thing about this business idea is that some candles have inspirational quotes on them and some are scented. But mine? Mine will be inspirational… *and* scented!'

'It's going to be great!' Alex says, finishing the last mouthfuls of his lasagna and patting his gently rounded tummy in satisfaction. 'Have you thought of any more quotes you can use?'

Donna nods, using her napkin to dab neatly at the corners of her mouth. 'I actually wrote some myself.' She takes a deep breath. 'Your love burns like a flame!' she announces triumphantly. 'Isn't it très romantic?'

I snort over my water glass until I realise that she's not joking. She's serious. *Your love burns like a flame?* That's not romantic. That's an STD.

'I like it!' Alex says tactfully, ever the people pleaser. 'We should come up with a bunch more over the week-end, darling. And did you get your final list of scents decided?'

'I've got lemon, of course, and vanilla and freshly cut grass.' Donna counts off on her fingers. 'I can't decide on the last two though… Maybe lavender for a candle that says "Dream, Sleep, Love, Live". Or maybe a rose-scented one for my "Live every moment of your life!" one.'

'What do you think, Olive?' Alex asks, sweetly bringing me in to the conversation. Even he can see Donna's tendency to completely overtake all dinner chat. I wonder if he's ever brought it up with her? Hmm. Probably not. Alex likes an easy life and criticising Donna in any way would likely bring him a world of hassle.

I shrug. 'Why don't you do one or two wildcard scents?' I say. 'Like maybe a candle scent that no one has ever come up with before? Like… your high school crush's leather jacket? Or the cold side of the pillow? Or maybe even long grass instead of freshly cut grass? So many candles are freshly cut grass. But long grass smells delicious! Especially if there are daisies in there. Long grass is so underrated.'

Now it's Donna's turn to snort… 'A leather jacket candle? Thanks for your input, Olive, but I think I'll pass.'

Before I can say anything else Donna turns back to Alex and launches into a speech about different types of wax moulds, which I can already tell is going to be long and extra detailed. At that point I decide to make my excuses and take off to bed.

'But… It's *The Big Bang Theory* in twenty minutes!' Alex points out.

'It's cool, I'll catch up tomorrow!'

'If Olive wants to miss out on Sheldon's hilarious antics, that's her choice,' Donna says, patting Alex on the shoulder.

'Are you sure?' Alex asks me as I back away towards the stairs.

'Definitely! I need an early night anyway. I'm visiting Birdie tomorrow.'

The pair of them bow their heads, nodding super sympathetically like they do each time I mention Birdie. I take the opportunity to quickly wave goodnight and leg it up the stairs two at a time.

After a quick scroll through Instagram and an episode of *Fawlty Towers* on my laptop, I lay my head on the pillow and close my eyes. But as I try to fall to sleep I can think of only two things: that bloody library scene in *Atonement* and Norris' out of the blue change to sea bass…

CHAPTER THREE

Text from Birdie: Hurry up, Brewster, I miss yoooou. Don't forget coffee. Also, there is a new doctor here and he is hot. I plan to take him as a lover. Fucked-up kidneys or no fucked-up kidneys, ya girl gotta get laid!!!

The next morning, I wake up with a strange sense of excitement and dread in my stomach. It's the feeling I always get when I'm visiting Birdie in the hospital. I'm eager to see her because she's my favourite person who ever existed. But I'm visiting her in the hospital where her most recent lupus-related organ troubles have had her stuck for the past eight weeks. Which is horrible. So horrible that I can only think of the whole thing in a vague abstract way. I still can't get my head around the fact that the doctors don't know how long she's got left to live. I push the thought out of my head as soon as it arrives and focus on thinking of ways I can brighten her day.

After a quick shower, I change into a mustard-coloured shirt dress, slip on my comfy black flats and leave the house, grabbing a takeaway coffee for Birdie on the way. After men, glittery clothes and the art of Egon Schiele, coffee is her favourite thing. But the hospital stuff tastes like a stagnant puddle so I bring her the good stuff. Plus, she won't let me through the door of her room if I turn up without it.

On the bus to Manchester Royal Hospital, I replay, for the gazillionth time recently, the moment I met Birdie. I love daydreaming about it because it was one of those rare moments when you know something amazing is happening *exactly* as it's occurring.

I was at the library in my first year of university, trying my very hardest to focus on writing my essay about *The Canterbury Tales*, when a short girl with a brunette pixie crop plonked herself down at the table noisily, spilling a little splodge of hot coffee onto the table.

'Fuck sorry! Sorry, you guys!' she said loudly to the other students at the communal table, mopping up the spill with her big orange woolly scarf. Her accent was pure New York, but she looked French in that totally cool Parisian way. Big sad eyes, bluntly lopped off hair, pale, haughty cheekbones and a dinky nose. She was wearing a chic black vest and black tulle skirt that fanned out far too widely to be appropriate in a dowdy old Mancunian library.

I remember being annoyed at the interruption. I barely found enough time to study as it was, working so many hours at Joan's Fresh Fish in order to even afford my tuition. And here was this American, gabbing on and spilling her coffee, no respect for the sacrosanct ways of the library.

'Oh, I've ticked you off!' she said to me, as she opened up an old tatty laptop where the ping of it booting up was set at full volume.

I rolled my eyes. 'No.' I whispered, pointing at my notepad. 'I just have to get this done.'

'Will you be quiet?' Another guy at the communal table shushed us furiously. 'It's basic library etiquette, gosh.'

Ignoring him, the girl leaned over to peer at my book. 'Chaucer. What a bore! But better than Van Gogh. Total nutcase.' She pointed at her own book: *Masters of Post-Impressionism.*

At that point I couldn't help but smile. This girl didn't give a single shit that she was annoying everyone. And because I was completely the opposite of that, it fascinated me.

'What's your name?' the girl said, her voice cheerful and booming.

The other lad at the table was starting to turn puce in the face. To avoid him blowing a gasket, I tore a sheet of paper from my notebook and scribbled on it.

Shhh! My name is Olive Brewster.

With a nod, the girl read it, took my pen and scrawled on the paper, her handwriting big and loopy.

I'm Birdie. Birdie Lively. I just moved here after a terrible heartbreak in my homeland, USA. I don't know anyone yet and I like the look of you. We should become best of friends, probably. What do you think? Tick this box for yes. There isn't a box for no, so you can't say no.

My eyes almost popped out of my face when I read it.

English people didn't make friends this way! I certainly didn't. And not with a gutsy American who flouted library quiet rules. But how could I resist? At the very least I wanted to hear all about this terrible heartbreak in her homeland USA. That sounded very intriguing to a girl who had never even been on a date.

I slowly picked up my pen and ticked the little 'yes' box Birdie had drawn.

And when she smiled at me, dazzling white American teeth sparkling, her big sad eyes shining in a way that made me feel like I was way cooler than I was, I fell in love with Birdie Lively. And from that instant onwards, as simple as that, we became best of friends.

At the hospital, I walk quickly through the sterile green-floored corridors. There are brightly coloured murals all over the walls in an attempt to brighten up the place. But the effort is futile because most everyone walking past the art looks too sad or poorly or tired to notice it. I turn a corner and enter the double doors that lead to Birdie's ward.

Poking my head around the door of her room, I grimace as I see she's had even more framed prints of her favourite modern art hung up onto the walls. I don't like that's she's settling in here. It's like she thinks she's not going to be coming home. In a frame next to her bed is a picture of her and I on a summer picnic at Heaton Park. She's giving the middle finger to the camera. I'm laughing at her doing it. I have the exact same photo beside my bed at home.

'What's the magic word?' she calls out when she spots me.

'I come bearing actual real coffee.'

'Then… you may come in.' She grins, ushering me inside from where she's sitting crossed-leg in a big pale blue chair by the window.

I hand her the takeaway coffee which she pounces upon as if it's the uninvented medical treatment that will save her life. I'm pleased to see that Birdie's cheeks are less pale today. Other than the drip in her arm, she looks completely normal in worn jeans, a soft wheat-coloured jumper and sparkly gold slippers. You'd have no idea she was so poorly.

'You look good!' I say, wandering over to her bed and emptying the plastic bag of things I've brought with me. Nail polish in a daring crimson red that I know Birdie will love, a big bag of chocolate buttons, some of those Korean sheet face masks that make you look like something from a horror movie and a jigsaw puzzle I found in the hospital gift shop.

'Thank you, my Brewster,' Birdie says, immediately opening the buttons and offering me one. 'Is that jigsaw puzzle for you?'

'No, it's for us?'

'You can fuck off if you think I'm doing a jigsaw puzzle.'

I blink. 'Jigsaw puzzles are fun! And therapeutic.'

'I agree.' Birdie nods. 'If you're eighty. And living in 1973.'

I pick up the box and clasp it to my chest. I love a good jigsaw puzzle! All the pieces fit together exactly as they're supposed to. You can't lose at jigsaws! 'This one is of a beautiful house! Look!' I point at the picture on the front of the box. It's a big detached country house surrounded by pretty flowers and magnificent trees. A bit like the house in *Atonement*.

'It's creepy as fuck. Look. The front door is a bit open.'

I squint at the picture on the box and see that she's right. The front door of the house is ajar.

'So? It's probably a hot day.'

'Or someone broke in and did a murder? I'm telling you, shit went down in that jigsaw house. I can just tell.' She raises an eyebrow and munches down on another chocolate button.

I laugh. 'Fine. It's a *bit* creepy.'

Birdie shuffles in her chair, moving her slippered feet under her bum. She looks so elegant doing it. I could never sit cross-legged on a chair without looking all awkward and smooshed up wrong.

Instead I perch on Birdie's hospital bed as we chat about what's been going on with us in the few days since we last saw each other. If it was up to me, I'd visit her every day! But Birdie vetoed that on account of the fact that she doesn't want me stuck in here as well as her. She's thoughtful like that. We text multiple times a day, but there are always new things to discuss with best friends. At uni, we would spend all day together and then call each other in the evening to discuss what we were going to have for tea.

Birdie clutches her stomach and laughs loudly when I tell her about Donna's shit candle quotes. I embellish the story and add a few made-up rubbish quotes for her amusement.

'Live, Listen, Look, Laugh, Life, Love, Listen again!' I say. 'Enjoy life and love and dreams and live! In the rain! Also believe!' I do a little impression of Donna as I joke around, looking faux contemplatively out of the window, a finger to my chin. Then I mime smelling a candle and put on an Italian accent. 'Ooh, Mamma mia. This one smells like the most authentic *lasagna!*'

Birdie shrieks with mirth and, although I feel a bit mean about taking the mickey out of Donna, having

Birdie be impressed with me, the sound of her laughter echoing around the room, is completely worth it.

When she's finally stopped giggling, Birdie finishes the last of her coffee and takes a deep breath. 'So. Brewster. I have been thinking about a guy.'

'Ooh, yes the doctor you texted me about!' I rub my hands together. 'What's his name? What's he like? Do you think he fancies you back? He obviously will do.'

Just because I'm not interested in love affairs for myself, it doesn't mean I don't like hearing about Birdie's (many) dalliances. She's definitely more equipped than me to deal with the inevitable fallouts and heartbreaks from love and sex. Though after seeing it destroy my family, I do worry that one day she'll fall too hard and it will break her. But it hasn't happened yet. Emotionally, this girl is as strong as steel. But I guess knowing you're going to die young will do that to you.

'The doctor is hot,' Birdie says. 'His name is BJ. Not ideal, but I can get over that because his muscled arms are the size of legs and he's got this Irish accent that gives me the flutters.'

'Are you sure that's not your arrhythmia?' I ask worriedly.

Birdie rolls her eyes. 'My heart might be weak as shit but I know the difference between a medical palpitation and a horny one.'

'Fair enough,' I say, wondering what on earth a horny palpitation feels like. It sounds terrible.

'Anyway, the man I'm talking about is not Doctor BJ. I've been thinking about a different man.'

'Oh! Who?'

Her big dark eyes meet mine.

'Chuck.'

'Who?'

'Chuck Allen.'

My mouth drops open. Chuck Allen is the man who broke her heart in her 'hometown USA'. The one she mentioned in her note to me that day we first met in the library. He was supposed to be coming to England with her to study in Manchester, but at the last minute accepted a place at Princeton and stayed in the US. Birdie couldn't afford the tuition there, so came to the UK alone and heartbroken. I don't know much more about Chuck than this. Birdie always got tearful when I asked, told me he was ancient history and changed the subject to something more upbeat.

'Why are you thinking about *him*?' I ask. 'Don't we hate him? *I* hate him. I don't know him but he made you sad. So I super hate him.'

Birdie smiles sadly. 'No. I never hated him. He did break my heart though. But he's been on my mind a lot these past few weeks.'

'Don't think about Chuck Allen!' I say, taking hold of her hands. 'Think about happy stuff! Like Doctor BJ's leg-sized arms and nice coffee and shit performance art and YouTube videos where two species of animals are best friends, and glittery things… and getting better!'

Birdie sighs, her smile dropping for a moment. I mentally punch myself in the face. We both know she's not getting better. The surgery she's having on her kidney in two weeks will hopefully give her more time, but beyond that, it's pretty hopeless.

'Sorry,' I say.

'Don't be daft,' she replies, squeezing my hand. Even here, now, stuck in the hospital, Birdie is tougher and braver than I will ever be. 'And I wasn't thinking about Chuck in a bad way. I was thinking about him in a good way. I've actually been thinking that, well, maybe he was the one. I mean, I've never met any other man I felt that way about.'

'What about Chef Greg?'

'No.'

'What about Big Peen Pablo?

'No.'

'What about Aaron the clumsy drummer with a heart of gold?'

'No. Although I did like him a hell of a lot... But none of them meant as much to me as Chuck.'

'Oh!' I say. 'Right! Wow. I always assumed he was nothing more than a distant memory to you!'

Birdie tucks her dark cropped hair behind her ears. 'I've had so much time to reflect in here, and in my situation you do a lot of thinking. And, well, I *think* that Chuck Allen might have been... my Big Sexy Love.'

'No!' I gasp. 'Your Big Sexy Love? Seriously? After all this time? After he broke your heart? No! Really?'

Birdie nods and shrugs one shoulder. 'Really.'

Wow. That's pretty big. Scratch that. It's *epic*.

The pursuit of Big Sexy Love is a thing Birdie told me about that first night after we'd met in the library. We'd headed off on a long walk around the campus, shared our entire life stories and discussed what we hoped for in our futures. She said that she wanted to experience love. But not just any love, Big Sexy Love, as she called it. The kind of love that made you sleepless and excited and devoted and crazy. Dramatic, all-encompassing, can't live without them, the sun shines out of their bum love. Big Sexy Love.

I countered with the notion that feeling so over the top in love about anyone sounded horrible and uncomfortable. How would you get anything done if you were feeling all those feelings all of the time? And what if they let you down? What if they buggered off and left you behind, like my parents did? Then what? Nah. I told her that my version of Big Sexy Love would be a dependable love. Steady. Someone who had a reliable job and turned up on time, and didn't make you lose your head. Someone lovely and consistent and secure. Someone who would never leave. In my fantasy at the time, this someone had sideburns and an unwavering five-year plan.

'Oh Birdie, I'm sorry,' I say, my heart squeezing with pity. How awful to be so young and thinking about lost love. Lost Big Sexy Love, even! As if her life isn't already totally unfair. Shit.

She fiddles with a bit of fabric on her jumper sleeve and bites her lip. 'I want Chuck to know that I forgive him. For choosing to go to Princeton instead of coming with me to England. I… want him to know what he meant to me. I don't want to… *go*… with him thinking that I hate him. I want him to know he was my Big Sexy Love.'

I nod, touched at her generous heart, and try to hold down the tears that spring to my eyes. She's so sweet. She's got all this going on and she's worried about letting an old boyfriend - who sounds like a bit of a shit to be honest - know that she loved him big time.

'Shall I help you write an email?' I ask, looking at my watch. 'I can stay a while, I don't have any plans. No plans at all.'

'No plans at all? On a Friday night? Jeez, Olive.' Birdie shakes her head in exasperation.

'Shuddup,' I say. 'I like a good Friday night in!'

'And Saturdays and Sundays and Mondays and all of the days… Oh Brewster, what am I gonna do with you?'

'We're not talking about me,' I grumble. 'What I'm saying is that I'd be happy to stay and write an email with you. Even if I did have plans, I'd cancel them.'

'Well, the thing is,' Birdie says, pulling a face, 'I don't have Chuck's email address. Or his phone number. No contact details at all.'

'Did you check Facebook? Google him? He must be on Twitter or Instagram.'

Birdie nods. 'Yeah I checked, but there's nothing on there. He doesn't have any social media accounts. It's weird. It's like… he's vanished.'

'No online footprint? That is weird,' I agree, my imagination immediately going into overdrive as it tends to do. 'Hmmm. Maybe he's in prison now? Or maybe he's in witness protection and had to change his name? Maybe he lives in the jungle as a nomad with no contact to the outside world?'

Birdie shushes me before my ideas about Chuck's potential demise become more and more outlandish. 'I couldn't find anything about him online,' she says. 'But I *do* have his parents' last known address. That's where Chuck lived when we were dating. And… I was hoping you'd do me a huge favour.'

'Anything!' I say at once. 'Whatever you need, I'm your girl. Ya grrrrl.'

With a small smile Birdie gets up from her chair and, pulling her IV bag with her, strolls over to the little cabinet at the side of the bed. She opens it up and pulls out a thick, creamy white envelope.

'I wrote Chuck a letter.'

'Great! Okay, I'll go and post it, of course. I'll do it now, shall I?'

I reach to take the letter from her.

'No… I… I need you to take it to Chuck. In person.'

I blink, what is she on about?

'To America,' she says. 'To New York. And… I need you to leave tomorrow.'

CHAPTER FOUR

Text from Donna Pickering: What time will you be back, Olive? You never mentioned and it would be super appreciated to know when exactly you'll be returning to the house! Alex and I are watching a movie and don't want to be interrupted if poss. Thanks!

Frowning, I shake my head at Birdie. 'Actual America? The… country America? New York, *America*?'

I feel the blood drain from my face. I've never even left the north-west of England, let alone been on a plane. Planes go in the sky and my fear of heights is legendary. I won't even sit on the top deck of the bus! And planes fly across the sea and since the time I almost drowned in a community centre pool when I was fourteen, I have a fear of water too! I can't go on a plane! Across an ocean! To a foreign country! On my own! Without prior notice! That's not a thing a person like me does!

'You don't know that Chuck's even there in New York, though,' I say quickly. 'And if you have his parents' address can't we just post the letter there? That seems like a less… *bonkers* plan?'

Birdie grimaces. 'I know it's a lot to ask, but I wouldn't if it weren't truly important. I just really feel like I need Chuck to get this letter. I can't stop thinking about it and I don't want any regrets.' She buries her head in her hands. 'I feel like a real shit for asking. But if we post the letter it could get lost. And his relationship with his parents was always rocky. Even if they still live at that address – I think they probably do, but I don't know for sure because its unlisted and I can't call – they might not give it to him. And… it's not like I have a great deal of time left to wait around.'

My heart drops.

'You might?' I say weakly.

Birdie shakes her head no. 'I was thinking that if you go in person you could start at his parents' house. Or their old house. Whatever it turns out to be. And go from there. Chuck loved New York City. I can't imagine him being anywhere else. We have to at least try! You're the only person I trust to get my letter into his hands. You're my best chance. My only chance, really. And I know you're scared. I know you *hate* the thought of international travel. But… I need this. I really do. I've got my surgery in two weeks and… I'm scared. What if it doesn't go well? What if I don't have all my affairs sorted and…?'

Fuck. *Fuck.*

I think… I think Birdie's giving me a last request.

Shit. This is crazy! This is a horrible, crazy conversation that two twenty-something best friends should never have.

Tears spring to my eyes. I wipe them away before they can splodge onto my face and clear my throat.

'What about work? And where will I stay?' I ask, starting to pace the floor around the small room.

Birdie sits up straighter in her chair, her eyes shining. 'You're not saying no...? Okay. Gosh. Okay. Well, you never take time off. Joan and Joan will let you go if you tell them why. And an old high-school acquaintance is letting me use her Airbnb rental. I will pay. I'll pay for everything, your food and drink, your taxi fares, everything.'

When she's not in hospital, Birdie works as a freelance digital artist. She doesn't make a lot of new stuff these days but her huge colourful prints sell pretty well online. But this sounds expensive...

'I promise I can afford it,' she says. 'My friend is giving me an amazing deal on her studio apartment and the last-minute flights are really quite cheap.'

My insides wobble. She really means this. She's properly thought about it. She's *planned* it, even.

I can't say no.

What kind of person says no to a dying wish?

I look at her looking at me desperately and feel a swell of love and sadness for my dear friend.

'I'll do it,' I say, much to my own surprise.

Birdie exhales with relief, clapping her hands and pulling me into a hug, her skinny arms squeezing me tight. 'Thank you. Thank you. Thank you,' she whispers, leaning her head onto my shoulder. 'Hey, you never know, you might like it.'

A massive busy city in a country that I don't know? Strangers? Planes? Someone else's bed? Trying to find a man called Chuck with no solid knowledge of where he might be?

'Yeah, you never know!' I say brightly, hugging her back, the pair of us getting tangled in her IV wire.

But I seriously doubt it.

* * *

It's late afternoon when I leave the hospital. I walk out into the cold, cloudy spring air, gulping it in as I head towards the bus stop into town. Joan and Joan work the stall on Fridays so I agreed with Birdie that I'd pay them a visit and ask to take some days off. I think they're going to be pretty peeved with me. I'm usually so reliable. Taller Joan once told me that I was as regular as clockwork, which I took as a great compliment.

Once I'd said yes to going to New York to deliver her letter, Birdie swung into action, her energy and excitement doing little to quell the swirling nerves in my stomach. She got out her laptop and in less than half an hour she'd booked the flights, arranged the Airbnb and bought my insurance all while I watched, still stunned that this was even happening.

I get on the bus, clutching the jigsaw puzzle to my chest. After Birdie said she didn't want it, I tried to give it to one of the geriatric wards. They didn't want it either, though, on account that it was 'so very eerie-looking'. I suppose I'll just keep it for myself.

When I reach the market, I pass the stalls I've been passing for the last nine years, waving to the friendly faces of the stallholders I see each day. There's Old Bob with his fabric stall, Mr Rishi who sells shoes and trainers. And there's Camembert Cath, shouting out to all potential customers nearby that she has the most reasonably priced cheese in town and that they should come check out her Sussex Slipcote, taste a bit of her old Gallybagger, sample her glorious Balcombe Brown Ring.

The fish stall is pretty quiet for a Friday afternoon and I spot Joan and Joan leaning against the wall, sipping paper cups of tea and nattering intently.

'Ladies… do you sell goldfish?' I ask when I reach the counter, putting on a daft deep voice.

'Look who it is!' Taller Joan trills when she sees me, her tanned, wrinkled face breaking into a warm smile.

'Hiya love! What the bloody hell are you doing here on your day off?' Tall Joan mock-scolds me.

My cheeks get all warm and I bite my lip nervously. 'I… Well… I'm here because… I was actually wondering if I could… take a few days off?' I say, shoving my hands into the pocket of my coat. 'Five days to be exact.'

The Joans look at each other in surprise. 'Of course love!' Tallest Joan says right away. '*Absolutely.*'

Shit. I think a part of me was hoping she'd refuse. Or at least make it seem like me going would be a hardship, rather than sounding as if she'll pack my cases herself!

'Is everything okay, flower?' Tall Joan asks.

I nod and explain about Birdie's request that I go to New York, find her ex-boyfriend and give him her letter.

'I wouldn't ask, but she's getting sicker every month and she really wants me to do this,' I finish.

'What is it that's wrong with her again?' Tallest Joan asks, putting her hands into the front pocket of her apron.

'Lupus,' I say. 'It's an autoimmune disease.'

Tall Joan shakes her head. 'My friend Margie has that. And she's all right most of the time! I didn't think it was serious!'

'It's manageable in most people,' I explain. 'But Birdie already had heart issues and now the lupus is affecting her kidneys pretty badly. She's had a gazillion treatments over the years, but things are getting worse.'

'How terrible.' Taller Joan shakes her head sadly. 'Well you must go and find this Chunk.'

'Chuck.'

'Right, yes. It all sounds very urgent.'

I step to the side as a customer approaches the counter and orders some scallops.

I nod. 'I suppose it is,' I say with a grimace. I hate urgency. Urgent is never a good state to be in. 'My flight is at 6 a.m. in the morning,' I add, thinking about how little time I have to prepare. At the hospital Birdie stressed how little time she had to waste, that of course the Joans would say yes and that she got a much better deal on a last minute flight booking.

'You take as much time off as you need,' Tall Joan says as she puts the scallops into a tray. 'It'll be good for you to experience a new place.'

I like this place just fine!

'Yeah…' I say faintly.

'Here,' Taller Joan smiles, pressing the till so that the money tray shoots open with a lovely round ringing sound. She pulls out three twenty-pound notes. 'Call it a bonus.' She holds out the cash in my direction.

'I can't take that!' I wave her away. 'I haven't earned it.'

'You bloody have,' Tall Joan says firmly. 'You work so hard here. And you're never sick. You're going to need some spends for the airport. Get yourself a new perfume from duty-free. Or a nice book to read on the plane.'

I do love perfume. And books. But not airports. I mean, I've never been to one, but I'm pretty certain I do not like them. They're full of strangers for a start.

'Take it, you daft sod, before someone runs past and nicks it.'

Heartened by her generosity, I take the money from Taller Joan and tuck it carefully into my satchel.

They're being really nice about this. Like they really want me to go.

'Will you even manage without me?' I ask. 'I don't want to inconvenience you!'

'We'll manage fine, won't we, Joan!'

'Of course we will, Joan.'

'We'll keep this place ticking over!'

'Right! Um. Okay.' I look at each of them suspiciously. They seem very, very keen for me to go. Almost too keen.

'You best get packing,' Tall Joan says with a bright, innocent smile. 'See you when you get back.'

'Bye now, Olive!' Taller Joan adds before turning to serve a new customer.

Okay.

I guess that's sorted.

I give the Joans a goodbye wave and shuffle off back through the market to the tram stop.

Right then.

I'm really doing this.

I'm going to New York City.

On my own.

Shit!

CHAPTER FIVE

Olive's recent search history:

- **Packing for America + tips??**
- **Chances of 27-year-old getting deep-vein thrombosis on long-haul flight**
- **Plane crash statistics**
- ***Final Destination* plane crash scene**
- **What is Jack out of *Dawson's Creek* up to now?**
- **Airbnb safe?**
- **Airbnb murders**
- **(incognito search) *Atonement* library sex scene**

The last time I went away for any length of time was in 2013. Birdie bought me a spa trip to Cheshire in an effort to get me to 'unclench my uptight butt'. And that was only two days away from home in a nearby county, so hardly an epic voyage. I found the whole thing pretty stressful, to be honest. The duvet at the spa was different to my duvet and I couldn't get to sleep. And there was a big open fire in one of the communal areas that I dreamt was going to somehow catch onto the curtains and set the whole place aflame, chargrilling us all to our untimely deaths. That was two days in a place less than an hour away from my house. This? This is a whole different story.

I try to distract myself from the nerves swishing in my belly, by applying myself wholeheartedly to the task of packing. I glance across my bed. I can no longer see the crisp white duvet cover because it is absolutely crowded with stuff. Clothes for every occasion, toiletries for every occasion, reading glasses, books for every mood, my favourite Miller Harris perfume for when I need to feel confident and my old faithful Avon perfume for when I need comfort, my entire skin care regimen, a mini first aid kit, big coat, little coat, shoes for walking slowly, shoes for running, shoes for casual dinner, shoes for fancy dinner, slippers, slipper socks, all kinds of footwear. In a neat pile next to it I have my selection of bras. Comfy bra, sleep bra, strapless bra, padded bra, bra that makes my boobs look very pointy but goes well underneath my red tea dress, bra that doesn't really do anything at all and went pinky grey in the wash but I am immovably attached to.

I glance down at my average-sized suitcase and bury my head into my hands. How do people do this? I need more time to figure this out! How on earth am I going to get this all done by 3 a.m. when I need to set off to the airport?

For the gazillionth time since I left the hospital, I pick up my phone and open up my texts to Birdie. And then for the gazillionth time I close it seconds later. What am I going to do? Cancel? I can't! I won't. Birdie is relying on me and there's no way I'm going to let her down, not now, not when it matters so much.

While I'm staring at the pile of gloves I have managed to accumulate into the mix, there's a light knock on my door.

'You may enter,' I call out.

Alex pops his head round the door, his soft round face grimacing as he sees the state of my room. There was a time when he wouldn't even knock, just burst in and plonk himself down onto my bed for a natter. But since he's been with Donna we seem to have settled into a polite awkwardness.

'Oh dear,' he says, wandering in, eyes searching for a place to sit and unable to find one.

'I know.' I gesture around the room, shaking my head. 'I've been trying to reduce the piles for the past hour but I'm finding it… tricky.'

Alex picks up a pile of scarves from where they're laid out over my easy chair.

'Well you can start here. Nobody needs to take ten scarves anywhere.'

'An attendee of a scarf festival would,' I say reasonably.

'There's no such thing as a scarf festival.'

'Actually yeah, there is! Where else would folk gather to celebrate the beauty of a well-woven chunky knit?'

Alex shakes his head, but I'm actually telling the truth. There is such a festival and if it wasn't held in some remote Scottish village with a history of terrible stormy weather then I would definitely be going.

I gather the scarves to my chest. I cannot choose between them. It took me thirty minutes to choose these final ten that were still in the running towards becoming America's Next Top Scarf For My Neck. 'I have scarves for all occasions here, every type of weather, every type of outfit. What if I leave the wrong ones behind?'

'You're going to New York, not Easter Island. If you find yourself in need of a different scarf you will be able to buy one. If you find yourself in need of a different hat, or coat or pair of shoes, they have shops! They have lots of shops in New York! It's all shops, pretty much. And you're only there for five days!'

'Yeah,' I say. Of course he's right. I am being daft. I just don't want to come unstuck when I'm there.

Alex puts his hand on my arm. 'You know you *don't* have to go, right?'

I frown. 'I'm helping Birdie! I have to!'

Donna pops her head around the door. 'You don't actually, Olive,' she says, casually joining in the conversation as if she's been listening behind the door.

'Of course I do! She's my best friend. She's…' I swallow hard. 'She's dying. She's requested this of me.'

Donna nods. 'It's terrible, truly terrible that she's so unwell.'

'Dying.'

'Yes. Of course, Olive. But a true friend wouldn't ask you to just up and leave your life, to go to America of all places to look for a complete stranger! It's dangerous there. Guns, mobsters, super-sized portions.'

Alex nods sagely.

'Birdie *is* a true friend,' I tell them. 'She wouldn't ask this of me if it weren't desperately important to her.'

Alex and Donna look at each other. 'We're just worried about you is all,' Alex says. 'You're not exactly, you know, worldly. Have you ever left Greater Manchester?'

'I went to Chester once!'

'Chester,' Donna says. 'That's not even an hour away from here.'

'You like things just so,' Alex points out. 'You get grumpy if things are different, if anything changes unexpectedly. You once told the BBC weatherman on the telly to go fuck himself because he'd predicted no rain and it did rain and you didn't have an umbrella.'

'I trusted that weatherman!'

'You like your routine,' Donna adds, smiling benevolently. 'And, Olive, we're just worried that you'll get all the way to New York and get yourself into some sort of pickle.'

'A pickle?'

Alex shrugs. 'That you'll get lost or in trouble or homesick.'

'And it will be left for us to fix things when it all goes wrong,' Donna adds, as if she's the parent talking to a problem child. 'I'm not being funny but, we just know you. We know what you're like.'

I don't *want* to go. I don't want to do this. Everything they're saying about me is completely correct. But still, I feel a flicker of sadness that they think so little of me, assume that I'm incapable.

'I can get in touch with Birdie, if you don't want to go,' Alex says, patting my arm. 'I mean, it is a bit of an awkward situation. I can tell her that it's too much to ask of you. That you can't just take off to New York out of bloody nowhere! You're not the sort of person who can do that. And that's *okay*.'

The flicker of sadness turns into a flame of anger at their complete lack of belief in me. I'm allowed to not believe in myself. Donna doesn't have to either. But Alex? He's my brother! He should trust me.

Like Birdie does.

She trusts me.

She trusts me to do this.

I take a deep breath.

'Wait a minute…' I say as something occurs to me. 'Are you guys trying to reverse psychology me? Are you trying to piss me off by saying I can't do something so that I retaliate with impressive courage and I do it?'

Donna and Alex shake their heads.

'No,' Donna says. 'We genuinely think this is a terrible idea and that you shouldn't go and that your friend is desperate, of course, but also a little selfish for asking this of you.'

Before I have chance to respond, my phone dings with a text. I open it up. It's from Birdie.

I know you're probably shitting yourself right now. But I just want you to know that I appreciate this so much, Brewster. I upgraded your flight to first class so it's a little comfier, I know how you hate small spaces.

I smile. And in that moment any wobbles I had seem to fade a little.

'Is that Birdie?' Alex asks. 'Shall I ring her now? Tell her you're staying.'

I stand up and put my hands on my hips. 'No. Because I am going. And I will find Chuck Allen. I will do this for my friend because I love her and that's what friends do.'

'Doesn't she have family in America who can send this letter?' Donna asks.

I shake my head. 'She was a foster kid. She doesn't have family. *I* am her family. I will be back in less than a week. So, you can either support me and help me sort out this shit heap,' I say, indicating the room of doom. 'Or you can bugger off. I'm already nervous as it is and I don't need you two here trying to talk me out of it.'

There. That told them. I am Olive Brewster. Strong, capable woman and they can eat their words.

Alex and Donna blink at my little speech, shake their heads sadly and leave the room.

Oh.

'You're not going to help me pack?' I yell. 'Guys? GUYS?'

I hear them tread softly down the stairs.

'Guys, come on,' I call out again.' Help meeeeee!'

They've gone. They're seriously not on my side?

'Alex?' I shout. 'Come back, dude!'

No answer.

Fine. *Fine.*

Looks like I'm doing this alone.

Totally, completely alone…

I am an adult woman and I *can* do this alone.

Can't I?

CHAPTER SIX

Olive's phone reminders:

Passport, money, tickets!
Remember: Air travel is the SAFEST mode of transport
Listen to 'Still Minds' app in taxi to airport
Don't freak the fuck out, you massive worrywart

Arriving at Manchester airport, I poke my head between the two front seats to pay the driver. As I hand him the money, I notice that my dumb hand is trembling. It's 4 a.m. and I have spent the entire night getting all of my earthly belongings into my suitcase, plus a smaller suitcase I borrowed from Donna (who informed me that I should be careful with it as it scuffs 'super-duper easily' and she's already doing me a huge favour lending it to me). I'm operating on zero sleep.

The taxi driver accompanies me to the boot of the car

and heaves out my suitcases, his face turning fuchsia with the effort.

'Great! Thanks!' I place a firm hand on each suitcase handle and start to yank them to the airport doors. They're so ridiculously heavy that my rate of movement is around 0.001 miles per hour. As I'm dragging them, I'm making a sort of guttural animal noise, like a contender on The World's Strongest Man contest pulling a lorry.

The cab driver pops his head out of the car window and laughs at me. 'You want a trolley, love!'

'Sorry?' I say. A trolley?

He points over to a big line of upright metal contraptions on wheels. I notice that everyone else in the vicinity is using these trolleys to push around their luggage.

'Ah! Yes, of course!' I say.

Of course!

It all makes sense now.

'Have you never *been* to an airport?' The driver laughs, judging me.

'Ha ha!' I laugh back. 'Duh. Of course! What kind of human woman aged twenty-seven has never even been to an airport? That would make me a loser, right? Nope. I come to the airport all the time! I practically live here! I'm like Tom Hanks in that film where he lives in the airport.'

The taxi driver gives me a pitying smile.

Shaking my head with mirth, like I'm in on the joke, I lug my cases over to the trolleys and heave them up, making a strained 'eeeeehuuh' sort of noise as I plonk them on. There we go! That wasn't too hard in the end! I allow myself a little smile while I catch my breath. I'm doing this. I'm actually doing it!

As I enter the main part of the airport, my positive feelings increase. Oooh. It's very quiet and organised. Runs of check-in desks line the huge expanse of back wall.

Before each desk stands an orderly queue, filled with people patiently waiting to check in their luggage. I love a queue, me! I once made the joke that 'everyone knows where they stand with a queue'. I thought it was quite a witty joke, sadly no one else laughed. But the point is that with a queue you know what to expect. Everyone in a queue has made an unspoken pact to follow the rules, to respect the right order of things, something about that speaks to me on a deep level.

I scan across the check-in desks until I spot one with a British Airways logo and, with a yank, set my trolley in motion, trundling towards my queue.

At the back of the line, a couple of people ahead of me turn around and give me a friendly smile. Queue buddies! I have queue buddies! One of them gives a nod of approval at the bumbag slung around my waist. I smile back and pat my bumbag proudly. What a find that was! While rummaging around the house for a pair of light gloves for if the weather turns cold but not cold enough for the heavy-duty mittens I had already packed, I found this old bumbag stuffed in the bottom of a plastic storage box full of things Alex has been asking me to throw away for years. I loved this bumbag when I was twelve. For a start, it's luminous pink and on the front there's a shiny hologram picture of the sun. Plus it's super waterproof, *plus* it has a secret pocket inside. I used to carry it around with me everywhere, put in cool-ass daisies I'd picked on the field behind our house, store my Hubba Bubba supply so that Alex wouldn't nick them. I'd keep my Walkman in the front and my chapstick in the secret pocket along with a fifty-pence piece I found on the street and wanted to keep safe in case the person who lost it tracked me down and asked for it back. It was fantastic to have a little pouch tied around my belly like a kangaroo. And since it's so much more secure than a handbag that could be lost, or snatched away by a thug at any moment, I decided, at around one this morning, to extend the belt to its largest possible width and bring it with me for my trip. It's perfect! Even if Donna did point and laugh when she saw me in it. What does Donna know? Nothing, that's what.

In the secret pocket, tucked very safely away, is the thick white envelope containing Birdie's precious letter to Chuck Allen. In the main bag part is my phone, my passport, flight tickets, antacids, paracetamol, chewing gum and some wire headphones. I know it might not be the most stylish apparel, but everything I may need at any moment is literally clasped around my waist and in that there's a certain security that transcends the need to look cool to people I don't even know. And even so, a part of me suspects that it actually does look pretty fucking cool in a hipstery, ironic, retro sort of way.

I'm almost at the front of the queue when a loud American voice makes me jump.

'Excuse me! Excuse me! Sorry, folks!'

I whip my head around and notice a slim man approaching our line. He has messy, slightly too long light brown hair and dark, thick-framed glasses perched on his face.

'Excuse me!' he repeats, striding past everyone with a sense of great importance.

I frown as he marches ahead of me, shuffles in front of the woman before me in the line and leans his forearms casually on the check-in desk. He plonks his passport down, running a hand through his hair.

Is… is he pushing in?

'Excuse me, miss. Sorry!' he says, this time to the check-in assistant, a young dark-haired woman with tired eyes. 'My name's Seth.'

'Hello sir.' The woman gives a slight forehead wrinkle. 'Um… is everything okay?'

'I'm incredibly sorry about this,' the guy says, 'but I'm a TV writer and I have to file a last-minute change to a script that's needed immediately. But the thing is, my laptop and my phone are out of juice and I need to get through to the departure lounge charging station so I can charge them up and send the script changes by email.'

He's cutting the queue because he needs to charge his electrical equipment? I let out a little snort. That's not a reason to jump a queue! Maybe he should have been more organised. *Maybe* he should have done what I did and charged all of his electrical stuff before leaving the house, while also packing spare batteries and one of those wind-up chargers you can use in emergencies.

I turn back to the rest of the queue with an eye roll that says 'get a load of this guy'.

A few of my queue buddies nod in agreement. One sighs, one curls her lip discreetly, but mostly they look at their feet.

I turn around, peeved, tutting loudly to myself.

The man turns around at my tut, a look of surprise on his face.

'I'm sorry, ma'am,' he says with a wide smile. 'I wouldn't do this if it wasn't kind of a work emergency.'

Ma'am? Isn't that American slang for women of a certain age? I'm only twenty-seven. I found a grey hair last month, and I may be make-up-free because it is stupid o clock, but I don't think I could be mistaken for a ma'am. This guy looks older than me! Behind the glasses he has little crow's feet around his eyes.

'In England we queue,' I tell him, immediately realising that I sound like a real dick, or Donna. I don't mean to but his self-entitled line cutting is really getting my goat.

'Which TV show?' the check-in assistant asks him, her tired eyes perking up a little.

Seriously?

The guy lowers his voice but I'm close enough to hear him say, '*Sunday Night Live*'.

Wow. *Sunday Night Live* is a huge American sketch comedy show. Even I know that.

'Oh, I love that show!' check-in woman says, fully awake now. 'That Beyoncé Lemonade Parody you guys did. I saw it on YouTube. It made me laugh so much!'

'Thanks,' I hear the man reply. 'If you let me through you will be saving the next episode from disaster, I swear!'

God, how dramatic. Who would even fall for that?

Then, to my outrage, the woman puts her hand out to take the man's passport. He only has a large record bag lobbed across his body and a tiny hand-luggage-sized suitcase, so with a few clicks on the computer he's checked in and she's ushering him through to the departure lounge before anyone can protest.

'Thank you, thank you!' he mutters, hurrying through the walkway by the check-in desk. But before he disappears from sight, he turns on his heel, points at me and calls out, completely straight-faced: 'Nice fanny pack.'

Oh my god. WHAT did he just say to me? I blush a crimson red, my mouth opening and closing like a Hungry Hungry Hippo.

It takes me a moment to figure out that fanny pack is American for bumbag and that this bespectacled stranger wasn't complimenting my vajeen. But before I can respond with anything more than a disgusted shake of the head, the queue jumper has disappeared.

Honestly, some people are just *so rude.*

* * *

Turns out I was completely duped about what the airport would be like based on the check-in area. It is not calm and organised and serene. It is Freaking Crazy!

I stand stock-still in the departure lounge, eyes wide in disbelief as to how totally different it is to the zen-like check-in area. Here, it's crowded and loud and grim. There are children running around unattended, huge groups of men wearing matching T-shirts and women in headbands with miniature penises atop them.

I blink and try not to let the chaos terrify me into turning around and going right back home to my bed and to my job and to my little life that's safe and comforting and wonderfully predictable.

I shuffle forward a few steps, wondering where the perfume shops are and where I might buy a book, when I hear a kid behind me yelling with glee.

'Look at it! Look at it go!' he squeals.

I turn around curiously, following his gaze to a huge glass window wall on the other side of the departure lounge and my throat freezes up. I do an actual gasp. Because, right there, through the window is a massive airplane speeding down the runway, the front wheels tilted off the ground at an angle that does not, in any way, look okay. I swallow hard, my eyes wide. Of course I've seen airplanes take off before on TV and in movies, but seeing it up close and knowing that in a few short hours I will be sitting on one of them as it cranks away into the sky. Argh!

I waddle slowly towards the massive window, watching as the back of the airplane lifts off from the ground. It looks so heavy and unstable. It can't possibly be safe. It looks ridiculous. How is it doing that? Why is it tilting? Surely, that can't be right?

'Check out that lass! She's turned green!'

My thoughts of doom are interrupted by deep voices

and laughing from my left. I turn around to where a group of muscular men are sitting around an open-plan bar table, guzzling pints while laughing and pointing at me.

'You look a bit unwell there, love,' one of them, a huge muscled guy with tanned skin and nice sideburns, says to me.

'Green in the face,' another of the group adds, helpfully.

'Do you, like, need to puke?'

'Uh, I'm fine,' I say, my eyes flicking to the now empty space outside where the airplane once was. Where is it? Is that it right up there? That dot going into the clouds? How is it in the sky? Why have I never really thought about this before?

'You don't look it,' another guy with curly blonde hair says. 'You definitely look like you're going to puke!'

I shake my head. 'Just a bit nervous about flying, I think. I'll be all right!'

I make to leave, to find somewhere quiet to sit, to maybe listen to that Still Minds app I've been meaning to listen to, when the hunk with the sideburns asks, 'Where are you off to then?'

'New York,' I answer, feeling a little flicker of pride as I do. It does sound super cool when I say it out loud. 'Manhattan, actually,' I add.

'Hey! New York! Get me a cup of cawfee! And a chilli dawg!' the men start saying over each other, laughing loudly at their terrible impressions of a New York accent. I can't help but laugh a little as one of them adds 'I like brunch!' and when he can't think of anything else to say, he says 'Get me a cup of cawfee' again, to which they all laugh uproariously.

'We're going to Australia for the rugby,' Sideburns says. 'But our flight's been delayed. We've been sitting here for three hours already.'

Behind me I hear another plane taking off. I spin around, my eyes wide, my stomach dipping as it wobbles its way into the air.

'Fuuuuuuck,' I groan to myself.

'You're really frightened, aren't you?' Sideburns asks, elbowing curly blonde to stop doing his terrible Robert De Niro 'You talkin' to me' impression.

'Pretty much, yeah,' I say, pulling a face. 'It's weird seeing it all up close! The planes look so big and cumbersome!'

'Well, Dan here is shit-scared of flying,' Sideburns tells me, pointing at curly blonde guy.

Dan gives a thumbs up. 'It's pretty much my worst fear,' he confirms, not looking at all bothered about it.

'No one really *likes* flying,' a hunky dark-skinned man says. 'We just do what we have to do to get through it.'

'And what's that?' I ask, desperate for any information that will make this whole prospect less alarming. 'Tell me the secret! Please!'

Sideburns waves his arm across their table, indicating the graveyard of empty pint glasses. 'We drink.'

'It helps,' Dan says with a burp.

I pull a face and look at my watch: 4.45 a.m. 'I'm more of a Weetabix for breakfast kind of girl, to be honest.'

Sideburns laughs. 'Dan, get this lady a pint. I'm Colin, by the way. This is Bob, Matty, Paulo and, of course, Dan.'

Colin holds his hand out, brown eyes sparkling with friendliness and alcohol.

I tense up as I hear the roar of another plane taking off behind me.

'Olive,' I say, shaking Colin's big hand and then waving at the other guys, all dressed in matching blue rugby shirts. 'And I'll have a small glass of red wine, thanks. Make sure it's small, though! I don't drink dead often.'

But before I've finished speaking, Dan's already on his way to the bar.

I don't think he heard me…

CHAPTER SEVEN

Text from Olive to Birdie: I love you sooooo much!!! Am at airport. It's okay here, have met nice peeps and one not so nice peep who jumped Q and made fun of my bumbag!!! I will do this for you. I promise I will find your BIG SEXY LOVE and everything will be okay, I promise! I PROMISE YOU THIS. Also, do you think libraries are sexy? Why are they sexy?

From Birdie: It's so early, Brewster! You sound drunk? Are you drunk? You're never drunk. Oh god, please be drunk. Shit! I'm laughing at the very thought of it. P.S. Yes, libraries are sexy, IF YOU'RE A GIANT NERD. P.P.S. A bumbag?? Wtf?!

Wow. I am feeling sooo much better about everything. It's crazy! I'm feeling better about flying through the air on a tin can, about going to a new country on my own. I still feel awful about Birdie, of course, but the ache in my heart has been diluted by a warm, fuzzy feeling in my cheeks.

I *feel* like I've drunk quite a lot of beer, but I'm looking at the pint glass (Dan ignored my request for a small glass of wine and got me a pint of beer like everyone else) and it's still almost full. Weird.

Either way, I've been having a nice time chatting to Colin and his sideburns. As it happens, he lives not too far away from me in Greater Manchester. He's been telling me all about his love of mending old cars, how passionate he is about playing rugby every Sunday morning and how he loves nothing more than hunkering down on a Saturday night, all cosy with a blanket, cup of cocoa and a good movie.

'Yes!' I shouted when he told me about his fondness for the indoors. 'Me too! Everything you need is at home. Why would you want to go out to a busy club full of people who you don't even know!'

'Exactly.' He nodded fervently. 'The beauty of a cosy night in is vastly underrated.'

To which we clinked pints and beamed at each other.

He's great. Unexpectedly lovely. And since I've been sitting here I've barely thought about the planes at all.

The screens on the wall of the bar area update and I realise that my flight is boarding.

'Time to go!' I stand up from my chair. 'Woah!' I wobble. 'I feel pretty blummin tipsy.' I peer at my pint. 'I've not drunk much though,' I say, pointing at it.

'Um, love, you've had two of those!' Dan says with a chuckle.

'What?'

Matty points to a big jug of beer on the table. 'We've been topping up. Didn't you know?'

I gasp. 'No!'

The entire table bursts into laughter.

Shit. No wonder I feel so drunk.

'Oh no!' I half grumble, half laugh.

'Are you okay?' Colin asks me gently. 'Do you want me to walk you to the gate?'

'I'm all right, thanks.'

'I'd like to,' he says, smiling sweetly.

'Oh. Okay then. Bye lads!' I wave goodbye at the other lads on the table who wish me luck in New York.

'If you get scared again,' Dan yells as Colin and I start to walk away, 'just remember, booze is the answer!' To which all of the others roar their agreement and down their pints.

When we reach the gate, Colin turns to me and gives me a big grin, displaying a row of small, but very clean teeth.

'I have really enjoyed meeting you, Olive,' he says, his long-lashed eyes sparkling. 'I'd love to get your number. Take you out sometime? Or *in*, if you prefer? Ha ha.'

'Oh!' I say, surprised. Wow. People don't ask for my number very often. And when they do, they're usually fish-market customers and over sixty. But Colin seems nice. Reliable. Steady. Sweet Exactly like I told Birdie my idea of Big Sexy Love would be.

I think about how impressed she would be if I'd managed to bag a date at the airport. That would definitely cheer her up!

I don't know if it's because of the alcohol making me feel loosey-goosey or maybe it's because Colin seems very safe and kind and is as fond as staying in as I am. Or maybe it's the flash of a thought in my head that if I want to have a family of my own one day I'm going to have to start dipping my toe in somewhere. Why not here? I can get to know him a little by text, risk-free. Whatever the reason, I find myself saying yes and tap my number into Colin's phone.

'I'm in Australia for three weeks, so I'll call you when I'm back.' He takes his phone back from me and puts it into his front jeans pocket. 'But… we could text in the meantime, right?'

'Right,' I say. 'Definitely!'

He really does have a pleasant face. And nice big arms. And sideburns. I've always had positive feelings towards sideburns.

'Okay then!' he says.

'Okay then!' I say.

'Safe flight!'

'I hope so!'

'Bye Olive!'

'Bye Colin!'

I watch him walk away and feel a little swoosh of excitement in my tummy.

At the gate entrance I hand my passport and boarding pass to the assistant, wobbling tipsily to the left as I do. I walk down a little tunnel and all of a sudden I see a very beautiful woman in a peacock-coloured suit and matching hat.

'Good morning, may I have your ticket and boarding pass, please?'

Taking them out of my bumbag, I hand them over, wondering if the beautiful flight attendant can tell that I've been drinking. I'm sure I read somewhere that you're not allowed to be intoxicated on an aircraft. But then… why do they have bars at the airport?

When I'm handed back my passport and boarding pass, I turn to the right and am about to head down the aisle to find my seat when the flight attendant grabs my arm.

Shit. I'm caught. Can she smell booze on my breath? Are they going to throw me off the flight?

'Miss, you're actually on that side,' the woman tells me with a friendly smile, thumbing to the left where there's a heavy blue curtain draped across the aisle. 'Your ticket is first class!'

'Oh. Oh!' I say, relief sweeping over me. 'So I am!'

I flick my curls back as if this is all totally normal for me, slide open the soft curtain and walk into a part of the plane that looks nothing like the cramped, bus-like version I just saw on the right-hand side.

Woah. It's like Air Force One in here! Okay… this isn't so bad…

I search my ticket for my seat number. 34b. That's my bra size! That's got to be a sign that everything will be okay, surely?

I wander down the aisle until I reach my seat. It's so roomy on this plane. I look down at the floor – it's carpeted! I notice that all the seats are almost like little private pods, one pod on each side of the aisle. Wow! I wiggle my eyebrows, impressed.

34b! Here I am! I settle myself into my little pod and gasp as I realise that there's a massive flat-screen TV all to myself, and that the seat reclines so that I can put my feet up!

I have two big windows to the left of me, which is not ideal considering that I need to pretend that I'm *not* in the sky. And so I pull down on the blinds. Now I can pretend I'm just in a really small hotel. Or on a really fancy bus or something. Beyoncé's tour bus!

As the other passengers file onto the plane, I mess around with the TV, pressing my fingers against it. It's touchscreen! My TV at home is massive, yes, but it's from 2004 so it still has a whole box at the back.

Man. If only I could just hang out here without actually having to go somewhere. It's so cool!

I reach into my bumbag and grab my phone, texting Birdie.

This airplane is so cool! I cannot believe you got me first class. The comfort level is definitely helping my fear of flying. P.S. I am a bit drunk. It was an accident. P.P.S. I am not a giant nerd. You are.

My phone pings back immediately, but it's not from Birdie, it's from Colin!

I'm watching your plane from the lounge and wishing I was coming with you x.

My eyebrows shoot up. Well that's very forward. And nice… right? It's nice that he's thinking of me even though we only just said goodbye less than five minutes ago. I smile to myself and text back.

Thank you! Hope you're well.

Even as I'm pressing send I realise that my reply might be the stiffest flirt text anyone has ever sent. But that's because I've never sent one before! Frowning, I quickly send a kissy face emoji to soften my formality and shove my phone back into my bumbag.

Plugging my headphones into the TV, I switch the channels until I find an old episode of *Curb Your Enthusiasm* – my favourite TV show.

'Jackpot!' I mutter with a grin.

I see a flash of green out of the corner of my eye. Looking up, I notice it's that guy from the check-in queue. The queue pusher. The one who made fun of my bumbag in front of my queue buddies. Ugh. His pod is the one directly opposite mine on the other side of the aisle. Damn. He looks so smug sitting in his seat, his white button-down shirt all crumpled, like he's too busy and clever to iron it, those big pretentious hipster glasses on his face. He thinks he's so high and mighty in his fancy TV job.

I realise I'm staring at him and quickly turn my head away before he spots me. In fact, I don't want to have to engage at all. I do what I always do when I want to signal to other people that I am not available for interaction – I pull the hood up on my hoodie and tug the string at the bottom so that only a tiny portion of my eyes nose and mouth are poking through the gap.

Okay, so I've never done it in public before – it's a pretty intimidating look – but it works when I'm trying to get Donna to leave me alone, and that's not generally an easy task.

'Oh it's you. Fanny pack!'

Shit. He's seen me. And he's calling me Fanny pack! Ugh.

'In England we call it a bumbag,' I say, giving him a firm but polite smile.

'Why are you so obsessed with England?' he asks, turning his pod seat so it's sort of facing mine. Jeez. What part of 'I have my hoodie hood up so bugger off!' doesn't he understand?

'Excuse me?'

'*In England* we queue. *In England* we call it a bumbag,' he mimics in a terribly whiny Liam Gallagher type accent.

'I'm not obsessed with England,' I respond, my nostrils flaring a little. 'I'm *leaving* it, aren't I?'

The guy just laughs and pulls out his precious laptop that he was so desperate to get charged up earlier. It's got stickers all over the back of it. UCB, SECOND CITY,

MAD TV, I HEART IMPROV and one that says 'There are no mistakes, only opportunities.' Which is blatantly wrong. What a weirdo. Who covers a nice fresh MacBook with stickers? What is he? Fourteen years old?

I snort to myself.

'What's that, Fanny pack?' he says. 'Did you say something?'

I look at him wide-eyed and point to my headphones to indicate that I am engaged in another activity.

He laughs again and with a nod spins the pod chair back to facing his window.

At that moment an air hostess arrives and offers me a selection of beverages for take-off.

'I thought there was no drinking on flights?' I ask.

The woman laughs. 'Of course there is. As long as no one is intoxicated then it's fine by us. Champagne?'

'Why not?' I say, feeling fairly relaxed by my earlier beers. The woman hands me a little bottle of champagne. In the top of it is a copper spout. You drink it straight from the bottle. This is so cool! I take a picture to send to Birdie and settle in to watch my show. And just as I've forgotten where I am, the plane engine whirs up noisily and we start to move.

Instantly I sober up.

Shit.

I lift up my window blind a tiny bit and peek through. We're nowhere near the runway, yet, but we are definitely moving. The plane is definitely moving. I look around to see if anyone else is panicking. Nope. Everyone else on the place gives zero fucks that we are now *moving*.

An air hostess stands in the aisle and on my TV, *Curb Your Enthusiasm* disappears and a new video flashes up. It's showing scenarios in which we might have to exit the plane in an emergency. Oh god!

The air hostess mimics the character on the screen.

Most people aren't even watching her, but I am *glued*. It's horrible. She is calmly telling us everything that could possibly go wrong on the plane, *while we are on the plane*!

And then something truly awful happens, the video on the TV shows a hypothetical plane emergency. And if I was feeling more relaxed about all this before, I am definitely not now. No siree. On screen a woman in her plane seat looks super chill as oxygen masks fall down from overhead. This is not realistic at all. Why is she so chill about the fact that she now needs emergency oxygen? Surely she should be screaming and yelling, 'Oh no! The oxygen masks! This is bad, guys!'

'Secure your own oxygen mask before helping others to secure theirs,' the narrator says in a soothing tone.

I peek over to queue jumper. He's clicking on his phone not even paying attention. I bet *he* would secure his own mask right away and not even help anyone else to secure theirs. I bet, if his mask was even slightly faulty he'd steal someone else's. Probably mine. I tut at him in disgust.

As the real life plane starts to speed up, the video shows a queue of plane passengers making their way to the airplane door in an orderly fashion.

What the fuck? Now the airplane door is opening and all the passengers start sliding down a slide. Not even a real slide. It's inflatable. It's… a bouncy castle slide! Are they still in the air? Are they dropping down into the *sea*? Why do they look so calm? How are they so coolly accepting their impending deaths? They look like they were *expecting* their plane to crash the whole time. 'Oh well, time to die, let me just get on this death slide! Byeeee!'

Jeeeeeeeeez.

Now the air hostess is holding up a whistle. What is that for? Why is she trying to make music in an emergency scenario? I'm so confused. And then, all at once, the video ends. Just like that! What happened to the people who went down the slide? *Where did they end up?* ARE THEY ALIVE?

Oh god.

The air hostess calmly takes a seat and buckles her seatbelt, totally at ease with this whole shitshow. I look down to triple-check I've done mine. I pull the tag a little tighter. The seatbelt is now so snug that it's digging painfully into my pelvis. I'm totally fine with that. This belt buckle might be the only thing between me and that fucking balloon slide.

The noise around us increases as the plane speeds up even more.

I try to swallow but my throat feels dry. Holy crap. It's really loud. Is it supposed to be this loud? Why does it sound so clunky? Like bits of machinery are rattling around, unsecured.

I grab my little bottle of champagne with trembling hands and gulp it back, not caring as the bubbles fizz up a little, dripping down my neck and all over my hoodie.

I take a deep breath. I knew this would be scary but *this is really fucking scary*. I was completely right to not want to do this.

My heart starts to pound. I hear the *Jaws* theme tune in my head. I feel the blood drain out of my face as my entire body is tilted backward and the nose of the plane points skywards.

This is it. We're leaving the ground.

We are leaving the earth, kind of.

I am mid-air.

Argh. I am mid-air. I'm stuck here, mid-air!

I do not like it!

Shiiiiiiiiiit.

CHAPTER EIGHT

Text from Colin: I am well. I hope you are too. I can see your flight taking off from here! I am waving at you. Hi, Olive!

I feel myself start to gasp for air. I do it quietly because everyone else is super calm. One woman further down the aisle is putting on a face mask, a man over there is reading a magazine and eating peanuts joyfully. The queue jumper is tap tapping away on his laptop with a half-smile on his face. Meanwhile I'm completely malfunctioning over in my fancy little pod.

Why is the champagne not working? I felt much more tranquil before.

I squeeze my eyes shut and as the plane rumbles and tilts its ways into the air I let out a tiny squeak of fear.

I grip the armrests of my luxury chair tightly when someone grabs my hand. I look up sharply to see queue jumper leaning over from his pod, still buckled into his seat, his arm outstretched across the aisle to hold my hand in his. It vaguely occurs to me to snatch my hand back because this seems very intimate and weird. But… it's helping, so I just leave it there.

'Not long until the bad part's over, Fanny Pack,' he says with a small smile. 'And then another nine hours until we land and it happens again. Just breathe.'

I seize onto his hand like it's a life raft. The plane sways a bit more and with my free hand I clutch my champagne bottle in the hopes there are a few drops I've missed. Nope. Nada. I look over the aisle. Queue jumper has three drinks. A mini bottle of champagne like I had and two mini bottles of whisky.

He notices me eyeing them and passes them over.

'Whatever you gotta do.' He shrugs.

I grab the drinks and down one after the other.

'People usually take Xanax when they're this scared of flying,' he says, one hand still holding mine, the other continuing to tap out onto his laptop keyboard.

'It's my first time,' I explain in a weird high-pitched voice. 'And last minute. I didn't have time to prepare, mentally or physically!'

I focus on queue jumper's hand, squeezing it extra tight when all at once, the clunking sounds settle down, a gentle ding tinkles out and a woman's confident, soothing voice comes through the speakers of the cabin.

'Good morning, I'm Anna Cooper and I'm your pilot today. After a smooth take-off the fasten seatbelt sign has been turned off and you are free to move around the cabin. We will arrive at JFK in approximately nine hours. The cabin crew will be with you shortly with snacks and drinks.'

I look up to find that the seatbelt light above me has gone out. I think I will keep my seatbelt on, ta.

'That's better, right?' queue jumper asks.

I notice I'm still gripping onto his hand. I let go quickly. 'Thanks for the hand.'

He shakes it with a grimace. Eek. I must really have squeezed it. 'No problem.' He points at his laptop. 'I should get back to it, I guess.'

'Oh!' I nod. 'Yeah, of course. Sorry. I'll just…'

I don't know what to say, I'm feeling a bit embarrassed about my freak out, and so I spin my pod seat round to face away from him.

Rummaging in my bumbag, I pull out the Rescue Remedy I carry with me everywhere and squirt a couple of drops under my tongue. When, five minutes later, the flight attendant comes to take our drink orders, I order another champagne.

'Of course! What size would you like?'

Um. I don't know… I look at the cart. There are small bottles like the one I just had and full-size bottles. If I get the full-size one it could keep me slightly tipsy for the whole flight. I wouldn't have to worry about asking for more… And I still have that money that Taller Joan gave me. I didn't spend at the airport…

'A… full-sized bottle, please?' I ask.

'A full bottle for you! Are you sure?' the hostess responds in a perfectly clipped accent.

Hmmm. Is she judging me? Is it weird to be having a whole bottle of champagne to myself? I know it probably is but, like Dan said at the airport, when in doubt, 'booze is the answer!'

'I'm, er, celebrating,' I blurt out to the air hostess before I can stop myself.

'Fantastic!' she says, with a wide approving smile.

There. Justified! Hah! No one can judge anyone for having champagne for celebration.

'What are you celebrating?' she asks.

Oh. Uh…

What am I celebrating? Nothing. Nowt. I have nothing celebratory going on in my life right now.

On the TV in front of me Larry David is in a jewellery shop buying a ring for his wife.

'I, er, just got engaged?' I blurt, my unexpected words tilt up at the end as if I'm asking a question.

What the hell?

'Wow, amazing!' the air hostess says, a little more loudly than necessary. Her eyes sparkle. She actually seems genuinely chuffed for me. 'Well in that case the champagne is on us!'

'Are you serious?'

'Oh, of course! Our first-class passengers are very important to us and you've just made one of the biggest, most exciting decisions of your life!'

'Yes. I… suppose I have! Brilliant.' I smile, feeling a flicker of guilt at my lie that disappears quite quickly at the thought of more angst-reducing champagne and the fact that it's going to be for free. This is totally the kind of thing Birdie would do!

I laugh at the thought of telling her.

'Ah, are you thinking of him right now?' the air hostess says, digging into her trolley, taking out a small silver bucket, filling it with ice and popping open a massive bottle of champagne.

'Yes,' I say with the kind of dreamy/smug combo smile I imagine an engaged person would pull.

'What's his name?' she asks, putting a crystal flute onto my table and pouring a stream of the sparkling amber liquid into it.

'Colin. His name is … Colin,' is what pops out. I go with it. 'Yeah, um Colin… Collins.'

Oops.

'You don't sound so sure!' she giggles. 'Colin Collins? What an unusual name!'

I giggle too. I'm not a natural giggler. I sound weird. Like an engaged person. 'I'm still in shock,' I say. 'He did it this morning at the airport. Spur of the moment. Didn't even have chance to get a ring!' I wave my naked left hand in her direction as if I'm proving something.

Why am I lying, still? I have my champagne. I got what I wanted. I am behaving like a psycho.

The woman congratulates me again before making her way off down the rest of the aisle where absolutely nobody else is obnoxious enough to order a whole bottle of champagne all to themselves.

I tuck into my bubbles with a sigh of delight. Okay. I just have to drink this and watch the whole series of *Curb Your Enthusiasm* and soon I will be in New York, I'll find Chuck Allen, deliver the letter, come home and get back to normal life, safe and sound.

I'm about to put my headphones back in when the ding sounds out of the cabin speaker again.

'Hello this is your captain speaking,' comes the voice.

My stomach dips and my head quickly runs through all the scenarios she could be about to announce. We've run out of fuel, we have to do an emergency landing, someone is holding her hostage in the cockpit, the blow up slide has got a puncture, the cast of *Friends* have definitively announced that they will never ever ever do a *Friends* movie.

But no. It's an altogether different kind of disaster.

'We here at BA would just like to wish some hearty congratulations to one of our first-class passengers Olive Maudine Brewster of seat 34b on her recent engagement to Colin Collins.'

Oh good lord.

I turn very red indeed as I hear scattered applause break out around me. Why did they have to announce my fake engagement? And tell people my middle name? I never share that with anyone – it's an amalgamation of Maude and Nadine that my mum thought was so cool and unique and actually just sounds like it's not even a real name. But, of course it's on my ticket.

Gah.

'Is that you?' queue jumper says, spinning around in his chair to face me. 'Olive Maudine Brewster?'

'Oh. Um, yeah.'

'Congrats. Does Colin wear a little fanny pack too?' he asks, his face very serious. His face is so serious I don't believe for a moment he is really a comedy writer.

I frown. 'Actually no,' I say, thinking of Colin in the airport and his nice brown eyes and healthy head of hair. 'And my "fanny pack" isn't little. It's big and roomy. You can fit in more than you think at first glance,' I remark imperiously. Then my words echo back at me. The person sitting in front of me – an elderly gentleman – cranes his head round, looking at me in horror.

Queue guy snickers. I ignore him.

Rolling my eyes, I turn the volume up on my headphones and neck some more champagne, enjoying the warmed feeling it gives my cheeks.

The plane jerks from side to side for a second. I clutch the glass with both hands to stop them shaking.

Then I put my champagne down and look at my watch.

Only eight hours of peril to go…

CHAPTER NINE

Text from Birdie: Eek, Brewster, you're on a plane right now! Go you! I've sent you an email with details on places you might want to visit when you're in New York. No pressure! I know you're not there for a touristy trip, but you'll defo have time to have a little look around. And I'd love it if you took some pictures of stuff for me! I love being a British Citizen now, but it will be nice to see my bonkers home city through your fresh eyes! Hope flight going well and you are not freaking out too much. I bet you're totally fine and are wondering why you have never flown before, right? Am v proud of you!!

I have managed to hold my bladder for three hours, which has got to be some kind of record! But it's now so full from all of the champagne that I'm feeling all fidgety and uncomfortable.

I should probably go and deal with it. But the thought of actually unbuckling my safety belt, leaving behind my life-saving oxygen mask, standing up on this wobbly plane and walking to the loo feels like a thing I really do not want to do. Also I am pretty tipsy again now. Fine, that's an understatement. I am discreetly wasted. I say discreetly because nobody knows. I've just been quietly watching *Curb Your Enthusiasm*, drinking my champagne every time the plane shakes, which is a lot. Still, I am nowhere near inebriated enough to brave the toilet. I mean, what if something happens while I'm in there? There's turbulence or a plane emergency and there's no one there to help me? And the plane goes down, and I die mid-pee. I don't want to die mid-pee.

My bladder gives out another squeeze of desperation.

Argh! What other choice do I have? I can't piss myself right here in the plane seat. I mean, it's *first class*.

I look around desperately.

There's only one thing for it. I need a flight attendant to come with me. They can hold me steady while I walk down the aisle of the plane, stand outside and then if anything bad happens in the cubicle they can help me escape. Yes, that's it. That's what I'll do.

I press my cabin crew dinger.

I wait for a few minutes, but no one comes.

I press it again.

Nothing!

Where are they? Is there some sort of emergency? Something bigger than the emergency in my bladder?

Biting my lip, I peer around to see where the loo is. It's only a few seats away. Maybe I can make it…

And then the plane swings violently, quickly to the left. NO one else seems to notice but I do.

I press my dinger thing again.

Nada.

Shit. I can't wait any longer. Literally cannot wait.

There's only one thing for it…

I spin my pod seat around and knock on the back of queue guy's seat.

He spins around and takes his headphones off his head. 'What's up, Fanny Pack?'

Ugh. I cannot believe I am about to do this.

'I need you to come to the loo with me. I'm sorry. I wouldn't ask if I…'

Queue jumper's eyes widen, a flash of amusement in them. He pokes his head out of the pod and looks up and down the aisle.

'There are no flight attendants about,' I explain. 'I checked and double-checked, trust me.'

'Um, yeah, okay then.' He pushes his specs up his nose. 'Let's go then!'

I smile. That was easy! He's being really nice about it! Okay, this will be all right. A little embarrassing but better than the alternative.

I unbuckle my seatbelt and, as I stand, I grab onto Queue jumper's arm. He looks down in surprise.

'Wow, you're eager,' he says with a grin.

'I really need it. I need it bad,' I explain.

He nods with an expression of surprise and approval.

He's being so cool about escorting me to the loo. Maybe I had misjudged him. Maybe he's *not* what the Americans would call 'a jerk'.

In only a few shaky steps we have reached the toilet.

'Are you sure? The whole engaged thing,' he says weirdly.

I point at the toilet sign. 'It's not engaged. It's vacant.'

'Huh?' He looks confused. 'Uh, my name's Seth, by the way.' He takes off his glasses and slips them into the breast pocket of his button-down.

'Hiya Seth. And thanks for this. You're a lifesaver.'

'I do what I can,' he responds with an odd cocky look on his face.

I open the door to the loo and shuffle in. And just as I'm about to close the door, Seth also comes into the loo, kicks the door shut behind him, pushes me against the sink, grabs my face with both hands and kisses me.

Whaaaaat?

Aaaaaaargh!

I push away. 'What the hell? What are you doing? Get off!' I yell at him, using my hoodie sleeve to wipe my mouth of his surprise advance. 'Perv alert! Get out!'

He jumps away, holding his hands up as if I'm pointing a gun at him and he's showing his willingness to co-operate.

'What? You said wanted us to…?'

'Us to what?' I ask, wiggling desperately.

'Join the mile-high club. You said you needed it real bad? I thought you wanted to…'

'No!' I hiss, shaking my head in horror. 'I don't want to have sex with you on this death machine. I need a piddle. God, I really need to go right now!'

'SORRY, WHAT? A PIDDLE?'

He reaches his arm out to open the door.

'Don't open the door!' I say furiously. I can't wait a second longer. I yank down my jeans. 'Turn around!!' I yell, mortified. 'And… cover your ears. Oh no. It's happening!'

Seth gives me a horrified look before turning away and clamping his hands down over his ears.

Oh god. How embarrassing. It's one of those really long wees too.

When I'm all finished, I step over to the sink with a wobble and wash my hands.

'Sorry,' I say to Seth as he uncovers his eyes and just stares at me, shaking his head slowly in disbelief. 'I'm really sorry! I think… we got our wires crossed…'

Seth looks terrified, to be fair he has every right. He

thought I wanted to engage in a sensual sky-high rendezvous and instead I have forced him to witness me going to the loo against his will. I probably should not have any more champagne…

Wide-eyed, Seth take his specs back out of his shirt pocket and slides them back on his face.

'I'll um… I'll just um… wow.'

He tries to leave and I grab onto his arm with both hands.

'Just lead me back to my seat,' I say, feeling like the biggest dick in the entire world. 'And I'll leave you alone forever, I swear. I don't have a child or a pet to swear on. I mean, I used to have a cat called Mr Muscle, but in 1999 I swore on his life that I wasn't lying about something when I *was* lying and the next day he died in mysterious circumstances so—'

'Come on. Let's get you back to your seat,' he interrupts. He's speaking slowly, kindly. Like I'm a very young person or a very old person.

We open the door and as I walk out of the loo, clinging onto Seth's arm in case the plane gets shaky again, the air hostess from before catches sight of us. She looks at me with great distaste.

As Seth takes back his arm, sits in his pod, jams his headphones over his ears and starts furiously tapping away on his laptop keyboard, I sit down shakily and buckle myself up. As I do, the air hostess strides over and crouches down beside me, her lovely small nostrils flaring.

'On behalf of us here at BA, we rescind our congratulations,' she hisses, looking me up and down. 'Colin deserves better.'

CHAPTER TEN

Email to Olive from Still Minds App :

We hope you are enjoying the Still Minds meditation practices. We have added a new session for calming an overactive mind. Click here to try it out!

Those with overactive minds tend to feel the need for control. It's hard for these people to relax because they feel that by controlling their circumstances, they can control themselves and everything in their lives. But this is simply not possible! What will happen will happen, and by trying to control it you will only succeed in worrying needlessly and feeding your overactive mind. What you *can* do is live the current moment as best you can. Meditation practice can help with this.

I manage to fall asleep (pass out) for the next few hours on the plane and soon enough we have touched down safely. I made it! I drank too much champagne, screamed twice, made up a fake fiancé, got glared at by the cabin crew and forced a man to accompany me for a wee. But I made it!

At the baggage stand, I wait with my fellow passengers for my suitcases to appear. As I'm doing so, I spot Seth out of the corner of my eye, heading towards the exit. He scurried off as soon as the plane landed, giving me a quick awkward wave as he did so. No wonder. He must think I am bonkers. He's right. I clearly am.

I contemplate running after him before he disappears from sight, apologising for my behaviour. Especially after he was so kind about my terror during take-off. But just as I'm about to race in his direction, I see Donna's red suede suitcase chugging along the luggage carousel. And there's my suitcase behind it.

Shit. If I don't grab it now, I will have to wait for it to go all the way around again. The carousel is massive – it'll take ages. And what if someone steals the cases on the other side where I can't see them? I once read a news story about people who come to airports and hang around just so they can stand at baggage claim and nick people's bags. Then what would I do? All that careful packing for nothing. No scarves, no shoes for every eventuality, nothing!

I give one last regretful look at Seth striding out of the airport before grabbing my suitcases from the carousel. I reach both hands out and grab the handles, yanking with all my might. But the cases are so heavy and won't come all the way off the conveyor belt.

Shit.

Before I know what's happening I find myself being dragged along with my bags.

'Sorry!' I say, as I bash into the person next to me, trying my very best to retrieve my cases.

But I'm not strong enough. I keep heaving and pulling

as I'm moving along with the carousel but I simply can't get them off. As I knock a few more people out of the way, I hear cries of 'Just take one and wait for the other!' and 'Let go!' and 'Bitch, you crazy!'

'Aaaaaargh,' I hear someone saying quietly. Then I realise it's me. I'm basically just bent over, walking my cases around the baggage carousel like dogs on leads, making weird noises every time I try to lift them off.

'Heeeeelp!' I yell. 'Help me lift them!'

A few seconds later a beefy guy grabs one of the cases, leaving me with the strength to grab the other with a loud cry and a stumble backwards into more plane passengers.

'Oof! Sorry,' I say, looking up to see that the beefy guy is actually airport security. He doesn't look impressed.

'No problem, ma'am,' he sniffs. 'It's not like I have anything else to do beside, you know, protecting our great nation from the threat of those who want to attack the values of Lady Liberty.'

'I'm sorry.'

He responds with a roll of his eyes, striding off cockily. I feel my cheeks sting at his sarcasm. Everyone else at the baggage claim stares at me as if I am the worst. Worse than someone who wants to attack the values of Lady Liberty. Worse, even, than a queue jumper.

'Sorry!' I say to them, feeling beads of humiliation sweat forming on my forehead.

Man oh man, I am failing hard at every turn!

I've only been in New York for twenty minutes and already it's a total shit show.

* * *

After a series of gentle disasters (not being able to find a trolley, annoying the cab driver by pulling up the information about where I was going *after* getting into his car, and not being able to find my dollars when we reach the destination), we arrive outside a sixteen-storey building with a cream and red brick façade looking lovely in the bright sunshine.

Once the cab driver has deposited me onto the pavement, along with my cases, I look down at my phone to the email Birdie sent.

Apartment 3C, 400 Riverside Way, Upper West Side, Manhattan.

Here I am then. My home for the next five days.

Blowing the air out of my cheeks, I peer up and down the street. It's a really, really long, wide road with huge, attractive red and cream buildings as far as I can see. I look at my watch. It's only midday here, which feels weird. People are milling around, going about their days, walking their dogs and hailing yellow cabs to take them to lunch.

I try to gather the energy to heave-ho my cases towards the green canopied entrance when a middle-aged man in a blue uniform and matching hat hurries over and grabs them like they weigh nothing.

This must be the doorman. Birdie's instructions say he's the one who'll let me into the Airbnb.

'I'm Olive,' I tell him. 'I'm here for apartment 3C?'

'Of course!' he says warmly. 'I've been expecting you. My name is Lloyd. If you can let me see your passport, I've been instructed to give you the keys to the apartment.'

I pull out my passport and Lloyd checks it with a nod.

He grabs my cases and we get the lift up to the third floor.

After depositing my cases inside, Lloyd gives me the number of the superintendent of the building, and an extra spare key. When he's left, I take in my surroundings with a sigh of relief that I am *finally* still after an entire day of motion.

'Bloody freaking hell!' I groan, rubbing my eyes with a

mixture of pure tiredness and pleasure at the studio space before me. The room isn't big but it's lovely and, more importantly, neat and airy. The floor is a slightly scuffed parquet, the ceilings are high and there's panelling in the stark white walls. To the right of the room is a small open-plan kitchenette area with a full-size fridge and a two-hob cooker. I wander in and open cupboard doors and drawers. Plain white cups and plates, heavy steel cutlery and a small selection of pans. Nice. I open the fridge which holds nothing but bottled water, and the freezer which contains only a bottle of fancy-looking vodka and a tub of frozen yogurt. I'll definitely have to go shopping then.

In the centre of the room there's a small pale blue sofa that pulls out into a bed. I perch on it and give it a little bounce. As I do a little cloud of dust rises up, making me cough.

Ooh, I hope there are no bedbugs. I read something online about bedbugs being a serious issue in New York. I lean my face down to the fabric of the sofa to see if I can identify any bedbugs when I realise that I don't have any clue what a bedbug looks like or even if they're visible to the naked eye. I'm just a person pressing my forehead into a sofa cushion.

Wiping my hands on my jeans, I get up and open a door on the right wall and peek my head around. It's the world's teeniest bathroom. A tiny person-sized toilet, like the kind you'd get in junior school. There's also a very, very narrow glass column holding a shower. I try to step in. I barely fit! And, apart from my gigantic hair, I'm a pretty small person. I mime washing in the shower and realise I will have to keep my elbows in at my sides if I am to successfully do it.

Back in the main room, I walk over to what are surely the room's best features, two large rectangular windows.

I take a peek out, only to find myself looking directly into someone else's apartment in a different building! The person in there – a long-haired man of around forty who is wearing a khaki coloured vest and, from what I can ascertain, nothing on his bottom – half looks up at me from his rocking chair and scowls. Eeek. Creeptastic or what. I close the blinds as quickly as I possibly can and vow to never ever open them again.

Shudder.

After getting myself a bottle of water from the fridge and taking two painkillers to help ease the post-alcohol/stressfest thud in my brain, I text Alex, the Joans and Birdie to let them know I'm here safe. Immediately my phone starts ringing. It's Birdie FaceTiming!

I put on the brightest smile I can manage and press answer.

'Why are you smiling weird?' Birdie says immediately, her dark eyes narrowed in suspicion. She's wearing mascara and bright crimson lipstick, her eyebrows are perfectly filled in and there are huge colourful earrings hanging from her ears.

'It's a bright smile,' I explain. 'A *welcome to our FaceTime conversation* smile. I'm being perky. Like an American. Why are you wearing all that make-up?' I ask. Then I gasp. 'Did they let you leave the hospital?'

Birdie shakes her head, turning her phone camera around to reveal the same old hospital room she's been in for the past eight weeks. 'I wish. No. It's Doctor BJ's shift tonight. I'm peacocking for him.'

'Peacocking?' I ask, screwing up my face. 'What's that? It sounds rude… Are you sure you're up to it? Have you got protection?'

Birdie laughs. 'Peacocking is when you make yourself look fancy in order to attract a mate. Peacocks do it with their feathers. The make-up, the outlandish earrings.' She points the camera down to reveal a tight blue dress that clings to her, not inconsiderable, curves. 'I'm peacocking like a mofo up in here.'

'Ah.' I nod. 'Well, you look very pretty. I'm sure Dr BJ will feel super inappropriately attracted to you.'

'That's the plan!' She wiggles her eyebrows. 'Are you sober now, you sneaky drunkard? How was the flight? Anything interesting happen?'

I think back to forcing a rando TV writer into the loo. To the flight attendant getting mad at me. To the whole plane thinking I was fake engaged.

'I got a date…' I say, deciding to omit the more humiliating aspects of the whole experience. After all, Birdie is always telling me I should try to focus on the positives…

'Whaaaaaat? On the plane?' Birdie presses a hand to her cheek. 'That's badass! Wow, I'm *impressed*.'

'Not on the plane. Before the flight. I did meet a man on the plane but… well we didn't exactly hit it off. Anyway, the man I met at the airport is called Colin. He has sideburns.'

'Just like you wanted your Big Sexy Love to have!'

I nod, touched that she remembered.

Birdie shakes her head. 'I didn't think you were interested in dating? Don't get me wrong, I totally think you should be getting laid on the regular, but… this is a surprise. A good surprise, but, you know, *unexpected*!'

I shrug. 'I didn't think I was interested either. But… Colin was sweet. I felt comfy with him. He was nice.'

'Just nice?'

'Really nice!' I add.

'Did you want to climb him like a tree?'

My eyes widen. 'God, no. I mean, not yet, at least. I

don't really know him. Anyway, you know how I feel about sex. I don't get those kind of feelings like you. Especially with someone I don't even know!'

'Well, either way, I'm glad you've got a date. It's about time you opened yourself up to new things. You'll be as horny as the rest of us in no time.'

'I hope not,' I say, thinking back to that damn *Atonement* library scene and how it is constantly popping up my brain, making me feel peculiar. What if that was a real person I couldn't get out of my head? What a pain in the bum that would be!

I find myself yawning, despite the fact that I slept on the plane.

'You should get yourself all unpacked,' Birdie says softly, tilting her head to the side. 'If you're not shattered after that, you should try going up to the roof terrace of the building. The view from there is *insane*.'

My mouth turns down into a frown. 'No thanks. You know I don't do heights.'

'Hey, you were just on a plane! You already faced that fear! A roof should be easy-peasy now!'

'I had to get drunk to even get on the plane!'

Birdie bites the corner of her lip. 'Just consider it, okay. The New York skyline is... well, it's pretty special.'

'I'll think about it.'

That's a total lie. There's no way in hell I'm going up to a scary rooftop to look at a view of other scary rooftops. If it's so cool I can just Google what it looks like – I don't need to actually go up there and scare myself shitless.

Birdie makes me promise to send her pics and updates about what's happening as frequently as I can before hurriedly saying goodbye because 'Doctor BJ is outside my room and I need to arrange myself sexily on the bed.'

It takes me an hour to unpack my stuff and when I'm

done I slouch on the sofa bed and pull up Birdie's most recent email. It's a pretty long list of places she thinks I ought to visit while I'm here. I click on the link to the website of a deli she recommends for breakfast, but before the page even loads, I find my eyes drooping closed and soon enough I've completely dozed off.

CHAPTER ELEVEN

Excerpt of email from

birdielivelysayshello@gmail.com:

Chuck Allen's family owns, like, an entire block in Gramercy Park. His parents, him and even a cousin lived there! Unless they've sold the block (which I highly doubt because Manhattan real estate tends to stay in families for hundreds of years), he will be living in one of the luxury apartments. And if not, his parents or some elite who knows him will be there and they can tell you his whereabouts. I doubt he'll be too far away – the Allens are to Gramercy Park what Serena van der Woodsen and Blair Waldorf are to The Upper East Side. XOXO GOSSIP GIRL ;)

The next morning, after a long and patchy sleep, I squeeze myself into the world's narrowest shower cubicle and have a good old scrub, bruising my elbows in the process. I dry my hair as gently as possible so that it doesn't explode into its usual wild halo, but it's no use. Something in the water here has made it look even bigger than usual. I wouldn't mind – voluminous hair is lovely on most people – but I have quite a small head and a short body, so the effect is one of complete disproportion. I pull the disobedient chestnut waves back into a ponytail and get dressed into a navy blue T-shirt dress, maroon tights, long knitted cardi, black pumps and a turquoise cotton scarf on account of the mild weather.

I double, triple and quadruple-check that I have Birdie's letter to Chuck, my phone, dollars, Rescue Remedy and blister plasters (which, one of the apps tells me, is a must for walking around NYC) in my bumbag, make sure it is securely tied around my waist and leave the studio apartment.

Outside the building, the sweet doorman Lloyd starts chatting to me about the weather. Most people find talking about the weather to be dull. But I like it! I like having a fair idea of what the temperature will be and what kind of clothes I'll need. Lloyd seems to enjoy it too, although he suggests that the weather in New York can be somewhat capricious, which isn't great to hear. He's just recommending that I go and see the cherry blossom blooming at the Botanical Gardens (which sounds like a much more pleasant activity than standing on rooftops) when my phone beeps with a reminder.

Shit! According to the schedule I planned out on the travel planner app this morning, I should be arriving at the subway station in three minutes because the train is in six!

'I have to go!' I tell Lloyd, zooming into the map on my phone. 'Sorry, Lloyd! I need to catch my train, stat!'

'Yes! Go! Enjoy New York City! Have a wonderful day!' Lloyd cheerily calls after me as I scuttle off.

I wave goodbye and once I've rounded the corner of the street, I look at my watch and start to full-on sprint in order to make it to the subway station on time. I'm not particularly fond of running, and I'm not very good at it, but I definitely do not want to miss my planned train. If I miss it then all the connecting trains I planned for get thrown out of whack and everything messes up. It basically turns into the butterfly effect and the next thing I know I'm Ashton Kutcher waking up with no arms.

Or something.

Fortunately, I make it just in time, my freshly washed hair now sticky with sweat and my nice maroon tights – that I am now realising are just that tad bit small for me – rolling down my belly and hanging low at the crotch. The subway is crowded and awkward, but it's on the ground and there are no bouncy castle slides and judgey air hostesses so, you know, I'm not complaining.

Thanks to my collection of apps and their various alarms and notifications that inform me when I'm supposed to switch stations, I manage to change my subways without any major upsets.

As I step out onto the pavement at 23rd Street station, I'm struck by just how huge everything is here. The roads are so wide! Triple the size of British roads. The buildings are gigantic, even the windows are bigger than at home.

It's busy, as I expected it would be on a weekend, but not so busy as to cause me any hassle. Not Manchester Arndale on Christmas Eve busy. I did that once – a dire mistake that I will never make again.

Squinting down at my phone, I follow the map towards Chuck's last known address on East 18th street. I turn a corner and it's almost as if I'm in an entirely different place. Gone are the Starbucks and Radio Shacks, lines of yellow cabs and super-fast walkers. That's all been replaced with beautiful, majestic, old red-brick buildings with sophisticated facades, steps leading up to glossy front doors, all shaded by trees in full foliage. It's absolutely gorgeous!

As I get further down the street, I notice an elegant row of about four brownstones, the first and biggest of them covered with climbing ivy. I look at the email. This is the house! It looks like something from a movie! Wow.

I step onto the first stair leading up to the door and notice that there are lamps lit inside, glittering through the window. Someone is in. Maybe Chuck Allen is inside there *right now*. I wonder what he's like? If Birdie's past flings are any indicator, he'll be unbearably handsome, athletic and just a little bit dumb.

My stomach flips with nerves that I'm actually here. At how crazy this entire thing is. How is Chuck going to feel when he finds out I've been sent here by Birdie? Is her letter going to make him sad? Or will he pleased to know that she still holds a candle for him after all these years? Happy that she forgives him for being a douchebag and going to Princeton instead of Manchester Uni? Either way, it's pretty nerve-wracking to be the person bearing news of this magnitude.

I ascend the last four steps up to the sleek navy blue front door and grab hold of the brass knocker, knocking three times.

Eeeeeeek.

I wait for someone to answer, biting my thumbnail as I do so. Ooh! There's a shadow behind the door! Someone's coming!

Here goes!

I take a deep breath as the door is pulled open by a man wearing a haughty expression. He's around my age, very tall, very thin and icy blonde with long pale lashes. He's wearing a black linen shirt with extravagant ruffles at the sleeves. He's very striking in a way that's so symmetrical it's almost not real. He looks a bit like a villain in a movie set in the future. A handsome CGI villain. Not at all what I'd expect to be Birdie's type. But then she's been known to surprise me in the past…

This can't be Chuck Allen, can it?

'Hiya!' I say uncertainly. 'My name is Olive.'

The guy just stares at me, so I clear my throat and try again.

'Are… is your name Chuck Allen at all?'

'Who wants to know?'

'I'm Olive Brewster. I have a message from Birdie. Chuck's, um… teenage sweetheart?'

He nods slowly, looking me up and down.

'Yes, come in.'

Bingo!

CHAPTER TWELVE

Text from Birdie: Doctor BJ is single = yay! BJ stands for Bruce Jim = nooooo! I think that might be worse than BJ… What do you think? Anyway, I flirted up a storm with him after our call last night but he was entirely professional. Little does he know that his honourable ethics only make me fancy him more. Ah well. It's nice to have a crush, even if it is a futile activity. Sometimes meaningless things can be fun just for fun's sake. SO, did you go to the roof? Have you been to Gramercy Park yet? Is Chuck there? I'm DYING to know. (Is it still a sick joke if I am the one dying? It made me laugh anyways.) Tell me things. Xx

I follow Chuck Allen through a grand hallway. Looking up, I notice the high ceilings are etched with gorgeously intricate fleur-de-lis cornicing. We enter a living room that looks like something from a glitzy American period drama! It's large and grand, the walls painted in a dark bottle green, the sofas all made of velvet, lamps at every possible spare floor point and, best of all, a beautiful, huge open fire, flames flickering away. Wow. Chuck Allen is, as Taller Joan would say, 'Not short of a bob or two'.

'Drink?' he utters, indicating that I should sit down.

I perch myself on the end of a massive mustard-coloured sofa, hands folded in my lap like I'm about to meet the queen.

'Just a water will do, thanks,' I say, smacking my nervous, dry mouth together.

Chuck throws me a look of disgust. 'Water? How dreary.'

Ignoring me, he saunters over to a mahogany side table topped with crystal bottles full of amber liquids. He pours out two small glasses and hands one to me.

Frowning, I give it a sniff. 'Whisky?'

'That's a thousand-dollar bottle of bourbon,' he declares, as if he's bestowing me with the Holy Grail.

'Oh, a water will be fine.' I smile, handing him back the glass.

He takes it from me and pours the liquid into his own tumbler, but still doesn't get me a water.

He clears his throat. 'What's your name?' He stares at me, eyes icy and clear, not a wrinkle on his beautiful face. Does… does Chuck Allen Botox? The lack of movement in his expression is a bit eerie. I squint, trying my best to understand what Birdie saw in this guy. But I can't. He's much prettier than she would ordinarily go for.

'My name is Olive,' I tell him again. Digging into my bumbag, I pull out Birdie's letter.

'Olive is not a name, it's a snack food,' Chuck says, giving me that weird blank stare.

I laugh a little, because logic tells me that he's joking. But he doesn't even crack a smile. I'm not sure he *can* crack a smile. *Birdie, what the hell were you thinking?*

'You have delightful hair,' Chuck says, narrowing his pale blue eyes. 'Thick. At first glance it looks wild, but…'

he steps forward, his hand reaching out, almost touching my head. 'On closer inspection, one can see that there's a certain beautiful uniformity in each of the curls.'

A shudder runs down my back, beads of sweat form on the back of my neck.

I'm officially creeped out.

He gently touches my head. Argh!

I dive off the chair and start to back away from him.

'Yeah, thanks,' I mumble. I need to get out of here. 'I, um, just came to deliver this letter from Birdie.' I throw the letter in his general direction. He catches it with one hand, his reflexes faster than lightning. Even that is unsettling. 'I have lots to do,' I continue. 'Lots of sightseeing, et cetera.'

'Who is Birdie?' Chuck says, tilting his head to the side so that a strand of blonde hair falls over his face.

'Um, your teenage sweetheart? You left her to go to Princeton?' I remind him, feeling less and less sure that I'm in the right place. 'You… you are Chuck Allen right?'

He gives a delicate shake of his head. 'My name is Anders,' he says. 'Anders von Preen.'

'What?' I yell. 'Anders von Preen? Why did you let me in? Who even are you?'

He shrugs elegantly. Like all of this is completely normal. Anders von Preen sounds like a made-up name. Who is this guy? I instinctively hold my hands up into a sort of karate chop position, just in case I need to defend myself in any way.

'I invited you in because I am bored today.' His thin voice drawls, as if he can barely be bothered to speak. 'I am bored so much of the day.' His accent is slightly British-sounding. Like Madonna. 'But here *you* come knocking at my door so unexpectedly.' He sighs dramatically, his red lips turning down into a sulk, his pointy shoulders sagging. 'And it's not like I have anything else fun to do today.'

'Are you going to murder me?' I blurt in a panicked voice, looking around for the way out. 'I mean… um… do you know Chuck Allen? Do you know his parents?'

'Maybe… maybe not.'

'Maybe, maybe not you will murder me?! Or maybe, maybe not you know Chuck Allen?!'

Shit! This is not good.

Anders von Preen sits down on a plush armchair and takes a sip of his drink, holding the glass with only his thumb and forefinger. 'Don't fret,' he says quietly. 'You seem like a rather fretful person. Are you sure you won't have a drink?'

I have been in New York for less than twenty-four hours and I have managed to stumble upon what appears to be a bona fide psychopath who won't even tell me if he plans to murder me or not!

'Chuck?' I find myself calling out into the air. 'Chuck Allen? Are you here? Are you here, please? Are there any other humans nearby?'

'Shouting won't help,' Anders says calmly, placing his drink onto a small glass table beside him.

Shouting won't help? That's exactly what a psychopath says to a screaming victim before he bops them on the head with a blunt object.

I make a tiny little frightened groan. I don't intend to. It just pops out. I put my hand into my bumbag and fumble around for something I could potentially use as a weapon. The only reasonably heavy thing is my bottle of Rescue Remedy, the irony of which does not pass me by.

'Sorry, that sounded rather threatening didn't it?' Anders says.

'Yes.'

'I've been told I come across as quite sinister. Do you think that's true!'

'Yes!' I nod fervently. 'Very true!'

His face drops a little. 'I must work on that. I just meant that calling for Chuck Allen won't help because Chuck Allen isn't here. He hasn't been here for years. That's all.'

My heart leaps. 'So you *do* know him?'

'Of course I do, darling.' Anders smiles this time, and his face looks ever so slightly less creepy. *Ever so slightly.*

'Well, can you tell me where he is so I can give him this letter? It's really very important. And time-sensitive.'

Anders stands up from the chair and takes a step towards me. I take two steps backwards.

'I will tell you what I know.'

'Great. Yes, thank you. And then I will escape… I mean… leave you to your day.'

'I want something in exchange for the information.'

I pull a face. I have a very strong feeling he is going to ask if he can drink my blood.

'W-what is it?' I ask, my voice trembling.

'Darling, I want to do your hair.'

What the actual fuck?

* * *

Once you know the backstory of a psychopath they become a teensy bit less terrifying. Half an hour later and I've learned that while Anders is definitely bizarre, he doesn't seem to be a threat. In fact, I think he's a bit sad and a bit lonely. Still, that doesn't mean that having him do my hair feels any less excruciatingly awkward. But if this is the only way to find out where Chuck is, then a girl's gotta do what a girl's gotta do.

As I sit, stiff-shouldered, in a fancy Queen Anne chair,

Anders pulls and twists at my hair. In his thin, raspy voice, he tells me all about his tragic life as a privileged, wealthy white man who can never become the hairdresser that he has always longed to be because his parents would 'financially abandon' him if he did.

'I'm a von Preen,' He explains imperiously from behind me. 'We don't have jobs. It's just not the done thing. We are members of the board at Lincoln Centre and MOMA. We volunteer our time to styling charity balls for New York's elite, we eat at Manhattan's finest restaurants and make sure that we're seen doing it… but we don't have jobs. I mean… that's just vulgar.'

'Jobs aren't that bad,' I say, as if this entire conversation isn't completely bonkers. 'I have a job. I'm a fishmonger!'

'Good God, you poor thing,' Anders says with a gasp, patting my shoulder. 'How awful for you.'

I shrug. 'It's not that bad,' I protest. 'My boss is nice and—'

'Anyway,' he interrupts. 'I realised I had a deep interest in hair styling during my first year at college. Hair was all I could think about. After graduation I planned on standing up to my parents. Telling them that I would train as a stylist, be the first in three generations of von Preens to have a job.' His voice turns wistful. 'My roommate Warner had such beautiful hair. Fiery Titian red, long and silky. He had problematic ends, but I knew in my heart that we could fix those.'

'And did you? Fix his split ends?' I ask, begrudgingly interested.

'I tried… We had been out for dinner with other members of our secret society, drank a little too much vintage, indulged in a little too much cocaine. I…I was feeling bold. When we got back to our room I told him I could fix his split ends. He thought I was joking, told me to fire up the PlayStation. But… I persisted.' His voice turns dark. 'I got out the seven-inch molybdenum stainless steel professional scissors I had bought the week before and approached him.'

My eyes widen.

Anders continues. 'I was about to take the first snip when Warner... he... jumped in shock and I sliced his chin.'

'Shit.'

'Yes. He thought I was trying to attack him. And I... I was too ashamed to tell him I was just trying to cut his hair! And so I left Harvard in shame. Known only as the man who had tried to disfigure his lovely red-headed roommate.'

'Wow.'

Do not laugh. This is a tragic tale. It is not funny, Olive.

Anders sighs heavily. 'And now I spend my days hanging around here, bored out of my mind. Watching old episodes of *Shear Genius* and wondering what might have been.'

I shake my head sympathetically, feeling a little bit sad for this strange creepy man.

'Don't shake your head!' he barks, his thin voice scratchy with the volume.

I stop immediately, I do not want to incur the same fate as his old college roommate.

I peek at my watch. I've been here for forty minutes already! What on earth is he doing to my hair? Surely it must be nearly done? I need to get out of here, I need to get on with finding Chuck. It's not like I have unlimited time!

'Why don't you tell me where Chuck is?' I ask. 'You may as well, while I'm sitting here.'

'Oh, I don't know where he is!' Anders says casually. 'I haven't seen him, gosh, it must be six or seven years now.'

'What? You told me that if I let you do my hair, that you would tell me where Chuck was?'

I get up from the chair and furiously spin around to face this liar, to look him in his lying eyes.

Anders puts a hand on his tiny hip and shakes a platinum strand of hair away from his forehead.

'I said no such thing.'

I gasp. I have been conned! Donna warned me this would happen, and it's happened on my first day here. I've been conned by a creepy rich guy whose door I *literally* knocked at of my own volition.

'You *did*!!' I hiss, my head feeling heavy because whatever he's done to my hair seems to be weighing it down.

'Actually, I said I'll tell you what I know about Chuck. And that does not include his current whereabouts.'

I screw my eyes up, thinking back to our earlier deal. Maybe he did say that…

'Fine,' I huff. 'Tell me what you know. I really need to find Chuck and, frankly, you are not being very helpful at all!'

'I haven't finished your hair yet!' Anders points to the chair.

I plonk myself back down into it with a grumble of protest. What choice do I have?

'I can't stay much longer,' I tell him. 'I have things to do. Urgent things.'

'You're so tense. Are you sure you don't want a real drink?'

I kind of do now, but I feel like Anders might drug me in order to spend more time doing my hair. Or maybe steal my hair and store it in a precious jewellery box under his antique bed. And then use it to weave into wigs for some life-sized dolls that he happens to collect…

'No thanks,' I say firmly, thinking back to the last time I drank and the ensuing humiliation.

'What is so urgent?' he asks. 'Why are you in such a rush?'

I think about Birdie. Her lovely open face, with skin and lips pale because of organs that don't work properly.

I shake my head out of it. It's best to think of Birdie's condition in an abstract way. Otherwise I worry I'll just start crying and never stop.

I swallow hard. 'I just do. It's important.'

Anders must sense the desperation in my voice.

'Okay,' he says kindly. 'I will tell you what I know of Chuck while I finish your hair. It will take me another hour to complete my work.'

'Fifteen minutes,' I counter-offer.

'Thirty.'

'Deal.'

As Anders continues doing whatever the hell he's doing to my head, he tells me how Chuck was a friend of his in college at Princeton. How they were in the same classes and that he was renting this place from Chuck's parents.

'So you know where his parents are?'

'They live in Belize now. I still keep in touch with them – they're my landlords – but they had a terrible falling out with Chuck over something mysterious and they don't talk to each other anymore.'

I sigh, my stomach sinking. This isn't exactly helpful. I can hardly pop along to Belize to track down his parents and ask them about Chuck's where-abouts, can I? 'There's nothing about him online either,' I say in frustration.

Anders sniffs. 'The last I heard, he was working on Wall Street.'

'I thought rich people didn't have jobs?' I point out.

Anders laughs. 'Chuck Allen's family are mere millionaires, darling.'

My eyes almost pop out of my head. Anders is a

billionaire? Wowee. Does he dive onto a bed of money at night like Scrooge McDuck? Does he wear all his underwear once before throwing it away in favour of a brand new pair? So many questions…

Focus, Olive.

'Which bank was Chuck at?'

'Chimes Investment on Wall Street, I believe.'

'Does he still work there?'

'Who knows. I stopped caring about Chuck Allen the moment he dropped me after the Princeton scissor scandal. He was Team Warner. They were always very close to each other. Always leaving me out…'

I sigh. Chimes Investment. It's a lead, I guess. Even if Chuck isn't still working there, someone will know something, surely? They have to!

Anders clears his throat. 'Oh, I do have a picture of him, if that helps?'

'A recent one?'

'Well, from about six years ago.'

That's better than nothing. Birdie didn't have any photos of him, on account of burning them all on the demise of their relationship.

'Yes! That would be great. Thank you!'

Anders wanders off out of the room, I'm assuming, to get the photo. I get up from my chair and search the room for a mirror so I can see what he's done to my hair. But there are no mirrors anywhere! I spot a gigantic metallic vase holding an extravagant array of cream and pale pink flowers. I dash over it, but just as I crouch to see my reflection, Anders glides back in.

'I said no peeking,' he barks again. 'I want it to be a wonderful surprise. Sit!'

'Jeez.'

With a tut, I traipse back over to my chair. Anders hands me a photograph. It's an image of three young men with their arms around each other, grinning widely into the camera. One is clearly a young Anders, though he looks much more bro-like than he does now; beefier, and with his platinum blonde hair spiky like a Backstreet Boy. The middle guy is a redhead with the most beautiful long hair. That must be Warner before Anders attacked him with professional scissors. And the last man in the group must be Chuck. I look closely. He's gorgeous. Exactly Birdie's type. I can totally see what she saw in him. His hair is short and dark, and he's clean-cut and preppy with startlingly green eyes. He's smiling freely into the camera, completely confident with his picture being taken.

'Chuck Allen,' I whisper to myself.

For the hundredth time since Birdie gave it to me, I think of the letter, now safely back in my bumbag, and wonder what it says. I get a vision of Chuck flying back to England with me, him running into Birdie's arms, turning out not to be a douchebag at all. Maybe having the solution to a cure. Or knowing something, anything to save her.

Tears sting my throat and I immediately disregard this scenario. Birdie has already told me a million and one times that there's nothing that can be done. No transplant, no magic medicine, no holistic cure. They've done everything they can. It's happening. It's happening and I need to accept it, like she has.

Once again I force the thoughts about Birdie's illness off, like a light going out, and try to focus on the situation at hand.

'Thanks, Anders,' I say, moving my thumb over the corner of the photograph. 'I think this will really help.' I glance at my watch. 'I really do need to get going. How long until this is finished?'

Anders leans into me and as he gets close I notice his

cologne is a gorgeous boyish aquatic at odds with his stiff demeanour.

He puts a hand onto my head, fiddles with a strand or two and steps back.

'It's done! It's complete!'

Thank jeebus for that.

'Come and see!' Anders says, leading me out of the living room and into the grand hallway.

I follow him into a large marble downstairs bathroom and peer into the mirror expectantly.

Holy. Shit.

No.

Oh my goodness, no.

You know in those hairdressing competitions, where the contestants have to make – not a normal hairstyle – but a kind of sculpture out of hair. The more outlandish the better?

Yeah, well that is what Anders has done to me.

'You like it?' I hear him say through the mist of hair-spray he's currently applying all over to secure the disaster into place.

I blink gormlessly at my reflection. It's not even a beehive, or a bun. It's a ginormous twist.

Right at the front of my head.

Like a unicorn. It looks like I have a unicorn horn.

'It's… it's…'

I can't come up with an appropriate word.

'Do you love it? You love it, don't you?'

It's a fucking unicorn horn. I look batshit crazy.

I peer closer in the mirror and notice that he's twisted in strands of blue hair. When did he do that? Where did he get blue hair from? Does he have a collection of different-coloured hair? Not only do I look like a complete crazy person, I look like a crazy person who's stuck in a Christina Aguilera music video from 2002. I wonder if

Anders knows that strands of blue hair have been frowned upon for many years now…

'Here, let me take a picture!'

Before I can stop him, Anders is holding up his smartphone and snapping away. He looks so proud, one hand clasped to his chest in delight.

'It's lovely,' I say, trying my best to force a smile of enthusiasm. It's done now – there's no point in hurting his feelings by being truthful. 'It's really… unique.' I pat the top of the horn, but my hand can barely reach the tall point, it's so high up. 'It's so… solid!'

'Darling, I know! It's perfect.' Anders nods approvingly at his own work. Thank God his parents put a stop to him becoming a hairdresser! No-one deserves this.

'Right,' I say. 'Well, thanks… I best be going now. Lots to do!'

Anders sighs lightly, a sad smile on his perfectly symmetrical face. 'Yes. Of course. Thank you for letting me style your hair.'

I don't tell him that I have never felt more ridiculous in my life. That as soon as I get back to my Airbnb I'll spend an age taking out every kirby grip and shampooing my hair three times to get it back to normal.

Instead I say. 'It was my pleasure. You take care now.'

And then, carefully tucking the photo of Chuck Allen next to Birdie's letter in my bumbag, I get the bloody hell out of there as quickly as I can.

CHAPTER THIRTEEN

Text from Colin: Hello there, Olive! The lads and I just arrived in Australia safe and sound. It's very warm and sunny! How are you? How is 'The Big Apple' treating you so far? All good, I hope. X

Anders waves me away like an old friend, as if our whole interaction wasn't the most ridiculous thing that has ever occurred, although to be fair, for him, it's probably not. I shuffle speedily down the street, head bowed, looking back sporadically to see if he's still waving.

He is.

At the end of the very long road, I turn around one final time to see if he's gone back inside yet.

Nope. He's still waving.

I give him a quick wave in return and dive around the corner to catch my breath.

That might be one of the strangest things that's ever happened to me. And I recently peed in front of a total stranger. Holy moly.

I continue half walking/half jogging my way towards

the nearest underground station, but the quick movement means my too-small tights are falling down. If I move much further without rectifying the situation, they will be around my knees and that won't be pleasant for anyone.

I peer around me in search of a private corner or hidden doorway and spot a runner heading through a gate into some sort of park. I follow, pulling the gate closed behind me and waddling down a gravelled path.

The runner jogs off behind some trees and I try to find a secluded spot in which to rearrange my tights without anyone seeing. As I round the corner at the end of the gravelled path, I breathe in sharply.

Because this is one absolutely beautiful park. It's clipped and neat, but charmingly designed, with winding paths and trees that look like they've come straight out of a fairy-tale picture book.

This must be Gramercy Park! I can't help but smile to myself. How gorgeous that in the middle of the bustling city is a place that looks as serene and composed as this! I can almost block out the sound of the hubbub and traffic from the next street over.

It's not busy in here at all. I wonder why. Surely anyone with any sense would want to hang out here on such a fresh spring day. I shrug away my confusion. The lack of people around means there's no one to see me hitching my tights back up in the most unladylike fashion.

I spot a big oak tree and slink behind it, hitching my dress up slightly so that I can pull my tights back around my waist where they belong. But then I realise that my bumbag is so tight across my middle that I can't get the tights up far enough to stay put.

I quickly unclip the bumbag and place it on a little wooden bench beside me. I take another furtive look around – no one nearby. With all of my strength, I yank up my tights again, my dress bunched up around my thighs. They really are a bit small and so I squat, hitch them up my legs bit by bit and wiggle so that they'll come up over my belly. I'm almost there when I hear the worst sound a lady can hear when she is pulling up her tights. The sound of a rip.

Nooooo!

I look down to see how bad it is. Dammit. They've split right up the crotch. No! These are my favourite tights! They're maroon. Maroon tights! They make me feel like Zooey Deschanel. Maaaan. I pull at the hole with a sad, frustrated sigh.

'You!' comes a furious voice from behind me.

I spin around to see a snooty-looking woman staring at me in absolute disgust. She's frowning, her top lip is curled, the whole shebang.

'Are you okay?' I ask.

'What on earth are you doing?' she spits at me, a vein popping out of her smooth forehead. 'Where is your key?'

I pull my dress down hurriedly. 'My tights were… Wait, what key?'

Two spots of colour flush onto the woman's high cheeks. 'You don't have a key?' she asks, seemingly horrified. 'This is outrageous.'

What is she talking about? What key? Is Gramercy Park the go-to place for all the odd people in this city?

The woman looks down at my dress in horror, her mouth agog. I follow her gaze to find that I somehow haven't pulled the skirt of my dress all the way back down. In fact, a chunk of the fabric has tucked itself into the waistband of my tights. As I struggle to pull it out, the woman stares at the crotch hole in my tights and inhales sharply before taking out her phone and frantically pressing at the screen.

'I didn't think anyone could see me!' I explain. 'How embarrassing. Sorry!'

'Police, please,' the woman shouts into the phone, one arm outstretched, palm flat. 'You stay there. Don't move a muscle.'

'What's happening?' I ask, wondering why she's calling the police. 'Is there a criminal? Are you in danger?' I crane my head up to take a look in the near vicinity. I don't see anything suspect. What the heck is going on?

The woman ignores me, her hand trembling. 'There's a pervert in Gramercy Park,' she says into the phone.

I gasp, my heart starting to speed up in fear. A pervert in the park? Shit. I look around again, eyes wide. 'Shouldn't we be running away?' I ask frantically. 'We should get out of here!'

The woman's hand is still warding me off. She continues speaking into her phone. 'This is the second time this has happened!' she snarls furiously into the receiver. 'I want someone here immediately.'

The second time a pervert has been here? But it's such a classy park. It doesn't look like the kind of place a perv would visit, even a high-class perv.

'She can't leave because she doesn't have a key. She is keyless. She was touching herself in broad daylight. And… and she has some sort of phallus on her head.'

The pervert is female. That's unusual. And she has a phallus? What the hell is a… A hot feeling floods over me as it dawns on me that this woman is talking about me! That I am the one with a phallus on my head. That *I* am the pervert she's talking about.

'Wait!' I shout in disbelief. 'I'm not a pervert! I was just sorting out my tights! I was hitching them up and they ripped!'

Ending the call and dropping her phone into her handbag, the woman puts her other hand out, feet in a wide, defensive stance. 'You do not speak to me. Do not come near me. I will not have it. This is a private, decent park for private, decent people!'

This is nuts. I've got to get out of here! I make to leave, but the woman yells so loudly that I stop in my tracks.

'Don't even think of it. You cannot leave. You do not have a key! You can't get in or out without a key.'

I think back to the jogger running into the park before, how I followed her through the gate before it had fully closed. I didn't know this was a private park! How was I to know that?

'There is a cop two minutes away. You will not get away like the last one.'

I blink. Why is this happening to me? Why won't this woman understand that I was just hitching up my tights? Has she never encountered a saggy crotch?

'I was hitching my blimmin' tights!' I protest again. 'I swear!'

'I don't care what you Brits call it! It's disgusting and you should be ashamed of yourself! Maybe you can get away with this depravity across the pond. But not here. Oh no.'

The woman pulls out her phone again and takes a picture of me.

'What are you doing?' I ask, shielding my face with my arms.

'Taking a photograph for evidence. I will name and shame you!'

I feel myself starting to panic, sweat pooling under my arms and on my forehead. Why doesn't she believe me? Okay, it might look a little weird, a girl with a unicorn horn examining her own crotch hole by a tree. But that doesn't mean I'm a pervert. I mean, I'm so inexperienced in sex! I'm basically the opposite of a pervert. I have had sex one time. Ten years ago. In the missionary position. And it lasted for three minutes. And I didn't get off in any one of those minutes! I'm the least perverted person on earth, pretty much!

'How dare you say I'm a pervert,' I say, fury burning in my belly now. 'I don't even have sexual feelings.' Except for that library scene, I add to myself silently. 'You are completely wrong on this. Just let me leave!'

'NO!' she shouts. 'The only way you are getting out of here is with a New York City Police escort.'

Ugh! This woman is horrible! And judgey! I bet she just got out of bed this morning, hoping for some drama to tell all her snooty friends about. She thinks she's so important with her park key. 'They will be here any second now,' she says, taking another picture of me before I can cover my face again.

Holy shit. I can't get arrested! In America. I've only been here for one day. What if they deport me? Then I'll never find Chuck and Birdie will be devastated! What if they send me to prison? I would never survive in prison. I have no tattoos. And I am weak. I am physically very weak; how would I stand up for myself? Oh God. What would Colin think if I went to prison? Would he still be interested in me? Would he be willing to be a prison husband? Would I have to do a conjugal visit with him? I mean, I don't think I'm ready for conjugalities in general, let alone in prison!

As these scenarios flash through my head, I get more and more freaked out. It can't happen. This is not happening. This day cannot get any worse than it already has been!

I soften my voice, try to sound reasonable, polite, non-deviant. 'Look, I didn't know it was a key-only park! I'm sorry. Please let me out. I beg of you.'

'Everyone knows that Gramercy Park belongs only to its residents.'

Man, this woman is the worst.

'Well it seems unfair that only some people get to enjoy it!' I retort before I can stop myself. I don't think I've ever acted so cocky before. But then, I've never been accused of public indecency before and if anything will bring out a person's grumpy side then that surely is it.

The woman sneers at me. 'Don't talk to me. Don't even look at me with your kinky eyes.'

She's so mean. I feel tears rush to my kinky eyes.

I have to get out of here. I have to get out of here now. I can't just wait around for the police to come. Donna would have a field day if that happened. No. I won't do it.

I notice that the horrid woman has a little string around her neck. And on the end of it is a golden key, glinting in the spring sunlight. That must be the key. The key to the park. The key that makes her think she is so much better than everyone else.

And I must be a damn fool because before I can think too much about it, I've reached forward, snatched the key from around the woman's neck and I am legging it. I am legging it like the motherfucking wind.

From behind me I hear the woman scream after me. 'Thief! Pervert! Thief! Pervert and Thief!'

I feel the stupid tights falling all the way down my legs. But I don't care. I will not get arrested. Not today. Not ever!

The tights make my run more of a fast penguin waddle, so as I'm running I grab underneath where the hole is spreading and I rip it as hard as I can. Reaching the gate, I slide the key into the lock, turn it, and get the hell out of there!

Now that I'm on a busy New York City street, no one seems to notice me, my ripped tights and my unicorn horn, and those that do don't care. I look behind me for any sign of the cops, and spot one leaning on a wall, eating a gigantic slice of pizza folded in half. He looks pretty chill but it could be a ruse.

I take no chances and continue scampering all the way to the underground. Once I'm on the train I take the only free seat and try to catch my breath. A weird buzzy feeling courses through my body. I feel full of energy, like I could take on a bear. I think it's adrenaline. Or endorphins. I need to calm down.

I yank the rest of my ripped tights off, bundle them up and shove them into my bumbag. A girl sitting opposite gives me a thumbs up as she watches me do it.

'Walk of shame!' she laughs. 'Alright!'

If only she knew.

I return her smile with an exhausted one of my own, close my eyes for a moment and try to breathe my heart rate back to normal.

What the fuck just happened?

I realise I'm gripping onto something extra tightly. I open my fist to see the little golden park key sitting there.

Oh my god, I just stole a key!

My stomach churns. What if the police are hunting for me right now!

I tuck the key into a little coin pouch and shove it into the secret pocket of the bumbag next to Birdie's letter.

Jeeeeeez.

I shake my head in disbelief as the subway whizzes away from the scene of my crime.

I'm not having the best luck *at all* today. I need to get this letter to Chuck as soon as possible before it gets any worse.

I take out my phone, open up my apps and plan a new travel route.

Next stop: Wall Street.

* * *

My run of bad luck is not over yet. Because it turns out that not only is Chimes Investment closed on a Sunday, but pretty much the entirety of Wall Street. Of course. It's *Sunday*. Duh. Obviously I should have thought of that, but with a random socialite doing my hair in return for Chuck intel, being accused of public indecency and stealing a key from the most horrid woman in NYC, my head is a teensy bit full.

A doorman at Chuck's company tells me that the stock market is strictly a 9-5 Monday to Friday situation like I'm some sort of idiot, which, of course, I am.

Out in the street, it seems oddly quiet and a little bit eerie. The buildings surrounding me are huge and beautiful, if a little intimidating. It's nothing like the genteel beauty of Gramercy or the leafy family vibe of the Upper West Side. On the subway over here no one seemed to care about my weird hair. But in the financial district people very definitely notice it. One besuited gentleman actually does a double take.

I plonk down onto some steps opposite a bronze sculpture of an aggressive-looking bull and get out my phone, pressing the FaceTime option to call Birdie and update her on the situation regarding Chuck.

When she answers, her lovely pixie face flashes up on the screen. She's smiling but she looks bone-tired. My heart lurches a little. Poor Birdie.

No matter how awful my day has been and how knackered I feel right now, I'm lucky. I'm lucky not to be stuck in a hospital room, awaiting a surgery that might give me a little more time before the inevitable.

I shake away my self-pity and plaster a smile on my face.

'Heya!' I say, full of enthusiasm. 'I'm in Wall Street! Sitting next to a statue of a very hostile-looking bull!'

Birdie stares at me for a moment and then her face

crumples. At first I think she might be crying. But then I realise that she is laughing. She is cry-laughing.

And she won't stop.

She points at me as she laughs.

Oh yes. My very own horn.

'I know,' I say, reaching up to feel the offending structure atop my head. 'I've had the weirdest morning!'

But Birdie can't even respond, she's laughing that hard. Tears stream out of her eyes, the phone camera shaking as she squeals with delight.

'All right. Calm down.' I roll my eyes, although her laughter is making me laugh too.

When she's caught her breath, she wipes the tears away from her eyes.

'What the fuck happened?' she eventually gets out.

'You don't think it suits me?' I strike a pose, hand on hip, smiling into the mid-distance. 'Unicorn chic?'

'You look insane.'

'I feel insane. And it's really heavy. I feel like my head is drooping. My neck actually aches a bit.'

'Wait, let me take a screenshot.'

'This.' I point to my head. 'Was my payment for a Chuck lead.'

'I'm guessing he wasn't at the place on East 18th Street?'

'No.' I shake my head. 'I'm sorry.'

Birdie nods, not looking all that surprised by the information.

'I did meet his old friend from Princeton, though,' I continue. 'His name was Anders. He was living in the house, renting from Chuck's parents who, apparently, haven't seen or heard from Chuck in six years.'

'Wow. He always did have a weird relationship with them. I wonder what tipped it over the edge into complete estrangement.'

I shrug. 'Maybe they had affairs and ran away like my parents did.'

'Oh sweetie,' Birdie says sympathetically.

'I'm just messing,' I say quickly, annoyed at myself for being negative in front of her, especially when she doesn't even have a family to complain about. 'Anyway. Anders gave me a picture of Chuck in exchange for letting him do my hair.'

'*What the shit?*'

'Yep. He invited me in, letting me believe that he was in fact Chuck Allen and then told me there was a "certain beautiful uniformity" to my curls.'

'Wow. Only in New York.' Birdie laughs gleefully. 'Show me the picture of Chuck!'

I take the photograph out of my bumbag and hold it up to the screen.

Birdie squints and smiles sadly.

'Ah, I bought him that shirt,' she says with a nostalgic sigh.

'He's very handsome,' I say.

'He was gorgeous,' Birdie agrees.

'Well, according to Anders, Chuck works in Wall Street. Or at least he did. So that's why I'm here.'

'But… it's Sunday.'

'I know that now! I didn't even think until I got here. I'll have to wait until Monday,' I say. 'Hopefully he'll be working at the bank still, I can give him the letter and I'll be back with you as soon as possible.'

Birdie nods. 'Thanks, Brewster. This really does mean a whole bunch to me.'

'I know,' I say. 'I'll find him, don't worry.'

I see a flash of emotion cross Birdie's face, but before I can decipher what it is, it's gone and she's smiling again.

'Hey, make sure you read my list of recommendations, won't you?'

'I will.' I grin back. 'You always did say that you'd show me NYC one day,' I point out with a wobble in my voice.

Birdie sighs. 'Well, there you go.' Her voice wobbles a bit too. 'Take pictures of everything, okay? I'm getting such a kick out of you being there!'

'Definitely.' I'm pleased that I agreed to do this for her, despite the fact that it's been a teensy bit traumatic so far.

'Anything else interesting happened today? Besides your crazy-ass hair?'

I cover my face because I can't believe what I'm about to say. I can't believe it actually happened.

'Oh, nothing much,' I say breezily. 'Except… I was just accused of having a public wank in Gramercy Park. Plus, I stole a key.'

And although I'm not really up for reliving my humiliation, the fact that Birdie is laughing before I've even started relaying the story means that I tell her every last detail.

CHAPTER FOURTEEN

@ElissaJohnson to @NYPD

I apprehended a pervert in Gramercy Park today. Upon phoning police, I was told that someone would be with me in two minutes. 1/2

@ElissaJohnson to @NYPD

20 mins later a cop FINALLY arrived. The pervert had fled, stealing a valuable key from around my neck. Appalled and disappointed in NYPD!!! 2/2

@ElissaJohnson

Everyone! Beware of a deranged British woman wearing her hair in an aggressive phallic arrangement. She is a pervert and thief

@ElissaJohnson

Thanks for your well wishes @Designermommy23 and @organic_hemingway_brooklyn. I am recovering

at @GuerlainSpa. Just hope the police find her! Am filing complaint as we speak.

By the time I get back to the handsome leafy streets of the Upper West Side, I can barely keep my eyes open. I grabbed a few groceries on the way back, so at least I'll be able to make a coffee to keep myself awake!

Up in the apartment it takes me an hour to remove all the kirby grips in my hair and even when they're all out, every strand remains in perfect place. Anders must have used some extra-super-strength hairspray; my hair is all crunchy. I step into the narrow shower and wash my hair vigorously until the horn structure starts to disintegrate and the gross blue hair drops out, pooling disgustingly in the plughole. Slipping into my white cotton dressing gown, I dry my hair, lay the sheets out on the sofa bed and switch on the TV.

Oh, *The Big Bang Theory* is on! I think of Alex and Donna at home. I wonder how they're finding it without me in the house. This is only the second time in my life that I've not slept in my own room. Donna's probably loving it. I wonder if Alex is too. He's not been in touch since I left so I'm guessing the answer is yes.

I thought I would hate staying in an apartment here alone. But it's actually quite nice. I can just sit here with no worries of Donna knocking on my door, or Alex bursting in to tell me that Donna is getting on his case because I've left the toothpaste lid off again. I look around me. No one is going to interrupt me in here. I can do anything I like.

I glance over to the blinds to make sure they're definitely shut and then I take off my robe so that I am naked.

There.

I am completely in the buff.

And no one can do anything about it!

It's not bad.

It's actually quite comfortable.

And then something even more exciting occurs to me. I don't *have* to watch *The Big Bang Theory*. I'm here alone. I have the power. I can do whatever I damn well please in this tiny studio apartment.

I've never really experienced that before!

So I pick up the remote control, point it at the TV and, with a flourish, turn *The Big Bang Theory* over to a completely different channel.

And, honestly, it's the best I've felt all day.

I snuggle myself down into the sofa bed with a massive yawn. And before I've even found something I want to watch, my eyes drift close.

* * *

I don't know how long I doze off for. It must be ages because it's dark when I wake up. The TV is still on, colourful lights casting a blue glow around the room.

Dammit. I didn't mean to fall asleep. I should have made a coffee as soon as I got back earlier. I squint at my watch. 11 p.m. Nooooo! Now I'll be awake all night!

I sit up, feeling a slight chill on my naked body. Grabbing my robe, I wrap it around me and pad over to the kitchenette to make a cup of tea and a piece of toast.

I notice I have a sweet text from Colin asking me what my favourite breakfast food is. I smile to myself and type back 'Weetabix.' A few seconds later, he sends a reply. 'Weetabix for me too!' it says.

Not many people would choose Weetabix. This has got to be a sign of some sort. Of what, I don't know… But, still. It's got to be a good thing, right?

Outside on the street I hear the sound of a police siren fly past and feel my shoulders bunch up.

I tell myself that *of course* they're not coming for me. I made a clean escape from Gramercy Park, they don't even know I'm here! But nevertheless the sound of the siren makes me feel a bit on edge. I grab the remote and turn the telly down to mask any outdoor noise.

Oh! Look! It's that show, *Sunday Night Live*! The show that Seth the queue jumper said he wrote for. We don't get it in the UK, but I see the clips floating around the internet every Monday morning.

The actors on screen are dressed as aliens, and they're all hanging out at a bar in outer space playing some alien version of pool. It's a bizarre and funny sketch and pretty soon I find myself laughing along with the live audience. I wonder if Seth wrote this sketch? If this was what he was typing away at on the plane? I watch with renewed interest until the advert break.

Having finished my tea and toast, I head to the kitchenette to rinse the crockery. When I return there's a new sketch playing out on the screen. Set on a turbulent airplane, from the looks of things. How they'll make a turbulent airplane funny, I have no clue.

'This is my first time on an airplane,' one of the actresses screeches, swigging back from a bottle of champagne. 'I live in England, don't you know,' she's saying to one of the other passengers – a bespectacled man. 'It's the best country in the whole wiiiiiide world.'

She's putting on a British accent.

A really twangy northern accent.

Like mine.

How weird.

I frown. And then, almost as if in slow motion, I notice that the actress on screen is in a wig of massive brown wavy hair. Like mine. And – oh my god – is wearing a bumbag. A pink bumbag. *Like mine.*

All at once my jaw clenches, my cheeks get very, very hot and I can only stare, mouth agog, as the actress on the screen invites a bespectacled fellow plane passenger to join her in the mile-high club.

'I need it,' she says. 'I need it reeeeeal bad.'

When the actress who looks like me and the bespectacled guy enter the airplane toilet, the actress rips off her top, sits onto the loo and says, 'Olivia likes to be watched! WATCH ME! WATCH ME PIDDLE.'

Oh. My. God.

My mouth completely dries up as the bespectacled man tries to escape the airplane loo but the woman makes him stay and watch her have a wee.

No. *No!* That is not what happened.

What the hell?

How did he? *Why* did he?

I jump up from the sofa bed and switch the telly off in shock.

That damn queue jumper! He has completely screwed me over. He used my fear of planes against me! How mean is that! Stunned tears cloud my vision. *He didn't even disguise me.* Olivia? From England? Wearing a beautiful pink bumbag?

The adrenaline I felt earlier today is back in full force and I am wide awake.

And there I was thinking this trip couldn't go any more terribly.

Boy, was I wrong.

* * *

I spend the next twenty minutes pacing around the tiny apartment angrily. But it doesn't calm me down. Not at all. I suppose it doesn't help that the entire length of the room is about seven steps end to end.

I peek out of the window blind. The man in the flat opposite is sitting bottomless on his sofa again, *watching Sunday Night Live!*

Seth. That absolute bellend.

I grab my phone and log onto the internet. I Google 'Seth writer Sunday Night Live idiot'.

I don't know what I'm expecting to find. His home address, so I can go over there and kick him right in the goolies?

Nope. No home address. There is an article, though, published a few days ago on a comedy website called Splitsider. The title of the article says 'Seth Hartman. *Sunday Night Live*'s Rising Star'.

I furiously click on the article and growl in rage as the screen fills up with a picture of the man from the plane. Ugh. His smug eyes are trying to look like the eyes of a normal, innocent kind person who once helped an anxious woman to navigate a long haul flight.

Those eyes lie!

I scroll down and start to read.

Seth Hartman has been a staple at the writer's desk of Sunday Night Live for the last five years. The thirty-five-year-old Harvard graduate came up through Second City Chicago as part of the popular comedy improv troupe 'Everybody Loves Dumplings' and while originally auditioning for spot as a performer on the show, he has become a solid part of the writing team. As well as his writing duties, he still regularly performs and teaches improv in New York and was recently the keynote speaker at the UK's Comedy Sketch Festival held every year in Manchester.

With a huge eye roll, I click off the article and load up Twitter, desperately hoping that, by some fluke, everyone else's TVs crashed at the same time and no one but me saw that horrible sketch.

But no. The world is loving what has now been termed the 'Watch Me Piddle' sketch.

I furiously scroll the #watchmepiddle hashtag.

The funniest thing Sunday Night Live has done in years!!

Kelly Cannon shines as Olivia the kinky British girl on a tempestuous flight. lololol #watchmepiddle

Seth Hartman is the new Steve Martin. Put him on the screen already @SundayNightLive.

Omg. That piddle sketch was bizarre. In a good way. Funny AF. WTF??

I scroll through the endless tweets for far too long. My hands shaking, my face burning with shame.

I need to talk to someone. I go to FaceTime Birdie, but realise that it's about 5 a.m. in England and the hospital makes everyone turn their phones off between 11 p.m. and 7 a.m.

Instead, I FaceTime my brother. He's usually up pretty early.

It rings for a while before Alex answers, his shell-shocked face popping up onto the screen.

Okay, maybe this is a bit *too* early.

'Olive? What is it? Are you alright? Are you safe?'

'Sorry,' I say. 'I know it's early. I… I just needed to talk to someone…'

'It's okay,' Alex says gently, wiping his eyes.

Beside him Donna's head pops up from the pillow. 'It's 5 a.m., Alex! Who is it?'

'It's Olive,' he replies. 'You go back to sleep, love.'

Donna moves her face right up to the screen. Her usually perfect hair is all mussed up, her eyes puffy.

'Oh, Olive,' she says. 'What have you done? Are you in trouble? Do you need money? You need money, don't you? Has she messed it up already? Oh darling.'

'Harsh, Donna!' I grumble.

'What's wrong?' Alex says, his eyebrows lowering worriedly. 'You look like you've been crying.'

I want to tell him. I want to tell him how weird and tough this day has been. How I've just been humiliated on live TV, how I'm so stunned I'm not quite sure what to do with myself. But Donna's there, staring at me through the phone screen. And I can feel her judgement from here.

'It's nothing to worry about!' I say. 'But… it is kind of private…'

'You want to talk to me alone?' Alex says, climbing out of the bed.

'Oh, nice!' Donna mumbles. 'I don't exist, do I?'

'No!' I say. 'I just …want to talk to my brother.'

Donna rolls her eyes. 'Donna's just second fiddle. That's fine, I guess.'

Argh!

Alex shakes his head and climbs back into the bed. 'Of course not, Donna.' He turns back to me. 'Are you sure you can't speak in front of Donna? She's part of this family too.'

I'm well aware. It used to be that Alex and I were our

own little team. A bit sad, a bit messed up, but a team, nevertheless. He never judged me for being so particular, for being easily spooked by so many things. He was the same for a while after our parents left. But now Donna is here. Don't get me wrong, I'm grateful that she makes him happy. I mean, she's clearly helped him to deal with all the shit Mum and Dad dumped on us when they left him in charge of a house and an eighteen-year-old sister when he was only twenty-two years old himself. But she's *always* there now. I never get to talk to him properly anymore. I miss that.

I shake my head. 'Ah, it doesn't matter. It was nothing. Just wanted to hear your voice!'

'Are you sure?' Alex says. To his credit, he does look slightly apologetic for Donna's behaviour. But not enough to leave the room and talk to me alone. 'Do you need to come back early?' he adds. 'Because I can lend you the money for an early flight, just about?'

Donna huffs. 'Although that wouldn't be ideal,' she points out, nudging Alex with her elbow. 'We have a filing cabinet to order and I've just seen some candle moulds in the shape of Siamese cats that I think will be perfect for the "Creamy Nights" candle scent. We could do without spending the money on a flight, Olive.'

I sigh. 'I don't need an early flight. Everything's absolutely fine. I'll see you guys when I'm back.'

And before they can say anything else, I end the call feeling utterly, guttingly alone. I have a little cry and a sniff which makes me feel a bit better.

As I plug my phone into the charger beside the bed there's a loud knock at my door.

Who the heck is that at this time?

CHAPTER FIFTEEN

@ElissaJohnson

Don't usually watch @SundayNightLive but I'm sure that the #watchmepiddle woman is based on vile menace who robbed me.

@ElissaJohnson

Had forgotten she was wearing a fannypack. Has anyone else encountered her? Pls RT.

Don't be the police. Do not be the police.

I head over to the door and take a peek through the spy-hole. It's a very short round woman of about sixty with silver hair down to her waist, and fifty-pence shaped glasses. She doesn't look like po-po. She's leaning on one crutch, a bandage wrapped around her knee, which is poking out from beneath the red and yellow polka dot nightdress she's wearing.

I open the door.

'Can I help you?'

The woman pokes her head in my flat and looks around nosily. 'Are you all right? I can hear you crying through the walls!'

Her voice is lilting and melodic, her accent a cross between New York and Spanish.

'Oh bugger, I'm so sorry!' I say, wiping away my tears with a piece of toilet tissue. 'I genuinely thought I was doing my quiet cry.'

The woman shrugs a shoulder. 'Maybe you were, but these walls are as thin as a water biscuit. I've complained to the building managers but, eh, they don't listen to me. "Old Mrs Ramirez, complaining once more," they say. They think that just because my rent is controlled that I'll never leave no matter what. They think…' she looks up and down the hallway with a confrontational expression, as if 'they' are listening '…that I don't know they talk about me. But I know. I know everything that goes on around here.'

I nod. 'Oh dear. Well… I'm really very sorry. I'll keep it down. I should probably stop crying actually. It's no help!'

The woman looks down into my hand at the screwed-up loo roll and blows the air out from her cheeks, giving a little shake of her head.

'Come with me, cariño,' she commands, promptly spinning around and marching across the hall into the flat opposite mine.

Hmmm. Perhaps it's not such a good idea to enter into a second stranger's house in the same day. But… this Mrs Ramirez looks harmless. I don't think she'll want to do my hair… God, I hope not.

Not everyone in New York is a weirdo, Olive.

I pop my head outside into the hallway. She's left her front door open for me.

I step out of my flat and tentatively cross the hall into hers.

As I enter, I notice that Mrs Ramirez's studio is exactly the same as mine, only everything's the other way around.

Her walls are filled with framed pictures of landscapes and seascapes and mountainscapes and there are little ornaments dotted here there and everywhere. Glass ducks, and matryoshka dolls, tiny cactuses and exotic-looking bowls and vases.

'I've travelled,' Mrs Ramirez explains, noticing me taking it all in. She sits herself down on a comfy-looking armchair and props her crutch up beside her. 'I like to bring something back from every place I've visited. Come.'

She ushers me in from where she's sitting and holds out a small handkerchief embroidered with wispy swirls of red, gold and silver. I sit on another armchair opposite her. She places the handkerchief into my hands.

'It's beautiful!' I remark, marvelling at the elaborate stitching.

'I got it from a fabric market in Bali,' she says. 'It's yours now.'

She gives me a kindly smile. And despite my fed-up mood, I can't help but smile back, touched.

'Now, I'll take that.' She plucks the toilet tissue from where it's bunched up in my hand.

'I can't actually use this handkerchief on my nose!' I say. 'It's much too precious.'

Mrs Ramirez dismisses me with a quick flick of her hand. 'Oh, my *pobrecita*, what else are you gonna do with it? Go ahead now.'

She's pretty forceful, like a mum telling off her toddler. I press the soft square of fabric against my eyes, and remove the last of the teardrops.

'Isn't that better? Now, what will you have to drink? How about a soothing Salabat tea? I brought it back last year from the Philippines. It's something special, I'll tell you.'

Salabat tea? What the hell is Salabat tea? I don't like the sound of it.

'Oh, don't go to any trouble. I'm okay, I promise.'

'It's no trouble for me. I need you to make me one, so you may as well have one yourself.'

'Excuse me?'

'It's the middle of the night! You woke me up!' She points at her bandaged leg. 'And I'm recovering from a sprained knee. The least you can do is make me a soothing tea,' she says it with a smile, but she definitely is not joking.

Tucking the handkerchief into my dressing gown pocket, I potter over to Mrs Ramirez's kitchenette area. All of the fittings are exactly the same as in my room, but the space looks completely different. The counters are covered with spice jars and cookbooks and exotic-looking knick-knacks from who knows where. There's even a big wooden sculpture of a face hanging on one of the cupboard doors. I reach out to touch it. It's rough and primitive looking. It's so unusual.

'I got that from Papua New Guinea,' Mrs Ramirez says. 'Wonderful place. It's a ceremonial mask, made by the craftsmen of the Sawos people.'

I nod, not wanting to admit that I've never even heard of Papua New Guinea, never mind the Sawos people.

'You must go sometime!'

'Maybe I will!' I say. I neglect to tell her that that I am a twenty-seven-year-old woman who left her home country for the very first time less than forty-eight hours ago.

'The tea is in the jar on the middle shelf of the cupboard on the right,' she points out.

As I make two cups of this tea which smells like lovely

cosy ginger, Mrs Ramirez tells me about her bad leg and how it's kept her indoors for the last two weeks, how she hates being stuck inside. She tells me about how she has lived here for twenty years and she knows all the comings and goings of the various Airbnb guests next door. 'None so pretty as you. Or crying so noisily and with so much self-pity.'

All right, jeez.

'It's just been a crazy, crazy day,' I say, taking a sip of the tea.

Mrs Ramirez nods, slurping from her cup and making an 'aaaaaah' noise. 'What happened?'

I must really need to get it out, or maybe it's this tea making me relax a little, but I tell Mrs Ramirez –a total stranger– everything. I blurt about the flight and Seth, about Anders and the Gramercy Park getaway, and then about that wretched sketch on *Sunday Night Live*.

When I've finished telling her, I take a breath. 'And that's why I'm crying. I've never experienced this many emotions in such a short space of time!'

'New York can be… a little challenging,' Mrs Ramirez remarks. 'But it is the most magical place in the world. Anything can happen here – as you are finding out. Most people dream of coming to New York.'

'Oh. Well, yeah. I never expected to be here. I've come for my friend. Birdie. She's dying and wants me to deliver a letter to a man called Chuck.'

Mrs Ramirez's hands fly to her mouth. 'Oh my goodness. How terrible. What is wrong with her?'

'It's lupus,' I say. 'She's had it for a while. It's just a matter of time now until it gets the better of her. She's a had a few close calls and she's gotten through them. But she's starting to get poorlier as the months go by.'

Mrs Ramirez narrows her eyes. 'It is very interesting how bluntly you tell me this.'

I frown. 'How do you mean?'

'Like… it doesn't bother you. You are so matter-of-fact about your friend dying.'

I wave her away. 'Of course it bothers me. I just don't think about it too hard. I can't, because if I do…'

I trail off, not bearing to even think about it.

Mrs Ramirez gives me an odd sort of look. Like she's trying to work me out. 'Forgive me. I just… grieving is very important.'

'Birdie's not dead yet,' I say heatedly.

Mrs Ramirez's soft tanned cheeks flush pink. 'Of course. I'm sorry.'

There's an awkward moment.

'Sorry. I didn't mean to get grumpy. It's just…'

'I know, chica,' Mrs Ramirez says, leaning across to pat my knee. 'I know.'

'I should probably let you get back to bed,' I say, talk of Birdie's illness lodging like a stone stuck into my throat, neither coming up nor going down. Just there. Waiting for me to confront it.

'Wait!' Mrs Ramirez says as I stand up to leave. 'Why don't you just call this TV show and tell them you don't like what they said about you.'

I fight the urge to laugh. For someone so well-travelled Mrs Ramirez doesn't seem to have a great handle on how these things work.

'You can't just phone a TV show. And even if you can, they won't do anything. It's already happened! It was live TV!'

'I suppose…'

I approach the door when Mrs Ramirez calls me again.

'Will you do me a kindness? My knee is not quite healed and I need to post these letters to my pen pals. They have been sitting on my dresser for two weeks and I would very much like to get them in the post. Do you think you might take them for me?'

'Oh, sure,' I say. 'No problem.'

She stands up, leaning on her walking stick and hobbles over to a large mahogany dresser where a small stack of postcards are arranged neatly in a pile. She picks them up and limps her way back over to me.

'You have a lot of pen pals,' I remark, taking them from her.

'I met them on my travels,' she says. 'My friends come from all over the world! I'm very lucky! Maybe you will meet a special friend in New York City!' she says with a chuckle.

'I've met you!' I smile at her. 'Thanks for the tea and the chat. I really needed it.'

'It was my pleasure,' she says, pulling me in for a spontaneous hug that, to my surprise, makes my heart swell. 'You come see me again anytime?'

'I will,' I say, hugging her back, her soft round body comforting and oddly protective. 'I definitely will.'

CHAPTER SIXTEEN

Email from Donna@candledreams.me:

Dear Olive,

Hope you're well.

I am writing regarding the phone call you made to your brother and I in the early hours of this morning. It was unfair of you to get in touch at daft o'clock, merely because you wanted to talk to your brother on your timeline and not ours.

Alex already worries enough about you. Of course he always will – you are his baby sister after all. But I think he – we – expected that as the years went on there would be less of the baby and that you would be able to take care of yourself.

Don't get me wrong, I know that you were upset

about something, but it isn't Alex's or my place to fix things for you. We told you we thought it was a bad idea for you to fly to a new country on a whim, when your experience of new situations is, well, less than stellar. But you went, and while we are soooo proud of you for doing something new, we are not at your beck and call when things fall out of your control and you become upset.

I know you are back soon, but I wanted to say this now before my upset dissipates and I decide that the best course of action would be to say nothing at all for the sake of tension.

With truth, care and love,

Donna

By Monday morning, I've managed to convince myself that no one will know that the Watch Me Piddle sketch was based on me. And even if people in the UK see it on the internet today, beyond the Joans, Birdie and Alex and Donna, I don't really know many other people who would recognise me. There's nothing I can do about it now and even though I am generally embarrassed and mad as hell at that stupid Seth Hartman, being consumed with my own humiliation will only take my mind off the task at hand. Which is to get to Wall Street and give Birdie's letter to Chuck.

As I leave the apartment building, it immediately starts drizzling. I open the little umbrella I brought with me, congratulating myself on being so resourceful. See? It was worth bringing two types of umbrella for my trip – one compact one that will fit in my bumbag and a bigger one for when I'm carrying my over the shoulder handbag!

Despite the drizzle, Manhattan is in full flow. I say hello and goodbye to Lloyd the doorman and make my way down Riverside Drive. My plan this morning is for a quick breakfast at a deli Birdie has recommended, post Mrs Ramirez's postcards and, from there, head right back to Chimes Investment in Wall Street and get this letter to Chuck Allen.

It only takes me a few minutes to reach the deli, which is called Zabar's, and before I've opened the big glass doors, I'm salivating at the delicious bakery smell wafting out. I take down my brolly, shake it off and wander inside.

Wow, it's enormous in here! Not only is it a place for breakfast, but a grocery store too! It's already busy with people filling up trolleys full of artisanal cheeses and fresh bread and meats.

I head over to a small seating area, delighted to find that one of the few tables is miraculously free. Perfect! Maybe today is going to be a success!

As I take a seat, I notice a young woman nearby staring at me. For a moment, I wonder if my hair is tangled, or if I have toothpaste on my boob – both things that happen to me more regularly than is necessary. And then see exactly where she's looking. Right at my pink bumbag!

Does… does she recognise me? No. Only people who know me would know that the Olivia character on *Sunday Night Live* was based on me, surely? Apart from the curly hair and bumbag, the actress didn't look at all like me… She must just be admiring the lovely bright shade of pink.

I turn my chair away from the staring woman and pick up my menu. As I do, a waitress in a crisp white shirt and a black checked skirt approaches. 'Good morning! May I take your order?'

'Ooh, I haven't had time to look at the menu properly yet! Can I have another few minutes?'

As I speak, I notice even more people in the cafe start to look at me.

The waitress narrows her eyes slightly. 'Do I… know you?' she asks.

I shake my head. 'No, I don't think so.'

'Are you sure you haven't been here before?'

'I am pretty sure I haven't. This is my first time in Manhattan, actually!'

The waitress frowns, her eyes flicking down to my bumbag. Then she shrieks. Really loudly. 'Watch me piddle!' she cries. 'That's it! Watch me piddle!'

Oh *shit.*

She shouts so loud that all surrounding noise comes to a halt and everyone in the place turns around to stare. One person even lifts up the phone to take a picture of me.

Noooooo!

'I don't know what you're talking about,' I lie immediately, trying to act casual. 'Ooh, the smoked salmon on bagel sounds amazing. Can I have that please? Thank you!'

The waitress shakes her pretty blonde head in confusion. 'But… you sound like the piddle woman and you look like the piddle woman and your pink fanny pack is *identical.*'

'Actually mine has this cool sunshine hologram on it,' I point out, realising a split second too late that I sound like an absolute nerd.

'Oh, it's definitely you!' a hipstery-looking bloke says from the table opposite, beaming with pleasure. 'You are *exactly* the same as the piddle woman. Did you really make someone watch you pee on a plane? Why would you do that? Is it a sexual thing?'

'NO!' I yell, my throat starting to tighten as everyone looks my way. 'I don't know what any of you are talking about! I just want to have some breakfast!' I look at the waitress. 'I just want a bagel with some smoked salmon!'

'Whether you know or not, you were definitely impersonated on *Sunday Night Live* last night,' hipstery bloke's female companion says. 'I would watch it if I were you…'

'Definitely,' the waitress adds, completely ignoring my order.

This is so very awkward. I don't think I've ever had this many people looking at me at the same time! I feel my brow start to get sweaty. I want to just spiral down onto the floor so they all stop staring. Does *everyone* in New York watch *Sunday Night Live*? Argh!

A few other customers of the deli start to approach the area to ogle at me. One requests an autograph and a selfie. Another asks me if I want to accompany them to the nearest public bathroom.

And that's when I decide that enough is enough.

Face flaming, I jump up from the table, chair screeching across the floor. I jog out of Zabar's and into the street. My stomach rumbles at my missed bagel, my whole body smarts with embarrassment.

I put up my umbrella and stand dumbly in the middle of the street, feeling completely exposed. I can't go through the rest of my day like this!

Across the road I notice a grocery store. A little plan forms in my mind. I go in and ask them for a paper bag. Back outside, on the street, I unclip my pink bumbag and stuff it in the paper bag like it is some sort of contraband.

I breathe a sigh of relief. I love that bumbag, but thanks to horrible Seth Hartman, it is now a major identifiable feature of the piddle woman. I really loved wearing that as well. Right. I definitely need to hide my curls too. They made a big deal about how big my hair was in the sketch. And with the water quality here in New York they're looking even more poofty than usual. I spot a chunky middle-aged man striding in my direction. He's wearing a black beret.

'Excuse me?' I call, jumping in front of him to get his attention.

'I ain't interested, whatever it is!' he grumbles, stomping past.

Damn. I need a hat right away. I need *that* hat!

'Please, sir!' I yell after him. 'I want to buy your hat!'

The man stops walking and spins around. He takes a closer look at me under my umbrella. 'You wanna buy this?' he points at his head, eyebrows shooting up. 'How much?'

I shrug and lift my chin. 'How much you want?'

'Fifty dollars.'

'Ten dollars,' I counter-offer, folding my arms.

The man's scowling face breaks into a warm smile. He takes the beret off his head and hands it to me. 'It cost me five bucks from a thrift store. It's not even my favourite beret.'

'Thank you, sir,' I say, giving him his money and taking the beret.

'Hey,' his eyes glint with recognition. 'Don't I know you?'

Poop. Another *Sunday Night Live* fan. 'No. It's not me. I was not on *Sunday Night Live*. Goodbye. All the best to you.'

I back away, shielding my face from the man. He's calling after me, something about the New York Daily paper, I think. But I ignore him, spin around and hurry off down the street, pulling on the beret as I do and tucking as many of my curls as I can up into it.

Securing my umbrella underneath my chin, I take out

my phone and turn the camera on to check if I'm still recognisable.

Aha! My disguise worked. Without my mass of mad curls, I just look like any other girl in New York, casually wearing a beret like I'm the kind of person who can pull it off! No one will recognise me now. I feel sweet relief sweep over me. *Now* I can get back to my day.

But before I do, I pout into the camera, snap a pic and immediately send it to Birdie with a text.

Who would have guessed I would suit a beret so much? I feel like maybe this is who I truly am. Do you like it?

Within 30 seconds she sends a reply.

You look like Samuel L Jackson.

I lift my chin defiantly.

I will choose to take that as a compliment.

Using trusty old Google, I find that the nearest mailbox isn't too far away on 106th Street and West End Avenue.

As I approach it, I pull the bumbag out of the grocery bag and unzip the back pocket to find Mrs Ramirez's post-cards, and as I do I hear a vaguely familiar voice.

Huh? I don't know anyone in New York? Ooh, is it someone famous? I turn my head around to follow the sound of the voice and… Oh. My. Goodness.

What the hell?

Standing under a red bar canopy, waiting out the rainfall and chatting casually to a beautiful strawberry blonde woman with the kind of good skin that comes only from a true dedication to expensive face masks, is that absolute turd.

Seth Hartman.

The dirty, rotten queue-jumping identity thief.

CHAPTER SEVENTEEN

Text from Colin: G'day from sunny Australia! Hope NYC treating you well and weather good. What do you think we should do on our indoor date? You know I give an excellent Indian head massage ;) ;)

Fury immediately sparks through my entire body. Even my earlobes and toes and my butt cheeks. There is fury *everywhere!*

What are the chances? In a city so big and busy, what are the chances that the person I have spent the entire morning wanting to kick in the goolies is here? A few metres away, ripe for the kicking?

I take a deep breath, adrenaline whizzing through my blood, geeing me up to race over there and destroy those goolies.

Then I stop myself. Violence is never the answer. Except in 1994 when Tracy Henshall stole my beloved Ninja Turtles pencil case and I threatened to snap her rainbow pen in half, unless she gave it me back at once. But I'm a grown-up now. And I've already gotten myself into enough trouble. I should just go over there. Calmly tell him that I think he is a bad person. That he has made me upset, that sharing my likeness on national TV is simply Not Fucking Cool.

The blonde woman throws her head back and laughs at something Seth is saying. Ugh. I bet it's not even that funny.

I feel anger bubbling up in my chest like hot lava about to boil over.

No, Olive. Keep calm. Be a grown-up. Do not lose control. You are not a woman who loses control.

'Oi!' I bellow, not calm at *all.* 'Oi, you!'

Seth, the blonde woman, and another five surrounding people all swing their heads around.

'You!' I shout, pointing at him. If I had a vein in my head it would be throbbing right now for sure! 'Yoooooou. Seth! Queue jumper!'

He screws his face up, trying to place me. Without my bumbag and with my curls tucked into the beret, he doesn't have a clue who I am. He steps out from under the canopy, into the rain, to get a closer look. 'Sorry, do I know you?' he asks, a quizzical look on his dumb face.

'Watch me piddle?' I hiss furiously, marching up to him and yanking off the beret so he can see who I am 'Really? *Really*?'

His jaw falls open and he does an actual, audible gasp. With big round eyes, he starts to shake his head in astonishment. He's pretty much doing a replica impression of me last night, you know, *when I saw myself on national TV.*

'It's you! Wow.' He steps cautiously closer to me, like he's approaching a bear or some other badass kind of animal who might kick him in the goolies at any moment.

The rain splats down on his head. The blonde woman, still under the canopy, gives me a curious look.

'Seth?' she calls over. 'Is everything alright?'

Seth looks back at her. 'Sharon, um… thanks for breakfast. I'll call you later, okay?'

He puts his arm out into the street for a cab. One immediately screeches up. The woman looks a little put out at my interrupting the two of them but, after giving Seth a kiss on the cheek, gets into the cab and zooms off.

He turns back to me. 'Hi. Um… I didn't think I would ever see you again. This is… awkward.' He looks around as if searching for an escape.

'Yeah. Awkward!' I say, my voice all high-pitched. 'You humiliated me on live television. You used me for a joke! How could you?'

'Umm…' Seth grimaces, rubbing a hand on the back of his neck. 'I… I don't know what to say… I'm, um, actually in a bit of a rush right now I have to be some—'

'Oh no you don't!' I cut in furiously before he tries to slink away. 'You can explain yourself. And apologise! People have been stopping me all morning shouting *Watch Me Piddle.* I pull the beret back onto my head with a tug. 'I have to wear this hat so people don't recognise me.'

Seth looks skywards and the rain starts to properly come down. No longer a drizzle but chubby cold rain-drops plopping down at speed. 'Shit.'

Ha! I feel a dart of joy. Of course he doesn't have an umbrella. This guy doesn't charge his electrical equipment before taking trips, he jumps queues, he thinks women want to have sex with him in airplane bathrooms, he steals people's likeness and manipulates it for a TV show. *Of course* he doesn't have an umbrella.

'Can I just…' he says, shuffling forward and ducking his head down to try to get underneath my brolly with me.

'No way!' I say, taking a step backwards. 'You don't get to share my umbrella!'

His eyes widen. He flings his arms protectively over his

head, as if that will be any use. 'Seriously? I'm going to drown here!'

I shrug. 'It's the least you deserve.' I lift my chin. 'I won't keep you long. I just want to say that I think you're a horrible person. I was really scared on that flight and you used it for jokes. And now everyone in Manhattan seems to recognise me! How many people even watch that show? It seems like everybody does!'

A proud little smile lifts the corners of his mouth, before he quickly realises how inappropriate that is and puts it back into a straight line.

A drop of rain falls off his hair into one of his eyes and he winces.

'It's only rain,' I scoff.

'I'm wearing hair gel!' he protests, blinking quickly. 'It stings.'

I sigh. It does sting when you get hair gel in your eye. As someone who used mousse every day during her teenage years, I'm only too aware of the pain that product in eyes can cause.

I don't want him to go blind.

I suppose.

'Just get under, already,' I grumble.

He dives quickly under my umbrella. He's much taller than me so he has to stand there with bended knees. All at once, his stoopid face is really close to mine and I notice that his eyes aren't blue, like I thought. But more like a pale turquoise. I don't think I've ever seen anyone with turquoise eyes before.

Another drop of water falls from his eyelashes and onto his jaw which, I notice, is covered in a light golden stubble that you can't see unless you are mere centimetres away. It seems to shimmer. It must be the water or the sunlight or something. It looks like little flecks of gold.

I must be staring because the next thing I know Seth

has leaned in so close that I feel the heat of his breath on my face. 'Hello? Olive? Earth to Olive?'

What the hell am I staring at his five o'clock shadow for? I immediately snap out of it. 'Earth to Olive?' I sniff. 'Who even says "earth to" anymore? What is this? *Saved by The Bell*?'

Seth snorts with mirth. 'You're mean! You look very sweet with those eyes and those rosy cheeks.' He waves his hand dismissively in the direction of my face. 'But you are mean.'

'Actually I'm not mean!' I protest. 'I am the opposite of mean. I have no problems with anyone. Except for my sister-in-law Donna who is a true dick, but other than that everyone likes me. Even Mr Rishi on the market – who hates everyone – loves me. YOU,' I say, poking a finger onto his wet shirt. 'YOU are mean.'

'It was all in good fun!' Seth says with a shrug. 'You *were* a little crazy on that flight.'

'I was freaking out!'

'You let me believe you wanted us to…' he trails off, pushing his glasses up his nose and raising a suggestive eyebrow. Ugh!

'That was your filthy mind. I was just hoping you would accompany me down the airplane aisle. It was so shaky. I didn't want to fall! I was scared, and you used it against me. On TV!'

Seth stares at me for a moment. I think he's going to apologise but instead he says, 'It's my job. I was just doing my job.'

'It's your *job*?' I repeat, raising my voice so that he can hear me over the thud of the rainfall on the top of my umbrella. Is he for real? 'So it doesn't matter who you hurt, or humiliate in front of an entire country, if it's your job? That's what… assassins say. *I was just doing my job. My job of murder!* Doesn't make it okay, dude!'

He glances from side to side as if looking for an escape. 'Look, *dude,* I don't know what I can do beyond say, my bad!'

'My bad?'

He pulls his phone out of his shirt pocket and looks at it. 'And I wasn't lying when I said I was on my way somewhere. I have to go. I really am late for something.'

Ugh. What an absolute turd this man is. 'You are a lying turd,' I say.

Amusement sparks in his eyes. 'A lying turd? Nice phrase. Maybe I'll use that in next week's show.'

I'm so angry that my mouth opens and closes. How dare he?

'Seriously, Olive Maudine Brewster. I'm being truthful. I was due at the Riverside Theatre five minutes ago.'

'Oh the theatre!' I repeat in a fancy voice. 'How lovely for you! Well don't let my humiliation keep you from the *theatre*.'

He looks at me and shakes his head in astonishment.

I don't think I've ever felt so mad at a person in my entire life. How can he not see that what he did to me was completely wrong! He's acting like I'm the nutcase when he is obviously some sort of sociopath.

'Jeez,' I sigh, clearly getting nowhere. I pull Mrs Ramirez's postcards out of my bumbag and push them angrily into the mailbox. Then I shoo him away with my hand. 'Go. Go to wherever you're going. You're not the only one with things to do and places to be.'

He holds his hands up innocently. 'I'm sorry if you're upset,' he says, which is the flimsiest apology on earth. 'It was all just a bit of fun.'

I stare after him as he turns around and darts off back down the street, holding his arm out for a cab as he does so.

I realise that my heart is pounding in my chest. I shake

my head in disbelief. Shouting and pointing in the middle of the street in a beret. That's just not me! I am a woman who complains via a well thought out email, or the contact form on a retailer's website. But that idiot? I don't think anyone has ever infuriated me so much.

I watch through narrowed eyes as he gets into a cab and zooms off.

I go to zip up the bumbag dangling from my hand.

Something is amiss. I frown and peer down into the bag. My phone, Rescue Remedy, earphones, painkillers and hand sanitiser are all there…

No.

Oh no.

Nooooooo.

My stomach lurches as the familiar and comforting sight of Birdie's letter to Chuck is no longer there where it has been safely nestled for the past three days.

'Noooooo,' I mutter to myself. 'No. NO. NO.'

I frantically open the other zips in the bag, desperately hoping that I moved Birdie's letter to one of the other compartments.

Nope.

This is not happening. This cannot be happening.

I quickly lean forward, pull down the shutter on the mailbox and peek inside. I can see nothing. Just blackness. And the smell of paper, which ordinarily I like but today makes me feel sick.

My cheeks start to burn.

Birdie's letter.

Birdie's final letter.

Oh my god.

CHAPTER EIGHTEEN

@janeyjaneyjaneyUWS

I swear to god the Watch Me Piddle woman just came into Zabar's. Here's a picture. It's definitely her, right??? #watchmepiddle

@NewYorkDailyNews to @janeyjaneyjaneyUWS

Hi! We'd love to use your picture. Can we DM you?

@janeyjaneyjaneyUWS

Sure thing!

It's okay. It's fine. Everything is going to be *just fine.* I can get it. I can get the letter. I have long enough arms to reach down into the mailbox, don't I? I can just get it. It's one of those thick-papered expensive envelopes. I'll be able to feel it, pull it out and then everything will be okay. I can deliver it to Chuck at the bank and all will be fine. Fine! *Fine.*

I peek out from beneath my umbrella. It's so busy on this street and everyone's moving quickly to avoid being out in the rain. No one is looking at me. No one would see…

As casually as I can manage, I lean to the left and discreetly snake my arm into the mailbox.

I feel around. There's a mass of papers and… ew, something soggy?

'Ugh,' I shudder, moving my hand to the right to feel for Birdie's letter.

My hand grabs onto a large thick envelope. It's the right size, the right weight…

I pull it out hopefully.

This envelope's brown.

Birdie's is cream.

Shit.

Keeping hold of the brown envelope so I don't repeat grab it, I reach my hand down again and clutch about, like one of those fairground machine claws.

'Excuse me,' comes a voice from my left. 'What are you doing?'

I jolt upright from the mailbox so quickly that my beret falls off, my curls springing free.

The person asking the question is a handsome besuited dark-skinned man with a sour look on his face.

'I… I accidentally posted a letter,' I explain.

The man's mouth turns down. 'I know you…'

'Nope,' I say, pulling the hat back on quickly. 'I don't think you do.'

The man examines my face suspiciously. 'I know you, I'm sure… And it's not for a good reason… Are you, wait, are you stealing mail?'

'No!' I assure him. 'Of course not! I'm trying to get back the letter I accidentally posted!'

I really don't need some busybody interrupting me

right now. And then I notice that the guy has got longer arms than me.

'Ooh, will you have a try for me?' I ask. 'Your arms are longer, you might be able to get further down.'

Pursing his lips, the man steps away from me, looking around worriedly.

'It'll only take you a second!' I add. 'Just have a dig around. The envelope is thick. High-quality paper. I beg of you. This is a life or death situation and your help would be much appreciated.'

'Excuse me!' the man yells out into the busy street. 'I need some assistance here!'

I follow the man's line of sight and notice that he is calling over a cop.

'Good idea!' I say. 'He'll probably know what to do with lost mail. Shit. What a nightmare!'

The cop comes over – a short, skinny man with pock-marked skin.

'This woman is fishing for mail! I think she's looking for cheques.' The besuited man tells the cop, like a kid telling over another kid. I throw him a dirty look.

'Of course I'm bloody not!' I protest. 'I dropped my friend's letter in there by mistake! I promise I'm not a mail thief. I'm Olive. I'm from England. I respect the postal service very much. Can you help?'

The cop nods and smiles at me, pulling out his phone.

'Thank you!' I say in relief as he taps onto the screen. 'Anything at all you can do to assist. Maybe have someone unlock it and I can just take my letter and then I'll be going.'

Forehead crinkling, the cop stares at his phone and then at my face. Then at his phone and at my face again.

'Ma'am, do you know anything about an incident in Gramercy Park yesterday?' he asks.

'Nope,' I say immediately. 'What, um, is Gramercy Park? Incident? No, thank you.'

Eek. I sound super guilty. They must have that stupid picture the woman in the park took on file. How on earth does he recognise me, though? I have a regular face. My eyes are a bit far apart from each other, but not in a freaky, instantly recognisable way. And I'm not wearing a unicorn horn today.

Then I realise the pink bumbag is still dangling from my arm after I posted all of the stuff. Damn. This beautiful bag is causing me more problems than it's worth.

My instinct – the safest option – is to try to reason with the cop. To tell him that yes, it was I in Gramercy Park yesterday, but the whole situation was a misunderstanding. I could reasonably explain to him that the incident in Gramercy Park was just me being wrongly accused of something I did not do. And that also today I am once again being accused of something I didn't do.

Hmmmm.

Even to me that sounds highly suspect. A cop won't believe that I was in the wrong place at the wrong time, two days in a row? Even if it is completely true, it sounds like a total lie!

'Ma'am?' the cop says again, glancing down at his phone and then at my bumbag. 'Can you tell me your name, please?

I look around me in panic. And in that moment, I make a decision I may well come to regret. But, honestly, all I care about right now is Birdie and getting that letter back for Chuck.

'Oh wow!' I exclaim loudly, pointing into the distance. 'It's beloved pop icon Beyoncé!'

The two men whip their heads around – no one is immune to Beyoncé. And when their heads are turned, I leg it and dive behind a nearby hot dog cart. I crouch down, I hear the cop yelling into his walkie-talkie. 'Menace located at the mailbox on 106th and West End Avenue. On foot. Holding a pink fanny pack, a brown grocery bag and a Samuel L Jackson style beret.'

Menace? He's calling me a menace? Rude.

The cop looks up and down the street, assuming I've run far away. I feel a dart of cleverness at my decision to hide unexpectedly nearby.

As the grumpy besuited man walks off shaking his head, and the cop heads to his car, I take the opportunity to run away, as fast as I can.

Running away from the law twice in two days.

I think technically that makes me a fugitive.

Holy Fuck.

* * *

I'm intermittently looking at my Citymapper app and walking quickly through the streets of NYC. Damn that Seth Hartman. If I hadn't been so focused on calling him out on his awful behaviour, I wouldn't have been distracted enough to post Birdie's letter along with Mrs Ramirez's postcards and had to run away from the mailbox to avoid getting arrested!

'Riverside Theatre,' I mutter to myself. He got me into this mess and he can bloody well get me out of it. I bet he's in the theatre right now having a ball, while I'm out here on the run from the NYPD. I bet he's with all his thespian mates and they're congratulating him on his sketch comedy glory. I wonder if they know that it didn't even come from his own brain, but from a real person. Me! I wonder if he's even allowed to impersonate a real person so closely on a TV show. I mean, of course he is, *Sunday Night Live* is full of celebrity impressions and such.

But I'm not a celebrity. I'm a sweet and innocent person who didn't ask to be in the public eye.

I follow my travel app map towards the Riverside Theatre, and as I do, the streets become less and less desirable. Where previously there were trees and fancy buildings, there is now graffiti and boarded windows.

A group of teenagers on the corner stare at me as I walk past.

'Hey look, it's Samuel L Jackson!' one of them shouts and they all start laughing.

I speed up my walk and turn the corner, finally reaching the theatre. Although it doesn't look like the upmarket theatre I was expecting. It's an unattractive concrete building with a big green door, the paint a scuffed off to reveal splintered wood beneath. There's a ramp leading up to the door and the metal bar at each side is rusty and covered with splats of bird turd.

I spot a small rusted, dull plaque above the door. *Riverside Community Theatre*. Oh! I expected something with nice lights on the façade and posters of musical theatre stars looking dramatically into the distance.

Hmmm. Seth is a comedy writer for a huge TV Show. What is he doing in a run-down theatre like this?

I take down my umbrella and shake the rain off heartily onto the pavement. I prop it up against the door, step inside and wander through a quiet lobby. The right wall is plastered in notices and leaflets. Over-60s Zumba classes, bridge club, and an am-dram production of *Cats*). I wonder what Seth is here for. Is he in *Cats*? I bet he's playing Macavity the sneaky, villainous cat. That would suit him perfectly.

I hear joyful voices from a room down the hall. I go and look through a little window in the door.

There he is. His too-long hair still damp from the rain. He's not wearing the button down shirt he had on before though. He's wearing a white T-shirt imprinted with the words West Side Knitters.

Huh.

I notice that everyone else in the room is aged between about thirteen and sixteen and they're all listening to Seth talk, wide-eyed, like he is telling them the guaranteed secret to acne-free skin.

I stop nosying, remember why I'm here and gently push open the door. Ordinarily I would wait politely outside until whatever it is that's going on is finished. But I haven't exactly got a great deal of time, and whatever *is* going on in here can't be as important as Birdie's lost letter.

I check that my beret is securely on. I can't have all these teenagers recognising me too. I try to enter the room without drawing too much attention but my trainers are wet and they squeak on the gym floor obnoxiously. Seth and about twenty teenagers stop what they're doing and spin around to look at me.

Eek.

'Sorry! Really sorry!' I say, holding my hands up as I creep past. But then, remembering that it was my Mancunian accent that got me recognised in the deli this morning I decide to change it into something less recognisable. 'Sorry!' I say again in an Australian accent. 'I'm sorry to interrupt, I just need a quick word with Seth?'

Seth comes out as Sith.

Why did you choose an Australian accent, Olive?

I mentally berate myself. Australian is definitely the hardest accent! And I have tried every accent out in the mirror at one point or another.

At my terrible Australian impression, Seth's eyes widen, his brows dipping and creating a mini crevice in his forehead. He glares at me in disbelief, like I'm a hallucination. Like he cannot believe I have tracked him down to a tiny community theatre on the outer fringes of the Upper West Side. Like a crazy stalker.

'Just a second, guys,' Seth says, walking across the hall towards me.

'Oooooooh!' some of the teens shout. 'It's your girlfriend! You loooooove her!'

'Give me some credit!' Seth fires back. Which actually hurts my feelings. I may not look very attractive in this beret and red-cheeked from my trek through New York to find him. But still…

'I need to talk to you!' I explain when he reaches me. 'I need your help and it's *urgent.*'

Seth bites at his lower lip. 'This is all incredibly weird but okay… Can you wait? I'll be finished up here in around thirty minutes.'

I sigh, thinking of that letter on the move to god knows where. And then I get a vision of Birdie's face when I have to tell her that whoops, I lost her letter and this was all a waste of time.

'Actually, it's really important,' I say. 'I need you now.'

He raises an eyebrow.

I tut. 'I mean I need to *talk* to you now. I'll only be a few minutes, I—'

Seth interrupts me, an expression of irritation flitting crossing his face. 'Look, this is the only time these kids get away from a school that writes them off, a home that's dysfunctional or, for some of them, the streets where they hang out with an older, shittier crowd. I volunteer and they only get one hour with me every week. I already arrived late…' He gives me a pointed look. 'I mean, if it's another bathroom related request, you're on your own. But otherwise, you can wait another thirty minutes, right?

I feel embarrassed at my storming in here. He volunteers? That doesn't fit with my current impression of him. He's clearly having some kind of *Dangerous Minds* moment. Or maybe he's volunteering just so he can *tell* people he volunteers and act all worthy about it. Yes, that must be it. There's no way someone so self-important would volunteer out of the goodness of their heart. Either way. I suppose I can manage another thirty minutes. I really could do with his help.

'Fine,' I sniff.

'In half an hour you can have as much of me as you want,' Seth says loudly so the kids can hear.

What a dick.

'Give me some credit,' I call back to his retreating form, to which some of the kids whoop and cheer me on.

I amble into the corner, every squelchy footstep amplified by the acoustics of the room, and plop down on an errant plastic yellow chair.

I take a breath and pull out my phone and earphones. Now would be a great time to listen to that meditation app I've been meaning to try. Thirty minutes of Still Minds sounds like a positive and sensible thing to do right now.

I press the buttons on my phone to load it up but am soon distracted by Seth's voice booming into the room.

'Alan, Trey, Lauren. You're up!' he's saying. 'Your theme is…' He holds his hands to his chin as if he's thinking very hard. 'Birthday.'

Three of the kids step out from the crowd and form their own group.

'Remember,' Seth says. 'Relax! It's all about relaxing.'

At Seth's instruction the kids shake out their legs and arms.

'Okay, go!'

'I got you a gift,' one of the kids says, pretending to hand something to one of the others. 'It's a really cute little teddy bear.'

The other kid, a skinny little thing, folds his arms. 'That's not a teddy bear,' he says. 'It's a killer drone!'

'Hold up!' Seth interrupts. 'Okay, Alan,' he says to drone boy. 'The point with improvisation is that you always have to say *yes*. No matter what. So if your team-mate starts the scene by saying that they are giving you a cute little teddy bear, they are giving you a cute little teddy bear. You have to go *with* it. Say *yes*.'

Alan nods, his little cheeks turning a bit pink.

'Try again,' Seth says, patting him on the shoulder. 'Go from the start.'

'I got you a gift,' the girl says again. 'it's a really cute little teddy bear.'

Alan takes the invisible teddy bear from Lauren and gasps. 'This is the most beautiful teddy bear I've seen in my entire life. And lord knows I've seen a lot of teddy bears.' Alan pretends to look at the floor sadly. 'Too many teddy bears...' he says mysteriously.

A big laugh goes up around the room and I find myself joining in.

I put down my earbuds and watch with interest as an entire scene is created in front of me, totally off the cuff. With the guidance of Seth, the kids concoct a whole story in which the teddy bear is secretly stuffed with stolen pot.

I watch as the kids go from tentative and nervous to being fully into the scene, putting on voices and being silly. They make more and more outlandish suggestions each time and support each other's choices. It's brilliant and I find myself clapping and cheering along from my seat in the corner.

The thirty minutes whizz by and soon enough Seth is ending the class.

'See you next week,' he says with a little wave. 'And sorry I was late.'

'You're always late,' one of the kids retorts.

'Yeah yeah.' Seth shoos him away. 'And remember, guys…'

'Just say yes!' the kids call back.

'That's right.'

As the kids file out of the hall, Seth strides over to me and takes a seat in one of the other plastic chairs.

'So. Olive Maudine. What can I do for you?'

'Just Olive,' I correct him. Then I tell him about the accidental letter being posted.

He shrugs. 'That sucks.'

Understatement.

'You don't understand. It's a life or death letter,' I tell him. 'It was supposed to be hand-delivered. There's no stamp on it, or address so if I can't rescue it, it'll probably just get chucked in the bin.'

'Why is it so important? Just write another one.'

'It's private,' I tell him, not feeling very keen on the idea of divulging anything to this guy – who knows what will show up on the TV next week if I do. 'But please trust me when I say that this letter is the only letter of its kind and it is truly, truly important that I get it back.'

I feel my throat swell with unshed tears.

Seth's cocky face softens slightly. 'This really matters to you, huh?'

'Yes.' I nod fervently. 'It really, really does.'

Seth blows the air out from his cheeks. 'I don't want to come off as a jackass, but what do you want me to do about it?'

'You are very much coming off as a jackass,' I mutter. 'It's *your* fault I posted it. If I hadn't been so concerned with being angry at you for your stupid sketch, then I would have been my usual organised self and I would still have the letter. So you have to help me get it back. I don't know how. But you are responsible too now. So just help me already.'

God, what is wrong with this guy?

He holds up his hands. 'Fine, relax!'

'You relax,' I spit back.

Seth laughs, though I'm not sure why. None of this is a laughing situation. 'Okay. I'll tell you what to do. You have to go to the sorting office on Staten Island. That's where all the mail gets routed to before it's rerouted to the boroughs. It used to be Brooklyn, but the rents are so high these days that they moved it to Staten Island.'

I goggle at him. 'How on earth do you know so much about the US postal system?'

'I get sent news headlines every week as part of my job. We use them to generate jokes and sketch ideas. The Staten Island postal re-route was a headline a few months ago.'

'Oh!' I fold my arms. 'So some of your sketches *aren't* based on poor innocent strangers who needed your help on a plane?'

'I said sorry.'

'Did you?'

'Yeah.' He holds his arms out wide. 'I'm sorry!'

'Well, I don't forgive you. And I don't even know where Staten Island is. I'm assuming it's an actual island?'

Seth runs his hands over his stubbled jaw. 'Look. I've got to get to work now, but I don't start until 2 p.m. tomorrow. How about I go with you to the sorting office tomorrow morning? The letters from today's mail won't get there until then anyway and I know Staten Island pretty well, as it happens. We can get the letter; I know a place that does a great pizza. I'll buy you lunch. And *then* will you forgive me?'

Tomorrow isn't ideal. I could really do with getting this sorted today… But things have a lot better chance of going smoothly if I'm with someone who actually knows this place. I can't risk getting lost or something going wrong again! And at this point I'm almost expecting it to!

'Okay. Yes,' I say quietly. 'Thank you.'

'Great.' Seth stands up and crosses the hall to grab his still damp shirt from where it's laid on top of his record bag. 'I will meet you at The Whitehall Ferry Terminal in Lower Manhattan. Nine thirty a.m.?'

'Ferry terminal?' I repeat, feeling suddenly sick at the thought of being on the water. I have never been on a boat in my life! Not even the rowing boats at Heaton Park. Plus, I'm a terrible swimmer. The very thought of a ferry makes me want to hurl.

'Yeah' he says. 'It's the best way to get to Staten island. And the most pleasant. Hopefully this rain will clear and you'll get to see the view of Manhattan from the water. It's really something to behold.'

I bite my lip and nod very slowly.

He already thinks I'm crazy. I can't be afraid of planes *and* ferries. Even to my mind that sounds super neurotic.

'Fine. 9 a.m. tomorrow,' I say. And then, for some reason, I hold out my hand for him to shake. Like we are making some sort of formal business deal.

Olive, you geek!

'Fine,' Seth replies.

'Fine.'

'Fine.'

'Can we stop saying fine now, please?'

'Fine.'

CHAPTER NINETEEN

Text from Olive to Colin: NYC is raining, sadly. Hope it's still sunny there in OZ. I like head massages, sounds like a good idea for our indoor date ;) Now it's my turn to ask you a question. What makes you laugh? X

Text from Colin: Still sunny here! About to have a BBQ. Put another shrimp on the barbie! Haha. What makes me laugh… hmmm. I really enjoy The Lad Bible. Do you know it? It's a meme site. I love memes. All kinds of memes!

On the walk back to the flat, Birdie FaceTimes me.

My stomach lurches. Do I need to tell her about the lost letter? I mean, is it worth stressing her out if I'm just going to get it back from the sorting office tomorrow? I decide to tell her the truth. She must be desperate to hear my updates regarding Chuck.

I press answer. And I find out that Chuck appears to be the furthest thing from her mind.

'WATCH ME PIDDLE!' she yells into the screen in a stupid voice. 'Waaaaatch meeeeee!'

'You saw it!' I hiss into the screen. 'Nooooooo!'

Birdie laughs. 'Seems you omitted to tell me a little something about your flight to New York. Why the hell are you being impersonated on *Sunday Night Live*? And why didn't you tell me?'

With a very red face and over the sound of her squealing laughter, I tell her about Seth and the misunderstanding on the plane. And then I tell her about people recognising me in the street, how I accidentally posted the letter, how Seth was right there in the street and how he's coming to the sorting office with me tomorrow and that I will absolutely get it back and that she mustn't worry. I expect her to be at least slightly upset about the letter, but she's far more interested in that damn *Sunday Night Live* sketch.

'I was hoping it wouldn't make its way to the UK,' I say, approaching Riverside Drive and walking by Central Park.

'It showed up on my Facebook feed this morning.'

'Noooo! I am mortified.'

'It's badass!'

'What?'

'Who can say that they got impersonated on an American institution of a TV show? You must have made quite an impression on this writer guy.'

'Yeah, peeing in front of someone will do that.'

Looking up and noticing that the grey clouds above have cleared a little, I take a seat on a wooden bench by the park.

'I hoped that you might have had a little adventure in Manhattan, but this is insane.'

'I know. I've only been here two days and it's been completely mental.'

'Well it's cheering me up no end!'

'My misery is cheering you up no end?'

Birdie rolls her eyes. 'Are you really fed up? More miserable than you are most of the time at home?'

I'm about to protest that I'm not at all miserable at home. But I bite the inside of my cheek and think about Birdie's words.

Hmmm. I'm het up, and a bit panicked, embarrassed and having a complete rollercoaster of emotions right now. But I'm certainly not *bored.* And that's the thing about home. I'm happy enough there, I'm not miserable, not at all, but maybe... I don't know, I'm a little bored?

No. I can't be. I like my life. Everything is simple and easy in Saddleworth. These past two days have been the opposite of simple and easy. They have been crazy and non-stop. That's not my goal state.

I shrug. 'It's certainly entertaining here.'

'So what are you doing tonight?' Birdie asks.

'There's a new Aziz Ansari stand-up special on Netflix. I might order a pizza. It's an early morning tomorrow.'

Birdie pulls a face and mimes hanging herself with a rope.

'Oi!' I tell her off. 'Netflix and chill! What's wrong with that?'

'Netflix and chill is a millennial euphemism for sex, you know?'

'Is it?' My eyebrows shoot up. 'I don't get it?'

'Me either.' She shrugs. 'But I'd be more than happy if you plan to Netflix and Chill in *that* way. Might be a good method to work off some of those high-octane emotions you're experiencing.'

She stands up and starts thrusting saucily at her hospital bed.

'Stop!' I laugh. 'You're gross!'

'Ooh Colin!' she yells. 'Make me feel like a woman, Colin.'

'I'm hanging up.'

'Noooo!'

She picks up a pillow and starts pretending to snog it. 'Colin! Oh Colin! Watch me piddle, Colin.'

Getting cross with her, I lean right into the phone camera.

'Dr BJ! Ooh Bruce Jim! Your name is so cool! What a turn-on! Ooh, can I interest you in a pleasant BJ, Dr BJ.' Birdie snorts with laughter and it's my favourite sound ever. I ham it up some more. I fan myself. 'My, my, I've got a fever, Dr BJ! And the only cure is your peen. Gimme that peen, Dr Bruce Jim. Gimme that peen in mah sweet vajeen!'

I'm closing my eyes and making kissy faces into the camera when I realise that Birdie is no longer laughing.

I open my eyes to see that she is looking in the direction of her hospital room door.

'Doctor BJ!' she says, her pale cheeks reddening. 'Hi. Ahem. Sorry. Um…'

The screen goes blank as Birdie quickly ends the call.

I spend the next fifteen minutes sitting on the bench and laughing so hard that I cry.

God, I love her.

* * *

The next morning, my phone alarm yanks me out of a really weird dream. I'm dreaming that Birdie is a ghost and we're at the top of the Empire State Building and she wants me to jump off. She says that I'll be able to fly, but I know, for sure, that I will splat onto the top of a yellow cab and make a mess. Then I'm in a big old library, watching the sex scene from *Atonement* again. Only James

McAvoy is actually Colin from the airport. But he can't seem to get it up.

'This has never happened before!' Dream Colin says.

'That's all right. I'm not that bothered about sex anyway!' Dream version of me replies. But in the dream I'm feeling very disappointed indeed.

As the alarm sounds, I grumble and sit up in the sofa bed. Last night I did Netflix and chill (in the non-millennial way) and while I did enjoy the Aziz Ansari stand-up special, it was finished in about an hour. At home I'd have been content enough to scroll through Instagram, take a bath, organise my closet or read a book, but last night none of those things appealed.

I briefly considered venturing out. Maybe treating myself to a dinner in one of the restaurants Birdie suggested, or going for a walk somewhere. But I soon dismissed the idea when I realised that I am not brave enough to go out for dinner alone. Breakfast and lunch is one thing. But dinner? In a restaurant? *Alone?* That sounds terrifying!

In the end I knocked on Mrs Ramirez's door and she was only too happy to feed me soup and tell me tales of all the exotic places she's visited and which ones I should definitely go to on 'my next trip abroad'.

After my shower, I peek out of the blind and check the weather. From what I can see, the sky is looking pretty dark and ominous, to be honest. Like something out of *Ghostbusters*. Plus, it's raining again. I swallow down my reservations about getting on a ferry in this weather, and get dressed in jeans, my favourite T-shirt with a picture of Bill Murray on the front, and a big maroon-coloured jumper over the top. Layers seem like the right call for a treacherous ferry trip.

I blow-dry my curls straight in an effort to make myself less recognisable. I don't have straighteners, but I do have serum (a must in every curly girl's arsenal), and after a lengthy battle with the hairdryer and a flat paddle brush, my hair looks pretty damn straight. There! No need to wear the beret!

After necking a strong coffee, I pull on my duffel coat, grab an across-the-body satchel, sadly leaving my attention-grabbing bumbag behind, and leave the apartment.

Because I'm already late I decide to forgo the subway, and hail a cab out on the street. But I mustn't be doing it right because none of the cabs stop for me! I look at my watch. Shit, I need to get a move on. I wave over to Lloyd in the entrance of the building, but he's chatting intently to another resident and doesn't notice me.

I hold my hand out and shake it about, like I see people do on the movies. But it still doesn't work.

An elderly Jewish woman holding a massive red umbrella shuffles past me. 'Doll, ya gotta be more aggressive than that!' She chuckles before continuing on down the street.

I'm not an aggressive person, though! How does one even aggressively hail a cab? Do I flip the middle finger instead of waving my hand? Do I do some of my best karate chop moves to get their attention?

Oh man. I haven't got time to ponder this if I'm to get to the ferry port on time. So I take a deep breath and yell at the next cab that drives in my direction.

'Oi!!!! Stop! STOOOOOOOPPPPP!'

To my surprise and delight it works! The cab zooms to a stop right in front of me. I climb in quickly, a little buzz rushing through me. I don't think I've ever shouted that loud before in my whole life!

'Where to?' the cabby asks bluntly.

'The Whitehall Ferry Terminal,' I say. 'And step on it.'

The driver grins at me in the wing mirror and puts his

foot down onto the pedal so hard that we take off with a noisy screech, just like in the movies!

I nod, satisfied, allowing myself a little proud smile.

Maybe I'm starting to get the hang of this whole New York thing!

* * *

Nothing dents the burgeoning confidence of a scaredy-cat quite like turning up at a rainy ferry port and seeing the ferry – that you're about to climb on to – rocking from side to side in this alarming weather.

'Olive? Over here!'

I spot Seth running over from across the road. He's wearing a scruffy black T-shirt, a black hoodie and faded black jeans. His hair is all mussed up, like he forgot to comb it.

'I didn't recognise you without your…' Seth says, gesturing to his head.

'My curls. Yeah. I'm more incognito like this,' I say, touching my straight locks. 'No random people shouting "watch me piddle" in the street.'

Seth grimaces. 'I'm sorry!' he says. 'Will you ever forgive me?'

'I will if you help me get my letter back.'

'That's what I'm here for!'

'Good.'

'Are you all right?' Seth asks as we start to board the ferry after getting our tickets.

'Fine!' I lie.

'You look a funny colour.' He puts a hand on my arm.

I jump a little at his touch and move my arm away. 'I'm fine! Totally fine!'

The drizzle has abated somewhat and so, once we're on the ferry, we go straight onto the deck. I sit down on one of the red painted benches. Seth stands right at the bow, facing into the wind, like this is the Titanic and he is Leonardo DiCaprio.

As the ferry sets off, it rolls from side to side and I try not to think too much about all of the deep murky water beneath us and all the terrible things that could happen if the ferry crashed, or the captain had a heart attack, or the wind became really strong and flipped us over, or if I got sea sick and just started puking and some of the puke got on people's shoes.

And then I notice that there's a little cabin full of life jackets. With wobbly legs, I head over and grab one. I look around. No one else is wearing one. Not even the six-year-old twins taking the ferry with their elderly grandpa.

I pull it on and tie the straps as tightly as they can go. It's not comfortable. Plus, the neck bit is really high and makes me look neckless. I look like a berk, I'm sure. But at least I'm a safe berk!

I take my seat again, my fists clenched, willing this journey to hurry up. Seth turns around from where he's standing. His face lights up as he takes in my life jacket. Then he purses his lips and I get the feeling he is trying very hard not to take the piss.

I ignore him, and focus on staring at the floor and not puking.

My phone dings with a text. It's from Colin! I smile as I open it, trying not think of him being flaccid in my dream, and also trying not to be perturbed by the fact that he said the thing that makes him laugh the most is *The Lad Bible*. Out of all the great comedy out there!

I am at a beach party. We are drinking punch. None of the girls here are as pretty as you. Or as *sexy*. ;)

I laugh. Our text conversations have been pretty staid so far. He must be tipsy!

I immediately type back.

Wish I was there! I am on a boat in the rain.

I pause and consider what I should type next.

I think you are sexy too.

I send it quickly, before I can change my mind. He said I was sexy. It's nice to return the compliment. And I *think* it's true. I like his sideburns. And texting with him is pleasant. And maybe, if we did start dating, I could wean him off *The Lad Bible* and introduce him to some real comedy…

Seth comes back to sit beside me. He fiddles with the cuff of his hoodie. 'Don't fret, it's only another twenty minutes until we get there.'

'I'm fine, Seth!' I say again.

'I can hear your dry heaves.'

My cheeks warm. Maaan. I thought I was doing a really good job of keeping them under wraps!

'Stand up,' Seth instructs me.

'Sorry?'

'Stand up!' Seth repeats, taking my arm and pulling me up from my bench. Argh!

He points into the distance.

'Look!' he says.

Oh wow.

Wow.

It's Manhattan. Looking like a postcard. An eerie postcard with dark skies and ominous clouds, but a postcard nonetheless.

It's pretty spectacular.

'Woah,' I say.

It almost doesn't look real.

'That's the reason you should always take the ferry to Staten Island,' Seth says, gazing ahead in wonder. 'The view of Lower Manhattan never disappoints.'

I hold my phone up and snap a picture. Not just for Birdie, this time, but for myself too. Seth's right. It's out of this world!

Behind us, a couple of teenagers pass by and point at me in my life jacket, laughing at what a dork I am.

I stick my tongue out at them, only thankful that I straightened my hair and they don't recognise me from the TV too.

And then, to my surprise Seth strides over to the life jacket booth, gets one and pulls it on.

He looks like even more of a berk than me.

And then, without a word he comes and stands back next to me.

'Yo, take a picture, maybe it'll last longer!' he yells to the cocky teenagers. They laugh and point at him then, instead of me.

And I get the feeling that was very much his intention.

CHAPTER TWENTY

Email from birdielivelysayshello@gmail.com:

OMG. Doctor BJ heard you talking about his peen! I had to turn my phone off, so I couldn't text back last night but I am mortified! He came in, his voice all stuttery and his face all red. He said: 'Do you have something you wish to discuss, Birdie.' And so I just told him that my friend – you – has a major crush on him. I know you've never even seen him, but *he* doesn't know that. I'm sorry, Brewster. I had to throw you under the bus to save myself!! I apologise for being glib about you feeling so embarrassed re. *Sunday Night Live*. I have had a taste of my own medicine fo sho!!! Argh! Good luck getting Chuck's letter back today!

As I step off the ferry with wobbly legs, I stand for a moment with closed eyes, feeling immensely grateful to be back on solid ground.

I follow Seth as he walks confidently out of the large

bright terminal and purposely down the street, not even looking at a map on his phone.

'You know this place well?' I ask, walking quickly to keep up with his long-legged strides.

'I grew up here, actually.'

As an ominous roll of thunder booms above us, the rain starts pelting down once more. I put up my umbrella and quicken my walking speed.

'Can I get under there with you?' Seth asks, crouching down.

'Seriously? It's been raining for two days straight. How do you not have an umbrella of your own?'

Seth shrugs. 'I forgot, I guess.'

I wonder how someone can just go through life not being prepared for anything. I bet he thinks he can just charm his way out of any trouble he might get himself into. Jumping queues because he didn't charge his laptop, getting under other people's umbrellas in the rain, avoiding getting kicked in the goolies by women he publicly humiliated for a laugh.

Above us a huge roll of thunder booms out of the sky. I decide to be generous.

'Well, you'll be no use to me with hypothermia,' I say, handing the umbrella to Seth so he doesn't have to crouch, and getting under it with him.

'We're about five minutes away from the Post Office,' Seth shouts over the sounds of the rain spattering onto the brolly above us.

'Cool,' I reply, feeling strangely self-conscious as we try to walk in sequence under the umbrella, our arms bumping up against each other.

Eventually we reach the Post Office building – a big tan-coloured structure that looks like it was airlifted in straight from the nineteen-seventies. Seth pushes open the glass door and holds it for me.

The décor inside is beige and drab – a bit like how Donna decorated the living room at our house in Saddleworth. Thankfully it's pretty quiet and we don't have to wait too long to see someone. My balloon is popped, though, when I realise that the man assigned to help us is a real jobsworth who doesn't seem to want to help at all.

'You posted an unaddressed letter?' he says for the millionth time.

'It was an ACCIDENT,' I reply for the millionth time.

As the man rants and raves about the amount of stupid people in New York who don't send mail correctly, I make a kind of snarly noise. Beside me, Seth laughs, which doesn't help at all.

'Well, of course you will need to submit a formal request in writing,' Jobsworth says, running his hand up and down his tie. 'And then that will have to be processed. Could take a week. Could take a month. You never can tell.'

I put my head in my hands. 'Dude, can't you just go into a back room and search through the lost and found? I only sent it yesterday!'

The man folds his arms. I think he's getting mad at me.

'Do you watch *Sunday Night Live*?' Seth asks suddenly, leaning his elbows onto the counter and smiling at the man in a chummy way.

I roll my eyes. He's so arrogant. Expecting that he can just charm his way around any problem, like he did with the check-in assistant at the airport.

'Of course,' the man says, as surely as if Seth had just asked him if he had a nose.

Seth lowers his voice. 'I work on that show.'

The man frowns. 'I don't recognise you.'

'I'm not a cast member – not yet at least – I'm a writer

for the show and if you can get me this letter, I have two tickets for you. Front row.'

The man studies us both with an expression of deep distrust. 'I don't believe you.'

Seth reaches into his back pocket and pulls out a worn, childish-looking wallet. It looks like the kind of canvas wallet Alex had when he was about thirteen. Seth slides out a lanyard. I peer at it.

Seth Hartman Senior Writer – Sunday Night Live. Rockefella Centre.

The Post Office man goggles. And immediately disappears into a back room.

Twenty minutes later, he returns brandishing the letter like it's the golden snitch. I grab it off him and immediately burst into tears, hugging the letter to my chest.

'Thank God, thank God, thank God!' I whisper, kissing the letter, my hands shaking. I hadn't quite realised how terrified I'd been about losing it until now.

'Thanks to you!' I say to Post Office guy, reaching up to give him a kiss on the cheek.

'Thanks to you!' I say to Seth, not kissing his cheek but holding my hand out to formally shake his again.

Why the floop do I keep doing that?

* * *

I know I said I would go to lunch with Seth, but now I have the letter, I just want to get it safely into Chuck Allen's hands as quickly as possible. Plus it's only eleven a.m.!

I'm about to suggest we just head straight back to the ferry terminal when Seth casually mentions that he only gets six tickets a year to give away to friends and family. He used two of those to get my letter back? To be fair, it is entirely his fault that I accidentally posted it. But still, it's another forty-five minutes until the next ferry and he *is* offering free pizza. I would be a true moron to turn that down.

Following a five-minute walk, the pair of us once more clumsily squished beneath my brolly, we arrive at what looks less like a respectable pizza place and more like a bar. I glance at the flashing neon pink sign in the window. This place is called 'Trickys'. No apostrophe!

'A bar?'

'I didn't say it was a pizza restaurant, just that it did the best pizza. Come on!' Seth beams, showing teeth as white and American as Birdie's. It occurs to me that it's the first time he's properly smiled since I met him. This must be some top-drawer pizza.

I follow him in. Yep. This is a bar. What might be kindly termed a 'dive' bar. The floor is dusty, there's a TV blaring high behind the bar, competing with the sounds of blues music coming from the vintage jukebox. My eyes widen. Never in my life have I been in a place like this. And Greater Manchester is full of dubious pubs!

It's busier than one would expect, it being pre-lunch on a weekday and all, and everyone in here is drinking beer. Morning beer.

At the back of the room is a pool table being used by a man and a woman in brightly coloured loungewear. The woman's loungewear has the word 'sweetcheeks' written in a cursive script across her backside. I can't help but admire her confidence and, indeed, her sweet cheeks.

'This place is…' I trail off, unable to find just one word to describe this subterranean boozetastic roadhouse. My eyes goggle at the fact that just off that quiet little street, this place exists. *And I'm in it.* I suppress a giggle thinking about what Donna would make of it.

'Lil' Hartman, baby!'

The woman's voice is very loud – it would have to be to be heard over the hullabaloo.

'Phyllis!' Seth yells back, so raucously that it makes me jump. He embraces the extraordinarily skinny woman so tightly I'm afraid she might crack. Her hair is bright red. Not in an elegant ginger way – in an actual crimson red way. It's piled atop her head in a very high bouffant. Her black eyeliner is expertly smudged heavily around her wrinkled blue eyes and she's wearing a gold chain with the words 'fuck you' written out in an incongruously pretty font. 'Hey, less of the 'little, please?' Seth laughs, kissing her on the cheek.

'You'll always be a baby to me.' She reaches to ruffle his hair. 'Who are you?' she says, turning to me. 'Another girlfriend? What happened to Blondie?'

'Not girlfriend,' I say at the same time as Seth says, 'Not my girlfriend, Phyllis. This is my friend Olive. She's engaged.'

I screw my face up as I shake Phyllis's tiny hand. *Engaged?*

'Good for you, honey,' she says. 'What's his name? Is he from Staten Island? I might know him. Is he as handsome as our lil' Hartman here?'

I blink for a few moments, wondering what on earth she's talking about.

Phyllis pulls a face at Seth as if to ask, 'who the heck is this moron?'

'I believe her fiancé's names is Colin Collins,' Seth explains, throwing me an odd look.

'Yes, yes of course!' I stammer quickly. Colin! My made up fiancé! '*Colin.* Colin! Yes… he's very handsome. He… has sideburns.'

I allow myself a brief second to think of Colin's lovely sideburns and his pleasant text messages.

Phyllis pats me on the arm. 'Very nice. Now you two kids take a seat, what can I get you?'

'Two beers and a meatball pizza,' Seth says, as we slide into one of the three booths opposite the bar. He turns to me. 'Sorry, I don't mean to be the jerk who orders without asking, but I promise you the meatball pizza is outta this world.'

'Great,' I say, the thought of meatballs and pizza together making me feel both nervous and excited. 'I'll just have a water, though,' I say. 'Bit early for me!'

'We don't serve water,' Phyllis says stonily. I look to Seth to see if she's joking but his face is as straight as hers. She might be old and skinny but she's also kind of terrifying.

'Um. Okay. A beer,' I say.

Phyllis wiggles off to the bar, telling a rowdy customer to 'go and fuck himself' as she does so. The guy, a very large, bald-headed man immediately apologises for whatever he's done to upset her.

'How do you know Phyllis?' I say, fascinated by this small fierce woman.

'She was a groupie of my dad's.'

'A groupie?!' I look over at Phyllis. I can see it actually. The loud pink dress, the clashing red hair, the big earrings. She looks like a rock chick. 'Your dad was a musician? That must have been cool.'

'He was a stand-up comedian, actually.'

I raise my eyebrows. 'That's even cooler.'

Seth smiles, almost to himself more than to me. 'It was. He was amazing.'

'Would I have heard of him?'

'Nah. But he was pretty popular around Manhattan, at the Comedy Cellar and Dangerfield's. He even did a spot on the Letterman show once.'

'Wow.'

'Yep. But he never quite made it big.' Seth shrugs. 'And now he's in a nursing home upstate making the other residents laugh in their old age.'

A short, stocky dark-haired fella treads over to the booth and plonks down two bottles of beer so enthusiastically that they foam up, spilling out of the bottle neck.

'Thanks, Sonny!' Seth says, giving the man a big grin.

'How's it going, hotshot? How's the fancy life? Clearly treating you pretty well.' Sonny nods in my direction. I give him a smile.

'Yeah, it's all right!' says Seth, his cheeks turning a little red.

'Will we actually see you on TV at any point? Or they still keeping you locked up behind the scenes. Ain't no one wanna put your ugly mug on screen!' The guy punches Seth's shoulder jokily.

'I have an audition tomorrow actually,' Seth tells him. 'For a cast member position.'

Sonny's eyes widen. 'Oh wow! Seth, that's amazing.' He clears his throat, his face turning serious. 'Your pops would be proud.'

Seth shrugs a shoulder. 'We'll see… Keep your fingers crossed for me.'

When Sonny has returned to the kitchen to get our food, I look at Seth curiously.

'You have an audition tomorrow?' I ask. 'Shouldn't you be preparing right now?'

Seth waves me away. 'Ah, I've auditioned a gazillion times before,' he tells me. 'I never get it. They like me as a writer, but I always flake out on the stage.'

'Flake out?'

'I forget my lines.' He pushes his glasses up his nose with his forefinger. 'Which is crazy because it's the same routine I've been doing for years.'

'Well, do you prepare? Do you practise?'

Seth laughs. 'That'll take all the fun out of it!'

I shake my head, horrified. 'Do you even want to be a cast member?'

'Sure I do.'

'Maybe you should prepare. So you won't flake out this time?'

Seth puts his arms behind his head and leans back against the booth. His top rides up a little, revealing a tiny bit of stomach. I think of James McAvoy and Keira Knightly in the library. I swipe the image quickly away. 'What will be will be, I guess.' Seth sighs.

'*What will be will be*?' I say incredulously. 'That sounds like an awful way to live.' I shudder at the very thought. 'I like to know exactly what's going to happen. In the words of Radiohead, *No surprises, please*.'

'Where's the excitement in that?' Seth argues, taking a gulp of his beer.

'Who says I'm looking for excitement?'

'Aren't we all?'

I think of Mum leaving our family in her selfish bid for excitement. Of Alex and me sitting in the kitchen, crying because Dad was so sad and we didn't know how to help him. I think of the past few days in New York. They've been what most people would call exciting. But I am technically on the run from the police and semi-famous for pissing in front of a stranger. That is *not* a positive thing.

'Excitement is overrated.' I lift my chin and take a small sip of beer. 'Excitement is just terror with PR spin.'

'You're nuts,' Seth laughs lightly.

'Maybe I'm the sane one,' I counter, tucking my hair behind my ear.

'So… how is the *prepare for every eventuality* approach working out for you, huh?'

'In general, absolutely *fine*.' I fiddle with the strap on

my satchel. 'Obviously the past few days have been... complicated. But that's only because I've been *completely unprepared.* I'm sure if I'd have known earlier that I was coming to New York, if I'd had time to arrange and organise everything, things would be going a lot more smoothly right now.'

'Oh really?'

'Yes! I mean, I only knew I was coming here hours before I flew out. I had no time to psyche myself to get on a plane, to get hold of Xanax, or whatever it was you suggested. If I had been adequately prepared I wouldn't have acted so mental. Then I wouldn't have been parodied on TV by an unscrupulous writer. *Then* I wouldn't have had to collar you in the street, accidentally posting Birdie's letter.'

'And we wouldn't be here enjoying this beer, about to have the world's best meatball pizza,' Seth adds with a lopsided grin. He rests his chin on his hand. 'I think if you prepare too much in life, you end up stifling yourself, stifling your creativity. You leave no room for anything amazing to happen unexpectedly.'

I scrunch my nose. 'Unexpected things happening is my worst nightmare.' I take a sip of my beer, enjoying the light pop and fizz of the bubbles on my tongue. 'Surely a show like *Sunday Night Live* takes massive preparation. It's live!'

'Sure, it does. Most of the sketches are written on a Wednesday night. We work on them off the cuff, sometimes responding to news stories that have only just broken, or celebrities that have just said something ridiculous on Twitter. But things constantly change. So even if I prepared a perfectly written sketch, there's a huge chance that it's going to get rewritten and changed multiple times before the show. Sometimes things change even seconds before they're due to air.'

I wince at the thought.

'And,' Seth continues, slurping back his beer and following it with a highly satisfied 'aah' noise, 'the best moments the show has ever had have come out of the unprepared moments. When cast members improvise, or break character, or a musical guest does something controversial. That's what people love the most.'

I nod. 'I get it. But if you've auditioned so many times to be on the cast and you've never gotten it, doesn't it make sense to try something you haven't done before – like practising? So you don't flake out?'

'I probably won't get it anyway.' He looks down at the table for a moment. 'If I prepare and build it up too much, it'll feel even shittier when it doesn't work out. And I like being a writer. It's *almost* my dream. And having that is pretty good going, you know?'

I nod, thinking about what my dream is. Am I close to it? It takes me a few seconds to realise with a jolt that I don't really have a dream. Not even an almost dream like Seth. No real goals I want to reach or heights to aspire to.

Hmmm. Do I need a dream? Why do I need one? Can't I be content with a steady life, a steady job, maybe a future with someone sweet like Colin. It might not set the world alight, but I'd be happy enough.

Wouldn't I?

CHAPTER TWENTY-ONE

Olive's recent search history:

- **Seth Hartman Sunday Night Live Idiot**
- **Lost post NYC**
- **Prison Sentence for stealing a key in USA?**
- ***Orange Is the New Black***
- **Improv**
- **Improv Manchester**
- **Lupus**
- **Lupus cure**
- **Kidney disease cure**
- **Why no cure for kidney disease????**
- **Staten Island Ferry safe?**
- **Dr BJ Manchester Royal Hospital**
- **Where was *Atonement* Library scene filmed? Which library?**
- **Am I happy quiz**
- **How to tell if you are bored with your life quiz**

Sonny arrives at our booth with a massive pizza topped with meatballs. It's ginormous. And it smells delicious, all tomatoey and spicy and terrible for me.

'How *you* doin?' Seth says to the pizza, an eyebrow raised flirtatiously. He picks up the pizza slicer and separates it into slices. 'You lookin' real fine.'

Chuckling, I pick up a slice. It's all doughy and heavy, the slice drooping in my hand, cheese sliding precariously to the left.

'Hold it like this!' Seth folds it slightly at the end. 'Trust me, I am a pizza expert.'

I follow Seth's instructions and take a small bite.

Oh.

Oh.

I take another, bigger bite, the salted tomato sauce bursting with flavour in my mouth, combined with the gooey cheese.

'Oh my god,' I whisper. 'Great Scott! Meatballs. On pizza. Fuck yes.'

Seth looks me in the eye, nodding slowly, chewing down on another mouthful. 'Fuck. Yes.'

We go quiet while we munch down. At home I try to keep my meal choices simple and healthy – rice and veggies, chicken salads, lentil soup. Right now I realise I have been an idiot the whole time. I should have just been eating meatball pizza my entire life.

I'm just finishing up my last slice when the alarm goes off on my phone. I wipe my tomatoey mouth with a paper napkin, and pull my phone out of my satchel to turn the alarm off.

'Time to go!' I say, folding the napkin and placing it neatly on top of my plate.

'You set an alarm?' Seth asks incredulously.

'Of course!' I say, patting my stomach in satisfaction. 'I can't miss the next ferry? I really do need to get to Wall Street.'

'Fair enough,' Seth says, looking slightly disappointed. When he goes to the bar to settle the bill, I double- and triple-check that I have the letter in my satchel. I do. I definitely have it. It's right there and it's not going anywhere except for right into Chuck's hands.

I pull my umbrella out in anticipation of the rainy walk back to the terminal.

When Seth's paid and hugged Phyllis and Sonny goodbye, I call out my thanks for a delicious meal, drain the last of my beer and head to the door.

As I step out of the bar and flip open my umbrella, the wind blows so fiercely that it turns completely inside out.

Argh!

I yelp, trying to wrestle my brolly back into shape, meanwhile getting absolutely soaked through by rainfall that feels like someone chucking a bucket of water over my head.

'Help!' I yell as I grapple with the umbrella, ducking as one of the spokes almost stabs me in the boob.

Seth appears behind me, mouth agape at the state of the sky. He grabs the top of the parasol and yanks hard, but the wind howls past us so quickly that it's no use. This isn't wind. It's super wind.

Across the street my eyes widen, horrified, as a wooden gate opens and closes so furiously that it almost comes off its hinges. I try once more to make the umbrella work. I turn into the gale and hold the edges, but before I can stop it, it flies open again and hits Seth in the eyebrow. Shit! His eyebrow is bleeding. I've maimed him! I've maimed him with my umbrella! Oh no!

I try to yell sorry over the sound of the storm, but it's

too loud. Seth grabs my hand and yanks me back inside the bar, blood trickling from his forehead.

'Shit! Shit! I'm so sorry!' I shriek, panting as Seth touches a hand to his head. 'Are you all right?'

Phyllis hurries over at the commotion.

'Baby, your head! Let me get you a Band-Aid.' She jogs off behind the bar.

'I'm fine!' Seth assures me. But there's blood everywhere!

I reach into my satchel and pull out the handkerchief Mrs Ramirez gave to me, pressing it against the cut.

'Thanks,' Seth says, putting his hand over mine to stop the bleeding. 'Honestly, I'm completely fine.'

'Good. Good,' I say, removing my hand from underneath his.

'Looks like we're gonna need to get a cab back to the ferry port.'

'Definitely,' I say wide-eyed. There's no way I'm going back out there again without the cover of a car!

Phyllis returns with a plaster and some cotton wool, instructing Seth to sit back down in a booth so she can tend to him. While she's fussing over him, Seth pulls his phone out of his hoodie pocket and taps out a minicab number, while I unbutton my coat and use my dry jumper sleeve to dab at my wet face.

'A cab from Trickys on St Mark's Place to St George Terminal, please.'

Seth frowns.

'What? Really? Why? Well… can we get a cab straight to Manhattan then? And the ferries?'

'What are they saying?' I whisper nervously. 'Is there a long wait? I mean, I'll be okay as long as I can get to Wall Street before close of business.'

Seth presses a button on his phone, ending the call.

'I can't believe it!' he says. 'The cabs aren't running.

The storm is getting really bad. The drivers have been told to stay off the roads.'

Shit!

I start to pull my coat back on. I'm gonna have to walk it. I need to get to Wall Street this afternoon! 'You stay here,' I say. 'But I really need to go. I'll just brave it.'

Seth puts his hand on my arm. 'Olive… the ferries have been cancelled until the storm clears.'

I frown. 'When… when will that be? An hour? Oh jeez, two hours? It's Tuesday and my flight back is on Thursday morning at 3 a.m. I don't have much time to get this letter delivered!'

'I'm not sure,' Seth says apologetically. 'The cab guy just told me they were all cancelled.'

'Oh no!'

'Sonny!' Phyllis shouts into the kitchen. 'Have you heard anything about this storm?'

Sonny shuffles into the room, grim-faced. He grabs the remote control and flicks through the channels on the TV. I've already got my phone out and am googling *Staten Island Storm Ferries*. But I needn't bother because Sonny finds a news channel showing pictures of a very stormy Hudson river.

The news anchor on screen looks into the camera solemnly. 'Sources suggest that the eye of the storm will pass through at around 1 a.m. While some treacherous weather was expected, a gale of this magnitude was not.'

I flop onto the booth. 'One a.m.?' I mutter worriedly. 'What?'

'Both of you will stay here,' Phyllis says, clapping her hands together, stirred into action. 'I have a bunch of rooms upstairs.'

'Are you sure, Phyllis?' Seth asks. 'That's real kind of you.'

'Nonsense. I got the room.'

Stay here? I don't have my stuff. I don't have my pyjamas. And what about Chuck? I've already been here for three days and I've still not delivered the letter. What if he's not there tomorrow? I can't let Birdie down. I promised her!

My heart thuds very slowly. I can hear it in my head. Boom. Boom. Boom. I feel like I'm going to be sick. Shit. I think I'm having a panic attack. I fumble in my bag distractedly for my bottle of Rescue Remedy. But it's not there. Of course. It's in the pink bumbag back at the Airbnb.

I close my eyes, willing this uneasiness to bugger the hell off. Ugh. It's horrid! I haven't had a real panic attack for years. But then, not much has happened to me for years either!

'Hey. Hey, Olive!' I hear Phyllis's voice saying my name, but it sounds all echoey and weird and I can't focus. Then I feel something sharp and painful on my arm.

'Motherfucker!' I yell in pain.

'There you are, honey.'

My vision comes sharply into focus and I look across the booth where Phyllis is staring at me worriedly, Seth by her side wearing the exact same expression.

'Did you… did you just pinch me?' I gasp, rubbing my arm.

'Yeah,' Phyllis says with a nod. She takes hold of my hand. 'You're having a panic attack.'

I nod, my heart still thudding slowly in my ears. I feel all hot and queasy.

'I want you to focus on my face,' Phyllis says

I nod and focus on Phyllis's tanned, pointed face.

'That's it,' she says. 'You are okay. Everything is okay. Say it back to me, honey.'

'I am okay, everything is okay.'

'Great! If I relax, this will pass.'

'If I relax, this will pass.'

'That's correct! Now, I want you to watch me and I'm going to breathe in for four and out for four and I want you to copy me. Breathe in right from your belly, honey. Nice and slow now.'

Holding Phyllis's hand, I copy her as she breathes in and out. As we breathe and count, Seth leaves the booth, but I barely notice.

I'm not sure how long we're breathing for, but I feel my heart speed back up, my cheeks feel less warm, my shoulders less scrunched. I'm okay. Everything is okay.

'That's it,' Phyllis says in a soothing voice. 'There you go.'

I wipe my wet hair back from my face. 'Wow. Thank you. How did you do that?'

'Fuckin' anxiety. I used to have a lot of it.'

'How did you get it to stop?'

Phyllis shrugs. 'It still visits occasionally. The best I can do is work at prevention. I've had to learn to relax with meditation and yoga. You can't just expect it to go away on its own. You feeling better?'

I blink, smiling in relief.

Phyllis returns to the bar to serve the customers who now seem to be taking this storm as a signal to hunker down and get even more day drunk then they already are.

Okay. Everything is okay.

Except I now have less than thirty-six hours to find Chuck and deliver Birdie's letter.

I reach into my satchel and pull out my phone.

I need to speak to Birdie.

CHAPTER TWENTY-TWO

@ElissaJohnson

So I spoke to the cops this morning for an update on my stolen key, and they say that the suspect was spotted trying to fish for cheques in a West Side mailbox!

@ElissaJohnson

She ran away! She ran away *again*. Does anyone know who she is?? Someone at @SundayNightLive MUST know. They impersonated her. I'm so confused and #angry.

@ElissaJohnson

Oh great. Now The Gramercy Neighbourhood Society say it will be another two weeks until I can get a new key!!! This is #horrendous

@NewYorkDailyNews

Hi Elissa. Follow us. We'd like to DM you about this.

'Hello you! Where are you? It's all dark!'

'I'm in a bar bathroom in Staten Island,' I tell Birdie, to which she gasps in delight. 'I got the letter back!' I say, deciding to start with a positive.

'Amazing! You are the best. What a relief. I gotta say, I was panicking a bit. I put my whole heart into that letter. Phew!'

'There's bad news too… I'm stuck in Staten Island overnight. There's a storm and there's no way to get back to Manhattan.'

Birdie's face clouds over. 'Are you all right? Where will you stay? Are you there alone? Shit, Olive.'

'I'm fine,' I wave away her concern. 'I'm here with Seth. He knows the owners of the bar.'

'Seth? *The TV show writer*?' Birdie raises an eyebrow.

'Yeah, him. Anyway. I'm just worried because I won't be able to get to Chuck today. Of course, there's tomorrow, but it's cutting it pretty fine, especially if he's not still working there.'

Birdie nods and bites her lip. She looks more tired than usual today. Her normally sleek pixie crop is a little messy and ruffled and her lips look pale.

'Are you okay?' I ask.' You don't look very well.'

Birdie laughs, absent-mindedly rubbing her chest. 'Oh I had a late night, you know. Giving a pleasant BJ to Dr BJ. We had a night of wild passion. Hence the messy hair.'

'WHAT?'

'I'm kidding!' she giggles. 'I *wish*. God, do I wish. I just didn't sleep well. I miss you.'

'I miss you too,' I sigh, resting my head against the

phone screen. Birdie does the same. We stay there for a moment.

I pull back and my phone screen flickers. The video image goes still so that Birdie looks like a smiling statue.

'Can you hear me?' I call into the phone. 'Birdie?'

'Yeah… patchy… storm.' Her voice is breaking up. The sound is all muffled.

Shit. The weather must be affecting the signal.

'Birdie?' I try again, holding my phone in the air, as if this will help. 'I will figure this all out, okay?' I say. 'Birdie? Don't worry about anything! Birdie?'

'Love… you… time… Chuck… relax…' Her voice comes back muffled and erratic. I can't tell what she's trying to say!

Then the screen goes black.

She's gone.

Stoopid storm.

When I return to the booth, Seth is sitting there, messing with his phone, two more beers on the table.

'It's not working.' He points to his phone.

'Me either,' I say, holding up mine.

'So… are you going to tell me about this letter?' he asks as I sit down opposite him.

I bite my lip. 'Okay. But Seth?'

'Olive?'

'Everything I'm going to talk to you about is private. Please don't tell anyone. Or write about it.'

He holds up his hands. 'We're friends now right?'

I feel a smile lift the corners of my mouth. 'Well, I suppose we have survived a major storm together.'

'Exactly.' Seth holds his hand out for a high five, which I promptly return. 'I only ever use the behaviour of complete strangers for comedy material. Not friends. So you're safe.'

I spend the next thirty minutes telling Seth all about Birdie and the mysteriously vanished Chuck. How the whole reason for me being here is to get this letter to the love of Birdie's life before she dies. He asks the usual questions about treatments and cures and how long she has left. To which I give him all the sad answers Birdie and I have known for a while. But mostly he just listens, his eyes serious.

'My flight back to Manchester is early Thursday morning. And I'm not even a hundred per cent sure that Chuck works at Chimes Investment! Hence the freak-out.'

'Can't you stay longer?' Seth asks, drinking from his bottle and nudging mine over to me.

I shake my head. 'Not really. Birdie's kidney surgery is a week Monday. I need to be back to help her prepare. She has no one else, you see.'

I lift my beer bottle and take a sip.

We both go quiet. Me thinking about what I've got to do. Seth thinking about who knows what.

Eventually Seth speaks. 'Why don't you call the bank and speak to this Chuck fella. Check he's definitely there? Arrange a time to meet him in the morning?'

I bang my hand against my head. 'Of course! Duh. That's a really sensible idea. Thank you!'

'I've never been called sensible before.' Seth pulls a face. 'I do not like it.'

I immediately pick my phone up off the booth table and Google Chimes Investment.

And then I remember that my reception is totally down, as is Seth's.

'We'll use the landline in the back,' Seth says.

I follow him to the bar, where Phyllis cheerfully waves us through to a tiny storeroom, with a Barbie-pink 90s telephone set hanging on the wall. On the table below it is a thick paper phone book.

'This is amazing,' I say gleefully, picking up the phone. 'So retro. And so pink!'

Seth flips through the book until he finds the number for the bank, reciting it as I push the buttons on the handset.

After a few rings someone answers.

'Good afternoon, Chimes Investment, how may I direct your call?'

'I'd like to speak to Chuck Allen please,' I say as clearly as I can. I sound like Donna.

'Putting you through to mergers and acquisitions.'

Ooh, mergers and acquisitions. That sounds fancy!

I tap my fingers against the phone, while Seth stands there, appearing to be studying an old calendar on the storeroom wall.

'Good afternoon, Mergers and Acquisitions.'

'Hi there. May I speak to Chuck Allen?'

Please let him still work there. Please, jeebus, let him still work there.

'Mr Allen has left for a meeting with a client,' the woman on the other end informs me. 'He will not be in the office until tomorrow. May I take a message'

I gasp. 'He'll be there tomorrow?' I do a little excited wiggle. 'In the morning? Definitely?'

'Yes he will,' the woman says in a clipped voice. 'May I ask who is calling?'

My heart lifts with relief. This is okay. I can make this work. I have located Chuck Allen!!

'It's Olive. Olive Brewster,' I say, a huge smile on my face. 'Can I make an appointment with Chuck? For tomorrow?'

The woman's voice turns suspicious. 'Mr Allen is a

very busy man. I'm afraid he's pretty tightly booked for the next month, at least. What is this regarding?'

'Oh… um… It's personal business. It's urgent.'

'Then you can get him on his personal number. We don't make appointments for personal business.'

Ugh, this woman is a right snooty patootie.

'Of course. And his personal number is?'

'Who are you? Is that you, Diane? Chuck said he never wanted to hear from you again! Stop calling. It's over, Diane! Over!'

This is going downhill very quickly.

Pull it back, Olive!

'Excuse me!' I say imperiously. 'This is not Diane! This is Olive. I… I need to see Chuck Allen immediately.'

My shift in tone causes Seth to turn around from the wall calendar, a surprised half-smile on his face. He leans right in close so he can hear what's going on. He's so close. Really close. His ear is almost touching my ear. I feel peculiar.

Focus Olive.

I clear my throat. Somehow I don't think the fact that I have a letter from Chuck's old girlfriend is going to cut it with this suspicious woman…

'I… I have a large investment to make,' I say. 'I am leaving Manhattan tomorrow evening on, um, a private plane. *My* private plane actually.' I make my voice sound much posher. 'This investment is of the utmost importance.'

Seth's eyebrows shoot up and he covers his mouth as he does a whispery laugh. He shoots a thumbs up.

'Your query is financial, not personal?' the woman says.

'Finance is personal to me,' I say haughtily. 'I have some investments and some acquisitions to make and… merge. You know. Always Be Closing, as I like to say. I don't mean to be crude but we are talking business worth at least… *nine* figures. Oh yes. It would be ghastly to have to tell your boss that he missed out on a very valuable client, especially after he was recommended to me so heartily by my friends at well… I shouldn't say. Billionaires are a discreet bunch, as you know.'

I have no clue what I am saying. Even if I'm making sense. I just know that I need this appointment with Chuck and I'm willing to do whatever it takes to get it. Seth is enjoying all of this immensely. His shoulders are shaking with silent laughter.

I think I might have completely fucked this up. I prepare to have the phone slammed down on me.

'Ahem,' the woman clears her throat. 'I am sorry, madam. I didn't realise you'd been personally recommended. Of course. Please excuse me. Mr Allen is very particular about who he meets with. Okay…Will ten thirty a.m. tomorrow suit? I can squeeze you in then?'

'Yes!' I yell. Then I cough and try to sound more like the character I've spontaneously concocted. 'That will be, um, amenable. Thank you and… best wishes.'

'Um, best wishes to you too, madam.'

I hang the phone back in its holder and Seth puts his palm out for a high five. Laughing, I smack my hand against his, adrenaline coursing through my body.

How the fuck did I just manage that? Yes! I will finally get to give Chuck Birdie's letter! I won't have let her down!

'That was kind of amazing,' Seth breathes, his eyes twinkling. We're so close to each other in this tiny storeroom, I can see the flecks of pale green that make his eyes looks so turquoise.

I take a deep breath. 'I didn't think she was going to believe me!'

I open the storeroom door and we head back past a couple having a row by the pool table, towards our booth.

'Have you ever tried improv?' Seth asks when we sit down. 'I have a feeling you'd be amazing at it. That phone call was insane.'

I take a sip of my beer, my mood considerably lifted by the fact that I have finally located the enigmatic Chuck. 'Is that what you were doing at the community theatre?'

'Yeah,' Seth smiles fondly. 'But that was beginner's stuff. We have a group at UCB – The Upright Citizen's Brigade – and that's professional improv and sketch comedy. A bunch of *Sunday Night Live* writers and cast members, including me, were discovered there. It's pretty much making stuff up on the spot, but in a team.'

'I'd be too scared. I wouldn't know what to say!'

'It can be nerve-wrecking at first but the buzz you get, the *adrenaline*. It's ridiculous. It's pure joy!'

He looks so happy.

'It sounds cool,' I say. 'And terrifying.'

His eyes light up. 'Oh man, Olive. You should definitely come and watch a show! You don't have to try it, even just to watch. I really think you'd like it.'

'I'm leaving Thursday morning, remember,' I laugh, running my finger in a circle on the booth table. 'But otherwise I would have really liked that.'

Seth's smile falls slightly. 'Oh, yeah, of course.' He taps the side of his beer bottle, 'This must be going to my head already.'

'Yeah. Three a.m. flight. And I'll definitely be taking some Night Nurse. If I can knock myself out beforehand that'll be for the best of everyone.'

I feel my cheeks turn red, just thinking of the last flight. It occurs to me then that Seth had thought I wanted to join the Mile High Club with him. And he was willing to. Does that mean he found me attractive?

Not that I'm bothered. Obviously. Seth is not even my type. He's a bit rumpled, his hair needs a good cut and he's way too laid-back. He's definitely not the kind of guy who would have a five-year plan. He probably doesn't even have a five-day plan. I mean, not that I *have* a type. People who don't date or have sex don't tend to have types. But if I *did* he would probably look a lot like Colin. Or maybe James McAvoy…

'Three a.m.?' Seth says, leaning his elbows on the table. 'So you'd have to be at JFK around 12.30 a.m.'

'Right…'

'So *technically*, you could come to my improv show tomorrow night. It's seven until nine. I have to go straight to work afterwards – it's our writing night – and you would have plenty of time to make your flight. You could even bring your cases to the theatre.'

I bite at my thumbnail, trying to work out my timings. I suppose I could book a cab in advance. Make sure I pack early…

'I mean, you don't have to,' Seth says his eyebrows shooting up. 'But you could… if you wanted to do. It might be fun. And it will *definitely* be funny.'

I take a swig of my beer. It's a bit last minute. But everything's been last minute this week and here I am, much to my own surprise, figuring it out. And by tomorrow night Chuck will have the letter and I'll have fulfilled my mission. And then I can get back to Birdie, where I belong.

'Okay, then,' I say, a smile lifting the corners of my mouth. 'I'm in!'

CHAPTER TWENTY-THREE

Text from Taller Joan: Hello, my love. Me and Joan were talking about you today! We want to say that we really hope your mission is going well and that you are finding time to HAVE SOME FUN!!!! We are so jealous of you being in New York New York! Make the most of it. Love Joan and Joan of Joan's Fresh Fish x

'Noooo, you're getting it wrong!' I scold Seth for the gazillionth time. 'You jump on the *Oi*. Heeeeey Macarena, *Oi*!'

'Isn't that what I did?'

'No, you jumped on the Macarena. Totally out of time. How are you not getting this?'

'The Macarena is hard,' Seth grumbles. 'And I don't think you're teaching it correctly.

'I'm a great teacher.' I put my hands on my hips. 'You just have a terrible sense of rhythm.'

'I've never had any complaints,' Seth says, his eyes glinting.

God. What is happening? We are totally, totally flirting. How have we ended up flirting? I haven't flirted in years. Maybe I have never even flirted at all? Even my conversations with Colin at the airport were all pretty polite and proper. We've flirted a little by text, but mostly we've been swapping information about the weather in our respective locales and asking questions like 'if you were an animal what kind of animal would you be?' and 'what's your favourite smell?' And while I do love a good chat about the weather, and one of my favourite things is finding out what kind of animal a person would be, it's not *really* flirting.

What I'm doing with Seth right now is one hundred per cent, completely and utterly flirting. Seth has touched me on the arm three times. I have nudged him once with my elbow and touched his arm twice! I know this because I counted.

Over the past hour or so I've found that I'm acting completely unlike my usual self around him. I'm laughing and quipping and flicking my hair and being daft like I usually only am with Birdie. Seth seems to find me genuinely funny. I told him about Donna's candle business earlier, doing the impression of her I did for Birdie at the hospital and he clutched his stomach he was laughing so hard. I even did a sexy wiggle when I taught him the Macarena.

Hmmm. Maybe I'm acting so out of character because the storm has been raging on for the past three hours and there's an energy of panic and dark excitement in the bar. Maybe the danger of it turns me on. *Maybe* all this time, my lack of sexual feelings was nothing to do with the breakdown of my family or my need for control, but because I can only get the horn in a storm? It must be a thing. Storm horn. I wonder if there is storm porn for people who have the storm horn… I will do an incognito Google search when my phone reception returns and see what I can find out.

I can't even blame this behaviour on booze. Unlike everyone else in the bar who is now completely sozzled, Seth and I stopped drinking beer after our first two bottles and now I'm sipping water and Seth is on root beer.

After a game of pool in which Seth won, mostly because we had to get it over and done quickly because a couple of the other bar attendees were giving us the daggers, we ate some peanuts and Seth taught me how to throw them up in the air and catch them every single time. The trick is to aim to where you think the nut is going to hit your nose and it will always land in your mouth. Such a pointless exercise, but fun.

And then we got onto the topic of Seth's audition tomorrow. I asked him to show me his routine, which he did. And it was brilliant! When he's not stealing my likeness for sketch material, he is actually very, very funny. I can see why it's his job. He told me he needed to do an impression as part of the audition and that he had settled on John Malkovich because it was the only one he could do. I asked him to show me and he did this whole bit where he was John Malkovich doing a red carpet interview. As he was talking, a little thought popped up in my head and really made me laugh.

'It's terrible isn't it?' Seth said as I giggled, his face flushing slightly pink.

'No! It's a really good John Malkovich. I just… An idea just burst into my head and it made me laugh.'

'Oh, well you have to tell me now.'

'It's daft.'

'Go on!'

I rolled my eyes. 'All right. I just thought that it might be funnier if, instead of having John Malkovich do a red carpet interview, he would maybe be…' I trailed off, feeling embarrassed. I had no right telling a comedy writer what might be a funnier thing to do.

'Yes?' Seth said. He looked genuinely interested.

So I carried on. 'So, like, John Malkovich could be teaching his friend the Macarena. I don't know why he would, but it just made me—'

'I love it!' Seth said immediately, with a big bark of laughter. 'It's ridiculous. I love it.'

'Really?' I beamed with pleasure. 'Ha ha!'

And so for the past forty minutes I've been teaching Seth the Macarena and making suggestions to the rest of his routine, most of which he's actually taken on. And to my great astonishment I am having the most fun I've had in years. The last time I laughed this much was when Donna tripped over a toddler in Asda and flailed forward, headbutting the toddler's dad in his goolies. She was not impressed when I suggested that she'd legit just cheated on Alex.

'Are you sure you've never written funny stuff before?' Seth says, shaking his head, after I suggest that John Malkovich dramatically recites the words to the Macarena, rather than sing them.

'God, no!' I say, embarrassed and pleased in a silly, vain kind of way.

'You're a natural.'

I feel my cheeks stretch into a gigantic smile. Maybe he's just being flirty. But I don't care. It's nice to feel like I might be good at something beyond filleting cod and noticing where all potential hazards within a five-metre radius might be.

After we've perfected the impression and the Macarena routine, much to the amusement of Phyllis, Sonny and a few of the other patrons, we take a seat back in our booth and order another pizza.

Over more delicious slices and with nothing else to do until the storm passes, Seth and I dive right in and talk about our lives. His attitude to things is so similar to

Birdie's. His main aim in life seems to be to have fun and if things go wrong then 'fuck it! It is what it is!!'

I shake my head in disbelief.

Seth takes his glasses off and cleans them with the edge of his T-shirt. 'So what happened?'

'Huh?'

'What happened to make you so het up all the time? Not to be an armchair psychologist, but everyone's defects can usually be traced back to events of their younger years. For example. I might seem easy and breezy to you, but part of me is just a tiny bit concerned that if I take things *too* seriously and they don't work out then I'll never fully recover. And that probably has a lot to do with my dad never making it as a stand-up. It was his whole life. His whole heart. And when it didn't work out, he never got over it.'

'So… if you don't try, you can't fail?'

'Exactly!'

'Yep, that's total armchair psychology.'

Seth laughs. 'So what about you? What's your mess?'

'It's boring,' I say, pulling a face. 'It's not even a big deal.'

'Tell me.'

I take a deep breath. The only person I've ever talked to about this is Birdie. After Dad moved to Scotland, Alex and I never really discussed it again. Just went along with our lives, pretending it was super normal for our parents to so easily leave us when we were still pretty damn young.

I pick up a beer mat and fiddle with the corners of it. 'My mum had an affair and left our family for a French dude. She lives in France. We barely speak. The whole thing broke my dad and he moved to Scotland. I had no clue it was coming. It knocked me and my brother for six. I was gutted. Really very gutted, you know?' I take a sip of water. 'I guess I decided that the best way to avoid feeling like that ever again was to make sure I kept my life as simple as possible, be prepared for any situation I could. If things are under my control, then there won't be any more nasty surprises. That was the worst I've ever felt. And I don't want to feel like that ever again.'

Seth gives me a sad smile. 'You know that's impossible though? You can't be prepared for everything.'

I shrug. 'I know. It's not ideal. Birdie is forever telling me to just relax. That I'm stronger than I think. I don't know… Life might not be a thrill a minute, but I've always been… fine.'

'But are you happy?' Seth asks bluntly. 'Do you ever feel, like joyful?'

'Of course!' I say, laughing as if it's a daft question. But even as I say it I'm not entirely sure it's true…

After the serious chatter has ended, Seth tries to lighten the mood by putting Bruce Springsteen on the jukebox and engaging the rest of the punters in a dance-off. The camaraderie in the bar is juxtaposed by the flashing images on the big-screen TV of the damage the storm is doing in some residential neighbourhoods. No-one has been hurt, but it's all pretty high-octane stuff.

I join Seth on the dance floor and try to bust a few moves in an effort to chase away the navel-gazing that our conversation has brought. But I keep thinking about going back to real life next week. To chomping my Weetabix every morning, getting my tram to work, serving the regular customers, moving my stuff into the box room, watching box sets with Alex and Donna. Week after week. *After week.*

Somehow, the notion doesn't sound quite so comforting as it did a few days ago.

'I think I might go to bed!' I yell to Seth over the booming music.

'Are you okay?' he shouts back.

'Yeah!' I nod, rubbing my eyes. 'Just, it's been a full-on day! And I've so much to do tomorrow. As do you! A good sleep will help you with your audition!'

Seth laughs. 'You really do think of everything.'

'Are the rooms just upstairs? I'd ask Phyllis, but I don't want to interrupt her fun,' I say, nodding over to where Phyllis is being twirled about on the pool table by one of the sloshed punters.

'I can show you,' Seth yells.

Following Seth round the back of the bar, we go through a door into a vestibule. A set of narrow stairs lead us to another hallway covered in flock wallpaper and framed pictures of the Staten Island Yankees.

'This is you!' Seth says, pushing his glasses up his nose. He giving me a sidelong glance.

The mood shifts. We both go quiet, the only sound the bassy beat of an Alabama Shakes song playing downstairs in the bar.

'Great!' My voice has gone all high-pitched. 'Where are you? I mean. Not that I … I mean… oh never mind.'

Shut yo mouth, Olive!

'I'm in that one.' Seth bites his bottom lip and points to the room next door to mine.

'Super!' I brush my hair out of my face and tuck it behind my ear. 'Okay! Well!'

'I've had a good day,' Seth murmurs, frowning slightly, almost as if he's surprised by the fact.

'Me too,' I nod, and realise that I'm not just being polite, that it's the truth. It's been complicated and hard and a bit scary. But I feel, I don't know… alive? 'Thank you for—'

'No problem.'

We stand there. Seth looks at me, scratches his jaw and gives a little laugh. I laugh too. I have no idea what we are laughing about.

I put my hand on the doorknob behind me.

But I don't want to go in yet.

Kiss him.

I want to kiss him.

What the fuck?

I really, really want to kiss him. I want to do more than that. I want to… be in a library with him. Argh.

Open the door and leave, Olive. This cannot be a good idea. Leave right now.

Seth takes a step towards me.

I freeze, my heart beating so loudly that it's reverberating through my whole body. Even my vajeen.

I swallow, making an audible gulp like someone in a cartoon.

Seth takes hold of my hand and runs his thumb over my palm. 'If you weren't engaged to another man, Olive, I'd kiss you so good right now that you'd never forget it, not for the rest of your life.'

I blink, baffled.

Engaged?

Engaged to who?

Oh shit! Colin! I had totally forgotten about Colin. Colin my fake fiancé! Colin the man I am planning to have an indoor date with upon my return to Manchester. Colin!

Seth's face is so close to mine that I can smell him – beer and clean skin and rain.

I want to…

I want to…

Oh my *goodness* I want to…

But before I can do anything, Seth has promptly turned around and walked straight into his room, closing the door behind him.

I blink, shocked, and slowly back into my room.

I lean back against the door.

I can't breathe. My head is all hot. I feel dizzy and tingly.

But not in a bad way. In… an awesome way.

What the fuck?

I jog into the little en suite and splash my face with icy water. I peer up at myself in the mirror.

I look different. Flushed and shiny-eyed. My lips look plumper.

I look… horny. I have honest to goodness storm horn!

I picture Colin's sweet face, his big arms, his stellar weather banter, his glorious sideburns, and try to recreate the zingy KAPOW feeling I just got from Seth.

But it doesn't bloody work. I try to picture Colin naked, sitting at a desk and working on a five-year plan. Then I picture Colin naked baking me a cake and just generally being a naked baker, frosting smudged sexily on his cheek. I even picture Colin pinning me up against a huge bookcase and kissing my neck.

None of it works!

I turn to the bed and throw myself on it dramatically.

Then I think about what Seth just said about kissing me so good that I'd never forget it, not for the rest of my life.

KAPOW. KAPOW! FIZZ! BLAM! WOO! YAAAASSS!

Well.

I definitely did not prepare for this.

* * *

I've had about an hour's sleep all night! I felt wired and alert and so literally *hot* that I had to sleep naked. The only thing I could think of was that all Seth would have to do is walk a few steps down the hall to my room. Or all I would have to do is walk a few steps down the hall.

And then…

Nothing. No. I live in England. He lives in America. I barely know him. Plus he has heard me pee. PLUS he put that little detail in our history on live television. Not sexy. Not sexy at all, Olive.

Bleary-eyed, I have a shower in the en suite, rub my hair dry with a towel – grumbling as it springs right back up into the mass of uncontrollable curls – and get dressed.

I grab my satchel, checking for the bazillionth time that Birdie's letter is safely tucked inside, open the door of the room and step out into the hallway.

At exactly the same time as Seth.

'Good morning!' he says brightly, cheerfully, as if *he* had a full night of sleep.

'Yes! It's morning!' I mumble nervously, like a psycho.

Seth shoves his hands into his jean pockets. 'Did you sleep well?'

'Yes, definitely!' I answer firmly. 'I slept so well. So well.'

'Great. Well, I Googled and the storm has cleared so we can get back to Manhattan right away.'

My heart kicks with relief.

'Amazing. I can *finally* get this letter to Chuck Allen! At last!'

'That's so great.'

'Yep.'

'Yeah!'

'Okay!'

'Okay.'

We study each other for a moment. I brush a curl away from my forehead. Seth cocks his head to the side. 'So, um, I've just got to—'

And then, all at once he steps towards me, pushing me up against my door, his body pressed against mine. He cups the side of my face with one hand and places the other hand on the back of my head. His gaze flicks down to my lips. Then back up to my eyes.

'Hi,' he murmurs, a slight frown on his face.

'H-hello,' I croak.

And before I can even make sense of what is happening right now, Seth's lips are on my lips. Or my lips are on his lips. Either way, we are *kissing*. We are kissing our lips together. We are kissing SO GOOD.

Seth moves his hands from my face to the small of my back, pulling me even closer to him. I swing my arms up around his neck and kiss him back like I am dehydrated and he is water. He runs his hand up my outer thigh, then his thumb down the front of my thigh and I can't quite catch my breath.

Boy oh boy oh *boy*.

'Hey! This is a respectable establishment!'

We immediately jump apart at the gruff sound of Sonny's voice. He's at the top of the stairs, chunky arms crossed, thick dark brows furrowed. Phyllis is standing next to him, wearing a very tight bandage dress and raising an eyebrow judgmentally.

'Oh my gosh, sorry!' I squeak. 'I didn't know you were there!'

Seth doesn't say anything. Just reaches for my hand lightly, trying to catch his breath.

I know for a fact that my face is turning crimson with guilt.

Sonny and Phyllis burst into laughter.

'Only kidding, ya dummies!' Sonny bellows.

'But if ya gonna fuck, do it in the room, right?' Phyllis says. 'I don't wanna see genitals in the communal areas.'

'At least not before lunch,' quips Sonny.

My face absolutely burns. Am I sweating? I feel like I'm sweating.

'We're leaving now!' I say in my most professional, polite voice. 'Thank you for your hospitality.'

'Anytime, honey. It was our pleasure.'

Sonny wiggles his eyebrows. 'But not as much as yours, huh?'

Oh god.

'Seth, your aunt Patty is in the kitchen. She heard you were here and wanted to say hi. She's making you waffles.'

Seth looks at me, a half-smile on his face. 'You want some waffles?'

I shake my head, feeling all flustered. 'I should, um, I should probably go. I have my appointment… I'll be fine to get back on my own.'

Seth squeezes my hand a little before letting go. 'Okay, so… I'll see you tonight? At the show?'

'Yeah!' I nod. 'Shall we swap numbers?'

I sound like a fifteen year old.

'Sure,' Seth says, taking my phone and handing me his.

We enter our numbers in to each other's phones, Phyllis and Sonny watching weirdly over us the whole time.

'Oh, and here.' Phyllis holds out her hand to drop something into mine. 'I wanted to give you this before you go. It will help you relax.'

I open my palm to find a small, fat, oddly rolled cigarette.

'It's clean, no resin. Just pure herb, top drawer. You'll see.'

Weed? *She's giving me weed?*

I make to give it her back – besides Rescue Remedy I have never taken a drug in my life and I don't plan on starting now – but Phyllis looks really thrilled at her kindness. And I must admit I'm touched that she thought to help me after she already helped so much yesterday.

I swallow and quickly shove the joint in my bag. 'This is really nice of you. Thank you, Phyllis.'

'You're welcome, honey. Hey, you should try screwing on that stuff. It's incredible, right Sonny.'

'Hell yeah!'

Okay. I definitely need to go now.

'Bye and thanks again!' I yelp, shifting past Seth and Sonny and Phyllis and jogging my way downstairs and out of the bar.

Once outside, I lean my head back against the bar window and take some deep breaths, gulping as much air in as I possibly can.

The sun is crazy bright today, and beyond the slightly damp glitter of the grey pavements you would never guess that last night this here was the scene of a treacherous storm. It looks serene and quiet, like nothing at all happened.

But something did happen. Something big. Something major. Something from which I don't think I can go back…

I had a sexual awakening. My vajeen has risen. And… I think I want more. Lots more.

CHAPTER TWENTY-FOUR

Text from Birdie: YOU KISSED THE COMEDY WRITER? YOU KISSED A STRANGER! YOU GOT STORM HORN? Not sure that's a real thing but OKAY! Who are you right now, Brewster? This is too exciting for me to handle. You know my heart is weak already! What does he look like? Wait… I'm gonna google him stat!

Text from Birdie: Oh Olive. YASSSS. He's got a Harrison Ford in the 1980s vibe going on. But, like, nerdier. In a good way. Hubba. Hubba indeed.

Text from Birdie: Don't know why you're freaking out! Maybe you can have a one-night fling with him? A quickie before you catch the plane back. Just have a ride on him, see how you like it. Super casual. What happens in Manhattan stays in Manhattan. Not everything has to be a big deal, you know?

Text from Birdie: Seriously. Hubba.

As the cab pulls up outside of Chimes Investment, I feel a mixture of trepidation and excitement. I'm finally going to meet the man who Birdie loved for so long. The one that got away. The man too cool for even the slightest whiff of social media presence: Chuck Allen! I have an appointment. I have the letter. I am in the right place. Nothing can go wrong.

At floor eighty-four I get out of the lift, my knees wobbling at the notion that I am really really really high up in the building. My chest tightens a little.

'Everything is fine. If I relax, it will pass,' I mutter to myself, breathing deeply like Phyllis showed me.

It helps. I still feel scared and I will be avoiding all windows up here. But I don't feel like I want to be sick and that's definitely an improvement!

I head over to the reception desk, where a very neat and pretty woman is sitting, tapping quickly on a keyboard.

She looks me up and down with a sneer. Can she tell that I am wearing yesterday's clothes? Is she judging my hair, which – due to a lack of straighteners at Trickys – is now poofed up in all of its gigantic curly glory. 'Yes? Can I help you?'

Hmmm. I don't like her attitude.

I find myself lifting my chin up and blasting into the plummy voice I used yesterday on the phone call to Chuck's assistant.

'I am Olive Brewster!' I declare. 'I have an appointment with Chuck Allen. I… would also like a coffee please. At once.'

The woman's eyebrows shoot up. 'Oh, of course! Sorry

Mrs Brewster. I spoke to you yesterday on the phone? I'm Lisa.'

'It's Ms. Muzzzz. If you don't mind, Lisa,' I say imperiously.

Lisa flusters, all traces of attitude gone now that she thinks I'm some rich investor. 'Yes, yes. Of course. If you'd like to take a seat.' She indicates a row of uncomfortable-looking chairs shaped like eggs. 'I will let Charles know you're here and I will get you that coffee.'

'Good,' I sniff.

'How do you take your coffee?'

'Like I take my men. Milk and one sugar.'

Okay, I took it too far. That doesn't even make any sense.

Lisa just nods.

I take a seat and pull Birdie's letter out of my bag. I clutch it to my chest. Shit! I'm about to do it. I'm about to meet Chuck Allen and give him Birdie's letter. My hands shake a little with the magnitude of it. Wow. I've done it. Me, Olive Brewster has conquered Manahttan! I may be on the NYPD's wanted list, but I have made my best friend's wish come true.

Lisa brings me the coffee – which I gulp back eagerly in a bid to wake up a little more, when the door to another office opens and a man walks out.

He strides over to me with a friendly smile, holding his hand out for me to shake.

Ooh. Who is this guy? Chuck's mate? His other assistant?

'Charles Allen,' the man says. 'Lovely to meet you.'

I… I don't understand.

This man isn't the man in the photo I have. This man is short. And bald. And in his fifties.

'Ha ha.' I nod slowly. 'Very amusing. Where is he really?'

The man's shiny round head turns from side to side. 'Excuse me?'

I sigh. I didn't sleep a wink last night. I really haven't got the time or the energy for this. 'Where is the real Chuck Allen?' I ask. I think I must say it pretty loudly because a few other people in the reception area turn around to look.

The man stutters a little. 'I… um… I *am* Chuck Allen. Charles. Only close friends and family call me Chuck.'

Huffing, I dig into my bag and pull out the photograph of Chuck in college.

'This is who I'm looking for.' I touch my finger to Chuck's smiling face. '*This* is Chuck Allen.'

Fake Chuck looks around uncomfortably. 'I… clearly that's not me.'

Lisa from the reception desk approaches us. 'Is there a problem, sir?'

Fake Chuck nods. 'Yes, Lisa. There appears to be some confusion.' He purses his lips, throwing Lisa a stern look. 'You arranged this appointment, correct?'

'I'm looking for Chuck Allen,' I say, handing her the picture. 'This guy. Chuck Allen.'

Lisa takes hold of the photograph, her eyes screwing up.

'Oh! Yeah. That's Chuck Allen. He used to work here in Private Equity.'

I'm so confused.

My stomach churns with a sense of dread. I turn to the bald man. 'So why are you saying you are him?'

Fake Chuck takes the photo from Lisa and holds it very close to his nose. 'Ah yes! I see. Yes. Chuck! He left about two years ago, I think. Isn't that correct Lisa?'

'Correct, sir.' Lisa smiles. 'It's funny, after he handed in his notice, he seemed to vanish from the face of the earth. My friend Jodie in Legal dated him for a little while. Lord knows what happened to him.' She turns to me. 'Do you know where he is?'

'Argh!' I cry to the ceiling, my temper – not helped by the lack of sleep last night – starting to bubble up in my chest. 'I thought he was here!' I point at the bald man. 'Who are you?'

'This is Charles "Chuck" Ellen.' Lisa says.

'Ellen with an E,' Fake Chuck says. He points to the picture. 'That's Chuck Allen. Allen with an A.'

No. No. NO.

'How funny!' Lisa simpers, seeming to find this all genuinely funny. 'It must be the British accent. I thought you were calling to ask for Chuck Ellen with an E!'

No. No. I cannot have misheard them saying Chuck Ellen instead of Chuck Allen. Nope. After everything, that cannot be what's happening here.

Lisa and new Chuck are chuckling over the confusion. 'I can still assist with your financial queries?' Chuck Ellen says, shaking his head like this mistaken identity is the most exciting thing that has happened here in years, which, to be fair, it probably is.

I go hot at the realisation that my flight home is in less than twenty-four hours and I have no clue in the world where the real Chuck Allen is.

This cannot be happening!

'Miss?' Chuck Ellen says. 'Shall we go step into my office and we can discuss those investments?'

I swallow hard, desperately trying to come up with a new option to track down Chuck before I leave.

'Miss?' Chuck Ellen repeats. 'Your investments?'

'There are no investments,' I say, my voice forceful with frustration. 'There is no money.'

'Excuse me?'

'I'm not a billionaire! I'm sorry but I lied on the phone so I could get an appointment to see Chuck

Allen. I have a letter for him and it's really really important.'

'Not a billionaire?'

A small crowd of besuited people has started to gather at the commotion.

'Not even a hundredaire at this point. There isn't any money!' I can hear my voice getting higher and higher. Holy crap. How can this day have started off so well and gone downhill this fast? 'I don't have any investments to make! I am poor! I work as a fish market assistant. I gut fish and sell the remains to northern people who want to eat the fish flesh. It does not pay well!'

There's a shocked silence around the room. It must be the talk of gutting fish. It always makes people a bit queasy.

'You have no money?' Chuck Ellen gasps like he's never encountered such a thing.

'Argh!' I yell, burying my head in my hands.

I hear the crowd of people muttering around me. Words like 'real life poor person' and 'maybe call security'. But I can barely pay them attention. All I can think about is the fact that this man is not Chuck Allen and I have no new leads! I have no more time!

I had one job! One job and I've well and truly messed it up. Shit. I should have found some way to get back to Manhattan yesterday. At least I would have had more time. I rested on my laurels. I didn't prepare.

'Nooooo!' I mutter, plonking down onto the egg seat. 'Gaaaah!'

'Is she all right?' I hear someone say.

'Is she staging a sit-in?'

'What is she protesting?' someone else says. 'They already put in the organic vending machine.'

'I think I recognise her…' A voice pipes up.

Great. Of course someone recognises me. Neither my hair, nor my accent is disguised.

I wait for someone to shout out 'Watch me piddle!' But instead I hear a sharp intake of breath.'

'Oh my god! It's her! It's the Menace of Manhattan!'

'Oh my goodness. I see it! Shall we call the police?'

'We definitely should. Don't let her get away.'

I look up sharply. They're talking about calling the police on me? Why are they calling me a menace? I'm just having a little meltdown is all. A tiny little meltdown. And with very good reason, I think!

'What are you talking about?' I ask, peering up at the small crowd of besuited people. 'Look, I've just had some bad news, okay? Sorry to be making such a fuss. I'll just go.' I stand up. 'You don't have to call the police! Talk about overdramatic.'

Lisa, the assistant, stands in front of me. 'Sit back down! You're not going anywhere. We know what you've been doing!'

'We all know,' Fake Chuck adds.

'The police are on their way,' someone in the crowd pipes up gleefully.

'Excuse me?' I stand up again and try to get past Lisa, but a few other people have joined her in an attempt to block me in. What the fuck is happening now?

A young man in a suit hurries over from a nearby office carrying a bunch of newspapers. 'This is you, is it not?'

Puzzled, I grab the papers off him. All of them are copies of a paper called the *New York Daily News*. I squint at the paper on top of the little pile.

'Ten per cent off at Patz Deli? Huh?'

I don't get it.

Lisa taps a manicured finger at a picture and small

column on the bottom left of the page. 'There! We know all about you.'

I look more closely at the newspaper and start splutter-coughing as I realise that the picture is a picture of me. In Gramercy Park. Unicorn horn atop my head.

Key Stolen in Gramercy Park reads the headline. I feel my cheeks flush. I quickly scan down the text. It's a report of a 'British girl with a pink fanny pack masturbating in Gramercy Park without a key'. And when confronted by a resident – one Elissa Johnson, a luxury mommy blogger – she stole a key from the local and ran away.

Oh my god.

I quickly pull out the next paper in the pile. There, again, in the bottom left corner, is another picture of me at the mailbox where I accidentally posted Birdie's letter. I'm clasping my pink bumbag to my chest. Next to me is the cop I ran away from and the dumb man who reported me. The headline here says '*Gramercy Park Thief Caught Stealing Mail*'. I read the accompanying text that outlines how I tried to groom a New York citizen into helping me to steal mail, then when confronted ran away again, escaping the cop who 'gave chase'.

What the hell? I wasn't stealing mail! I wasn't trying to *groom* anyone and that cop did not 'give chase'. And even worse, the picture is very obviously me. That beret, as it turns out, was not covering as many as my curls as I had hoped.

Right at the bottom there's a one-liner that suggests that the recent 'Watch me piddle' character in *Sunday Night Live* appears to be based on this 'Menace of Manhattan', as spotted by a waitress at Zabar's.

You've got to be kidding me!

I pull up the third paper and look at the bottom left corner.

It's another picture of me, taken when I was in Zabar's innocently trying to order a bagel with smoked salmon!

The headline here says: '*Menace of Manhattan pilfers hat from passerby.*'

Pilfers a hat? I've never pilfered a hat in my life! I read on, my eyes quickly skimming down the salubrious copy. Apparently I stole a hat from one Franklin Beckett.

'She whipped the beret right off the top of my head!' said Franklin, a 54-year-old saxophonist from Morningside Heights. 'And it was my favourite beret!'

'Outrageous!' I hiss at the newspaper, my hands trembling. 'That guy told me it *wasn't* his favourite beret! He sold it to me! I paid ten American dollars for it!'

This whole thing has become ridiculous. Now I'm the Menace of Manhattan? This is farcical. It can't be real!

'I need to leave,' I utter, trying to get past Lisa, Chuck Ellen and the mini barricade they've made.

'I'm sorry,' she says, arms folded. 'The police will be here any moment now. They'll know what to do with you. I knew you were a fake when you called us yesterday. Billionaires are *not* discreet.'

'You totally believed me,' I snipe back, feeling very angry indeed.

'Menace!' someone in the crowd heckles.

'Public fiddler!'

'Watch me piddle!'

These Wall Street people are horrible! They are properly ganging up on me! Ugh!

Two cops, one female and a male, push through the little crowd, looking slightly bored and unimpressed.

'What seems to be the problem here?' the woman policeman says.

I peek at her badge. Officer Parker.

'Officer Parker, there is an explanation for everything, I swear.' I hold my hands up in innocence. 'You've got to understand, these past few days have been a little tricky and everything is *not* as it seems.'

'Wait…' the male cops says slowly, leaning forward to get a proper look at me. 'I know you! You're the Menace of Manhattan!'

'We thought it was her,' Lisa says superiorly. 'We restrained her for you.' She's sucking up to the cops like a real goody-two shoes. I should introduce her to Donna, they'd got along great!

'I am *not* a menace!' I protest. 'I am Olive Maudine Brewster. Fishmonger. From Manchester. God, This stupid city! It's been a nightmare from start to finish! I'm just trying to deliver a letter, that's all! I'm just trying to help my friend!'

Officer Parker grimaces. 'We don't take kindly to foreigners calling our city stoopid. New York is the best city in the world.'

'Yeah!' the crowd agree. 'Go Knicks!'

'Actually it is not,' I say, my temper now wildly out of control… 'That's so arrogant to say that. Have you been to all the cities? Have you? No. I bet you haven't.'

'Miss, did you expose yourself in Gramercy Park?'

'No! I was hitching my tights.'

'Did you steal mail from a public mailbox on 106th Street and West End Avenue?'

'No! I accidentally posted a very important letter. This letter!' I wave Birdie's letter in the air. 'I was just trying to get it back! Please. I really need to go. I have a flight at 3 a.m. and I really need to find a man!'

'Don't we all,' Fake Chuck mutters to himself wistfully.

'Miss, did you steal a Gramercy Park key?' the male officer asks.

Shit. I did do that. I could deny it but… That key is in my satchel right now. Wait… is it in the bum bag at home? Argh! What if they search me? Take all of my private belongings out of my bag one by one, in front of all of the eighty-fourth floor Chimes Investments. I can't have that happen. Oh god. There's a joint in there. Phyllis's joint! They can't find that. Maybe they'll let me off lightly if I'm honest about the key. Cut me a deal.

'Yes,' I say, looking down at my feet. 'And I am truly sorry. I panicked. I can give it back to you right now. And then you have to let me go! Seriously!'

Officer Parker snorts. 'We don't have to do anything.' She turns to the male officer. 'Let's bring her in.'

I look at the male cop's badge – Officer Gallo. And I can only watch as – oh shit – he magics up a pair of handcuffs and before I can even protest he's snapped them around my wrists.

'Olive Brewster, you are under arrest.'

CHAPTER TWENTY-FIVE

Text from Colin: Hey Olive! You didn't reply to my last text. Is all okay? I am hung-over after the beach party, but it is very warm today. Poolside chill-out day, methinks!

Text from Colin: What's your email address? I have some amusing memes I can send to you, if you like! I have a folder of them on my iPad :D :D

The thing they don't show in TV shows is that in addition to it being super nerve-wracking, getting arrested involves a whole lot of admin. There was a queue. Usually I love a queue. But this was the worst queue I had ever encountered. Really shit queue mates. The woman in front of me said she would perform some erotic poetry for ten dollars and then called me a 'sumbitch' when I declined the offer. The man behind me wanted to sell me meth and didn't mind if I paid him or not. He just wanted a buddy to do the meth with. And the man behind *that* man just kept yelling that he had to get home immediately because his baby iguanas needed feeding.

After booking me in, taking my prints, mugshot and all of my personal belongings – including, much to my humiliation – the joint that Phyllis gifted me earlier, I was taken to a holding cell. That's where I am right now.

In a jail cell. A freaking *jail cell.* I don't even know what's going to happen next! Do I get a lawyer? Are they going to make me wear an orange jumpsuit? Will the British Embassy be informed? I think I'm in shock. It all feels like a crazy scary trippy dream. This time last week my biggest worry, after Birdie, was the fact that Alex and Donna were making me move into the box room. And now… I am in jail! Sitting next to a woman who tells me her name is Mandy Banana and that I should not look her directly in the eyes because she will 'fuck a bitch up'.

Oh Jeeeeebus.

I sit huddled on the cold bench of the holding cell – one of those real American movie ones with actual bars – and I shake. My hands, my legs, my bum, my chin, my ears, probably. All of it is trembling. Because at each stage of the booking-in process I've tried to explain why I'm here and what I'm trying to do for Birdie. I don't want to play the 'my friend is dying' card, but I do it. And no one seems to care. All they care about is the fact that I am 'The Menace of Manhattan' and that I called New York stoopid.

Okay, so I have done some pretty menacing things over the past few days. But I didn't mean to. It was all accidental. I didn't *really* have any choice! And this is New York! A massive, bonkers city. There are worse criminals than me! Since I've been here I've seen a person not pick up their dog's turd. I've seen multiple people having road rage. I've even seen a man throw a frosted cronut at a sightseeing tour bus. What about those people? *Those* are the real menaces.

But the NYPD don't care when I inform them of this. I don't think it helps that my voice is very high-pitched and my face is as red as a cherry. They just tell me to be quiet and wait. Wait for what? I don't know.

I do as I'm told and end up sitting in the holding cell for two entire uncomfortable hours before it occurs to me that I'm allowed to make a phone call! That's the thing isn't it? One phone call!

I stand up from the bench, avoiding eye contact with Mandy Banana, and wobble over to the front of the cell, putting my hands around the bars.

'What now, English?' the officer at the desk asks without even looking up. He's been calling me English since I got here. He thinks it's funny or insulting or something. Little does he know that I quite like it. I've always wanted a nickname. In primary school I tried to get everyone to call me Olli, but it never took. I tried again in secondary school, urging people to call me Liv, but that never caught on either. I tried to get both Joans to call me 'Speedy Brewster' because I'm the fastest filleter on the team. But sadly it never happened. Since being in New York I've aquired two whole nicknames. The Menace of Manhattan and English. I definitely prefer the latter.

'I need to ask you something,' I say to the officer.

He sighs. 'What do you want, English? Why can't you wait patiently for your assigned legal counsel like Mandy Banana over there, huh? I just want an easy day. That's all I want.'

'I get a phone call, right?'

The officer looks up. He seems weary, his blue eyes tired beneath his grey eyebrows. He has a kind face, though.

'You didn't make your call yet?'

'Nope. I get a call, don't I?'

'Yes. Yes, you do.'

Yes! Aha!

The officer unlocks the cell, attaches a handcuff to my wrist, which he then clips to his own wrist, and leads me over to his desk, pointing at a cream-coloured desk telephone.

'I need my mobile,' I say. 'It has all my numbers in it!'

'You don't know any of your numbers by heart?' he says in disbelief.

'Of course not! Humans stopped remembering phone numbers with the invention of the smartphone.'

With another laboured sigh, the officer takes the phone and dials a number. 'Joyce? It's Officer Leeland. Can you bring Olive Brewster's smartphone please…? No, she doesn't remember her numbers by heart… I know. Thanks.'

Within a minute or so, a pretty, chubby woman arrives in the office with my phone. I reach out to grab it from her.

'Not so fast!' Officer Leeland says, taking the mobile before I can. 'You can tell me the name of the person whose number you want and I will find it.'

'I can't give you my passcode! I have private things on there!'

'Oh yeah?'

'Not, like, sexy stuff. Just… lists and reminders and notes and links to videos of dogs and cats being friends. Sometimes turtles.'

'I won't look at anything. But I'm afraid you can't have your phone back.'

'What do you think I'm gonna do?' I blurt. 'Text my way out of jail?'

My sarcasm does not sit well.

'You are arrested,' Officer Leeland says sternly. 'You do not get your mobile phone, capiche?'

I nod, willing my ratty temper to simmer down. Now is not the time to get snappy.

With Officer Leeland looking at me expectantly, I realise that I don't actually have a large pool of people to call. I'm in a different country after all. Then I get an image of Seth giving me his number in the hallway at Trickys this morning. He will help me! 'Seth,' I cry. 'Call Seth. It's in the contacts app, under Seth.'

'You don't say,' Leeland deadpans, pulling up the number and tapping it into his landline.

He passes the handset to me and I press it to my ear, my stomach flipping at a) the prospect of talking to Seth again after this morning's kiss fest and b) having to tell him I'm in freaking jail. Very attractive. Olive. Not that I *care* about how attractive he thinks I am.

Except I totally do.

Olive Brewster, you are a damn fool.

Seth's phone rings.

And rings.

And rings.

When it eventually disconnects, I panic.

'He didn't answer! My one phone call and he didn't answer! He doesn't even have a voicemail.'

And then, I can't help it, I burst into tears. What the hell will I do now? I only get one phone call and he didn't bloody answer! Oh dear.

'Calm yourself, English!' the officer says sternly. 'It's not true that you only get one phone call. That's just in the movies. We're not total monsters. Just call someone else already.'

A river of relief runs over me. But then it occurs to me… I don't have anyone else I *can* call. Birdie or Alex and Donna can't do anything from the UK. And I don't have Mrs Ramirez's number.

Officer Leeland is scrolling through my contacts list. 'You don't got many friends, huh?'

How rude. 'I have friends,' I say, blowing my hair out of my face. 'I'm *very* well thought of in Manchester, England.'

But the truth is I have a great friend. Birdie. And soon she'll…

Nope. Do not think about that. This is not the time to think about that.

'Anders von Preen?' Officer Leeland snorts. 'Sounds like a made-up name. You makin' yourself up some friends, kid?'

Anders! The hair-obsessed socialite of Gramercy Park…

I couldn't…

Could I? I've only met him once. And he was really very strange…

But I don't have many options here.

'You want me to call someone or not, English?'

'Call Anders von Preen,' I instruct Leeland with a firm nod.

So he does.

But to my dismay, Anders doesn't answer either! Unlike Seth, though, he does have a voicemail facility on his phone.

I leave a frantic, jumbled message asking Anders to please come to the precinct and help me.

When I've put the phone down, I look at Officer Leeland in despair.

'So what am I supposed to do now?'

'You wait for your assigned legal counsel, like I already told you,' he answers, leading me back to the holding cell.

'How long will that be? I have a flight back to the UK

in…' I look at the clock on the wall. 'Thirteen hours! And I still have to track someone down before then.'

He shrugs. 'It takes as long as it takes. New York is a very big, very busy city.'

'You don't say,' I snip back. I've never had such a quick temper before. But I guess if anything is going to bring it out of a person, it's this!

'Sit down and keep it down, English. Manhattan Menaces do not get to answer back to New York city cops, all right?'

With slumped shoulders and still trembling legs I shuffle back to the bench of the holding cell, sitting as far away as possible from Mandy Banana.

'You're the Menace of Manhattan?' Mandy asks, giving me a sidelong glance.

'Oh, um… Yeah, but it's all a mistake, I didn't—'

'So cool! You're, like, famous or something!' She scooches down the bench to sit next to me. I dare to make eye contact and see that her angry face has transformed into a smiling one. Up close I notice she has little freckles all over the bridge of her nose. I thought she was in her early thirties when I first saw her, but she must only be about eighteen or nineteen. I think it's all the eyeliner she's wearing. 'I've been reading about you on the New York Daily News blog. You're a fuckin' baller! Not the jerking off in public – gross – but they did you on *Sunday Night Live*, right? I love that show!'

Mandy Banana's voice has completely changed from rough and aggressive, to sweet and interested. She seems very impressed by me.

'W-what are you in here for?' I ask, still too afraid to look her directly in the eye. She might, frankly, still want to cut a bitch.

'I just stole my boyfriend's car. The douche has been

putting his dick inside the whole of the fuckin' east village. Dirtbag.'

'Ah.' I nod. Stealing her boyfriend's car. That's not *so* bad… not really. And the guy sounds like he deserved a bit of a spook.

Mandy nods. 'Yeah. Then I set fire to the car. I drove it to a parking lot and just set it off. It was a biiiiiig fire.' She looks psyched, her eyes staring wistfully into the distance. 'It was fuckin' beautiful.'

'*Oh.* Gosh.'

Car on fire. That's a little more serious then.

Mandy pulls her purple furry jacket a little tighter around her shoulders. 'The idiot won't be cheating again anytime soon.' She says to herself with a wry smile. 'That's for sure.'

'Wait… you're staying with him?' I ask in astonishment. 'What about all his, um, hoes in different area codes?'

Why did I just say hoes in different area codes? It sounded hip and cool in my head, the kind of thing Mandy might be impressed by, but out loud I sound like I learned all of my cool lingo from a sexist 90s dance movie. Jeez.

Mandy laughs and shrugs. 'I love him. I love him so much I could die, ya know?'

Wow.

I wonder what it's like to be so in love with someone that you completely lose your shit and set fire to their car?

I shake my head in wonder.

But then it dawns on me… I *do* know how it feels to be so head over heels about someone that you behave in ways you never thought you would. Because that's what I feel about Birdie. About our friendship. This whole thing, the depth of my feelings for her has got me losing my shit like I never have in my life. I mean, I'm in a jail cell for goodness' sake.

Despite my daunting situation right now, I feel a bubble of laughter bounce in my chest. The irony of it. All these years I've been avoiding men and sex and anything that might make me 'feel' too much because I so desperately wanted to keep a tight hold on my emotions. But here I am! In a freaking jail cell for Birdie!

I look over at Mandy beside me. 'I get what you mean,' I say to her, a small smile lifting the corners of mouth. 'Love can make you do some crazy things.'

CHAPTER TWENTY-SIX

Text from Alex: Really looking forward to seeing you tomorrow, sis. We've missed having you here!

'Oh Olive, you poor poor goose. You poor frightened trembling little goose.'

I wake up to the sound of a very thin, drawling voice calling me a frightened goose. My eyes flutter open and I'm peeved to discover that I am not on a sofa bed in the Upper West Side, but still in a jail cell, my head resting on the furry-coated shoulder of Mandy Banana who is lightly snoring beside me. I rub my eyes. Anders is in front of the holding cell, his horrified face poking between the bars. He's wearing a tight white T-shirt and baggy white jeans on his skinny frame. With his white blonde hair and pale skin, the effect is startling.

'I came as soon as I could,' he says, grasping onto the bars of the cell with a quiet drama. 'I had my phone turned off – I was dyeing hair extensions and I didn't want to be disturbed – it's a very particular process. Anyway I'm here now, you poor sweet jail kitten. I'm so glad you called me. Surprised – people never seem to call me again – but glad.'

'What time is it?'I ask, suddenly wide awake.

'It's 3 a.m,' Anders says, his perfect face looking not at all sleepy. 'How long have you been here? Don't worry. I'm getting you out.'

My stomach drops into my feet. 3 a.m.? My flight home is in six minutes. I've missed it. I've missed my way out of here. And I haven't found Chuck. And Seth probably thinks I stood him up! Why did I fall asleep? Why isn't my legal counsel here? What am I going to do now?

'No, no. no,' I mutter to myself. 'I can't have missed my flight.'

Officer Leeland appears behind Anders. 'You're a lucky kid, English. Your friend here has a hotshot lawyer. She's spoken to the prosecution office, they've deemed this a low-priority case and are choosing not to file charges.

I blink.

'You mean, I can leave? I - I can go?'

'Yup,' Officer Leeland says, unlocking the cell, and letting me out. 'English, you are free to go.'

* * *

In the cab, I tell Anders how and why I got arrested. He seems thrilled with the drama of it all. 'And there I was thinking you were such a meek little thing!' He's even more thrilled that a photo of me with hair styled by him has appeared in the *New York Daily News*.

When the taxi pulls up to my apartment building and before I can even open the car door, Anders has dived out and done it for me. I get the sense that, like me, he doesn't have many friends and that he's quite pleased to be the one helping me. Or maybe he is just being nice until he can knock me out and have his way with my hair. Only one way to find out.

Upstairs, I take out my key, as Anders shudders at the 'miniscule dimensions' of the vestibule. I just want to flop on the sofa bed, FaceTime Birdie, eat some comfort food and figure out what the hell I'm going to do next.

But as I open the door to my apartment I'm greeted by the sight of a young red-haired woman painting her nails on the futon. She jumps up in fright at our arrival.

'What the hell?' she yells, the little pot of pink nail polish tumbling off the futon and spilling onto the parquet floor. 'Who are you? How did you get in here?'

I frown as I take in the apartment. None of my stuff is here!

'Who are *you*?' I step inside and glance around. Where are all my belongings? 'I… this is my apartment,' I say. 'Where's my stuff?'

'Oh!' the girl's confused face relaxes into a smile. 'Oh, yeah. The doorman said you might turn up. Yeah, so this is my Airbnb now. I checked in half an hour ago. The super said you were supposed to have left by now. He was gonna take your belongings down to the basement but the woman in the apartment opposite said she'd look after it for you, that you weren't the kind of girl who left without saying goodbye. I guess she was right!' She turns to Anders. 'Nice jeans.'

'I know,' he says. 'Prada.'

I shake my head in disbelief. Now I have no place to stay? How the ham sandwich has everything gone so completely and utterly wrong! This is chaos! Bona fide chaos!

Anders following me, I hurry out across to Mrs Ramirez's place and give it a gentle knock. It's almost 5 a.m. Man, I hope she's an early riser. I feel like a dick for potentially waking her up, but what else am I supposed to do? I need my stuff. I need to change out of these stinky clothes ASAP.

Within a few seconds of me knocking, the door swings open. Mrs Ramirez stands there, fully dressed, her long hair damp.

'Ah, I knew you hadn't run away! Come in, dear.'

I walk into Mrs Ramirez's apartment, Anders close behind.

'I'm Anders von Preen,' he tells Mrs Ramirez. 'I rescued Olive from jail.'

'Jail? Ay no! I'm Mrs Ramirez,' Mrs Ramirez replies, leaning over to shake Anders' bony hand before hobbling back over to her armchair, hand rubbing her injured knee.

While they're making introductions, I notice that there, in the corner of Mrs Ramirez's flat, is all my stuff. Piled up in a jumbled, unorganised way, nothing in its place. And while ordinarily the sight of such disorder would freak me out, today it seems so inconsequential compared to what else is going on. Like the fact that I've completely failed Birdie and I have no earthly idea how I'm going to fix it!

'I need some air,' I mutter, leaving the room while Anders dramatically relays to Mrs Ramirez the story of how I ended up in jail.

Out in the hall, I get into the elevator and am about to press the button for the ground floor when I notice the button at the top. *Roof Deck.* Before I can psyche myself out of it, I place my finger on the button and push. If I'm about to call Birdie and let her know that I've not found Chuck, I can at least go and see the view from the roof like she asked. I can fulfil that promise to her. Even if it does scare the living shit out of me.

When the lift comes to a shuddering stop, I really really really want to press the button that will take me back down. But I don't. I exit the elevator, walk up the corridor towards a door marked 'roof' and, with trembling hands, I push it open. I'll just step out for thirty seconds, have a little peek at the view Birdie was so excited about and then get back inside to safety.

But what I see when I step out onto the deck makes me suck in my breath, my heart filling with wonder.

The early morning sun is rising in the cornflower blue sky, casting a pink, orange and yellow glow over the buildings so that they look almost golden. Stretched out ahead is acres and acres of greenery and the gorgeous, lush trees of Central Park, and beyond that is the shimmering silvery blue Hudson river set against everlasting skyscape. New York City is waking up right in front of me, getting ready for all of the amazing moments that are going to happen today.

I take a few steps forward and take a seat at one of the teal painted chairs set out for residents of the building. My legs are wibbly at the thought of being so high up. But I am okay. I breathe in and out through my belly. And it works. Everything is okay. I am safe on this seat. I am safe here in the sky.

A gentle breeze whips its way through my messy hair and my eyes fill with exhausted, overwhelmed tears. I look out over miles and miles of city and shake my head at its magnitude. In that moment it occurs to me that I'm probably safer up here than anywhere else in the world right now. Everything that could possibly go wrong here has done. And at the end of it all, I'm still going to lose my best friend. And I'm fucking terrified. That's the worst thing in the world. What else do I have to be afraid of? There *is* nothing else to be afraid of.

Before me, the sun bursts right out into the blue sky as if to say 'Here I am!' It's glorious.

Imagine if I had missed this.

Imagine if I had never got to see this because I wanted to stay in my safe little world.

Even from the other side of the earth, Birdie's making my life better.

I bite the corner of my lip, take my phone out of my pocket and FaceTime her.

Her face flashes up on the screen, bright and happy. 'Hello, my Brewster. What is happening? Ooh, where are you? Wait – why are you not on the plane?'

I swallow hard and take a deep breath.

'I have some bad news and some good news.'

Birdie nods, eyes widening. 'Go on.'

'Right. Well the bad news is that the man at Chimes Investment was not Chuck Allen. It was Chuck Ellen. With an E. Oh, and also I got arrested, spent the night in jail and missed my plane.'

Birdie's eyebrows shoot up so high they almost disappear into her hair. 'What the fuck? Olive! Oh my god. How? Why? WHAT?'

I tell her everything, unable to believe what is coming out of my mouth, that any of it actually happened. When I'm done, Birdie runs a hand through her cropped hair.

'Okay. That's enough, Olive. Come home immediately. Come home. Get a flight. I will book it now. Get here. Shit. I'm so sorry for sending you over there! It's my fault you've gone through all this. I thought that—'

'Hush!' I interrupt her. 'You haven't heard the good news yet.'

'What? What is it?'

I grin, my heart lifting. 'Number one, I am on the roof. And you were right. It is amazing. Scary, but not as scary as I thought. In fact, nothing that's happened has been worse than what I've imagined in my head. And number two, I'm going to find that elusive motherfucking Chuck Allen.'

Birdie shakes her head. 'Olive, listen, seriously, don't worry about it – we can—'

'NO. I said I was going to do it. I promised. And I'm going to do it. I just need a few more days. And I will back before your surgery, okay?'

Birdie looks panicked. 'But you got arrested? Your eyes look all wild and glinty. What about work? What about—'

'Don't worry!' I say with a laugh. 'Unclench, why don't you!'

Birdie presses her lips together, a delighted smile in her eyes.

'You're a nutcase, Brewster.'

'I fucking love you, Birdie.'

'I fucking love you too.'

'Good.'

'Good.'

'Good.'

'Stop saying "Good" and go find that elusive mother-fucking Chuck Allen already!'

'On it.'

Ending the call, I run down the stairs instead of taking the lift and burst into Mrs Ramirez's flat, where she's sitting in a chair looking very happy while Anders brushes her hair.

I put my hands on my hips.

'Right! I have no earthly idea where he is and I don't have long until Birdie goes for her big surgery and I have to be back in England. But I am finding Chuck Allen and you two are going to help me. I hope. Please?'

CHAPTER TWENTY-SEVEN

@ElissaJohnson

I just spoke with the police. They caught the woman who stole my key. The Menace of Manhattan. And they let her go!!!!! Not enough evidence, low priority apparently.

@ElissaJohnson

This is #outrageous. My word is not good enough evidence? This is not a #lowpriority to me.

@ElissaJohnson

They say she is on her way back to the UK and I will not have to worry about her anymore. But where is my key? What about my trauma?

@ElissaJohnson

I have not slept a wink since I caught her caressing herself right in front of me in #broaddaylight

@ElissaJohnson

Please RT this thread for awareness. Private NY parks should be peaceful, protected #safespaces for parkside residents. So, so important!

@ElissaJohnson

Why are people unfollowing me?

Within thirty minutes of making my grand statement, it occurs to me that the adrenaline kick I got from being on the rooftop has made me slightly delirious – because while my intent to find Chuck Allen holds true, my usual nature of thinking of all the logistics has failed me. What about my job? Where will I stay? How will I afford to get a later flight back? What about the fact that Birdie and I were supposed to do the Harry Potter Marathon this weekend? And what will Donna and Alex say?

'I have never met anyone who frets so much!' Mrs Ramirez says from where she's sitting in the front of the cab. At Anders' insistence, we're in another taxi, whizzing our way to his house to hold a planning meeting because he *couldn't bear to be in a room the size of his shoe closet any longer.* Mrs Ramirez agreed that moving to Anders' house was a very good idea, especially since her poorly knee had kept her indoors for weeks and she was desperate to get out.

'I am learning to be more relaxed,' I point out from my place in the back seat beside Anders. 'But these are genuine logistical points!'

'Everything can be fixed,' Anders says.

'Birdie can't,' I say sadly.

'Most things can be fixed.'

'Where will I stay?'

'With me!'

'I can't do that!' I get a vision of waking up in the night to find Anders standing over me with a bottle of Olaplex and some high-end cutting razor.

'It's no problem!' he drawls, as if my protest is out of politeness rather than fear.

'And I can't afford a flight back. Shit.'

'I have air miles!' Mrs Ramirez shouts out from her place in the front. 'I have travelled all over the world. Now I am too old, I have so many air miles saved that I can no longer use!'

'Are you sure?' I ask, leaning forward towards her seat in the front. 'That's too generous. I can't possibly!'

Mrs Ramirez waves away my protest. 'What else am I gonna do with them? I go on a flight these days and my knee joint swells up to the size of a Santa Claus melon!'

'Thank you! Okay… well… what about my job?'

The Joans have been so good to me, but they're not going to let me have time off indefinitely, after all, I am the best fish filleter in the Greater Manchester area.

'Just call them up, ask them for some more time!'

'But…' I start. My mind is so used to coming up with potential problems and worries that it feels weird not to have one immediately at hand.

Huh.

I take out my phone and call Taller Joan's mobile.

'Hello Joan's Fresh Fish.'

'Joan, it's Olive!' I say.

'Olive! It's Olive,' I hear her repeat, presumably to Tall Joan. 'We miss you! We can't wait to see you tomorrow and hear all about the Big Apple. Did you have a fabulous time? Did you meet anyone interesting?'

'Well, that's the thing… I'm kind of… still here.'

There's silence on the other end for a moment. Shit. She's mad. They're going to fire me and hire someone else. Someone with the name Joan who will fit in way better than I ever did.

'Ah…Is everything okay, Olive?'

'Yes,' I lie. 'I just… would you be really mad if I took another four or five days?'

I expect Joan to at least fuss a little, to verbally try to figure out how they'll manage, what cover they'll have, how they will cope without me. But instead, to my great surprise, she answers immediately.

'Of course, love! Take as long as you want! If you need to stay longer, you can!'

'Well Birdie's surgery is next Monday so I'll definitely be back by then.'

'Great!' Joan says brightly. 'No worries at all, my love.'

'Are you sure? I mean… Won't you struggle without me?'

'It must be costing you a fortune to call from Manhattan!' Joan says, seeming to avoid my question. 'Give us a bell when you get back, won't you?'

'Okay… See you then, I guess.'

'Yes. Yes. Must go, there's a customer. Bye love!'

Joan ends the call.

'You fixed it?' Anders asks as I stare at my blank phone screen.

'Yeah.' I reply with a slight frown. 'It was all… very simple.'

Somehow, a little too simple.

* * *

At Anders' house, we sit down in his grand living room, while his housekeeper, Jan, makes us all breakfast. I go for toast and hot coffee, Anders sips on a strong Bloody Mary and Mrs Ramirez – who cannot stop marveling at the size of Anders' place – opts for a stack of pancakes with bacon, maple syrup, and scrambled eggs.

'You only have one life to live!' she says, patting her stomach happily.

After breakfast, another coffee and a long, soul-cleansing shower in Anders' luxurious wet room, the three of us gather at the dining table. Mrs Ramirez is holding a notepad and pen. Anders is poised over his laptop, wearing a headset. I'm not sure the headset is even switched on, I think it's just for show.

We spend the next hour or so coming up with plans to get the word out about Chuck. All of Mrs Ramirez's ideas are small and sweet – hold a raffle, send out leaflets, put a notice up in the window of her local deli, she can email her online friends and see if anyone knows anything. All of Anders' ideas are outlandish and ridiculous – hire every billboard in times square and put up a picture of Chuck with the words 'Where are you Chuck?' or pay for a Kardashian to do a sponsored Instagram post asking for people to just 'keep an eye out'.

'Oh! You can get in touch with the man from *Sunday Night Live*,' Mrs Ramirez says. 'He has access to the biggest show in America. He *must* be able to help.'

'I don't think he has that much power there,' I say. 'He's a behind the scenes person.'

At the thought of Seth my stomach flips happily. I wonder how his audition went? I wonder if he's upset that I never turned up to his show last night? Is that why he hasn't texted? He thinks that I stood him up without any notice? Shit, he probably thinks I'm back in the UK!

'Surely he'll know some PR people, darling?' Anders says. 'The kind of people who know exactly what it takes to hire every billboard in Times Square.'

That's true – the Times Square thing is clearly ridiculous – nobody could organise that – but Seth might have some good contacts in publicity… People who can get the word out about Chuck in a large-scale way that's also affordable and efficient.

And… I should definitely call him anyway. I don't like the idea of him thinking I just ignored his invitation. Even it was because I was briefly incarcerated!

I quickly pick up my phone from the table and press Seth's number. There's no answer. And, of course, he doesn't have voicemail.

'No answer,' I grumble. 'He must be busy'

'Or he saw you were calling and decided to ignore it,' Anders points out with a sniff. 'People do that, you know?'

'He must be upset that you stood him up,' Mrs Ramirez adds. 'Being stood up for a date is terrible. It happened to me once. Back in nineteen ninety-two. I was backpacking Brazil and I was supposed to be having a date with a man I'd met. Marco, his name was. I'd met him that morning at the market. And when he didn't turn up I was devastated. I'd dressed up in a beautiful blue dress—'

'How was your hair styled?' Anders interrupts.

'Loose. It was even longer back then.'

Anders nods with approval, a nostalgic smile on his face, almost as if he'd been there in Brazil with Mrs Ramirez.

'Anyway, I waited. And I waited. I sat at the bar feeling sadder and sadder. I was *humiliated.*'

'That's awful,' I say. 'Oh man. I hope Seth didn't feel like that.' I dial his number again. 'I was in jail. And it wasn't a date. It was just a casual invite to see his improv troupe.'

'Do you know that for sure…'

'Well yeah. I live in England. He lives in New York. He stitched me up on television. He… he jumps queues. It can't have been an actual proper date…'

But that kiss…

'I haven't had a date in ten years.' Anders says wistfully.

'Outrageous,' Mrs Ramirez says. 'But you are so handsome.'

'I know,' Anders responds. 'Maybe too handsome.'

I stare at the pair of them, suppressing a giggle, and stand up. 'Guys, I'm going to go to Seth's work.'

'Aaah!' Mrs Ramirez sings with a smile. 'Good girl. Life is too short.'

'No. I mean… just… for the PR thing. Like you said, he probably has great… contacts.'

Anders and Mrs Ramirez stare at me like they don't believe a word I'm saying.

Fair enough.

I don't believe me either.

* * *

After a speedy Google to find out where the *Sunday Night Live* studios are located, I hail a cab and whizz my way to the famous Rockefeller Center in midtown Manhattan. It's one good-looking skyscraper. I recognise it from so many of my favourite TV shows and movies.

The area outside the entrance is teeming with tourists excitedly taking pictures.

'Tourists, right?' a woman in jeans and a leather jacket says to me, as we both try to push past the crowd in a bid to get to the entrance.

She thinks I'm a New Yorker? A little spark of pride flares in my chest.

'Right?' I reply with an eye-roll. 'Totally!'

I finally reach the entrance and push through the doors into a large, glossy lobby. I look up at the ceiling – it's painted with a giant elaborate image of some beefy naked guys holding up the ceiling. Wow. This place is cool! I'm impressed that Seth works here. It feels like the centre of something exciting.

I march over to the main lobby desk and inform the young man behind it that I'd like to see Seth Hartman at *Sunday Night Live*.

The man looks me up and down. In a positive way or a negative way, I do not know. I think I look quite nice today, though, in blue jeans and a soft navy blouse with a little bow at the collar. 'Is he expecting you?'

'No. Um. Can you just tell him it's Olive. And that I really need to talk to him.'

'Well, we don't usually…' Then the guy blinks, his mouth slowly dropping open. 'Oh my god, it's you. You're here? Oh wow!' He starts to laugh and clap his hands together gleefully.

The daftest thing about this scenario is that I can't be sure where this guy recognises me from: *Sunday Night Live* or the fact that I've been a running story in the *New York Daily News*. Dammit. I should have remembered to wear the beret!

'Wow. I'll call Hartman now,' the young man says, enthusiastically. 'It's the main writing day today so he might not have much time to see you, if any at all. But I will try!'

'I don't need long.'

'Wow.' He clasps his hands to his chest. 'How lucky you are to have been immortalised in a New York institution like *Sunday Night Live*. What a tale to tell, right?'

I smile and nod, a little thrown that this young person clearly thinks that being impersonated on TV is a good thing. Something I should be happy about. Even if it's as a nutter with a fetish for bathroom voyeurism. Huh.

The guy calls Seth and within five minutes he's there in

the lobby. Standing right in front of me. My breath catches in my throat.

God. How did I not realise right away how sexy he is? He is very, very sexy.

'Hello!' I say, my heart already beating a drum through my whole body.

'Olive. I thought you'd be back in the UK by now?'

'Nope. Still here.'

After an odd pause in which we just stare at each other's faces really intently, Seth shrugs. 'Uh, is there anything I can help with?'

He sounds oddly formal. Professional. Peeved?

'I didn't stand you up!' I blast out. 'I mean, you probably didn't even notice my absence at your show, either way, I'm—'

'I noticed, Olive,' Seth murmurs in a low voice, looking me directly in the eye in a way that makes my mouth salivate.

'Oh. Well, I have a good excuse.'

'You do?' He asks, curious, despite himself.

'Yeah. Yeah I do. I was arrested!'

Seth's eyes go all round. 'That's a pretty good excuse. I guess they caught you!'

'Wait… you know about the whole New York menace thing?'

Seth starts laughing, his eyes crinkling behind his glasses. 'We get sent the papers every week to use for our sketches. I saw all the articles yesterday morning. I was gonna show you last night, help you come up with an escape plan, but—'

'They caught me. And, for your information, I was *not* masturbating in Gramercy Park.'

'Shame.'

My body goes instantly hot. I get a vision of Seth in the *Atonement* library. I try my very best to act normal.

'I did steal a key, though.' I say coolly. 'And they found Phyllis's joint in my satchel.'

'And now you've missed your flight.'

A ghost of a smile flits across his face.

'Yep.' I take a deep breath. 'I've decided to stay for a few more days. The guy at the bank turned out to be the wrong Chuck.'

'Another Chuck? That's crazy.'

'I know. I lost my shit. I confessed that I wasn't really a billionaire looking to invest and they made a barricade and wouldn't let me leave. It was not cool. Anyway, I'm still hunting the real Chuck down. And I came here to ask you for your help with something.'

Seth looks up at the giant ornate clock on the lobby wall.

He smiles at me, all formality gone. 'Are you free for lunch now? We'd have to eat it in my office, but…'

'Yes!' I almost shout. 'Yes,' I repeat at a more reasonable volume.

Seth leads me across the enormous lobby, grabbing me a guest pass from the reception desk.

'I thought you'd stood me up.' He laughs as we head over to the lifts. 'I'm sorry you were arrested but, as excuses go, that's a pretty stellar one.'

The lift door opens and we step in. A large group of tourists shuffle in behind, squeezing us all up against each other like sardines.

Seth does a loud spluttery cough. 'Three days of this virus and no sign of it going anywhere!' Then he gives a huge, fake cough and then a really over the top fake sneeze. 'And a rash too! It itches! It *burns*!'

The cluster of tourists give Seth a horrified glance before hurrying right back out of the elevator and into the lobby. One even covers their nose and mouth in an effort to avoid his 'germs'.

I can't help but laugh as the lift doors close and Seth gives the tourists a friendly goodbye wave.

Now it's just me and him here in the lift.

Alone.

Seth takes a step towards me.

'Fuck, I'm really glad to see you again,' he says, his voice so low I can barely hear him.

And before I can respond that I'm glad to see him again too, he's kissing me, his hands lacing up into my hair, his nose pressing against mine, my hand under his T-shirt running across the smooth hot skin of his broad upper back.

I don't have much experience of kissing, but with Seth, it feels like I'm doing it exactly right. Like I'm an expert kisser. Like if there were an annual convention of kissing, I would be appearing on a panel of some sort to instruct other people how to do it this perfectly.

My body zings with nerves and emotions and feelings, every hair on my body stands on end. I can't control it. Not one little bit. And right at this moment, that's absolutely fine by me.

CHAPTER TWENTY-EIGHT

Text from Colin: How was your flight back? Are you glad to be back in Manchester? I'm looking forward to coming home. It's a little hot out here! And I'm really looking forward to our date! Are you?

Text from Alex: If you need to stay longer, you need to stay longer! Fine by me. It sounds like a real adventure. I'm proud of you. Don't stay too long though, haha. I miss you! It's… different in the house without you here. Lots of love sis x

Text from Donna: Hi Olive! Hope all well! Make sure you give Alex plenty of notice when you want collecting from the airport so he can make plans accordingly. He was in the car about to set off to pick you up when he got your text. Just thought you should know! All best x

After a make-out session that lasts the duration of the lift ride up to the twenty-fifth floor of the Rockefeller Center (apart from between floors fifteen and twenty when some other people got on and we had to try to keep our hands off each other), we reach the *Sunday Night Live* floor. I step out into the carpeted corridor and wait for the icky sense of panic I would ordinarily get from being on such a high floor. And while it's definitely there, a little fizz of unease in my belly, it's nowhere near as bad as it was. After being on the roof this morning, and experiencing such a peaceful, gorgeous moment up there, it doesn't feel quite so scary to be this high up.

Moreover, any panic I do feel is overtaken by a massive sense of excitement. Is it possible for creativity to be airborne? It feels almost buzzy with expectation, just in the corridor. The walls are lines with framed pictures of movie stars, huge name comedians and musicians who have appeared on the show.

'Oh my god, it's Steve Martin!' I say, pointing at one of the pictures. 'And there's Goldie Hawn! Ooh, look it's Britney Spears! Argh Chris Rock, I love him!'

Seth laughs. I bet everyone he's ever brought up here does the exact same thing. I don't care if I look uncool though. This is well exciting!

We turn a corner and walk into an office. It's a tiny office but with an incredible view of the Empire State Building. Woah.

Seth invites me to sit in the office chair. He perches on the end of his desk.

'Oh, hey, did you hear about your audition yet?' I say. 'I can't believe I haven't asked. How did it go?'

Seth grins. 'It went really well. They loved the whole John Malkovich bit you wrote. It killed.'

I feel a pleasant warmth in my cheeks. I like being referred to as someone who 'wrote' a joke. It sounds so cool and crazy and badass!

'I should hear this week actually,' Seth continues, picking up a guitar pleck from the desk and turning it over in his hands. 'I don't know... there were a lotta people going up for it this year.'

Standing up from his desk, he heads over to a mini fridge in the corner. He opens it up and pulls out a huge takeaway container. He carries it back to the desk, opening a drawer and taking out two plastic forks from a packet full of plastic cutlery.

'I hope cold chicken avocado pasta is okay?' he asks. 'It's from this amazing deli down the road. I'm addicted.'

'It smells dreamy,' I say, grabbing a fork and helping myself to a mouthful.

'So, what can I help you with?' Seth asks, also tucking in.

I explain about how me and two friendly randos I have met in New York are trying to get the word out about Chuck in an effort to find him before I go back for Birdie's surgery. I ask Seth about the TV studio PR people and if they'd be willing to give us some tips for getting the word out.

'Absolutely!' Seth says. 'And I'll help all I can. I'll be working most days and some nights, but anything I can do.' He puts on a weird ET voice. 'I'll be... right... here.'

I hold my finger up and he presses his finger against it.

Then Seth leans forward, our noses almost touching and just smiles at me for a long moment.

Holy cow, he is sexy. He's so confident in his skin and laid-back and... *sexy*.

Seth's phone beeps with an alarm. 'Shit. Time flies like an arrow. I've gotta get back to work.'

'You set an alarm?' I ask incredulously. 'You laid into me for doing that at Trickys!'

Seth's face pinkens a tad. 'Everyone here gets mad at

me for being so late all the time. I… decided to take a leaf out of your book.'

'Next stop, a five-year plan,' I tease.

'Never utter those words in my presence again.'

I laugh. His pure abhorrence for any form of rigidity still seems utterly bonkers to me. But with arms like that. And legs like that. And eyes like that. And a tongue like that, it hardly seems important.

Seth looks thoughtful for a moment. 'Do you think you could stick around for another couple of hours? I've got a two-hour writers' pitch meeting – why don't you sit in on it, and when it's done I can introduce you to Sharon who runs PR for the show. She can give you some tips, some local media contacts and help you come up with a plan.'

A pitch meeting? Aren't TV writing rooms sacred spaces? And he's inviting me to watch? My heart leaps like I am a ten-year-old and it's Christmas morning. I'm a little surprised by how interesting the prospect of watching joke pitching sounds to me. But now that he's suggested it, I know that there is nothing else I would rather do for the next two hours. Anders and Mrs Ramirez are back at Anders' house making leaflets and doing internet research. And if I have to wait to see the PR woman anyway…

'What do you say?' Seth asks, grabbing a bottle of water from his desk, taking a long swig and grabbing the carton of pasta to take along to the meeting.

'I say yes please. Very much yes please.'

'Okay then! Let's go!'

* * *

The sensation of delight I'm getting, purely by being in a place so full of comedy legend and history, is getting bigger and more intense, until I'm so full of glee I legit worry I'm about to explode with it!

I'm seated at a large round table with around ten writers. After they ribbed me about the whole Watch Me Piddle thing, I curried their respect by ripping right back into them about 'maybe learning to create original characters'. I pulled up all my courage, lifted my chin and told them in no uncertain terms my propensity for piss play was no longer available for creative fodder but that they were welcome to use my desire to only make love to men dressed up like giant hot dogs. That, to my delight, made them properly laugh and I was welcomed into the fold.

Now, I watch in astonishment as these people invent sketches and jokes out of thin air! The energy is crazy. Everyone is laughing, no one seems scared to say the wrong thing and if they do say something unfunny everyone boos them – but it is a sort of playful, non-dickish way. And when someone picks up on the idea of a joke that the team likes, they develop it and riff with each other until the joke becomes progressively tighter and funnier. It's fascinating.

I watch, captivated as the sketch ideas go from rough, vague jumping-off points to fully fledged ideas with solid characters and catchphrases. Tomorrow all of the ideas will be presented to the executive producer of the show, the cast and the celebrity host. Then only a few will get chosen to air.

Seth comes up with a sketch idea that everyone likes. It's a parody commercial, advertising an invention for the socially awkward. The invention is for a food postbox that enables people to get takeaway delivered without having to interact face to face with another human. It's really weird and funny. His delivery is dry and relaxed and the rest of the writers clearly love him.

'What do you think?' he turns to me. I give him a

thumbs up. There's no way I would make a suggestion in a room like this, full of experts and people who are actually funny. I couldn't…

'Would you change anything?' Seth asks.

I shake my head. 'No!'

'Come on! If you *had* to change something, what would it be?'

I look at the table, my heart pounding. 'Um, well, I don't know… maybe it could be more specific. Like, a slot in the door just for pizza,' I say quietly. 'Like a tiny, narrow slot that would be useless for any other food except pizza. Not even pizza in a box. Just, like, unboxed pizza.'

Seth nods. 'Yeah. I like it. It's ridiculous.'

'You could call it Pizza Flap?' I add, which gets a huge laugh around the room. The sound of it ringing out and echoing around me makes my heart sing in a way I've never experienced before.

Seth gives me a huge grin.

'Where did you find her?' one of the other writers asks and I turn red with pride.

When the writing session is over, I'm buzzing with my tiny, tiny contribution and the fact that, no word of a lie, that past couple of hours was the most fun I think I've had in my entire life. I can't believe that somebody gets to do that for their actual job. It makes no sense. I've never really minded my job at Joan's Fresh Fish. I mean, I've never loved it, but it's been, you know, sufficient. But that? Seth gets paid to do that? No wonder he's so chilled out and confident all the time. He gets paid to have the most fun that anyone could possibly have. For a brief moment I picture myself getting up in the mornings, going to work somewhere where my entire job would be to write things to make people laugh.

My heart pangs with longing.

* * *

Seth's friend Sharon – the PR woman at *Sunday Night Live* – turns out to be the blonde woman I saw him with that day when I collared him for writing about our humiliating airplane dalliance. She's lovely and clever and super attractive. I wonder if she's the 'blondie' ex that Phyllis was referring to… She's so put together, so confident and sure and at ease with herself. Basically the opposite of me.

She's really keen to help with the cause and not only does she give me personal mobile numbers of people at local radio and news outlets, but she also says that she will send a tweet out from her personal Twitter account, which – she tells us proudly – has over twenty-thousand followers. I thank her profusely and in response she lays her head onto Seth's shoulder.

'Any friend of Hartman's is a friend of mine,' she grins. He doesn't seem particularly comfortable with the exchange and steps out of the way so that Sharon's head is left sort of dangling where Seth's shoulder once was.

Yes. Those two have definitely done sex together. I am alarmed at the spike of jealousy that flies through me. I haven't felt jealous of anyone or anything in years. Ugh. It's horrid, all burning and ragey. Ew! I do not like! I try my best to shove it aside and tell Sharon that I'll keep her updated with the search.

'I'll be writing all night tonight, but can I see you tomorrow night for dinner?' Seth asks as he walks me out of the Rockefeller Center.

'Yes,' I say at once.

'Awesome. I know a great place near Gramercy. I'll pick you up at eight.'

As I hail a cab, he leans in and I think we're going to start snogging again, right in the middle of the street, but instead he kisses me softly on the cheek and it makes my insides flip.

I grin at him and he grins at me.

'WATCH ME PIDDLE!'

I look up to see a group of *Sunday Night Live* fans, outside the building, pointing at me and snapping pictures. 'ENGLAND IS SOOOOO AMAZING!' they giggle. I think of what the guy at the Rockefeller reception said about how many people would love to be immortalised on a show that big. Even if it is for entirely nefarious reasons.

And these people taking pictures. They seem really happy to see me. They're laughing and smiling and waving. And for someone who, until this week, has gone pretty unnoticed in the world, it's a damn nice feeling.

CHAPTER TWENTY-NINE

Text from Birdie: A date! A real live date!

Text from Olive: It's not a date. It can't possibly be. We live in different countries. What would be the point?

Text from Birdie: Fair enough. But you could have a fling with him? If you fancy him that much it would be a great way to dip back in, so to speak! If it's not good it doesn't matter because you'll be back in Manchester soon, far far away!

Text from Olive: I do fancy him... I finally get what all the fuss is about. My loins are gagging for him.

Text from Birdie: Haha. Also, that's gross. Text me later. Doctor BJ just came in for his rounds and he's wearing a shirt with SHORT SLEEVES. He might be

too much of a professional to get it on with a sexy patient but that doesn't mean I can't do some high-quality ogling.

Text from Olive: He's a fool for not crossing the boundaries of patient-doctor relationships with you. A fool to resist you! A damn fool! Also do you know how much I love you? I miss you and I love you and I think you are amazing and brave and pretty and smart and cool and strong. Just thought I would tell you that.

Text from Birdie: Gush much?

Text from Olive: Shuddup. I love you, all right.

Text from Birdie: Not as much as I love you.

I wake up the next morning with a brand new feeling in my stomach. It's a feeling I've not had before, at least not that I can properly remember. Maybe I had it when I was in school – when I did my creative writing lessons and the teacher said I'd done well. Or maybe the day I met Birdie and we talked for six hours straight. I'm not sure. Either way, it feels entirely unfamiliar. Like everything is in colour. Like everything is louder and crisper and more and less terrifying all at the same time.

Like I'm alive.

After showering in Anders' wet room, stocked with as many Sisley products as I could ever hope to see and white towels that are as soft as puppies, I pull on my jade-green long-sleeved jersey dress, and head downstairs to the kitchen. Anders is already sitting at the large white marble table, Mrs Ramirez sitting right up next to him. The pair of them are hunched over a laptop, chattering away.

'You're here already?' I remark to Mrs Ramirez. 'Thank you! That's so kind of you.'

'Anders here had a car sent for me,' Mrs Ramirez says proudly. 'Not a cab. A *car*.'

'Of course,' Anders says with a benevolent smile on his tranquil face. 'You have to take care of that knee.'

I give them a curious look. They appear to have made firm friends. I'd never have put them together in a million years. But they seem completely relaxed in each other's company, Anders not quite as stiff and sinister-seeming as he was the day I met him.

'Why are you staring at us?' he asks.

'Come on!' Mrs Ramirez claps her hands together. 'We have work to do!'

Over three hundred brightly coloured leaflets are printed off, showcasing a close-up picture of Chuck's head from the old photo that Anders kept from college. The text at the top of the leaflet asks, 'Where In The World is Chuck Allen?' And below that there's the number (of a burner phone that Anders has acquired for the occasion) for people to call if they have any information.

We spend the rest of the morning walking all over Manhattan, giving out leaflets to everyone we see, asking shops, cafes and delis to display them in their windows. It takes us a little longer than anticipated: Mrs Ramirez's bad knee slows us down a tad, but mostly, we're held up because she wants to know the life story of everyone we meet and ends up exchanging phone numbers with around half of them. I've never met anyone who makes friends so easily. I don't know what we'd have done without her actually. I reckon Anders' ghostly aristocratic presence either intimidates or terrifies most people (I'll go for terrify), and me? Well I am polite and awkward and British. Not exactly great for getting busy New Yorkers to stop and talk to me.

Mrs Ramirez returns to the Upper West Side after lunch so she can take her usual siesta, while Anders and I head back to his place. While he slides off to do a yoga session in his home gym, I shoot off a bunch of emails to all the media contacts Sharon gave me. *Immediately* after sending them I refresh my emails about five times in the hope of speedy replies. The thought of going on the radio makes me want to burrow down into a hole of my own making, but I can't deny that the opportunity to reach people on a national level, to really have a great shot of finding Chuck, is too amazing to not completely go for.

When I FaceTime Birdie to update her on our progress, she answers not with her usual bright smile, but with tired, teary eyes.

'What is it? What's wrong?' I say at once, my chest tightening.

Birdie sighs, rubbing her hand across her face. 'I shouldn't have answered. I'm sorry. I'm not having a great day. I'm tired and achy. I feel rotten.'

'Oh Bird. Tell me. What's happening? How can I help?'

Birdie looks up into the screen. 'I'm just… I'm scared today. I'm really fucking scared. I'm fine most of the time. I know what's going to happen and I've made my peace with it. But today… I feel terrified.'

My eyes immediately sting with tears. Birdie always puts on a brave face about her situation. Through the surgeries and tests, through the hopes that they would find a way to fix her, and the disappointments when they couldn't. She's always always been stoic.

This is new. My heart cracks. I wish I was there with her right now.

'Tell me,' I say. 'Let's talk about it.'

Birdie fiddles with her earlobe and exhales through her cheeks, making a sound like a horse. 'I just keep thinking. What if, when I'm gone, no one remembers me?'

I almost laugh, it's so outrageous.

'That will never happen.' I say firmly. 'How could anyone forget you? You're literally unforgettable.'

Birdie half smiles. 'You won't forget me will you?'

'Are you for real? I could never forget you. There are some things about you I wish I *could* forget. Like your crap taste in music and the time you considered becoming vegan. But that shit's sticking around forever, dude.'

Birdie nods. 'Good.'

'And I will tell everyone I ever meet about you, for as long as I'm lucky enough to be walking this earth. I will bore them *silly* with stories of you and how amazing you are, how everyone who meets you falls in love with you—'

'Except Dr BJ.'

'Yes, except that fool Dr BJ.'

'Damn fool.' A small smile tugs at the corner of Birdie's mouth. That's better.

'Damn *fool*. Then I'll show them photos upon photos of you and all the wonderful times we've had together. It will be intense, Birdie. People in the street will start to avoid me in case I collar them to talk about you. They'll be like, "There's that curly-haired girl obsessed with Birdie Lively! I didn't think she had any more Birdie stories to tell us! But, oh boy, she does! She has never-ending Birdie stories!"'

Birdie laughs. 'Will you show them videos of me too?'

'I will make a fucking reel of them. And set them up on one of those projector thingies. I will project the videos of you onto Manchester Town Hall. It will be like an art installation. It will be a veritable fucking Birdie Fest.'

'Okay.'

'Okay.'

Birdie yawns. 'God, I'm really tired.'

'Have a nap.'

She nods, her voice going small. 'Will you stay on FaceTime. Just until I fall asleep? I just…'

'It would be my pleasure.'

As Birdie's eyes drift close, her breathing settling into a steady rythym, I watch her. Not in a creepy way. Just in a way that allows me to memorise every inch of her face. Which I guess sounds a little creepy. But I don't want to forget a thing.

I sigh, utterly full to the brim with adoration for this American livewire. And completely heartbroken that, in the not too distant future, she'll only be alive in videos and stories and dear, dear memories.

I lean down and whisper into the phone, into her dreams.

'Birdie, Lively, You will *never* be forgotten.'

* * *

Later, when Birdie is deep in Naptown, Snoozeville, I check my emails for any response on the Chuck search. But there's zilch. I turn the burner phone on and off a few times, just to make sure it's working properly. It is. And no-one has called.

Anders returns from his workout session, holding a black briefcase an excitable glint in his eyes. Hope blooms in my chest. Has he found something?

'Hair time!' he says.

Oh. Yeah. I agreed that in exchange for letting me stay here he could do my hair once a day.

He opens the briefcase onto the dining table to reveal that it is actually a briefcase full of hairdressing tools, gleaming like chef's knives. Wow. He means business. What have I let myself in for?

'I… can we do it tomorrow?' I ask. 'I'm, um, going for dinner tonight.'

'With the comedian?' Anders says, raising an eyebrow. From the way he says it, I can't tell if it's derogatory or complimentary. 'All the more reason to have a little pampering!'

I suspect our definitions of 'pampering' differ, somewhat.

Crap. I can't go to dinner with another unicorn horn.

'You promised,' Anders scolds. 'That was the deal, darling?'

He's right. I did promise. And Olive Brewster doesn't break her promises. Whatever he does to my bonce is going to have to stay like that for my date – I get the feeling that taking it out beforehand will hurt his feelings. And I definitely don't want to do that.

'Okay… Can… you keep it subtle?' I ask. 'Like, no structures. Bouffants or… horns.'

Anders shrugs a bony shoulder. 'I'm an artist, Olive. I do what the muse tells me to do. Do you not trust me, after all we've been through?'

'Um… I don't know you that well!'

'Yet you stay in my house, accept my hospitality.' He sniffs, looking hurt. 'Call *me* to rescue you from incarceration. I think we know each other well enough.'

'You're right,' I say. If it weren't for Anders, who knows what would be happening to me in jail right now. 'I'm sorry. Go for it.'

He licks his lips, pulls out his scissors and snaps them together in a way that looks entirely menacing.

Here goes.

* * *

Two hours later and Anders blasts my hair with a mist of extra-super-strength hairspray. Once again he has not allowed me to peek at the work in progress, which means that my bum has been glued to this chair for all that time and now I have a numb butt cheek, which I didn't even realise was a physical possibility. But it is. It really is.

I hobble across the parquet floor as Anders proudly leads me to the hallway mirror.

My shoulders hike up to ears, in anticipation of the possible monstrosity he has concocted atop my head. What will it be this time? Medusa style snakes? A ginormous mohawk? Antlers?

And then I see myself.

Oh wow.

Wow.

I look like me. But a polished, put together, confident, sexy version of me. Anders has waved and brushed my hair so that the curls are big and uniform, one half of my hair across my face, almost obscuring my eye, and the other side tucked behind my ear with a hidden clip. I'm practically a Hollywood starlet!

I shake my head in disbelief and look closer. There are shiny copper strands subtly laced throughout the do. They catch the light when I turn my head!

'How…?' I ask, putting a delicate hand to my hair. I vetoed any use of hair dye… But these strands of copper are astounding – they brighten my entire face!

'Extensions!' Anders declares, a huge grin stretched across his normally motionless face. I don't think I've ever seen him look so delighted. He looks crazy. But in a good, happy way.

'How the heck did you do that?' I ask. 'I can't see where you've added them? It looks like my own hair!'

'I've bonded them at the root. It's all very understated, like you asked.' He rolls his eyes. 'And you can take them out later.'

I've had the same hairstyle my entire life. I've never wanted to risk changing it in case it didn't suit me and I couldn't change it back. But this is epic. I don't look like oddball Olive, fastest fish filleter in the north anymore. I look like… I look like I belong in New York City.

I spin around and pull Anders into a hug. His lanky body stiffens – I wonder how long it's been since he had a genuine hug? I squeeze him a little until he relaxes. He hugs me back.

'You are talented,' I tell him with a grin. 'And your college room-mate, Warner, was it? Well, he totally missed out not getting those fiery red locks cut by you.'

'Really?' Anders says, cocking his hip to the side. 'Do you think?'

'Yeah!' I nod emphatically. 'This is the best my hair has ever looked. I love it. Thank you.'

Anders takes a deep breath, his eyes filling with tears. He flaps his hands in front of his face like a pageant winner. 'I think this is what happiness feels like, Olive,' he says. 'I've taken every drug that has ever been invented, dined at the finest restaurants the world has to offer and been blown by the sultriest male models of New York, Paris and Tokyo. But a happy hair client… there's nothing like it.'

And then he bursts into joyful laughter, pulling his phone out of his pocket and taking pictures of my hair from every angle.

'So much better than doing it on a mannequin!'

I laugh out loud at his laughing.

He may be the weirdest person I've ever met. But he's definitely growing on me…

CHAPTER THIRTY

Text from Birdie: Thanks for before, Brewster. Feeling a bit brighter after a long nap xxxx

Text from Birdie: Also: Good luck tonight. Don't put too much pressure on yourself. If you don't feel ready to DO IT, you don't have to! And if you do feel ready, for the love of Tina Fey USE PROTECTION. This has been a public service announcement.

Text from Birdie: ALSO remember everything. I want to know it all. ALL.

Seth picks me up at eight as promised. When Anders' doorbell goes, my forehead immediately breaks out in a light sweat. I'm nervous. But not in the all-encompassing way I have been so many times before. In an excited way.

After much discussion with Anders, I've decided to wear my lucky red tea dress. Lucky because I once found a two-pound coin on the street in Saddleworth and what was I wearing at the time? Oh yes. The red tea dress. As I fastened on the only bra that looks good underneath it, I felt very justified in bringing fifteen bras for what was supposed to be a five-day trip.

I don't *really* know how to do make-up and I don't like the feel of it on my skin, so I just curled my eyelashes, combed my unruly brows into submission and dabbed on some cherry-coloured lip-stain to match the dress. I don't wear high heels – the possibilities for falling over a bump in the pavement and breaking my leg are too much to contemplate – and so I wear my favourite chunky Doc Martens. I'm not sure they go with the tea dress but Anders told me it looks very 'Drew Barrymore.' Which I take as a compliment. I like Drew Barrymore. I like the way her mouth moves when she talks.

'Hey, girl,' Seth greets me in a daft voice when I open the door. He coughs straight after he says it and it strikes me that maybe he's a bit nervous too. The thought makes my shoulders drop comfortably. If confident, chilled Seth is feeling a bit nervy about this dinner of ours, then it's not just me being a fusspot.

He's noticeably made an effort and it takes all of my effort not to dive on him right there on the stoop. Instead of his usual T-shirt and hoodie he's wearing a white linen shirt with the sleeves rolled up to reveal lightly tanned, capable-looking forearms, and new-looking dark blue jeans. He leans in to kiss me on the cheek and I get a whiff of his lovely cologne. It smells like wood and figs and grown-up man. The scent sends a tingle of lust right through me.

Man, oh man. How the hell do people cope feeling this feeling and reining it in? How do horny people make it through the days without feeling themselves up the whole time just to keep the randiness at bay?

'Hey, boy,' I respond in the same daft voice and step out the door into the balmy spring evening. Just as I'm about to close the door behind me, Anders runs towards me out of nowhere, carrying his tin of hairspray like a weapon. He liberally spritzes it over me, causing all three us to cough dramatically.

'Apologies!' Anders says. 'I didn't think it would come out that rapidly.'

'Anders, this is Seth Hartman. Seth, this is Anders von Preen.'

Anders nods regally, one eyebrow raised, while Seth gives Anders a friendly, slightly befuddled handshake.

'I'm Olive's dear friend,' Anders says territorially. He crosses his arms and lowers his voice dramatically. 'If you hurt one hair on her head I will find you… It took me a long time to get it to shine like that.'

I laugh so that Seth knows that Anders isn't being serious (although I suspect he is) and shoo him inside, instructing him to call me if we get any important news regarding the search for Chuck. It's been nearly twelve hours and we've had zero responses. But I'm still hopeful. I've brought the burner phone with me, so I'm fully available if anyone calls.

As Seth and I walk down the glittering Manhattan street towards the restaurant Seth has chosen – The Bistro on Irving Place – we don't really say much. We just keep looking at each other and bursting into laughter, although nothing that funny is happening.

The restaurant is only a few minutes away yet it's a world away from Trickys. I walk in first, Seth behind me, and my heart dips at how lovely and pretty it is. It's busy, but in a quiet, gently buzzy way not in an overwhelming crowded way. The walls are all dark wood, the ceiling is strung with hundreds of tiny lanterns, and all the tables are intimate and private so that all conversation is strictly between you and your dinner guest.

This is not just dinner. This is a *date*. I'm on my first ever date!

Once we're seated, we order drinks – sparkling water for me – I have lots more Chuck searching to do tomorrow and need to keep a clear head – and a glass of merlot for Seth.

I take my phone out of my bag and quickly press refresh on my email. I don't mean to be rude, but, as I've already explained to Seth, I need to be completely present and ready for any Chuck-related news. I'm desperately hoping that one of the gazillion leaflets we sent out will lead to information soon. Impatiently, I wait for my inbox to load and feel a thud of disappointment when I see nothing about Chuck and nothing from any of the radio stations I contacted. All that trickles in is an offer to upgrade my Still Minds app for a discounted price. Masking my frustrated sigh as best I can, I put my phone away and once we've got our drinks, Seth lifts up his glass.

'I've got some great news. I… got the job!' His turquoise eyes glint with pride. 'I'm gonna be a cast member on *Sunday Night Live*!'

'Oh my goodness!' I jump out of my seat, my knee bumping into the table and making everything atop it wobble precariously. 'Wow! Come here!'

Despite my own dramas right now, I could not be happier for Seth. What an incredible thing for him to have achieved!

He stands up and does an adorable 'aw shucks' shrug. I give him a hug, my head barely reaching his chest. Would it be appropriate to just stay here for the rest of the night? Would it be terribly impolite to just unbutton a button on his shirt and maybe have a little lick of his chest. Right here in the restaurant.

Get a grip, Olive!

I reluctantly pull away. 'That's amazing, Seth! Actually incredible!'

He laughs as we sit back down. 'I found out this afternoon. It's going to be announced formally tomorrow and I'll be introduced on the live show this Sunday night.'

'Formally announced?' I ask.

'So, the press release will go out tomorrow and it should make *Deadline* and *Variety* as well as the comedy blogs. This dumb face is gonna be everywhere.' He points at his face and does a gormless expression. 'And then on Sunday night, I'll appear on the live show with the host. I'll be introduced as the new featured cast member, and then I'll actually start appearing in sketches next week.'

'Woah!' I shake my head. 'Are you nervous?'

'No,' Seth says, taking a sip of his wine. 'I'm fucking terrified.'

'You will be brilliant. Holy moly. Are you going to be famous now, then?'

'Little bit, yeah.' He sniffs and brushes some imaginary lint off his shoulder. 'I'll have to start wearing sunglasses indoors and shit. Drinking green juices, getting manicures, working out so I'm camera-ready.'

I have a little daydream of Seth working out. All sweaty. No top on. No bottoms on either, come to think of it. He still has his specs on though. Like a naked, cocky Clark Kent, lifting dumbbells. Maybe in the library from *Atonement*. Yes. Perfect. I feel like a cartoon wolf about to do a howl. I do not howl, though. This is a nice restaurant and if I'm going to start feeling these smutmuffin feelings I'm going to have to learn to control them at least a little. Instead of howling, I quip, 'Good idea. Everyone knows they don't let you on TV if your cuticles are ragged.'

Seth wiggles his eyebrows excitedly. 'Hey, maybe the woman who owns my local deli will finally remember my name. She's been calling me Ted for three years. I correct her every time I go in there. And I go in there a lot – they do the best soup in Manhattan, you have to try it – but it's like she decided I look more like a Ted than a Seth and opted to stick with that.'

I raise my glass of water. 'To Ted, featured cast member on *Sunday Night Live*.'

Seth raises his wine glass. 'And to Olive Brewster, without whom my John Malkovich impression wouldn't have knocked anyone's socks off.'

We eye one another, grinning madly as we toast. That I might have had a tiny something to do with him getting his dream job is a really great feeling.

'Seriously, Olive,' Seth says putting his glass back onto the table. 'I'm not trying to flatter you, but you have a natural ability for it. The team were really impressed with your input at the writers' meeting.'

I feel my cheeks turning red with pleasure. 'I barely did anything.'

'Of course you did. Pizza flap?' He pulls a face and slides his glasses up his nose. 'I mean, who comes up with pizza flap?'

'I had the best time,' I say with a wistful sigh. 'I can't *believe* people get to do that as a job.'

'You could get to do that as a job,' Seth says, his face turning serious. 'I mean, you know, you'd have to get experience, take improv classes, write practice sketches, maybe even do some formal comedy training. But it's completely possible.'

I shake my head and shield my embarrassment at his compliments by taking three large gulps of water.

As he continues talking about the opportunities out there for someone like me to get into comedy writing, my breath catches in my throat, my stomach flipping over in a pleasant way. Because all at once I know, I am *certain*, that that's exactly what I want to do with the rest of my life.

Who'd have thought?

* * *

After an incredible meal of roasted oysters followed by grilled garlic lamb with market greens, we leave the restaurant and step into the unseasonably warm evening. Seth suggests we wander around to a nearby ice cream shop to get a couple of small desserts.

On the way, we pass by Gramercy Park. I can't see much through the cast-iron fence but I notice that there are little twinkle lights strung up inside the garden. It looks so pretty.

And then something occurs to me.

'Wait,' I say to Seth. 'Hold on a sec.'

I reach into my bag and pull out my little coin pouch. I pinch my fingers inside and pull out the key I stole. I hold it up to Seth.

'You still have it? I thought the police took it back!'

I shake my head. 'It was in my pink bum bag, in this little pouch. The day I was arrested I was wearing my satchel!'

'We couldn't,' Seth breathes, eyes glittering.

I raise an eyebrow. 'What happened to super chill "*aren't we all looking for excitement*" Seth Hartman?'

I dramatically creep towards the gate and gently slide the key into the lock.

'You're really doing this?' Seth laughs. 'You're actually going to break in?'

'It's not breaking in if you have a key! It's gorgeous in there. You have to see it.'

I push open the gate door, grab Seth's hand and lead him inside.

'Wow,' he whispers.

'I know!' I look up at the hedges strung with fairy lights and the gravelled pathways lit by little lanterns.

We walk down the path into the centre of the garden, where Seth pulls out his phone and fiddles with the buttons until the gruff soulful voice of Otis Redding's *I've Been Loving You Too Long* rings its way into the air.

'Would you dance with me?' he asks, bowing his head a little.

I blink. I have never been asked to dance before in my life. I feel my cheeks turn red.

'Alright then,' I say quietly, reaching up to put my arms around his neck.

As the evening spring breeze whips around us, Seth presses his hands onto the small of my back and we sway underneath the trees and the stars, the only two people in this beautiful park, in this big old city. My heart thuds in my ribcage, and when I lay my head against his chest, I hear that his heart thudding too.

I lean back and study his face. I want to kiss him. If we kissed right here it would surely be the most romantic moment anyone had ever had in life.

But before anything kiss-related can happen, the music changes to the next Otis Redding track on the album – the super sexy *Love Man.*

I burst into laughter as Seth steps away from me and comically swirls his hips from side to side, a dumb pervy expression on his face. It's so funny that I decide to do the same thing, putting my hands on my hips and rolling them around like I'm doing a hula hoop. I pull a stupid face as I'm doing it and Seth starts to laugh too, clutching his stomach with amusement.

The two of us saucily dance our way around the park. Seth wiggles and twirls around a bush. Getting well and truly into the spirit of the bit, I start to fake hump a tree which causes tears of mirth to roll from Seth's eyes.

When the song ends it takes us a whole ten minutes to stop giggling. I can't remember the last time I had this much fun with anyone other than Birdie. In fact, I'm pretty sure I never have!

After sneaking back out of the park, we find a bench to sit on so I can check my email again and see if any leads have come through about Chuck. But nope. Nothing. Then I check the burner phone that Anders bought for our mission, making doubly sure that all the notification volumes are as high as they can go. But no-one has tried to get through on that, either! I sigh and put the phones back in my bag.

'No luck?' Seth asks.

'No.' I shake my head, confused. 'We must have given out a gazillion leaflets. I thought we'd have at least a few calls.'

'Did you hear from any of Sharon's contacts?'

'No.' I sigh. 'I'll chase them up tomorrow.'

'I'll text her, see if she can chase them. People don't generally leave Sharon hanging!'

I eye him as he taps a text out on his phone. He has her personal number then.

'You know her well?' I ask super, super casually.

Seth nods and leans back against the bench. 'We used to date.'

I knew it. I may not be clued up in the ways of sexual adulting, but I could completely tell that they had history.

'Cool. Cool,' I say nonchalantly. 'So what happened? Why did it end? When did you break up? What's the story?' I add, completely ruining my casual vibe.

Seth puts his phone pack into his shirt pocket and turns to me. 'We were together for about a year and she cheated on me,' he says it very matter-of-fact. So matter-of-factly that he was evidently hurt by it.

'Shit,' I say. 'That's horrible.'

Seth nods, giving a small empty laugh. 'It was. She always told fibs, little white lies, exaggerations. I hate liars – hate them – but I figured they were little lies, harmless. And she's in PR after all, and that whole deal is about putting a spin on shit. But she lied about sleeping with someone else for three months. Not such a little or harmless lie. I had completely trusted her. I felt like such an idiot.'

'Gross! I'm sorry that happened to you.'

'Yeah.'

'And you still have to work with her! Ick.'

Seth shrugs. 'Ah, I'm over it now. We're learning to be friends again. I mean, we were never right for each other in a romantic way so I'm glad it happened. I tend to stay in long relationships, so if she hadn't have cheated I'd probably still be with her now.'

Does that mean he still has feelings for her?

I hope not.

Not that it should matter to me…

'Oh.' I say casually.

Seth nods. 'Plus she farted in her sleep. At first I thought it was cute. But sometimes they were so loud they literally woke me up.'

'We all do farts in our sleep!'

'Sure. I bet yours smell like fresh spring blooms.'

'They do. And on *that* note I propose a subject change!'

And by subject change I mean that perhaps it's about time to do some kissing. I've been watching his lips moving all night and have been able to think of nothing but what they will feel like on my neck. Pressed against my belly. On my…

'Olive?'

Seth's voice interrupts my fantasy. I'm drooling a little bit.

He's grinning at me, his tongue poking out. I scooch towards him so that our thighs are touching.

His eyes run over my face like he wants to eat me up for a second dessert.

I nudge my knee against his and turn so that I'm properly facing him.

He moves his face closer to mine. Closer, closer, closer and then.

He sighs.

And it's not a sexy sigh full of longing and desire. It's a full-on negative sigh.

What?

Why is he sighing?

I lean back and look at him expectantly.

'Sorry. I'm just thinking about all that shit with Sharon.'

'Don't think about that!' I say, waving my hands madly as if I am shooing all thoughts of his ex away. 'Think about your new job! About those oysters we just had!' I force myself to be brave. 'Think about me!'

'That's the problem.' Seth looks down at his hands. 'I can't stop thinking about you.'

'Why… why is that a problem?' I ask, completely confused.

'Because Colin! I'm talking about Sharon cheating on me and here *we* are. You're engaged. Don't you feel bad? I know we've not… but…'

Colin? Who the hell is… Oh shit *Colin*. And my fake engagement.

I open my mouth to tell Seth that Colin is basically a

stranger. That I knew him for a very nerve-wracking hour in the airport and that, while we exchanged a few flirty texts and I thought he might have been a sensible option for a future date, he doesn't give me the wibbles like Seth. And I want those wibbles. Now that I've had them I want them all the time. Plus Colin emailed me, like, eighteen shit memes. That's unforgivable.

But… I can't confess that *now*! How can I? Seth clearly already knows I'm crazy, but he's just explicitly stated that he hates liars. And I… am a total liar. What happens if I tell him that I have been lying to him about being engaged? He's mentioned Colin on more than a few occasions and I've never corrected him. I didn't expect that we would see each other again! And if I tell him now, I might never get to have the fling that I am feeling, very very firmly, that I should have with him.

'You're feeling guilty, I know. You look so gloomy,' Seth says gently. 'Don't beat yourself up. We just got caught up, I guess… *Fuck*.' He shakes his head in frustration.

I'm not feeling gloomy about Colin. I'm feeling gloomy that the *one* time in my adult life I am feeling so attracted to someone that I can't quite control it, a *made-up* fiancé is getting in the way.

Argh. I fancy Seth so much. I mean… I'm going home in a few days. I'll probably never see him again… Who knows when I'll feel like this about anyone again. *If* I will.

I look at Seth's strong, stubble covered jaw. His twinkling, clever eyes behind his dorky glasses. His forearms. The way he smells. The way he tastes. I am ready. If I leave New York without having this little fling with Seth, I might regret it for the rest of my life. I'll just be thinking about it all the time, wondering what it would have been like. I won't be able to concentrate on anything else! Forever! And although I seem to becoming more comfortable with the idea of small risks, this is one I'm not willing to take.

So I take a deep breath and do the only thing that makes sense to do right now.

I do what Birdie would do: tell just a few more teeny, tiny fibs.

I fiddle with the clip in my hair. 'I feel so bad about Colin,' I say awkwardly. 'But… the truth is… I'm not sure about…'

'What?' He says, seeming to perk up a little.

'He's the only person I've ever been with…'

Seth's eyes widen, his mouth making an 'o' shape.

This is only a half-lie. I *have* only ever been with one person. I mean, it wasn't Colin. It was a guy called Guy during my Fresher's week at university. But still. A half-lie means it's a half truth. Which isn't *so* bad.

'One person? Wow.'

'Mmmhmm.' I nod. 'And the thing is… if I've only been with one person, how do I know if… he's the right person?'

Seth frowns. 'But you got engaged to him… surely you think he's the right person… don't you?'

Argh. He's making this hard. Why does he have to be so *honourable?* Ugh!

'Erm… I mean. I think… maybe in the future, what if I decide that I never got enough experience? And I feel resentful that I only ever slept with… Colin?' I nod, getting into my stride. 'And we end up getting divorced?'

Shit. Am I really going in with this angle?

A breeze whips past, rustling the trees above us, mussing Seth's light brown hair across his forehead and carrying that gorgeous fig cologne of his under my nose.

Yes. Yes, I most certainly am going in with this angle.

'What if we get divorced because I had never been with anyone else?' I ask. 'What if…' I hold a finger in the air like a professor giving a lecture. 'What if we have kids? And I get divorced! Think of the kids. The kids with no mum because she only ever slept with one man.'

Seth shakes his head. 'What are you saying?'

I'm no longer sure. But I'm saying it anyway.

'I'm… I'm saying… I'm just worried that I haven't had enough experience. And that maybe… a… fling… might be… okay.'

'A fling?'

I try to read his expression. To see if my ruthless shtick is working. But he's giving nothing away. He's just watching me very intently.

I swallow, my mouth feeling a bit dry. 'I'm going home in a few days.'

'Right.'

'And then we'll be entire continents apart, so *technically* it would never happen again.'

'Right.'

'And then I could spend the rest of my life with Colin, knowing that I had… um, sowed my wild oats.'

'*Technically*, this would be the kind thing to do. For Colin. And your future children?'

'Yes. Exactly. Not really cheating. Just… protecting against possible future doubts. For the, um, children.'

Seth's eyes flick to my lips. 'And we won't ever see each other again after next week,' he says. 'So…'

'So…' I add.

And I don't know who grabs who, but we are kissing again. And he is so clever at kissing that my body wants to climb atop his body and just cling to it like a koala on a tree.

Holy heck.

Seth somehow manoeuvres us into a standing position and moves us towards the road, where his arm is frantically waving for a cab.

Why aren't any cabs stopping? I can't hold out much longer!

Seth continues holding his hand out, but I'm not feeling quite so patient.

'OI!' I yell, super aggressive like the elderly woman on the Upper West Side taught me. 'OOOOIIIIII!' Immediately a cab comes to a screeching halt right beside us.

'Nice!' Seth says, impressed. 'You're definitely getting the hang of this whole New York thing.'

'Little bit,' I say, closing the cab door behind us and planting my lips immediately back onto his.

CHAPTER THIRTY-ONE

Text from Colin: Did you get the memes I sent? I didn't hear back… Let me know and I can send more. There are so many good ones. Hope you are all right and everything is going well back home in Manchester. How is the weather there? Still very hot here in the land of oz!! Not as hot as you though. Haha.

If the whole engagement to Colin was a real thing, it would be off. I'd have dumped him. Sayonara Colin. Your sideburns are cute but our textual chemistry is lacking and oh my goodness Seth.

Man. Oh. Man. *Seth.*

We're doing it. We are having sex. I am having sex. Seth is having sex with me. We are at his apartment in the Upper West Side. We didn't even stop for a drink or a brew or anything. As soon as we got in the door, he pushed me up against the hall and lifted my tea dress up over my head. I was so naked. And his hall light was on. And I *didn't care*. When he lifted me up, I wrapped my legs around him and kissed him while he carried me to the bedroom, pulled down my knickers and licked every part of me.

I feel completely new. Like an animal. A sexy wild animal. Like Madonna and Mae West and Marilyn Monroe all in one Olive-shaped Woman.

Seth rolls over so that I'm on top. He holds my hands, watching me as I move back and forth above him, rocking myself against him, feeling completely free and bold and safe and scared and hot, hot, hot.

'Olive,' he groans, his hands moving to my backside as we move more quickly together.

Oh. Wow.

This is amazing.

This feels amazing.

I finish a few seconds before Seth and lie back on his soft jersey pillows to catch my breath. My whole body is sparkling. My toes are all ticklish. My body is on over-drive, all of my senses on alert, and for the first time in forever it's not in a way that feels like an attack.

'Woah.' Seth grins, leaning over to press his forehead to mine, his cheeks hot and pink.

'Woah,' I reply, stretching like a cat, kissing him and wondering how soon until I can do that again.

The answer is thirty-five minutes.

The second time is slower, sweeter, gigglier, decadent and playful.

The second time we look at each other the entire time.

The second time I have to stop myself from choking up because there's this odd bittersweet ache in my chest that I don't want to think too hard about.

The second time is when I have to try very very hard to not fall for someone who, after this week, I'll never see again.

This is just a fling, Olive. That's all it is.

* * *

I wake up the next morning to the five missed calls. It's 8.30 a.m. I pick up my phone from Seth's bedside cabinet to see that all of the missed calls are from Anders. How did I miss those? I had all the volumes turned up. God, I must have slept super deeply. To be fair, I had a *very* physically active night.

My heart leaps at all the missed calls. Oh my goodness, I hope it's Chuck-related! Please let it be Chuck-related!

I try to call back but it goes to voicemail. I hope everything's alright… Turning over, I peek at Seth who is awake and who is smiling at me sleepily, his cheek lined with cotton pillow marks.

'How are you?' he murmurs.

'I am… really good,' I reply.

'Did I satiate you enough to never sleep with another man apart from Colin for the rest of your life?'

He raises an eyebrow cheekily and my heart drops to my toes.

Oh yeah. That. My lie to get Seth to 'cheat' with me. I mentally clear my head. Of course. That's what this was. He still thinks I'm engaged. That we'll never see each other again.

And… he seems fine with that.

Well I am fine with it too. This is a fling. Last night we 'flung'. I dipped my toe in as intended!

And that's all! Great!

'I should probably go!' I say brightly, sitting up and pulling the soft blanket around me. 'Anders has tried calling loads and I'm hoping it's good news about Chuck!'

'I hope it is! That would be awesome.' Seth stretches his tanned arms above his head. 'I have to be at work in half an hour.'

I nod.

He nods.

'Okay. Well…'

'Do you want to come and see the show on Sunday night?' he blurts out. 'It would be cool to have you there on my first night as a cast member.'

'Yeah,' I say immediately. 'Yes. I'd love to.'

'Great!'

'Great!' I parrot again.

Wrapping the blanket around me, I wander out into the hallway to retrieve my clothes.

Once dressed and at the front door, I open my mouth to ask Seth if he wants to hang out tonight again. To do more 'flinging'. But before I do, Seth leans in to give me a kiss on the cheek.

'Hey, um, listen… I'm gonna be pretty busy at work so… I probably won't see you until Sunday. I'll email you the tickets, um…'

He trails off, his cheeks turning a little red.

Awkward.

'Yeah. Yeah, no probs,' I reply, my voice a tad too high. 'Okay. Bye! See you then!'

'Goodbye, Olive.'

* * *

As I walk back from the subway station to Anders' house, the sun shines brightly, illuminating the buildings prettily. I try my best to not feel gutted about the fact that Seth seemingly couldn't wait to get rid of me. I have no right to feel gutted. I told him it was just a one-time thing. It *was* just a one-time thing. I should enjoy it for what it was: a toe well and truly dipped in. I stride purposefully through Gramercy Park, feeling proud of myself as I navigate most of the journey without my Citymapper app.

Before I turn onto Anders' street I hold up my phone and take a picture of myself squinting in the sun. Then I send it to Birdie, along with a text that says:

Sex is nice, isn't it? Why didn't you tell me ;)

I chuckle to myself as the text wings its way to her, but my laugh is cut short when I realise that there's a crowd of around thirty people outside of Anders' house. They're all jostling to get the front, elbowing each other out of the way.

What the heck is going on?

I push my way through the throng to Anders' front door.

I knock on, but there's no answer. I knock again as hard as I can.

'I *said* to form an orderly queue!' Anders yells from inside. 'No knocking. We will see to you all in good time! Dear me!'

I open the letter box and push my face up against it. 'It's Olive! Anders! Let me in! What the bloody hell is going on here? Let me in!'

After a few seconds the door swings open and Anders stands there dressed in shades of cream and grey. His usually pale face is glowing red.

A young man walks past him and out of the house, disappearing into the crowd outside.

'Goodbye,' Anders yells after him. 'We'll be in touch!'

'Who was that? Who are these strangers outside your house?' I ask, closing the door behind me. 'Why are you so pink of cheek?'

'Come through, come through,' Anders says, taking

my hand and dragging me into his kitchen. 'It is all happening at Chez von Preen this AM.'

What is going on?

In the kitchen, things look very hectic indeed. I blink. Mrs Ramirez is sticking polaroid photos up on the window, on the kitchen table there are tall stacks of papers, empty mugs of coffee and three burner mobile phones buzzing away!

'We have been very busy, sweet *guapa*. I hope you had good sex last night? You have the look of a woman well tended to.'

My cheeks warm and I avoid her question while wondering how on earth a well-tended woman looks and how this is so clearly visible to an ageing Spanish woman.

'Who are those pictures of?' I say, distracting Mrs Ramirez by pointing at the polaroids on the window. I turn to Anders. 'And will someone tell me who the people are outside!'

Anders gives me a look that's somewhere between guilty and excited.

'They are here regarding Chuck Allen,' he explains, one hand on his skinny hip.

'What?' My heart leaps. 'Wow. This is incredible news! The leaflets worked?'

'They did not,' Mrs Ramirez says, bustling over to the kitchen counter and pouring me a coffee from what I think is a crystal cafetière.

'Huh?'

'Ask him.' Mrs Ramirez thumbs in Anders' direction.

I turn to Anders, a quizzical look on my face.

'I might have put a little something up on Craigslist,' Anders says breezily. 'And it got a *great* response!'

'Anders, you are a genius! So what have you found out? Have you heard from Chuck himself? Does anyone know where he is?'

Yes! The search is finally coming together.

'We are not having great luck,' Mrs Ramirez says, sitting down at the kitchen table.

Oh.

'Not yet!' Anders interjects. 'But we will.'

'Mr von Preen here offered a reward on the internets. So the people outside are not, how shall I say… *trustworthy*.'

Anders tuts lightly. 'It's only five thousand dollars for goodness sake.'

'Five thousand dollars!' I goggle. 'Oh Anders. What are you like?'

'Ay! All that money!'

'It worked in *Annie*, darling. They put up a reward for information leading to the discovery of Annie's biological parents.'

'It didn't work in *Annie*! Tim Curry and Bernadette Peters used the whole thing as a ruse to con Daddy Warbucks. Remember? Mrs Hannigan was involved and everything.'

'It *didn't* work in Annie?' Anders puts a hand to his face, crestfallen. 'I thought… It's so long since I saw it. Oh dear. I was so hopeful last night. I'd had some cognac and thought that this would be a great help.'

'It could still work, I suppose,' I say brightly, touched that this unusual man has put up so much of his own money to help me and Birdie. 'Thanks for trying, Anders.'

Anders gives an elegant shrug. 'Besties help besties,' he says.

I guess now isn't the right time to tell him we're not besties.

'So, the pictures on the window are the people you've already met this morning?' I ask, heading over to the big kitchen window to have a look at the five polaroids stuck up there with Blu-Tack. 'Why are they on the window?

And how on earth did you get strangers to pose for pictures? Did they not think it was odd?'

'Mrs Ramirez said we should.' Anders pulls a face, speaking in a petulant voice, almost as if he wants to get back at Mrs Ramirez for shading his Annie reward idea.

'It is how Olivia Pope would do it,' Mrs Ramirez explains.

'Olivia Pope?'

'From *Scandal*. She is magnificent. She and all her gladiators in suits put photographs for their investigations on the window. Everyone we have seen was very happy to have their picture taken!'

'Oh. Cool. I think.'

I peer at the polaroids. Three are headshots of men and two are headshots of women. Written underneath in tiny writing are their phone numbers, email addresses, how they know Chuck and the condition of their hair. One says 'dry', one says 'oily roots', another says 'stressed follicles' and one says 'soft as feathers – follow up'.

'Why are there notes on here about these folks's hair?'

Anders rolls his eyes as if I am an idiot for even asking. 'Because one can tell everything one needs to know about a person based on their hair.'

'Of course! Right! And these people say they know Chuck?' I ask. 'Do you have any information we can use?'

'Nothing concrete… not yet, at least,' Anders tells me. 'But there are plenty more people waiting outside.'

It takes us six hours of interviewing randomers until we decide to send the rest of the people outside away, asking them to contact us via a specially set up email address if they have any verifiable information. Of the many people we spoke to, only three of them actually knew Chuck.

One was friends with Chuck at college but hadn't seen him in years. And then he scarpered as soon as he recognised Anders and called him 'the dude who cut that other dude's face with the scissors'. Which made Anders lock himself in one of his three bathrooms for a whole thirty minutes. The second person was a pretty young woman who fancied Chuck when they'd both worked at Chimes Investments. She didn't have any info to offer but wanted to be kept in the loop if we found him and he was still, by some miracle, single. The third guy said he had a friend who had been to an incredible party that Chuck had held at mansion in Brooklyn but that he'd never actually met him and he didn't know anyone who had.

'This Chuck Allen is like the Great Gatsby!' Mrs Ramirez pointed out, after she had done scolding Anders for hiding out in the bathroom, telling him that 'grown men do not tantrum'.

Everyone else we saw was a liar, a rubbernecker, or just wanted to get a look inside the beautiful Gramercy Park house they had admired for years and never been able to get into.

At the end of the day, Anders, Mrs Ramirez and I slump on Anders' living room sofas. Well, as much as we can slump on stiff, Chesterfield antique settees. I sigh, determined not to be downbeat, despite this feeling like a wasted day. Making an effort to try to see things in a more positive light, to try to relax when I can has made life feel so much brighter. And the search isn't over yet. There's still time! Not a lot of it… but still.

'All we can do is try again tomorrow,' Mrs Ramirez says with a sleepy sigh.

I nod. She's right. If there's one thing I've realised this past week, it's that you can't force things to happen, no matter how much you want them to. But it doesn't mean you can't try your best.

'Anyone care for a tipple?' Anders asks, slinking over to his living room bar cart. 'The cognac I had last night was divine. I would highly recommend it for taking the edge off.'

'Yes please,' Mrs Ramirez says. 'With ice please.'

'I'll just have…' I'm about to say I'll just have water, but hell. If I can't enjoy a glass of fancy-ass cognac when the opportunity arises, then what am I even doing? And it's not like I've got any other plans tonight. Seth palmed me off this morning and my inbox is still, sadly, all quiet on the Chuck front.

'I'll have one,' I say. 'Thank you.'

I stand up to help Anders make them, but he hisses that I should sit back down immediately because besties bring drinks to besties. I do as I'm told and recline back into my seat. After he's handed myself and Mrs Ramirez our drinks, Anders lights a small fire and a warmth settles over the grand room making us feel snug and cosy. I think of Birdie, hoping that at least one of the leads we got today comes to something solid. I've not got long left to find Chuck and I desperately don't want to let Birdie down.

Ramirez gives a happy sigh as Anders turns on his record player and the rich baritone notes of Frank Sinatra glide into the air.

'Well, if this isn't a lovely time then I don't know what is.'

I smile dozily, watching the flames of the fire crackle and fizz.

I completely agree.

I wish Birdie were here.

CHAPTER THIRTY-TWO

Text from Olive to Birdie: Did you get my text, Bird? Where you at?!

Three glasses of old cognac later and I am *quite* tipsy. It's only early evening, though, so I can drink plenty of water and get the early night I had planned.

I text Birdie again and am a little surprised when she doesn't text back immediately as she usually does. I realise that she didn't respond this morning either. My stomach kerplunks as I consider how this morning's text might have seemed to her. She's stuck in hospital feeling downright rotten and here I am gloating about amazing oyster dinners, sneaking dances in beautiful parks and having the kind of sex that can make a person feel brand new.

Way to rub it in, Olive. I mentally slap myself around the face and try calling Birdie's phone but it rings out. Looking at my watch, I realise that it's about midnight in England and she's probably tucked up in bed. I'll let her get a good night's rest and call her in the morning to apologise for being a self-absorbed goon.

As Anders and Mrs Ramirez chatter away about all the far-flung places they've visited in the world, I scroll through my recent texts and see Seth's name there.

He was so weird this morning. He seemed super into me last night. We got on so well. And got *it* on so well! But this morning he looked really uncomfortable as we said goodbye. Like he just wanted me out of there.

Before I can stop myself, I text him. All I put is, HI!!! I immediately regret it. The capital letters and the exclamation marks make it look like I'm being passive-aggressive. HI!!! is a text Donna would send. Hell, HI!!! is a text Donna *has* sent to me in the past when I haven't replied speedily enough!

Well, there's nothing I can do about it now.

I take a sip of my drink and ten minutes later, when there is zero response from Seth, something horrifying occurs to me. What if I was the *only* one who had a good time last night? Oh shit. What… what if Seth didn't enjoy our sexy times as much as I did. He seemed to, but… he's amazing at improv. What if he was… *improvising* his enjoyment? What if he thought I was lacklustre or freaky or selfish in bed? I've not had any real experience, so I can't exactly compare.

Shit, what if, when I was rocking away on top of him having such a lovely time, I leaned back too much in my rapture and *hurt his penis*? Maybe bruised it a little? And he felt too embarrassed to tell me? Or he *did* try to tell me but I was so caught up in getting off that I didn't hear him! The terrible possibilities are endless!

Oh god. Maybe Seth was trying to let me down gently this morning. Maybe those *Sunday Night Live* tickets were a pity gift. A 'thanks but no thanks' payoff. I'm not even sure how I would find out the answer to these questions. I can't exactly text him again. *HI!!! Hope all well. Did I bruise your dick last night? Sorry if so! Best wishes!*

Argh.

My brain starts to go off into one of its overthinking spirals and with great effort I use Phyllis's belly breathing technique to bring me back to the present moment where I am cosy and warm and mellow in Anders' house.

At the sound of my phone ringing, my heart lifts. I hope it's Birdie. It's rubbish going a whole day without speaking to her! I pick up my phone from where it's resting on the arm of my chair.

Oh! It's a New York number.

Maybe it's Seth? Calling to tell me that he is at the hospital with a peen bruise.

I hope not. I really really hope not.

With a deep breath, I answer the phone.

'Hi, is this Olive Brewster?' asks a forthright female voice.

'Yes?'

'Hello! This is Terri Wyatt from Perry Media. I got your details from Sharon at *Sunday Night Live*?'

'Oh!' I say excitedly, immediately putting the mobile on speakerphone so that Anders and Mrs Ramirez can listen in. 'Yes! Hello!'

'Hi! So, I was planning on emailing you to let you know that we weren't gonna be able to fit you in within the next week, but as it happens we've just had a guest cancel and we need a fill in.'

'Yes, YES!' I yell, standing up from the chair while Anders starts excitedly pacing the large room and Mrs Ramirez does a shoulder jig. 'We haven't had much of a response from anyone else, so this is great news! When—'

I trail off as Mrs Ramirez and Anders immediately start frowning and shaking their heads 'no'.

'One moment, please,' I say, interrupting myself and pressing the 'mute' button. 'What is it?'

'Never let them know that no one else is interested!' Mrs Ramirez admonishes, wagging her finger at me.

'You need to act like they are getting a *scoop*,' Anders adds, sipping from his glass of cognac. 'That's all the media wants. Scoops.'

'Scoops?'

'Scoops,' Anders nods.

'Scooooops,' Mrs Ramirez grumbles. 'Speak to her now! Don't keep her waiting. The media do not like to wait.'

I unmute the phone, rolling my eyes at the two sudden founts of all media-related knowledge here.

'Ahem. Terri. Sorry about that,' I say. 'I, um. I meant to say we haven't had much of a response… from people we'd be happy to speak to…'

'Right…?'

'I mean… like… this is a very *important* story. Only for very important… media.'

Anders and Mrs Ramirez nod approvingly at my improvisation skills. I give them a thumbs up.

'Riiiight,' Terri Wyatt repeats, clearly not quite as impressed. 'Look, can you come in or not? It's a ten-minute slot, presenter asks you about the search for this Chuck character, you tell them why you're doing it, we give the contact details out on air, everybody's happy.'

'Okay, yes. I will do it,' I say, sensing that Terri is not the kind of woman you act timid around. 'May I ask what date and time you would like me to be there and where I should go?'

'Now. It's tonight,' Terri says, sounding slightly exasperated. 'We need someone here in forty minutes to go on the air at ten.'

'Now?' I squeak.

But it's night. It's 8.30 p.m. I've had three cognacs.

'Yes,' Terri says. 'It's at Anchorage Studios on 6th

Avenue. Look, we wouldn't be calling you if we could get someone else at such short notice… Damn Ricky Martin for cancelling at the last minute.'

Ricky Martin. *The* Ricky Martin. This must be a really amazing radio station for them to have Ricky Martin on! But, oh god, I'm hardly Ricky Martin. Those are some big shoes to fill!

'Um…' I say, nerves starting to simmer up in my stomach. What if I speak too loudly into the microphone and no one can tell what I'm saying? What if I burp? What if I burp on the radio? What if a random made-up word pops out of my mouth? A word that means nothing. Like fleperty. What if I say fleperty! *Fleperty.*

Mrs Ramirez grabs the phone out of my hands. 'We'll be there,' she declares and then hangs up.

'Argh.' I stare at the phone. 'I'm not prepared. I'm tipsy. I have nothing to wear. My hair is a frizzy mess.'

'It's radio. No one cares what you look like,' Mrs Ramirez calls from the hall where she's grabbing my coat from the hat stand.

I stand still and take a deep breath, remembering all of the new things I have done this week. How I'm starting to feel like a totally different person. A braver, more badass Olive. I can do this! I have to!

Mrs Ramirez hands me my satchel. I squint at it, noting Birdie's letter tucked inside. I don't even like this satchel. It's nowhere near as cool as…

'I'm taking my bumbag,' I say firmly, adrenaline coursing through me.

'That horrible pink fanny pack?' Anders screws up his face. 'Why? *Why*?'

I lift my chin. 'Because I love it. And I'm sick of not being able to wear it in case people stop me in the street.'

'Yes!' Mrs Ramirez calls out.

I smile at her. 'I mean what am I so afraid of? A few

people yelling "Watch Me Piddle" at me? Pah! Worse things have happened.'

Mrs Ramirez starts clapping. 'Yes!'

'And it has a holographic sunshine on the front,' I add.

'Ick,' Anders drawls, pulling on a long dark coat.

'It's waterproof *and* has a secret pocket and did I *mention* the holographic sunshine? Way better than a safe, boring old satchel.'

'YES, CHICA!'

'And most importantly it's the safest place for Birdie's letter,' I say, grabbing the bumbag from where it lies atop my suitcase in the corner of the living room. I transfer everything from my satchel into it and clasp it firmly around my waist.

I turn around to Anders and Mrs Ramirez, my hands on my hips in a total superwoman stance.

'Let's do this!'

Anders sighs dramatically, smoothing his ice blonde hair back from his forehead. 'Midtown. Ugh. The lengths besties will go to.'

CHAPTER THIRTY-THREE

Olive's recent search history:

- **Improv Manchester**
- **Tips for being on radio interview**
- **How to suppress burps discreetly**
- **Bruised penis painful?**
- **Bruised penis common injury?**
- **Fleperty**

When the cab pulls up outside Anchorage Studios, I'm surprised to see how close it is to the Rockefeller Center. I think about what Seth's doing right this minute. He told me he was working tonight. He's probably up there right now. Studiously avoiding my text. Icing his bruise.

Myself and my two unlikely sidekicks march through the door. At the reception desk, the man behind it gives the three of us a confused look. Granted we don't look quite like the kind of people who frequent radio station studios on the regular. The last-minute nature of this whole thing means that my hair is all big and tangled around my head, my eyes tired and my dress crumpled. Mrs Ramirez looks like she should be sitting on a front porch, rocking in a chair somewhere. Anders looks impeccable as always but, you know, like Anders.

We're instructed up to the fourth floor and when the elevator doors open we are met by Terri who looks much like she sounds – cropped blonde hair, sturdy athletic figure and stylish no-fuss outfit of black jeans, a white shirt and high-heeled leather 'don't fuck with me' boots.

'Thank god you're here,' she says, grabbing my hand and speedily yanking me down a corridor without even saying hello. 'You don't look great but, fuck it, we don't have many options right now.'

Rude!

I look behind me, wide-eyed, as Mrs Ramirez and Anders try to keep up with Terri's rapid pace but don't quite manage it considering Mrs Ramirez's dodgy knee and the tightness of Anders' jeans. The pair of them look genuinely excited to be here, though, and that excitement ignites a little fire in my belly too. I'm going to be on the radio. Actual radio!

Terri pushes open a big set of double doors and into a huge, warehouse-type room covered in lights and lines of tape over the floors and massive expensive-looking cameras.

'Ooh it's a TV studio as well!' I say. 'Is the radio studio bit far?'

Terri throws me an annoyed look for slowing her pace. 'Excuse me?'

'The radio studio,' Mrs Ramirez enunciates very slowly from behind, her Spanish accent making the 'r's roll melodically. 'She said the radio studio.'

'Who gives a shit where the nearest radio station is!'

Terri barks. 'Who listens to radio these days! This is *Evenings with Craig and Diane*!'

'Oh my goodness! Oh my goodness, Olive!' Mrs Ramirez squeals, pressing a hand to her bosom. 'I love Craig and Diane!' She absolutely beams. 'I thought I recognised this set.'

'This is TV?' I yelp as Terri grabs my arm again and pulls me across the studio floor, pushing me into a small, bright room with mirrors across the wall, a row of spinny chairs and tons of hair and make-up products laid out on countertops.

'Live TV,' Terri corrects, looking at her watch. 'I'll be back in five. Hair and Make-up should be with you in two. Your friends can sit in here with you for now. There's a water cooler over there.' She points into the corner of the room.

'W-wait, what shall I—' I start, but before I can even finish the sentence Terri has left.

'How exciting!' Mrs Ramirez sings. 'Craig and Diane! Craig is my favourite. An American hunk!'

'Live TV!' I choke, my voice all wobbly. I was feeling so brave before. But that was when I thought I was going on radio! But TV? Live TV? 'Argh! Live TV? Oh man. I don't even know who Craig and Diane *are*!'

'It's a local talk show,' Anders says dismissively, picking up a hairbrush from the countertop and inspecting it. 'It's a five boroughs news TV show. So millions of people will definitely *not* be watching.'

'This is all a good thing!' Mrs Ramirez points out, admiring herself in the mirror. 'TV has much stronger reach than radio. We have a far better chance of someone who watches knowing where Chuck is!'

I peer at my terrified face in the mirror and think of my best friend. Mrs Ramirez is right. This isn't about me.

It's about Birdie and I will do *anything* to make this happen for her.

'I can do it,' I say to myself sternly. '*I* can do it.'

'You can do it,' Mrs Ramirez says, rubbing my shoulders as if I'm a boxer about to go into the ring.

'You can do it, Olive,' Anders says, picking up a comb and running it gently through my curls.

'I can fucking do it,' I say, taking off my coat and bumbag and brushing lint of my dress. I do some jumps in the mirror and a few karate chops to psyche myself out. 'I can *do* it!'

I *can* do it.

Can't I?

* * *

I have a little light concealer and powder pressed onto my face and my hair fluffed and combed by a woman who seems perturbed when Anders tells her that she's not doing it right and nudges her out of the way to do it himself and, after the gorgeous job he did for my dinner with Seth, I let him. Then, as Terri attaches a microphone to my dress, feeding a wire down past my bra and round my back, she, for the millionth time in the past ten minutes, goes over how this is all going to work. I will sit on the studio sofa with the presenters of the show, Craig and Diane. They will ask me about my search for Chuck Allen, why I'm looking for him and how people can get in touch with me. I absolutely must relax and act like I'm having a simple chilled out conversation with two friendly middle-aged people in primary-coloured suits. I absolutely must *not* curse or look directly into the camera.

'Got it!' I promise, my stomach starting to roll and jolt as the commercial break begins and Terri tells me it's time to go sit on the sofa.

Eek!

'Cariño, if you get scared all you have to do is imagine everyone in their underwear,' Mrs Ramirez says kindly.

'Or don't,' Anders adds.

'I've got this,' I yelp, my nostrils flaring a little. 'I've definitely got this. Live TV! No big deal!'

Don't puke, Olive. Do not puke.

I hand Mrs Ramirez my bumbag (I had wanted to keep it on, but Terri put a halt to that idea pretty quickly), clutch Birdie's letter to my chest and, with shaky legs, head across the studio to take a seat on the big purple sofa with Craig and Diane. Craig looks like a fifty-something superhero, with a dark quiff and a matinee idol jawline. Diane is very pretty and bright-eyed, with lovely long brunette hair that's been so perfectly blown out it shines like glass.

I inhale and breathe out slowly, thinking of all the people who might be watching this show. All the people who might have information leading to Chuck…

'Hello Olive,' Diane says with a dazzling smile, as the make-up artist comes over and dabs a shit-ton of powder on her forehead. 'Thanks for coming to the rescue.'

'No probs. Thanks for having me!'

She seems nice. This is going to be okay.

Craig gives me a brief smile, but is mostly busy reading over his paper notes. He's preparing. I can get on board with that.

Before I know it, someone I can't see is counting down from five to zero and saxophone theme music starts to play.

Goodness me. This is it.

The lights are ridiculously bright. And it's so warm. Really hot, actually. Why is it so hot in here? I can see the camera! Must not look into the camera.

When the theme music comes to an end, Diane and

Craig's faces magically zing into megawatt super-toothy smiles.

'Welcome back!' Diane says into the camera. 'Next up we have a guest with a very interesting story. This is Olive Brewster who has come to New York from England to find a man.'

Craig does a cheesy laugh. 'The lengths we go to, huh?'

Diane giggles too. 'Olive is here to find a man, but not in the way you might expect, Craig. Why don't you tell us why you're here in Manhattan, Olive.'

Holy moly.

My throat immediately goes dry. The lights beam down on my forehead making me sweat. *It's so warm.*

I take a big steadying breath and think of Birdie.

'I'm here for my friend,' I say to Diane and Craig. 'Her name is Birdie and she has lupus which, because of associated complications, has become terminal.'

Diane and Craig's faces immediately switch into sad sympathetic expressions.

'How awful.' Diane frowns, pressing a manicured hand to her chest.

'Yep. It is,' I say, stealth tears popping into my eyes. *Go away, tears! You are not welcome!* I carry on. 'Birdie's American. She was born and raised in Manhattan, but now she lives in England. Manchester, actually. She asked me to come to New York to deliver a letter.' I hold up Birdie's letter and wave it a little, discreetly fanning myself at the same time. 'She wants me to give it to a man she lost touch with long ago. His name is Chuck Allen and he was the love of her life.' I frown slightly. 'Chuck Allen. That's Allen *not* Ellen. *A* L L E N.'

Craig gives a little snicker of mirth at my spelling. I don't care. I'm not chancing another Chimes Investments wrong Chuck scenario.

'And why does Bertie—'

'Birdie. Birdie Lively.'

'Why does Birdie want to find this man now?'

'She… she hasn't got long left.' My voice shakes. 'And she's been thinking a lot about her life and her past. Chuck was her Big Sexy Love and she—'

'Sorry?' Craig interrupts with a slight frown. 'Big Sexy Love?'

I grin, fiddling with the corner of the letter. 'That's what Birdie calls epic love. We used to talk about one day finding our Big Sexy Love – the greatest love known to humankind. I guess it's kind of a private joke type thing…'

Craig nods, looking slightly befuddled.

'…And she wants me to deliver this letter,' I tap a finger to the envelope, 'so that Chuck can know how she truly felt about him. She never told him when they were younger and she doesn't want any regrets.'

Diane puts a finger to her chin, a thoughtful expression on her face. 'It certainly seems a long way to travel to deliver a letter! Is Chuck not on social media? Can she not reach him on the telephone?'

'Chuck is not on social media. Trust me, I've searched, she's searched. He is elusive.'

'Not on social media? He sounds like he might be in Brooklyn!' Craig chuckles.

'We've looked everywhere, handed out leaflets, posted online, offered a reward like in *Annie*, visited his last-known locations. But we can't find him. And I have to leave in a few days. Birdie's having kidney surgery next Monday and I need to be back before that. So it's… well, it's pretty desperate.'

'That sounds very risky,' Craig says. 'A surgery when she is already so unwell…'

I bite my lip. It does sound risky. It is risky.

'Are you scared?' Craig says, leaning closer towards me.

'Yeah.' I nod. 'Not as scared as Birdie, probably.'

I think of my friend. Her big eyes, her mischievous grin, her filthy laugh, her sweet, kind, failing heart.

I only realise I'm full-on crying when Diane hands me a box of tissues. Craig gives me a satisfied smile and I get the feeling it was his intention to make me cry.

A spark of anger flickers in my chest. This isn't a game. This isn't TV fodder. This is *serious*.

I fiercely wipe my tears away and when Craig starts talking I gather up all of my courage to interrupt him. I turn and look directly into the camera even though Terri told me to definitely not do that.

'Chuck Allen, if you are out there, you better blummin' well get in touch,' I say, quickly trying to keep my voice steady. 'If anyone watching knows where he is, they can reach me by emailing whereischuckallen@gmail.com. Please!'

'Um. Okay, there are the details!' Diane says brightly. 'Thanks for joining us Olive. And please give Birdie all of our love.'

That's it? I did it? It's done?

I look around, expecting Terri to come and lead me off the set when Craig presses his hand to his earpiece.

'Olive… one of our researchers has just informed us that…' he widens his eyes in glee, '…you are the Menace of Manhattan? That you were arrested for stealing a Gramercy Park key?'

'That was you?' Diane asks, her eyes squinting to get a closer look at me. 'It is you! You were in the *New York Daily News*!' Her expression changes from one of pity to one of absolute disgust.

Shit! No. No. I am not here for this. This is about Birdie and finding Chuck.

My mouth opens and shuts gormlessly. I'm not sure what to say.

I panic. 'Um… fleperty.' Gaaaah. I just said the made-up word I was worried about saying! Oh Olive.

'Excuse me, did you say fleperty?' Craig asks.

'Fleperty,' Diane repeats slowly. 'What is fleperty? Is it a British thing?'

'Do you steal things often, Olive?' Craig asks.

'Er… Um…'

'And do you only take keys? Or are you open to thieving a variety of items?' Diane adds.

'Do you steal so that you can feel something, Olive? Truly *feel* something. Something more than just the endless tedium of day to day life, staring into a lens, talking to people you will never ever meet and who care not one iota about you.'

Diane gives Craig an odd look. As do I. He turns red, clearly horrified at his little burst of emotion.

'Back to "fleperty",' Diane says, trying to retain an air of professionalism. 'Is that UK slang for, um… public masturbatory practices? Tell us more, Olive.'

Public masturbatory practices? Okay, this is getting out of hand now. Heart pounding, I stand up off the sofa and march over to the camera. 'Chuck Allen. I will be waiting for your call!' I say intensely before jogging off the set, much to the horror of Diane, Craig and Terri, who I jog past.

Anders and Mrs Ramirez stand on the sidelines just staring at me in absolute disbelief.

'Holy fucking turd alert!' I hiss, grabbing my coat and bumbag off Mrs Ramirez. 'Let's get out of here.'

I feel a huge yank on my back.

'Ouch!' I turn around to see Terri, her face flaming, holding wires in her hands.

'Your microphone was still on,' she spits, her eyes bulging angrily. 'You just said *Holy Fucking Turd Alert* to our entire audience!'

Oh no! This is not good. This is really not good. I really *am* The Menace of Manhattan.

I gawk at Anders and Mrs Ramirez in panic. Anders grabs my hand and then Mrs Ramirez's hands and in the highest volume his thin voice can manage, he yells, 'Ruuuuuuun!'

* * *

We only run about ten metres because Mrs Ramirez's knee means we can't take the stairs and we have to wait for the lift. So the three of us stand there feeling all kinds of awkward as various crew members walk past and throw us dirty looks.

Once we're outside the studio, Mrs Ramirez gets emotional. 'When you walked up to the camera and spoke directly to Chuck? Oh, I felt it in my heart, Olive.'

'Thanks, Mrs Ramirez. I just hope it works.'

I stare at the pair of them and suddenly I start to laugh with relief and adrenaline. They join in. 'That was bonkers,' I breathe. 'I can't believe they knew about that whole Manhattan Menace thing. There's been nothing in the papers about me for two whole days now! I thought people were losing interest in—'

'Olive?'

I turn around at the deep, warm voice behind me.

It's Seth.

Huh?

'Seth? What are—'

'This is Seth?' Mrs Ramirez holds out her hand to him. 'You are right, Olive. His eyes are turquoise. I didn't think it possible, but it is!'

'Um hi,' Seth shakes Mrs Ramirez's hand.

'Hello, again.' Anders says, leaning in to kiss Seth on the cheek, much to his surprise.

'What are you doing here?' I ask. 'How did you even know I was here?' I look up to the nearby Rockefeller Center. 'Did you see us out of the window?!'

'I just saw you on *Evenings with Craig and Diane.*'

'You watch it?' Anders pulls a face and then leans over to whispers in my ear. 'Bad taste in TV. Deal-breaker?'

'I told you it has an audience!' Mrs Ramirez adds.

'I don't watch it. One of the other writers at *Sunday Night Live* watches it religiously though. He ran into my office and told me you were on.'

'Oh!'

Seth shoves his hands in his pockets. 'I wanted to tell you something. I've been thinking about it all day and then when I saw you on Craig and Diane I raced over here to see if I could catch you in time.'

'Give us a second,' I say to Anders and Mrs Ramirez, indicating that Seth should come and stand by me near a tree. I have a feeling that whatever he's about to say – good, or bad – is not something I want anyone else to hear. And definitely not if he's about to tell me about a certain intimate contusion.

'Hey,' Seth grins, when we're out of earshot of Anders and Mrs Ramirez. 'Nice fanny pack.'

'Hey!' I say lightly, trying not to look at him with total heart eyes because my whole body is *pinging* in his presence. 'In England we call it a bumbag.'

We smile at each other like a pair of idiots.

'So… I kind of just wanted to say—' Seth begins

And then my phone rings. It occurs to me to ignore it, but it could be Birdie calling me back. Or it could be someone who's just seen me on TV and has Chuck intelligence. Terri promised to direct all calls to my mobile. But then I did just swear on her show so maybe she's no longer so keen to help. Damn.

'Just a sec!' I say, grabbing my phone from my bumbag. 'Hello!'

'Hello,' comes a man's voice. It's American and self-possessed. 'Is this Olive Brewster?'

'Yes,' I say, my breath catching in my throat. 'Who is this?' I ask.

But I don't even know why I'm asking. Because I already know who it is. Something inside me just *knows*. That this, right here on the phone, is the man I came to New York for.

This is Birdie's Big Sexy Love.

This is Chuck.

'It's Chuck. Chuck Allen,' the smooth voice responds, confirming what my heart already knew. 'I hear you've been looking for me?'

CHAPTER THIRTY-FOUR

@ElissaJohnson

That's the key thief/pervert on Craig and Diane! The @NYPD told me she was back in the UK. They #lied! I am so upset.

@ElissaJohnson

She just cursed on live TV! My six-year-old Amber heard it! #fuming

@AmyBNYC to @ElissaJohnson

I didn't know you had kids!

@ElissaJohnson to AmyBNYC

I don't. Amber is my dog

'Chuck! Chuck Allen!' I repeat back to him. Seth's mouth drops open. 'It's Chuck! The real Chuck!' I shout to

Anders and Mrs Ramirez. They hurry over to me, clutching each other in anticipation. 'You don't know how happy I am to hear from you!' I tell him.

'I must say I'm surprised. Birdie and I were so long ago,' Chuck says, somewhat stiffly. 'And we didn't end on the best of terms. I'm very sad to hear she's been so unwell.'

'I have a letter for you!' I squeak, barely able to contain my excitement!

'Yes, I gather. I've been reading about the Menace of Manhattan in the paper. And now, having just seen you on Craig and Diane, I realise that you are *in* Manhattan because of me. I felt I ought to get in touch.'

Did he just do an irritated sigh? No. Chuck Allen wouldn't sigh.

'Where are you?' I ask, concerned that my reception will go and I won't get his exact location.

'I'm on my yacht at New York Harbour. Some friends and I are having a party on the river before I leave for Bali tomorrow.'

'Bali?' I spit. 'Well I need to see you now. Right now.'

'Yeah, the yacht sets sail in about forty minutes. We're on Pier 78. You'll spot my yacht. It's the biggest one.'

'Okay! I'm on my way. Don't leave before I'm there. This is so important.'

Chuck sniffs. 'I'll do my best, but, as they say, the captain's word is law.'

I hang up feeling a swirl of disappointment in my chest. Chuck doesn't exactly sound like the swoonsome romantic hero I've been picturing in my head this past week. I shake the thought away. That doesn't matter. I've found him! Birdie will be so pleased!

'Right!' I say, shoving my phone into my bumbag and zipping it up. 'I have to get to New York Harbour, Pier 78 asap.'

'I could hire a helicopter,' Anders ponders. 'It will be a pleasant trip but perhaps a little time-consuming considering…'

'I think I'll just catch a cab.' I walk out into the pavement and stick out my hand.

'Shall we come?' Mrs Ramirez asks.

'I'd be happy to,' Seth says. 'I can take an hour out!'

I shake my head. 'No. No. Thanks for offering, but this is something I need to do alone. I want to sit down and talk to Chuck. To tell him about Birdie. To wait while he reads the letter.' I look at Anders and Mrs Ramirez. 'You guys wait back in Gramercy for me. I'll be there later.'

'Make sure you give him my number,' Anders instructs. 'Tell him that I retain my innocence regarding my intentions with Warner's face. I was just trying to fix his ends. I did *not* mean to cut his face with my scissors.'

Four cabs fly past me. I take a deep breath and shout super loudly and, as I'm a dab hand at this now, the next cab screeches to a halt right next to me.

That will never get old!

'Call me if you need any help,' Seth says. 'I guess I should go back to work but… I'll call you later?'

'Yeah,' I smile, getting in the cab and trying not to think about how sad I feel that our destiny was to be nothing more than fling. 'I'll speak to you in a little while.' I close the door of the cab. 'New York Harbor,' I say breathlessly to the driver.

He turns around, his dark eyebrows raised. 'You want me to step on it?'

I break into a massive smile. 'Yes please!'

So he does. And as he screeches off the sidewalk I turn to see Anders, Mrs Ramirez and Seth waving madly behind me.

My heart lifts at the sight of these three people. People

I never expected to meet. People I now really care about and, I think, care about me.

How lucky am I?

* * *

I reach New York Harbour exactly thirty-eight minutes later. Handing over a wad of dollar bills to the driver, I dive out of the taxi and race to Pier 78 as fast as I can, praying that he hasn't left yet. I look around for the biggest yacht, spotting a really ostentatious one right at the end of the pier, lit up with hundreds of twinkling lights.

It's breezy tonight and all the boats are rocking from side to side. I sprint towards the yacht, thanking heavens that I got here on time, but just as I reach the bow a massively obnoxious-sounding horn blares out and, oh my goodness, the ship starts to move!

Shiiiiit! It can't be leaving! I'm only two minutes late! Oh no! Nooooo.

'Stop! Don't leave,' I shout as loudly as I can, my voice cracking with desperation. But no one hears me! Argh. I run around in a little circle of panic. Chuck said he's going to Bali tomorrow. I have to see him now! I can't let him get away after all this. Fuck! I cannot let Birdie down. I promised her. I promised myself.

I hear Birdie's voice in my head.

Come on, Olive! Be brave!

And then I do one of the most dangerous, unsafe, ridiculous things I've done in my safe little life. I run at the pier, hoping that my legs are strong enough to jump far enough to land on the hull deck. They have to be! I've done so much walking this week!

With all my might and all my strength and every last speck of hope I possess, I make the jump.

And I *miss.*

It feels like slow motion as I drop into the ocean like a rock.

My whole body sinks deep under the river, the water flooding into my nose and ears. I feel my head start to swirl in panic, my limbs get shaky with fear.

Fuck. This isn't good. I knew I had a good reason for my fear of deep water!

I hear Birdie's voice again, as clear as a bell. *'Don't be a dick, Brewster. Don't drown. Swim! You're so close!'*

She's right. Drowning right now would be a total dick move. After everything, I cannot drown!

I try to relax my limbs and focus my brain like I've been practising since Phyllis showed me how. I repeat the words she taught me at Trickys. 'If I relax, this will pass.'

By not panicking, by allowing myself to relax, my legs and arms start to work. I kick and swim up to the surface of the water, my dress billowing softly around me. Taking in a huge gulp of air, I tread the water as best as I can without falling into freak-out mode again.

Above me, the yacht looms large, blurry from all the water in my eyes. I spot a couple chatting by the upper deck, sipping champagne, completely oblivious to my murky struggle.

'Help!' I call out. 'Heeeeellllp!'

But they can't hear me over the strains of shit dance music coming from the boat. I can't quite believe Birdie's Big Sexy Love listens to such shit music!

Kicking my legs furiously to stay afloat, I wonder what to do. It's brassic cold in this river, so I need to make a decision very quickly. I can swim back to the dock, risking the chance to ever get Birdie's letter to Chuck. Or I can…

I don't know! I don't know what to do!

Suddenly I see a flash of pink in the water. It's my bumbag.

I gasp, getting an idea! It's a long shot, but…

Still treading water, I reach into the front pocket of the bumbag, being careful not to disturb the main zip and damage the waterproof integrity of the bag and Birdie's letter, and yank out my Rescue Remedy. I haven't been using it these past few days so the bottle is still almost full!

I focus on the couple I can see on the yacht and, with all my might, I lob the bottle up towards the top deck. I watch as it sails slowly, beautifully through the night sky.

Don't miss! Don't miss!

The Rescue Remedy arcs down and – yes! It skims the man's shoulder!

Yesssss!

All at once the couple lean over the railings of the yacht.

I can't hear what they're saying over the sound of the shit music but they are pointing and gesturing dramatically.

Suddenly a bunch of other people appear at the barriers, peering down at me in shock.

One of them throws down a rope ladder so that it hangs over the side of the boat. With the last of my energy, I swim towards it and cling on.

Well, that was a close call.

* * *

After one of Chuck's staff takes me below deck to shower off the river water, I dress in a soft white robe monogrammed with CA initials, and wait in Chuck's private quarters, a sumptuous room decorated in burgundy and gold.

I'm waiting for fifteen minutes before the door opens and Chuck strides in. Woah. He is ridiculously, preposterously good-looking. I had wondered if, in the years since Anders' college picture was taken, Chuck might have aged like the rest of us humans. But nope. He still looks like a twenty-one-year-old god. He's wearing a black party tuxedo and his hair is dark, glossy and slicked to the side like Don Draper in *Mad Men*. He has a set of perfect white teeth, a tanned healthy face and gorgeous long-lashed brown eyes that put George Clooney's to shame.

'Hello!' I say, standing up and immediately handing him Birdie's letter, which, having been zipped tightly in the inside pocket of my waterproof bumbag is perfectly intact. Ha! Everyone who laughed at my bumbag can suck it! It totally saved the day!

'That was quite a risky move out there, don't you think?' Chuck says as he sits formally on an armchair opposite me and peers at the envelope. He doesn't even say hello!

'Um, well. I had to get this letter to you.'

'I see. You've certainly gone to great lengths.'

'Birdie is very important to me,' I tell him. 'I promised her I'd give you that letter. You've been so hard to find! I was starting to think you didn't exist for a moment there.'

'I like to live off the grid,' Chuck sniffs, his eyes running over my damp face. 'I found myself being locked into a world of screens and social media and the alpha world of investment banking. It was *suffocating*. It almost ruined my relationship.'

His relationship? Chuck is in a relationship? Huh. I suppose a part of me had been secretly hoping he'd read Birdie's letter and decide that she was his Big Sexy Love too. That he'd fly back to England with me to reunite with his sweetheart.

I guess not.

Chuck leans back into his chair and crosses his legs. 'I'm lucky enough to be able to travel the world. I have real adventures rather than watching those of other people play out on Instagram and Facebook. I chose to take it the opportunities my wealth has given to me. To privately enjoy my life with Warner.'

Warner? I screw up my face. Why do I know that name?

Wait. Warner? Anders' college room-mate Warners?

'Redheaded Warner?' I splutter.

Chuck nods, frowning. 'You know him?'

Wow. Chuck is *gay*. All this time, Anders thought that they left him out because they disliked him, when really it was because they were actually together?

'I know Anders von Preen. I believe you and Warner were at college with him?'

Chuck curls his lip a little. 'Von Preen? Wow, that's certainly a blast from the past. Anders von Preen! Creepy guy.'

'Actually he's a really lovely talented guy,' I snip. 'With a great sense of style and a kind heart.'

I cover an irritated huff. Chuck Allen is… not what I expected.

'Why don't you open the letter!' I say quickly. 'That's why I'm here, after all!'

Chuck nods. 'Yes. Yes, all right then.'

I watch, wide-eyed, as he slowly peels open the envelope, pulling out sheets of thick, expensive-looking paper.

I smile to myself as he unfolds the paper and starts to read. I can't believe he's here! I found him! He's here and he's actually, *finally* reading Birdie's letter! I wonder what it says!

Then Chuck's face turns from cool and serene to absolutely furious. His tanned cheeks flush beetroot red and he stands up from his chair with a gasp.

'What the hell is this?' he says angrily, holding the papers up in the air.

I stand up too. 'Wh-what is it? What's wrong?'

Chuck shakes his head. 'You think this is funny?"

I blink, completely confused. 'I don't understand,' I try. 'What's the matter?'

Chuck looks me up and down furiously. 'I'll have someone call a speedboat to come and collect you as soon as your clothes are dry. You are no longer a guest on my yacht.'

Chuck screws up the papers of Birdie's letter and throws them onto the floor, storming across the room. Before he leaves he whips around and takes one last angry look at me. 'You really are a menace. Get out of New York!'

As he slams the door behind him, I bend down to pick up Birdie's letter with shaking hands.

I start to read…

Dear Chuck,

I just wanted to say that you were a real dick of a boyfriend. I loved you. And you let me love you so that your parents wouldn't find out you were gay!! If you'd have told me, I'd have been happy to beard for you! I am cool like that. Or I could have helped you to come out to them when you were ready. But you let me fall in love with you. And you let me believe that you were straight. That you loved me too. That we would go to England, to university together. That sucks. And for me to find out the truth by walking in on you with my next door neighbour Quiet Bruce who turned out not to be so quiet at all? That was not cool, Chuck. Not. Cool. You were an asshole. I bet you are still an asshole. I hope not. But I bet you are.

ANYWAY. This whole thing is not about you. Please pass this letter back to my friend Olive who I am assuming is somewhere nearby. The next letter is for her.

Bye bye, Chuck. Be happy.

I half laugh in complete disbelief and quickly pull out the next sheet of paper. It's covered in Olive's loopy messy handwriting.

Olive,

There you are.

Hey.

Don't be mad at me! Oh god, you're going to be so mad at me, I know. But let me explain.

Okay, so I kind of tricked you into going to New York. But it wasn't meant to be a mean trick. It was meant to be a magical gift.

As you know, I won't be here for a great deal more time. I know you get sad when I'm so upfront about it, but I've made my peace with what's happening. I promise you. I've had a gorgeous life. I really, really have. I've travelled, I've loved, I've laughed 'til I peed my pants (mostly thanks to you) and cried until my nose was so blocked I could barely breathe, I've had heartbreaks and fights and scary times and joyful times. I've lived. I've really lived!

And I got to know you. I was so alone when I moved to Manchester. I was supposed to be here with Chuck, I was wrestling with this shitty illness and I didn't have anyone. And then you happened. And you loved me. Right away you loved me. You welcomed me into your life and let me talk at you for hours, helped me plot my adventures, rant about daft men, sat with me in hospital waiting rooms, introduced me to Kit Kats dipped in tea and bought me cool iridescent Band-Aids so that my blood draw marks were stylishly covered.

You've been my sidekick since the day we met, no questions asked, no mugging for the spotlight. And, I'll be honest, I've loved every minute of it. As you knew I would.

But now I have other plans (maybe we should pretend that I'm just going on a long holiday???) and I wonder about you. What will you do? Who will you be? Because the truth is, Brewster, as much as I adore you, I can see you're not happy. And I know you never want to talk about you, to talk about your shitty parents and all that worrying you do. But this is my letter. And you have to read it. So I'm gonna say what I need to say. So there.

My darling, you're living a half-life. I'm sorry if this sounds harsh. I don't mean to throw shade on your whole existence – I love you. But you are so much more than you think. You don't see how much you shine. But I do. I always have. You are a diamond-covered sunshine, dude. You're so comical and kind in a sophisticated non-martyrish way. Underneath all that scared demeanour is a total badass. I'm sure of it! And that's why I sent you on this trip.

I couldn't give a shit about Chuck Allen (don't be mad!!). Because Chuck Allen is not my Big Sexy Love. You are, Olive Brewster. You're my Big Sexy Love! My best buddy. My favourite person. The love I have for you is so much more epic than I've had for any boyfriend. And that's why, in a totally cruel-to-be-kind way, I forced you into going to New York under a misapprehension. I knew you wouldn't ever do anything like this without some serious forcing. And what works more than a dying wish? Nothing, that's what! I have all of the power, muu haaa (how do you spell the evil laugh? You get what I mean, right?).

So. You're due to arrive here at the hospital for a visit in less than an hour and I feel giddy at the thought of my big sneaky plan being put into motion. It's the most excited I've felt in years. You see, New York is the greatest city in the world for someone like you. I know that just by being in

NYC, by being terrified and thrown in at the deep end, you'll find adventure. Because that's what New York does. It gets under your skin! It drives you a little crazy! And sending you off on a wild goose chase seems like a good idea to me right now. I had a lot of medicine this morning though, so I'm a little bit high…

Shit. I hope this is the right idea. I hope you see some eye-opening things (the view from the roof at the Airbnb I've booked is insane! I hope you see that! The amount of people openly taking craps on the sidewalk is also insane in a different way – I hope you don't see that). I dearly hope you meet some interesting people. I hope that by doing this you will see how much you shine. Because I won't be here to keep telling you. And you need to know.

You are destined for great things, my darling.

I can't wait to see you when you get back.

Don't be mad at me. You can't be mad at a sick person. It's against the rules.

All my love forever,

Your Birdie.

I stare at the letter, my tears falling onto the paper. I don't want to smudge it, so I clasp it to my chest, laughing as I cry. I pull my mobile out of my bumbag and go to dial Birdie's number – sod sleep – I want to hear her voice right now! I cannot believe she has done this! The letter was for me! Chuck Allen was a gigantic ruse and all this time, it was for me!

Looking at my phone, I notice eight missed calls from Alex. Eight? He must have tried calling while I was doing my stupid yacht jump. Shit. I hope he's okay.

I immediately press his number on the screen. He answers after barely half a ring.

'Alex? It's Olive! Are you okay? Is Donna okay?'

'Olive,' he says, his voice full of anguish. 'I've been trying to ring you all night.'

'My phone has been on silent. I only just saw. What's the matter?'

Alex's voice breaks. 'It's… Birdie.'

Oh god. Oh god. No!

'She… Birdie had a heart attack. She was rushed into emergency surgery last night..'

'Oh my god. Is she okay?' I hear a funny clicking noise and realise it's the phone banging against my earring because my hands are shaking so much. 'Please tell me she's okay, Alex?'

'The emergency surgery went well but when they tried to wake her up she… Well, she's not responding now. She's in a coma. I'm so sorry, Olive.'

The room swims before me. Bile rises in my throat.

'I'm coming back now. Do not leave her side.'

'Donna wants me to—'

'I do not care what Donna wants. If you love me at all you will stay by Birdie's side and you will hold her hand until I get there.'

I hang up.

I need to get home right now.

CHAPTER THIRTY-FIVE

Text from Anders: Thinking of you, darling bestie.

Text from Mrs Ramirez: Chica, be brave for your friend. I am praying for her and for you.

Text from Seth: Sending my love, Olive. I'm here if you need anything.

Text from Colin: Where did you go? Did you get my memes?

The second time I fly on an airplane is much scarier than the first time. Not because of turbulence or oxygen masks falling or flying over the sea. But because the thing I've been most scared of this whole time, losing Birdie, is happening. I barely notice as the flight attendants ask me if I want anything. I barely notice anything. My whole head is blurry and tired and absolutely terrified. I don't even sleep. I couldn't even if I tried. My body is coursing with adrenaline. I need to be alert, I need to be ready.

As soon as I got back to Gramercy Park, Anders organised and paid for me to be on the next flight to Manchester, while Mrs Ramirez gathered my stuff, packed it and made me a cup of chamomile tea which I couldn't even hold because my hands were trembling so much.

Our goodbyes were hasty and hazy and apart from a quick exchange of phone numbers I didn't think to say a proper thank you for all the help they've given me.

Eventually, after the longest nine hours of my life, the flight touches down with a rickety bump and I walk into the cool, wet air of Manchester. As I do, New York immediately becomes a memory. A faraway, bonkers, dreamlike thing that happened to someone else. The only thing real to me now is that my best friend is in a coma, and she might never wake up.

When I reach Manchester Royal Hospital, I get out of the cab, race through the double doors and up the stairs to Birdie's ward. I heave my heavy suitcases behind me, tripping over and stumbling as I do so. The ward sister, recognising me, waves me right through to Birdie's room.

Heart pounding like a kick drum, I push open the door to find Alex sitting beside Birdie's bed, holding her hand. I feel a rush of love for him. He pulls me into a hug without saying a word.

'Can I go to the toilet now?' he quips, which makes me chuckle as much as anything can make me chuckle at a time like this.

'I suppose.' I wave him out of the room.

I sit down in the seat Alex just vacated and take Birdie's hand, peering worriedly down at her face. She looks like she's asleep.

'Hey Birdie!' I say brightly. 'I'm back! I got your letter, you turd. What the hell?'

I wait for her to open her eyes and laugh. To ask me to get her some coffee, to tell me about Dr BJ's arms, to make it all better. But she doesn't. Please don't let this be it. I have so much to tell her. So much to thank her for.

'Come on, Bird!' I try. 'Please?' Part of me stupidly thinks that the sound of my voice will wake her up. Magically snap her out of it.

But, of course, it doesn't.

'What did the doctors say?' I ask Alex when he returns from the loo. 'How did they know to ring you?"

Alex brushes his hair back from his chubby face, his eyes tired and sad. He sits down on another visitor chair opposite me. 'Our house phone was listed as the contact number for you, her next of kin. It's a good job they had it. There was no one else listed. When I got here the doctor told me that she'd had a heart attack and they'd had do an emergency angioplasty.'

I shake my head. Poor Birdie. Poor, poor Birdie.

'Why isn't she waking up?' I ask, the tears starting to fall. 'I don't understand.'

I press my hand to her cheek. It still feels warm. It still feels alive.

'They said physically, she seems absolutely fine. There's no sign of infection, but she could have had a small stroke, maybe? They said that sometimes the stress of these events in the body can cause patients to take a little longer to wake up.'

'So they don't know.'

'They don't know,' Alex confirms.

'Wake up, Birdie,' I say, trying to sound upbeat. 'Come on, you lazy ass! Wake up!'

But she just lies there.

* * *

The following morning, I wake up in Birdie's hospital hoping to find her miraculously back to normal, hoping that last night wast a terrible dream, an after effect of almost drowning at the harbour. But no. She's exactly the same.

'Wake up, dude,' I say for the millionth time since I've been here. My eyes fill with fresh tears as I squeeze her hand. 'You're being really ignorant you know,' I grump.

Alex is still here, asleep on the chair opposite. He wakes up, his hair all messed up, his round face all crumpled and sleepy-looking.

'You can go, if you want.' I say to Alex. 'Donna must be wondering where you've got to.'

Alex shrugs. 'I'm leaving her.'

'What?' I yell in such a high-pitched voice that I check to see if it roused Birdie. It didn't. 'What?' I repeat in a more reasonable tone of voice.

Alex sets his mouth into a grim line. 'She's *horrible*.'

'I know!' I nod fervently. 'Wait… how do *you* know? What happened?'

'It was like, without you at home, just hanging out with Donna alone, there was no buffer. And it just hit me… that I don't actually like her all that much anymore.'

I press a hand to my mouth.

Alex half smiles at my reaction.

'I thought you were super into her!' I gasp.

He fiddles with the sleeve of his brown jumper. 'I was at first. But… I wonder if I was just looking for some stability, something secure after Mum and Dad, you know… and Donna is very steady.'

'Yes.' I blow the air out through my cheeks. 'I thought I was the only one with Mum and Dad abandonment-related headfuckitis.'

'Nope.' Alex grins. 'Me too!'

'Well, it's better you realise it's wrong now before starting a family…'

'I know. I think that's what made me decide. She's packing her stuff up right now.'

'Oh my goodness. Was she upset?'

Alex looks thoughtful. 'She seemed more upset when I confessed that I didn't really like *The Big Bang Theory* as much as I had been making out.'

'Alex!'

I knew it!

He grimaces. 'I know. Then seeing you head off to Manhattan on your own. It just made me think… what's out there?'

'A lot,' I say, my head flashing with images of New York making my chest pang in a weird way. 'So, so much, Alex.' I stand up and pour us both a glass of water from the jug at the end of Birdie's bed. 'I guess I won't have to move into the box room then,' I remark, taking a sip of water. Last week I would have been thrilled about that. But it seems so small-fry now. Who cares about a box room? I feel like a different person now.

Alex takes his glass from me. 'Well that's the thing, Olive… I… I was thinking that maybe we should sell the house.'

My eyes widen. Gosh. This is the last thing I expected Alex to say. The house in Saddleworth is our sanctuary. The last remaining evidence of the life we had before our family fell apart. It's our home. The thought of no longer living there, of no longer sleeping in my childhood bedroom is… no longer as scary as I always thought it would be.

I plonk back down onto the chair, a sense of freedom floats over me. Sell the house? Alex doesn't even have to convince me. I'm as sure as I've ever been about anything that it's the right thing to do.

It's time to move on.

* * *

After Alex leaves to start making plans for his life without Donna, I spend the morning sitting with Birdie, willing her to be okay. I switch between crying so much that one of the nurses pops her head round the door to see what the wailing noise is, to singing songs from our university days, telling her jokes and relaying all my tales from Manhattan. I re-read her letter a million times. I read it to myself, I read it out loud, I read it so many times that I soon know it off by heart.

My phone continues to beep like crazy with texts from Colin who has become somewhat creepy in his efforts to find out if I am okay, and if I have received his memes, both of which seem of equal importance to him. I spend thirty minutes crafting a text that tells him I'm not looking to embark on anything romantic right now because I have other priorities, but that I hope we can be friends. I feel guilty as I press send but, even if Birdie was completely well, now that I know what real, whole-hearted attraction feels like, even if it was with somebody I'll never see again, I know that that's not what I felt for Colin. Despite his sideburns.

He doesn't text back.

I try not to think too much about Seth either. Now that I'm here, back in real life, it seems daft that we should stay in touch. I texted him back to say thank you for his nice message about Birdie, but otherwise I've left well alone. What would be the point? Nothing could ever come of it. We're on opposite sides of the world, for goodness sake. And right now, I don't have space to be thinking about anything other than Birdie.

At lunchtime, one of the nurses enters the room to tend to Birdie, changing her tubes and sheets, making sure she is clean and in a fresh gown. As she potters about the room, preparing everything, I burst into tears again. I can't help it. This is devastating.

'You might as well go for a coffee,' the nurse says kindly, 'I'll be about an hour or so and we don't usually allow visitors in the room at this point.'

'Oh, okay,' I say. 'Are you sure there's nothing I can do to help?'

'No, love. You get gone. You might want to get home for a shower?'

She says it kindly, but she's right. I must stink. I'm in the same clothes I've been wearing since my flight.

Alex took my cases back to the house this morning, so I grab my bumbag and head home to get cleaned up.

* * *

After a long, hot shower, I get dressed into jeans and a soft green jumper, pack a bag with some water, face wipes and a nice hand cream for Birdie and head back to the hospital. On the bus there, in my foggy, jet-lagged state, it occurs to me that it's Monday already. Which means last night would have been Seth's first show as a cast member on *Sunday Night Live*. I shouldn't watch it. I definitely shouldn't watch it. It'll make me miss him and I don't want to miss him, I *can't* miss him. Hmmm. Maybe I could just watch the first five minutes...

I pull out my phone and my earbuds and search the internet for somewhere I can stream the episode.

As the bus trundles along the streets of Greater Manchester, five minutes turns into a lot longer as I watch

Seth, handsome and self-assured, introduced as the newest cast member of one of the biggest shows in the world.

I smile and chuckle lightly as he appears as an overly positive old guy on a broken funfair carousel ride and then in the next sketch as an Italian teenager in an arthouse black and white film. He doesn't mess up once! He doesn't flake out, he doesn't even look slightly nervous! He looks like he belongs on that stage.

I know him! I think proudly. Well, I *knew* him. For one ridiculous, crazy week. The best week of my life, really.

At the thought, my heart blossoms and breaks in equal measure.

As the show draws to a close, I feel my stomach flip over when the cast do the final sketch and it's one that I recognise. Holy moly. It's the Pizza Flap sketch I helped to write! It's a little different than it was the day Seth came up with it; tighter, funnier, but the fact that they used some of my ideas makes me burst with delight. Wow. What a feeling!

As the end credits play, I peer out of the window. We're passing through Manchester town centre full of people in suits, staring at their phones, looking harassed by the busy traffic, walking a mile a minute, in a rush to get where they're going.

I think of Birdie, not rushing anywhere. Completely still.

Life is short. Unexpectedly short.

Before I know it my hand flies out and I press the bell so that the bus stops.

I'm not at the hospital yet, but I get off anyway.

There's something I need to do. And if I don't do it now, I might never do it at all.

* * *

'Quit?' Taller Joan gasps from behind the fish counter. 'You want to quit?'

'Hand in my notice, yeah,' I correct as Tall Joan puts her hands to her cheeks in shock.

'But… why?'

I hold out my hands. 'I think it's time for a change,' I explain. 'I've been working here for a long time and… well, I'm pretty sure it's not my passion. There are other things I'd really like to try.'

'Well!' Tall Joan says, wide-eyed. 'Olive Brewster!'

I bite my lip, worried that I've offended them both after they've been so kind to me. But then Taller Joan bursts into noisy laughter.

'Well thank buggering bugger for that!'

I blink. 'Um, what?'

'We've been fretting for a while now, wondering how we could let you go gently,' Tall Joan says, leaning her elbows onto the counter.

'Let me go?' My mouth drops open.

'We haven't needed you here for a long time,' Taller Joan explains, two spots of colour appearing on her cheeks. 'I don't know if you noticed, but we've not been getting enough custom for three staff. No offence, love, but you've been a bit surplus to requirements for about eight months now.'

I look between the two of them, unable to believe what I'm hearing. 'Why the bloody hell didn't you tell me?' I ask. 'Why didn't you just sack me?'

Tall Joan looks at her feet. 'Well, we love you, petal. And working here is all you've done for so long. We worried you'd panic if we let you go.'

'And you stay indoors so much, at least by working here you got to natter with us or the customers day to day.'

I feel a little spark of anger in my chest that, what, I've

been a pity hire? They should have told me! I'd have been fine!

But then I think back to me before New York. Obsessed with my routine, living firmly within my snug little comfort zone. They're right. I would have freaked out. I would have gotten another job that I didn't want for security's sake. I would maybe have had a panic attack, even.

'Oh!' I say, quietly. 'Wow.'

'You look different today, love,' Taller Joan says, squinting her eyes.

'Have you changed your hair?' Tall Joan adds.

'No,' I say, pulling them both in for long hugs.

'Well something's different about you,' they say, looking me up and down.

Everything, I think. *Everything is different.*

* * *

I hurry back to the hospital, picking up a bunch of wild-flowers on the way.

Outside Birdie's room, I take a deep breath, preparing myself for the gut-wrenching sight of her still, comatose body just lying there, so quietly.

I slowly push open the door and get the fright of my life to find Birdie not only sitting up in the bed fully awake, but being tended to by a gigantically muscled doctor who I assume is the infamous Dr BJ.

'What the fuuuuck?' I yell, running over and pulling Birdie in a hug.

'Watch the tubes!' the huge man warns, with a chuckle.

I jump back, not wanting to tangle the wires or hurt her in anyway. Then I lean forward again, more gently, and wrap my arms around my friend.

'Brewster,' she whispers.

'Bird!' I choke out.

The pair of us burst immediately into tears, clinging onto each other for dear life.

'Well, I will tell you something. That was a nap and a half,' Birdie quips, her voice croaky and dry.

'Too soon.' I lean back and take her in. Her face is white and her eyes are half closed. But she's here. She's *here*.

Once Dr BJ has checked all of Birdie's vitals, assuring us that she's doing really well considering, he leaves the room, giving me an odd sort of look as he does.

Birdie giggles lightly. 'You know he thinks you have a crush on him, right? I told him it was you who fancied him after he heard us on FaceTime that day, remember?'

'Yeah, you turd. I've got a good mind to go out there and tell him the truth. That it is in fact you who wants to bestow Dr BJ with a pleasant BJ.'

Birdie shakes her head, snickering with gentle laughter. 'You wouldn't do that to such a sick woman.'

I take hold of her hands. 'Thank you for my letter,' I whisper tears spilling out of my eyes and rolling speedily down my face. 'For what you did for me.'

Birdie looks at me. 'Anytime, Brewster.'

Laughing, and crying and snotting and shaking, we embrace each other once more.

And I don't plan to ever let go.

CHAPTER THIRTY-SIX

Birdie Lively Funeral Order of Service:

Piano performance of 'You're my Best Friend' by Queen
Reading of 'Funeral Blues' by W. H. Auden
Eulogy by Olive Brewster
Acknowledgements
Piano performance of 'Ain't No Sunshine' by Bill Withers

I wrap my coat more tightly around me to shield off the icy wind that blows my hair into my face, where it sticks to the lip gloss I put on because Birdie warned me I had 'better make a damn effort at the memorial'.

'I don't want to bloody leave,' I say to Birdie's headstone. Everyone else left an hour ago. But I haven't been able to bring myself to do it quite yet.

'You'll freeze to death,' I hear her answer in my head. *'That would be a dick move and you know it.'*

I look up at the sky. It's mostly grey, but right over there, the sun is trying its utmost to get a turn in, bolshily elbowing a few dark clouds out of the way.

After her heart attack, Birdie got another six months before it happened again and stole her away for good. It was more time than either of us expected to have and we both agreed, just last week, that it was the best six months of both of our lives. But it wasn't enough time. Another six years, another sixty years wouldn't have been enough time.

I plonk myself down on the ground in front of the headstone and cross my legs. I'm vaguely aware that the ground is cold. And that the wet grass is seeping into my skirt. But I don't really care.

After Birdie recovered from her surgery, she was allowed to leave hospital for a few days each week. And while I took on an evening job as a bartender at a Manchester Comedy club, I was free to spend my days with her. So we took a trip to London, because I've never been and Birdie said that if I was to continue to shine and not get stuck back in my boring old ways then I was to keep on trying new things. So we did it together.

We also went Segwaying in the Lake District, we ate Japanese food and Korean food and the spiciest Indian food we could find. We laughed and squealed our way through a Chippendales performance, did an overnight stay in an observatory and fell asleep looking at the stars. We sang karaoke in a private pod, went for massages and spa treatments in Cheshire, spent a day at Stonehenge and declared it 'incredibly boring'. And when Birdie had her hospital stays we embarked on major Harry Potter Marathons, flirted with Dr BJ until he got so embarrassed his eye would start twitching, and even once did a jigsaw (much to Birdie's annoyance).

If Birdie had a period of illness, then she would pick something bonkers for me to do and make me film the whole thing so she could laugh at my inevitable messing up. And that is why there is now a video on the internet, showcasing one Olive Brewster dramatically puking while on an Alton Towers rollercoaster.

I clutch my arms around myself, my bum starting to freeze on the floor. I can't believe my friend has gone. We both knew it was coming. We've known for a long time. But now it's here, I don't quite believe it. My chest feels empty. It aches and swirls with a pain I know I will always carry with me.

Above me, in a gnarly old oak tree, I notice a dark little bird peering down at me, it's head cocked to one side. And for a brief moment I wonder if…

Then I hear Birdie's giggly voice in my head. *'Nope. Not me. Of course I'm not a bird, you geek! If I was going to come back as something do you think it would be something so on the freakin' nose as a bird? Olive!'*

I laugh. And it turns into a cry. But not in a bad way. Just in a way that's needed.

I slouch there, before Birdie's headstone and chat to her until the sky gets dark and the chapel park-keeper tells me that it's time to go.

I touch my fingers to the headstone, my eyes blurry with tears, my throat aching with the words I never wanted to say.

'Goodbye, Birdie.'

CHAPTER THIRTY-SEVEN

Olive's phone reminders:

Send cheque to storage company
Find a new counsellor
Buy one of Donna's candles because no one else is buying them
Take flowers to Birdie
Double-check course registration details
Start level 3 of Still Minds app

'The planes are so big up close! How do they even stay in the air? I know it sounds dumb, but it doesn't make logical sense!'

'Alex, relax! I promise you it will be fine.' I pat my big brother's shoulder and hand him the pint I bought him, watching as he takes a nervous sip. 'You're going first-class too. It's great. They have pod seats and flat-screen TVs and everything.'

Alex nods, patting his coat pockets for the millionth time to check he's still got his passport and tickets to Japan. He's taken a year's sabbatical at work and some of the money we got from the house sale to travel Asia. It's been a long time in the planning and I couldn't be prouder of him for having the courage to embark on a new adventure.

'Told you you should wear a bumbag,' I say, stroking mine lovingly.

'Nah.' Alex laughs. 'I'm not a total nerd.'

I look pointedly at his hand luggage – a briefcase, and the book he's taking onto the plane called *The Visual Display of Quantitive Information.*

'I beg to differ.'

As we sit in the airport bar, nursing our pints, Alex keeps looking worriedly out of the huge windows. 'It's definitely going to snow.'

'It might,' I agree. 'It is Christmas. Snow tends to occur.'

'But will it affect the plane?'

'If it does, they'll just cancel it. Show some chill!'

Alex laughs. 'I never thought I'd hear Olive Brewster instructing someone to "Show some chill!".'

I grin thoughtfully. 'Me either. I like it. I like saying it.'

'It suits you.'

The airport speaker blares out, announcing boarding for Alex's flight. As we head to the gate, I notice that his hands are trembling. I stop him and grab them.

'You are going to be fine. You are going to be absolutely fine. If I can do it, lord knows you can.'

Alex takes a deep breath. 'Thanks, Sis.'

'Have fun, okay. And keep me updated with absolutely *everything*. But not, like, sex stuff, obviously.' A nearby couple give us an odd look. 'He's my brother,' I explain. To which they make a horrified sort of noise.

'And you too!' Alex calls, as he hands his tickets, boarding pass and passport to the pretty young flight attendant. 'Okay! Here I go!'

'There you go!' I yell back. 'Go Alex go!'

As he disappears through the gate, off on an adventure that will change him in ways he can't even fathom yet, I find myself smiling thoughtfully into mid-air. The pair of us are firmly back on a good footing with each other. I'm not saying it had anything to do with Donna leaving but… oh heck, I suppose I *am* saying that. She was pretty terrible. Living with Alex while we spruced up and sold the house turned out *not* to be the awkward tedium it was before I went to New York, but a sweet, comfortable time, full of long conversations, laughs and the watching of anything other than *The Big Bang Theory*.

My phone alarm yanks me out of my thoughts, buzzing incessantly from inside my bumbag.

Ooh! That's my reminder! Shit! I best get a move on.

I have my own flight to catch!

* * *

Nine hours later, I step out into the arrivals lounge wibbly-legged from a tumultuous flight. This time I didn't need alcohol or Rescue Remedy or Xanax to get through it – I just used every anxiety-reducing trick in my newly equipped mental arsenal. And it worked. *Mostly.* Hence the wibbly legs.

My cases have already been couriered over from Saddleworth and so the only luggage I have is my beautiful pink bumbag, wrapped snugly around my waist.

I walk through the melee of chauffeurs and reuniting families to a soundtrack of Christmas carols playing over the tannoy system. My eyes flick from left to right searching for…

'Olive!' I hear his thin, reedy drawl before I see him. I peek up and Anders is there, looking insane and a bit terrifying in tight white jeans, a tight white jumper and ginormous grey scarf, his icy hair in a quiff, his pale eyes super wide with excitement. He's holding a home-made cardboard sign that says 'Welcome (back) to NYC, Darling.'

Beside him, dressed in a rainbow-striped dress and with a very sleek new silvery bob is Mrs Ramirez. She waves madly as I approach, a big smile stretching her wrinkled cheeks smooth.

It's been over eight months since I've seen them. I can't believe I'm back here!

'Anders!' I yell as they embrace me. 'Mrs Ramirez!'

'You're here, Chica! You are finally here!'

'I love your bob. It looks great, Mrs Rami—'

'For goodness sake, call me Glorita.'

'Sorry! *Glorita*. Your bob looks beautiful!'

'That's not just any old bob, darling, that's a perfectly trimmed graduated bob with hand-painted babylights. We learned it last week during salon training. I got top marks, of course.' Anders beams. He's two months into his hair-dressing course and seems to love every minute of it! He's already asked if he can practise on me when I live with him. Of course I said yes. Except for unicorn horns. I said a firm no to having any kind of horn on my head ever again.

'Well, it looks brilliant.'

Mrs Ramirez pats her head proudly. Anders reaches out to stop her. 'Careful!'

I laugh at these two bonkers ex-strangers, who are now the most unlikeliest of friends. I'm so excited to be back here with them, part of their oddball gang. If it wasn't for

Birdie I never would have met them. The things that woman did for me.

After Birdie's funeral, and with Alex deciding to head off on his Asian adventure, I made the decision to use my share of the house sale money to come back to Manhattan and enrol into an improv course at the Upright Citizen's Brigade Theatre. I've been doing comedy-writing classes in Manchester for the last four months and the absolute heart-lifting, joyful feeling I got from it made the decision to take this bigger, scarier step much easier.

When I called Anders to tell him I was coming for a whole year, he insisted I stay with him. He's already taken Mrs Ramirez in. The two of them have become firm friends in the last year and when her studio apartment building announced that they were selling up in order to get rid of the rent-controlled tenants, it was a given that she would live with Anders in his big old house. They're an odd pair. They bicker a lot, they're completely different, but they love each other fiercely and in a city so big, they're each other's family. That I introduced them to each other will forever be one of the best accomplishments of my life.

In the snowy cab to Gramercy, the three of us catch up, although to be honest, with the daily texting and Face-Time sessions we're pretty much up to date on each other's news.

'Ah, turn this one up, please!' Mrs Ramirez yells at the cab driver. 'It is my favourite!'

The driver does as requested, and Andy Williams' *Most Wonderful Time of The Year* rings out around the car.

Anders turns to me from his seat in the front and rolls his eyes. But I can tell he loves it just as much as I do.

As the Manhattan skyline comes into view, my eyes brim with tears. I knew I missed it here. I knew it as soon as I got on the plane back. But seeing the magnificent buildings in the sky ahead of me, all of the new possibilities the city holds, a million experiences good *and* bad that I'm going to have, experiences I never would have had the guts to go for without my dear Birdie, overwhelms me.

'What's the matter?' Anders asks, his head cocked to the side. 'Are you *crying*? Is it the saccharine music?'

'Ay, she's happy, silly,' Mrs Ramirez says, handing me an embroidered handkerchief to dry my tears and then grabbing my hand between hers. 'She's just glad to be back home.'

I swallow hard and nod. She's absolutely right.

* * *

The house at Gramercy is lovely and warm when we get in. The fires have been lit, the smell of mulled wine wafts through from the kitchen and in the hall is a huge pine Christmas tree twinkling with hundreds of minuscule lights.

'All of your belongings are up in your room,' Anders says as he takes my coat. I pull my bobble hat off and he grimaces at my hair. 'Those ends! Don't worry, you're in safe hands now.'

I laugh as Mrs Ramirez hands me a glass of mulled wine and we all stand there in the hallway by the tree, thrilled to be seeing each other again, happy as heck that we're about to be the weirdest most mismatched group of roommates anyone ever saw.

'We got you a surprise!' Mrs Ramirez says, her eyes flicking secretively up to Anders who gives a little nod.

'A Christmas surprise,' he adds.

I press a hand to my chest. 'Lucky me! Well, what is it? Don't leave a girl hanging!'

Anders takes one of my arms and Mrs Ramirez takes

the other. The pair of them lead me into Anders' grand, ostentatious living room.

Holy shit.

There, standing in front of the crackling fire, looking gorgeous and ridiculous in equal measure, is Seth.

I stare at him, taking in every inch of the face I've been trying not to picture in my head every night for the last eight months.

After I came back to Manchester, Seth and I kept up with a few polite 'how are things going?' texts, which pretty quickly petered out. For me, it hurt too much to think of him, of the fact that I would never see him again, that I had developed real feelings for what could only ever be a 'fling'. Plus, the fact that he clearly wasn't as into it as I was, having sent me packing the day after we slept together, kept me well away.

Not to mention that all of my heart was taken up with Birdie. I didn't want anyone else to steal even a tiny bit of that space. She was my priority. But that didn't mean I didn't sneakily watch Seth's show each week, under the covers in my bed. Smiling proudly as he went from strength to strength, being named one of the year's rising comedy stars. I imagined calling him at that point. Just to offer my congratulations. Whereupon he would declare that he couldn't stop thinking about me and was going to fly to Manchester, just so he could kiss me again.

And then, when I saw a picture of Seth on a US gossip site, kissing one of the other *Sunday Night Live* cast members in Central Park, I quietly deleted his number from my phone and tried my hardest to not let it hurt. I didn't have room for that.

Now he's here. Wearing… a Christmas jumper? And a set of antlers?

I peer at Anders and Mrs Ramirez who are looking

from me to Seth and back again, mega-intense smiles on their faces.

'They made me wear this jumper and antlers,' Seth says, awkwardly pushing his glasses up his nose. 'If it were up to me, I'd be looking much cooler right now.'

'Well you don't look like a Christmas gift in any old shirt and pants!' Mrs Ramirez points out.

Anders nods in agreement.

A small smile lifts the corners of my mouth.

'We will leave you two alone…' Anders says, giving me a little wave with his bony hand.

Mrs Ramirez continues to stare at us, beaming, until Anders has to physically drag her out of the room.

My heart jolts as Seth gives me a daft smile. My body, which (apart from a couple of *Atonement* re-watches) has been fairly dormant in Manchester, lights right back up again.

Man alive.

I sit down on one of Anders' stiff velvet armchairs. Seth sits opposite me on the mauve sofa.

Then I notice that he's holding a small stack of letters, tied with a gold ribbon.

I frown. Weird…

'Hey,' Seth says. 'It's good to see you.'

'Hello…' I reply, noticing that he looks a lot more groomed than when I first met him. His usually messy long hair has a sharper cut now. His shoulders are broader, like he's been working out. His clothes are *ironed.* I guess that's what happens when you start to get famous. 'What are you doing here?' I ask.

'Birdie invited me.'

I frown. 'What? How? What are you talking about?'

Seth picks up the stack of letters and waves them at me.

'What?'

He gives a small single shoulder shrug. 'We were… kind of pen pals for a while.'

My jaw drops open. Birdie and her letters! What has she been playing at! How has she…? Why has she…?

I eagerly reach my hand out for the letters. Seth places the stack into my hand, his fingers briefly touching mine, giving me a little electric shock.

I pull a letter out of one of the envelopes. And sure enough, there is Birdie's loopy handwriting in a missive dated from six months ago.

I goggle at the letters, emotion bubbling up in my chest.

Seth smiles at me. 'She wrote to me because she thought I should be made aware that you weren't engaged. That it was a fib you made up on the plane and that you didn't tell me because I hated liars.'

I nod, in complete disbelief that Birdie wrote to Seth and didn't even tell me! Just like her to be so obnoxious. And… amazing. Even now she's managing to surprise me!

'You know that's why I cooled off after our night together?' Seth says, sitting forward on the settee.

I give him a quizzical look.

'I knew after we… um…' he trails off.

'Did *it*.'

'Yeah, *it*. I knew that I was falling for you. I think I knew earlier than that, if I'm being honest. I think I knew that rainy day in the Upper West Side. The day you lost your letter and followed me to the theatre.'

I knew I was falling for you too, I think.

That all seems so long ago now. But still, it makes my heart sing to hear him say it.

'I thought you were engaged!' Seth goes on. 'I didn't want to get in any deeper. There I was feeling things about you I never thought I'd feel in my whole life. And you were about to leave to marry Colin Collins.' He shrugs. 'It was too much.'

I bury my head in my hands, my face turning red. 'I thought you were trying to get rid of me because I was weird in bed.'

'Yep.' Seth laughs and points at the stack of letters in my lap. 'Birdie told me that too. And I'd like to take this opportunity to officially inform you that my penis was not bruised. It was, in fact, very happy after our encounter.'

'I'm pleased about that.'

'Me too.'

We smile at each other.

'Wait…' I ask. 'How did you know I'd be here? Even Birdie didn't know I was coming back to New York.'

Seth laughs. 'Actually, she did.'

'Huh?'

He takes out the letter at the bottom of the pile, pointing at a paragraph on the second page.

I quickly wipe away the tears I can feel running down my face as I read.

Olive doesn't know it yet, but she fell in love with New York. She'll be back, I know it. I have asked her friend Anders to get in touch with you when that happens. And then, if you are single, I want you to take her on an official date. Tell her that when you ask, she has to say yes or else I will haunt her. Not in a sweet gentle ghostly presence way. But in a scary gross way: blood and fangs and throwing things across the room. All that. It will be horrendous.

I burst into noisy, tearful laughter. 'Oh Birdie!'

'She seemed like she was one of a kind,' Seth says gently.

'She was,' I say with a heavy heart. 'She really, really was.'

Seth stands up and holds his hand out towards me. I stand up and take it. 'I *am* single,' he murmurs, his face close to mine, his eyes flicking down to my lips. 'And Birdie was right. You *did* come back. And so… Olive Maudine Brewster, will you go on an official date with me?'

I laugh some more and give a exaggerated shrug. 'Well I don't want to get *haunted*. So I guess my answer is—'

And then we are kissing. And my whole body, my whole heart is lit up. Seth pulls me closer, his hands weaving through my hair, I push him down on to the sofa and climb onto him like a rabid animal. We kiss breathlessly and it feels insane and amazing and *right* and…

'Ahem!'

'Olive! No! Not on the antique sofa!'

Seth and I reluctantly pull apart at the sound of Anders and Mrs Ramirez. They're standing at the entrance to the living room, bundled back up in their coats and scarves.

I laugh, pulling my clothes into some semblance of respectability. Seth does the same, his cheeks a little pink.

'There's a carol singing service in Gramercy Park,' Mrs Ramirez tells us happily. 'Would you like to come with us?'

'They're opening the park up to the public for one night only,' Anders adds. He raises a pale eyebrow, hip cocked. 'Although I suppose that's not quite as exciting to you with your stolen key.'

'You didn't return it?" Mrs Ramirez gasps.

I give her an innocent look as I grab my bumbag and coat from the hat stand. Seth wraps his scarf around his neck and takes my hand as the four of us step out into the cold Manhattan air.

As we walk down the city street to cries of 'Merry Christmas! Happy Hannukah!' from red-cheeked passersby, I peek up at the twinkling festive lights surrounding me, and then across at Seth who runs his thumb suggestively around the palm of my hand, and Anders and Mrs Ramirez who are arguing passionately about what the best holiday song is.

This is what I was afraid of?

We enter a snow-covered Gramercy Park, full of happy singers and locals handing out glasses of champagne.

'Thank you for saving my life, Birdie,' I whisper under my breath.

And I know that while my best friend might be gone from the world, she will always, always be chilling out right here in my heart. In every moment I live – I truly, outrageously, honestly and bravely live – Birdie Lively will be leading the way.

Because *that* is Big Sexy Love.

@ElissaJohnson

So #excited to be carolling in Gramercy Park today! Not ideal that they've opened up the park to the public, but all in the #festivespirit, I suppose! Who else will be there?

THE END

* * *

DEAR READER

Thank you for reading BIG SEXY LOVE. Did you like it? DID YOU? I hope so. It's a bit bonkers, right? I loved writing it so much.

Reader reviews are massively helpful to an author. Especially authors like me who don't have the budget of a big publisher behind them. These reviews help to bring attention (and sales, of course!) to my books, but also help other readers to figure out whether they might enjoy what I write!

If you enjoyed reading BIG SEXY LOVE, I would be *so* grateful if you could spend a few minutes leaving a review. Even a really short one would be amazing. I read all of them. I probably shouldn't but I have zero chill about these things.

Thanks a million and until we meet again,

Kirsty x

www.kirstygreenwood.com

YOU CAN READ MORE KIRSTY GREENWOOD BOOKS!

Yours Truly
The Vintage Guide to Love and Romance

ACKNOWLEDGMENTS

Thank you to my fantastic (and super patient) agent Hannah Ferguson, and the talented team at Hardman & Swainson for everything you do.

Thank you to Caroline Hogg, amazing friend and kickass editor, who always helps to make my books SO much better than they would be without her. I shudder to think what my novels would be like without you.

Thank you to Jade Craddock for the rescue! And for such a thorough copyedit. I loved working with you!

Thank you so much to Angie Jordan for the proofing!

Thank you to my darling writing bestie Cesca Major. This book *literally* wouldn't be here without you, for so many reasons. I am eternally grateful and I like you a lot.

Thank you to my Notting Hill Girl Gang: Celia Ferrari, Elizabeth Keach and my little pumpkin Ophelia. The times I spent with you guys have been some of my favourites ever and your support means the world! Thanks also to Fabien and Louis for making my time in London even more enjoyable!

Thank you to the Book Camp gang and the brilliant Basia Martin who looked after us so perfectly. I had the most fun writing (and talking about writing, cuddling Barnaby, making music videos, drinking bubbles and perving over A and his tractor) with you all. Any writers reading this? You GOTS to go to Bookcamp!

Thank you to my writing friends: all of them supremely talented and supportive. Isabelle Broom, Cressida McLaughlin, Holly Martin, Poppy Dolan, Rosie Blake, Jennifer Joyce, Katie Marsh, Lynsey James and Keris Stainton.

Thank you to Victoria Stone for your amazing cheerleading and belief in me. I hope this book makes you like me as much as you like Mick Dundee.

Thank you to the amazingly supportive bloggers who read and review my books and make me feel like I'm doing something right. Particularly the lovely Leah Graham, Amanda Moran, Jennie Shaw, Kevin Loh, Natalie McCormack Eve Chong and Catriona Merryweather.

Thank you to my beloved family: Edd, Mum, Dad, Lynette, Nic, Tony, Mary, William and C-Dawg. I love you all so, so much and hope to make you as proud as you make me.

Finally, thank you to my readers! I am so grateful to have you. And I really, really, *really* hope this book brings you joy.

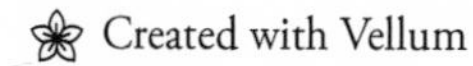
Created with Vellum

Made in the USA
San Bernardino,
CA

56358155R00214